1

The Life of Bret Harte, with Some Account of the California Pioneers

by Henry Childs Merwin

Copyright © 7/15/2015
Jefferson Publication

ISBN-13: 978-1515094388

Contents

CHAPTER I

BRET HARTE'S ANCESTRY

Francis Brett Harte was born at Albany in the State of New York, on August twenty-fifth, 1836. By his relatives and early friends he was called Frank; but soon after beginning his career as an author in San Francisco he signed his name as "Brett," then as "Bret," and finally as "Bret Harte." "Bret Harte," therefore, is in some degree a *nom de guerre*, and it was commonly supposed at first, both in the Eastern States and in England, to be wholly such. Our great New England novelist had a similar experience, for "Nathaniel Hawthorne" was long regarded by most of his readers as an assumed name, happily chosen to indicate the quaint and poetic character of the tales to which it was signed. Bret Harte's father was Henry Hart; but before we trace his ancestry, let us endeavor to see how he looked. Fanny Kemble met him at Lenox, in the year 1875, and was much impressed by his appearance. In a letter to a relative she wrote: "He reminded me a good deal of our old pirate and bandit friend, Trelawney, though the latter was an almost orientally dark-complexioned man, and Mr. Bret Harte was comparatively fair. They were both tall, well-made men of fine figure; both, too, were handsome, with a peculiar expression of face which suggested small sucsuccess to any one who might engage in personal conflict with them."

In reality Bret Harte was not tall, though others beside Mrs. Kemble thought him to be so; his height was five feet, eight and a half inches. His face was smooth and regular, without much color; the chin firm and well rounded; the nose straight and rather large, "the nose of generosity and genius"; the under-lip having what Mr. Howells called a "fascinating, forward thrust."

The following description dates from the time when he left California: "He was a handsome, distinguished-looking man, and although his oval face was slightly marred by scars of small-pox, and his abundant dark hair was already streaked with gray, he carried his slight, upright figure with a quiet elegance that would have made an impression, even when the refinement of face, voice and manner had not been recognized."

Mr. Howells says of him at the same period: "He was, as one could not help seeing, thickly pitted, but after the first glance one forgot this, so that a lady who met him for the first time could say to him, 'Mr. Harte, aren't you afraid to go about in the cars so recklessly when there is this scare about small-pox?' 'No! madam!' he said, in that rich note of his, with an irony touched by pseudo-pathos, 'I bear a charmèd life.'"

Almost every one who met Bret Harte was struck by his low, rich, well-modulated voice. Mr. Howells speaks of "the mellow cordial of a voice that was like no other." His handwriting was small, firm and graceful.

Chance acquaintances made in England were sometimes surprised at Bret Harte's appearance. They had formed, writes Mme. Van de Velde, "a vague, intangible idea of a wild, reckless Californian, impatient of social trammels, whose life among the Argonauts must have fashioned him after a type differing widely from the reality. These idealists were partly disappointed, partly relieved, when their American writer turned out to be a quiet, low-voiced, easy-mannered, polished gentleman, who smilingly confessed that precisely because he had roughed it a good deal in his youth he was inclined to enjoy the comforts and avail himself of the facilities of an older civilization, when placed within his reach."

Bret Harte's knowledge of these disappointed expectations may have suggested the plot of that amusing story *Their Uncle from California*, the hero of which presents a similar contrast to the barbaric ideal which had been formed by his Eastern relatives.

The photographs of Bret Harte, taken at various periods in his life, reveal great changes, apart from those of age. The first one, at seventeen, shows an intellectual youth, very mature for his age, with a fine forehead, the hair parted at one side, and something of a rustic appearance. In the next picture, taken at the age of thirty-five or thereabout, we see a determined-looking man, with slight side-whiskers, a drooping mustache, and clothes a little "loud." Five years afterward there is another photograph in which the whiskers have disappeared, the hair seems longer and more curly, the clothes are unquestionably "loud," and the picture, taken altogether, has a slight tinge of Bohemian-like vulgarity. In the later photographs the hair is shorter, and parted in the middle, the mustache subdued, the dress handsome and in perfect taste, and the whole appearance is that of a refined, sophisticated, aristocratic man of the world, dignified, and yet perfectly simple, unaffected and free from self-consciousness.

In a measure Bret Harte seems to have undergone that process of development which Mr. Henry James has described in "The American." The Reader may remember how the American (far from a typical one, by the way) began with sky-blue neckties and large plaids, and ended with clothes and adornments of the most chastened, correct and elegant character. Actors are apt to go through a similar process. The first great exponent of the "suppressed emotion" school began, and in California too, as it happened, by splitting the ears of the groundlings and sawing the air with both arms.

Bret Harte had something of a Hebrew look, and not unnaturally so, for he came of mixed English, Dutch and Hebrew stock. To be exact, he was half English, one quarter Dutch, and one quarter Hebrew. The Hebrew strain also was derived from English soil, so that with the exception of a Dutch great-grandmother, all his ancestors emigrated from England, and not very remotely.

The Hebrew in the pedigree was his paternal grandfather, Bernard Hart. Mr. Hart was born in London, on Christmas Day, 1763 or 1764, but as a boy of thirteen he went out to Canada, where his relatives were numerous. These Canadian Harts were a marked family, energetic,

4

forceful, strong-willed, prosperous, given to hospitality, warm-hearted, and pleasure-loving. One of Bernard Hart's Canadian cousins left behind him at his death no less than fourteen families, all established in the world with a good degree of comfort, and with a sufficient degree of respectability. Now the impropriety, to say nothing about the extravagance, of maintaining fourteen separate families is so great that no Reader of this book (the author feels confident) need be warned against it; and yet it indicates a large, free-handed, lordly way of doing things. It was no ordinary man, and no ordinary strain of blood that could produce such a record.

Bernard Hart remained but three years in Canada, and in 1780 moved to New York where, although scarcely more than a boy, he acted as the business representative of his Canadian kinsfolk. The Canadian Harts had many commercial and social relations with the metropolis, and there was much "cousining," much going back and forth between the two places. Bernard Hart lived in New York for the rest of his life, and attained a high rank in the community. "Towering aloft among the magnates of the city of the last and present century," writes a local historian, "is Bernard Hart." He was successful in business, very active in social and charitable affairs, and prominent in the synagogue. In 1802 he formed a partnership with Leonard Lispenard, under the name of Lispenard and Hart. They were commission merchants and auctioneers, and did a large business. In 1803 the firm was dissolved, and Mr. Hart continued in trade by himself. In 1831 he became Secretary to the New York Stock Exchange Board, and held that office for twenty-two years, resigning at the age of eighty-nine. In 1795, the year of the yellow fever plague, Bernard Hart rendered heroic service, as is testified by a contemporary annalist. "Mr. Hart and Mr. Pell, who kept store at 108 Market Street, a few doors from Mr. Hart, were unceasing in their exertions. Night and day, hardly giving themselves time to sleep or eat, they were among the sick and dying, relieving their wants. They were angels of mercy in those awful days of the first great pestilence."

Bernard Hart was also a military man, and in 1797 became quartermaster of a militia regiment, composed wholly of citizens of New York. That he was a "clubable" man, too, is very apparent. It was an era of clubs, and Bernard Hart founded the association known as "The Friary." It met on the first and third Sundays of every month at 56 Pine Street. He was also President of The House of Lords, a merchants' club, which met at Baker's City Tavern every week-day night, at 7 o'clock, adjourning at 10 o'clock. Each member was allowed a limited quantity of liquor, business was discussed, contracts were made, and sociability was promoted. He was, too, a member of the St. George Society, and is said, also, to have been a Mason, belonging to Holland Lodge No. 8, of which John Jacob Astor was master in 1798. Bernard Hart was a devout Jew, and his name frequently appears in the records of the Spanish and Portuguese Synagogue, known as the Congregation Shearith Israel, the first synagogue established in New York. He lived in various houses,—at 86 Water Street, at 24 Cedar Street, at 12 Lispenard Street, at 20 Varick Street, and finally at 23 White Street. A picture of him still hangs in the counting-room of Messrs. Arthur Lipper and Co., in Broad Street.

How came it that this orthodox Jew, this pillar of the synagogue, married a Christian woman? The romance, if there was one, is imperfectly preserved even in the family traditions. It is known only that in 1799 Bernard Hart married Catharine Brett, a woman of good family; that after living together for a year or less, they separated; that there was one son, Henry Hart, born February 1, 1800, who lived with his mother, and who became the father of Bret Harte.

A few years later, in 1806, Bernard Hart married Zipporah Seixas, one of the sixteen children, eight sons and eight daughters, born to Benjamin Mendez Seixas. These young women were noted for their beauty and amiability, and so strong was the impression which they produced that it lasted even until the succeeding generation. The marriage ceremony was performed by Gershom Mendez Seixas, a brother of the bride's father, and rabbi of the synagogue already mentioned. From this marriage came numerous sons and daughters, whose careers were honorable. Emanuel B. Hart was a merchant and broker, an alderman, a member of Congress in 1851 and 1852, and Surveyor of the Port of New York from 1859 to 1861. Benjamin I. Hart was a broker in New York. David Hart, a teller in the Pacific Bank, fought gallantly at the battle of Bull Run and was badly wounded there. Theodore and Daniel Hart were merchants in New York.

BERNARD HART
Bret Harte's Grandfather

One of Bernard Hart's sons by the Hebrew wife was named Henry. He was born in 1817, and died of consumption in his father's house in White Street on November 16, 1850. He was unmarried. Bernard Hart himself died in 1855, at the age of ninety-one. His wife was then living at the age of seventy-nine.

None of his descendants on the Hebrew side knew of his marriage to Catharine Brett or of the existence of his son, the first Henry Hart, until some years after Bret Harte's death. It seems almost incredible that this Hebrew merchant, prominent as he was in business and social life, in clubs and societies, in the militia and the synagogue, should have been able to keep the fact of his first marriage so secret that it remained a secret for a hundred years; it seems very unlikely that a woman of good English birth and family should in that era have married a Jew; it is highly improbable that a father should give to a son by a second marriage the same name already given to his son by a former marriage. And yet all these things are indisputable facts. There are members of Bret Harte's family still living who remember Bernard Hart, and his occasional visits to the family of Henry Hart, his son by Catharine Brett, whom he assisted with money and advice so long as he lived. Bret Harte himself remembered being taken to the New York Stock Exchange by his father, who there pointed out to him his grandfather, Bernard Hart. It may be added that between the descendants of Bernard Hart and Catharine Brett and those of Bernard Hart and Zipporah Seixas there is a marked resemblance.

How far was the venerable Jew from suspecting that the one fact in his life which he was so anxious to conceal was the very fact which would rescue his name from oblivion, and preserve it so long as English literature shall exist! Even if the marriage to Catharine Brett, a Christian woman, had been known it would not, according to Jewish law, have invalidated the second marriage, but it would doubtless have prevented that marriage. What rendered the long concealment possible was, of course, the deep gulf which then separated Jew from Gentile. Catharine Brett had been warned by her father that he would cast her off if she married the Jew; and this threat was fulfilled. Thenceforth, she lived a lonely and secluded life, supported, it is believed, by her husband, but having no other relation with him. The marriage was so improbable, so ill-assorted, so productive of unhappiness, and yet so splendid in its ultimate results, that it seems almost atheistic to ascribe it to chance. Is the world governed in that haphazard manner!

But who was this unfortunate Catharine Brett? She was a granddaughter of Roger Brett, an Englishman, and, it is supposed, a lieutenant in the British Navy, who first appears in New York, about the year 1700, as a friend of Lord Cornbury, then Governor of the Province. The coat of arms which Roger Brett brought over, and which is still preserved on a pewter placque, is identical with that borne by Judge, Sir

Balliol Brett, before his elevation to the peerage as Viscount Esher. Roger Brett was a vestryman of Trinity Church from 1703 to 1706. In November, 1703, he married Catharyna Rombout, daughter of Francis Rombout, who was one of the early and successful merchants in the city of New York. Her mother, Helena Teller, daughter of William Teller, a captain in the Indian wars, was married three times, Francis Rombout being her third husband. Schuyler Colfax, once Vice-President of the United States, was descended from her. Francis Rombout was born at Hasselt in Belgium, and came to New Amsterdam while it still belonged to the Dutch. He was an elder in the Dutch Church, served as lieutenant in an expedition against the Swedes, was Schepen under the Dutch municipal government, alderman under the reorganized British government, and, in 1679, became the twelfth Mayor of New York.

Francis Rombout left to his daughter, Roger Brett's wife, an immense estate on the Hudson River, which included the Fishkills, and consisted chiefly of forest land. There, in 1709, the young couple built for their home a manor house, which is still standing and is occupied by a descendant of Roger Brett, to whom it has come down in direct line through the female branch. A few years later, at least before 1720, Roger Brett was drowned at the mouth of Fishkill Creek in the Hudson River. Catharyna, his widow, survived him for many years. She was a woman of marked character and ability, known through all that region as Madame Brett. She administered her large estate, leased and sold much land to settlers, controlled the Indians who were numerous, superintended a mill to which both Dutchess County and Orange County sent their grist, owned the sloops which were the only carriers between this outpost of the Colony and the city of New York, and was one of the founders of the Fishkill Dutch Church. In that church, a tablet to her memory was recently erected by the Rombout-Brett Association, formed a few years ago by her descendants. The tablet is inscribed as follows:—

In memory of Catharyna Brett, widow of Lieutenant Roger Brett, R.N., and daughter of Francis Rombout, a grantee of Rombout patent, born in the city of New York 1687, died in Rombout Precinct, Fishkill, 1764. To this church she was a liberal contributor, and underneath its pulpit her body is interred. This tablet was erected by her descendants and others interested in the Colonial history of Fishkill, A. D. 1904.

Roger Brett had four sons, of whom two died young and unmarried, and two, Francis and Robert, married, and left many children. Whether the Catharine Brett who married Bernard Hart was descended from Francis or from Robert is not certainly known. Francis Brett's wife was a descendant of Cornelius Van Wyck, one of the earliest settlers on Long Island. Robert Brett's wife was a Miss Dubois.

Such was the ancestry of Bret Harte's paternal grandmother. Her son, Henry Hart, lived with her until, on May 5, 1817, he entered Union College, Schenectady, as a member of the class of 1820. He remained in college until the end of his Senior year, and passed all his examinations for graduation, but failed to receive his degree because a college bill amounting to ninety dollars had not been paid. The previous bills were paid by his mother, "Catharine Hart." Alas! the non-payment of this bill was an omen of the future. Henry Hart and his illustrious son were both the reverse of thrifty or economical. Money seemed to fly away from them; they had no capacity for keeping it, and no discretion in spending it. Unpaid bills were the bane of their existence. Henry Hart's improvidence is ascribed, in part, by those who knew him, to the irregular manner in which his father supplied him with money, Bernard Hart being sometimes very lavish and sometimes very parsimonious with his son.

Henry Hart was a well-built, athletic-looking man, with rather large features, and dark hair and complexion. His height was five feet ten inches, and his weight one hundred and seventy pounds. He was an accomplished scholar, speaking French, Spanish and Italian, and being well versed in Greek and Latin. He passed his short life as school-teacher, tutor, lecturer and translator.

On May 16, 1830, he married Elizabeth Rebecca, daughter of Henry Philip Ostrander, an "upstate" surveyor and farmer, who belonged to a prominent Dutch family which settled at Kingston on the Hudson in 1659. It will be remembered that the hero of Bret Harte's story, *Two Americans*, is Major Philip Ostrander. The mother of Elizabeth Ostrander, Henry Hart's wife, was Abigail Truesdale, of English descent. Henry Hart was brought up by his mother in the Dutch Reformed faith, but soon after leaving college, owing to what influence is unknown, he became a Catholic, and remained such until his death. His wife was an Episcopalian, and his children were of that, if of any persuasion.

In 1833 we find Henry Hart at Albany, and there he remained until 1836, the year of Bret Harte's birth. In 1833 and 1834, he was instructor in the Albany Female Academy, a girls' school, famous in its day, where he taught reading and writing, rhetoric and mathematics. Early in 1835 he left the Academy, and for two years he conducted a private school of his own at 15 Columbia Street, but this appears not to have been successful, for he ceased to be a resident of the city in the latter part of 1836, or early in 1837. One event in Henry Hart's life at Albany is significant. In December, 1833, a meeting was held in the Mayor's Court Room to organize a Young Men's Association, which proved to be a great success, and which has played an important part in the life of the city down to the present day. Henry Hart, though a comparative stranger in Albany, was chosen to explain the objects of the Association at this meeting, and at the next meeting he was elected one of the Managers. When Bret Harte came East from California, he went to Albany and addressed the Association, upon the invitation of its members.

After leaving Albany the family led an unsettled, uncomfortable life, going from place to place, with occasional returns to the home of an Ostrander relative in Hudson Street in the city of New York. The late Mr. A. V. S. Anthony, the well-known engraver, was a neighbor of Bret Harte in Hudson Street, and played and fought with him there, when they were both about seven or eight years old. Afterward they met in California, and again in London. From Albany the Henry Hart family went to Hudson, where Mr. Hart acted as principal of an academy; and subsequently they lived in New Brunswick, New Jersey; in Philadelphia; in Providence, Rhode Island; in Lowell, Massachusetts; in Boston and elsewhere.

A few years before her death Mrs. Hart read the life of Bronson Alcott, and when she laid down the book she remarked that the troubles and privations endured by the Alcott family bore a striking resemblance to those which she and her children had undergone. Some want of balance in Henry Hart's character prevented him, notwithstanding his undoubted talents, his enthusiasm, and his accomplishments, from ever obtaining any material success in life, or even a home for his family and himself. But he was a man of warm impulses and deep feeling. When Henry Clay was nominated for the Presidency in 1844, Henry Hart espoused his cause almost with fury. He gave up all other employment to electioneer in behalf of the Whig candidate, and the defeat of his idol was a crushing blow from which he never recovered. It was the first time that a really great man, as Clay certainly was, had been outvoted in a contest for the Presidency by a commonplace man, like Polk; and Clay's defeat was regarded by his adherents not only as a hideous injustice, but as a national calamity. It is not given to every one to take any impersonal matter so seriously as Henry Hart took the defeat of his political chieftain; and his death a year later, in 1845, may justly be regarded as a really noble ending to a troubled and unsuccessful life.

CHAPTER II

BRET HARTE'S BOYHOOD

After the death of Henry Hart, his widow remained with her children in New York and Brooklyn until 1853. They were supported in part by her family, the Ostranders, and in part by Bernard Hart. There were four children, two sons and two daughters. Eliza, the eldest, who is still living, and to whom the author is indebted for information about the family, was married in 1851 to Mr. F. F. Knaufft, and her life has been passed mainly in New York and New Jersey. Mr. Ernest Knaufft, editor of the "Art Student," and well known as a critic and writer, is her son. Unfortunately, Mrs. Knaufft's house was burned in 1868, and with it many letters and papers relating to her father and his parents, and also the MSS. of various lectures delivered by him.

The younger daughter, Margaret B., went to California with Bret Harte, and preceded him as a contributor of stories and sketches to the "Golden Era," and other papers in San Francisco. She married Mr. B. H. Wyman, and is still a resident of California. Bret Harte's sisters are women of distinguished appearance, and remarkable for force of character.

Bret Harte's only brother, Henry, had a short but striking career, which displayed, even more perhaps than did the career of Bret Harte himself, that intensity which seems to have been their chief inheritance from the Hebrew strain. The following account of him is furnished by Mrs. Knaufft:

"My brother Henry was two years and six months older than his brother Francis Brett Harte. Henry began reading history when he was six years old, and from that time until he was twelve years of age, he read history, ancient and modern, daily, sometimes only one hour, at other times from two to three hours. What interested him was the wars; he would read for two or three hours, and then if a battle had been won by his favorite warriors, he would spring to his feet, shouting, 'Victory is ours,' repeatedly. He would read lying on the floor, and often we would say ridiculous and provoking things about him, and sometimes pull his hair, but he never paid the slightest attention to us, being perfectly oblivious of his surroundings. His memory was phenomenal. He read Froissart's Chronicles when he was about ten years old, and could repeat page after page accurately. One evening an old professor was talking with my mother about some event in ancient history, and he mentioned the date of a decisive battle. Henry, who was listening intently, said, 'I beg pardon, Professor, you are wrong. That battle was fought on such a date.' The professor was astonished. 'Where did you hear about that battle?' he asked. 'I read that history last year,' replied Henry.

"When the boy was twelve years old, he came home from school one day, and rushing into his mother's room, shouted, 'War is declared! War is declared!' 'What in the name of common sense has that got to do with you?' asked my mother. 'Mother,' said Henry, 'I am going to fight for my country; that is what I was created for.'

"After some four or five months of constant anxiety, caused by Henry's offering himself to every captain whose ship was going to or near Mexico, a friend of my mother's told Lieutenant Benjamin Dove of the Navy about Henry, and he became greatly interested, and finally, through his efforts, Henry was taken on his ship. Henry was so small that his uniform had to be made for him. The ship went ashore on the Island of Eleuthera, to the great delight of my brother, who wrote his mother a startling account of the shipwreck. I cannot remember whether the ship was able to go on her voyage, or whether the men were all transferred to Commander Tatnall's ship the 'Spitfire.' I know that Henry was on Commander Tatnall's ship at the Bombardment of Vera Cruz, and was in the fort or forts at Tuxpan, where the Commander and Henry were both wounded. Commander Tatnall wrote my mother that when Henry was wounded, he exclaimed, 'Thank God, I am shot in the face,' and that when he inquired for Henry, he was told that he was hiding because he did not want his wound dressed. When the Commander found Henry, he asked him why he did not want his wound dressed. With tears in his eyes Henry said, 'Because I'm afraid it won't show any scar if the surgeon dresses it.'

"When my brother returned from Mexico, he became very restless. The sea had cast its spell about him, and finally a friend, captain of a ship, took Henry on a very long voyage, going around Cape Horn to California. When they arrived at San Francisco, my brother, who was then just sixteen, was taken in charge by a relative. I never heard of his doing anything remarkable during his short life. As the irony of fate would have it, he died suddenly from pneumonia, just before the Civil War."

Bret Harte was equally precocious, and he was precocious even in respect to the sense of humor, which commonly requires some little experience for its development. It is a family tradition that he burlesqued the rather bald language of his primer at the age of five; and his sisters distinctly remember that, a year later, he came home from a school exhibition, and made them scream with laughter by mimicking the boy who spoke "My name is Norval." He was naturally a very quiet, studious child; and this tendency was increased by ill health. From his sixth to his tenth year, he was unable to lead an active life. At the age of six he was reading Shakspere and Froissart, and at seven he took up "Dombey and Son," and so began his acquaintance with that author who was to influence him far more than any other. From Dickens he proceeded to Fielding, Goldsmith, Smollett, Cervantes, and Washington Irving. During an illness of two months, when he was fourteen years old, he learned to read Greek sufficiently well to astonish his mother.

If the Hart family resembled the Alcott family in the matter of misfortunes and privations, so it did, also, in its intellectual atmosphere. Mrs. Hart shared her husband's passion for literature; and she had a keen, critical faculty, to which, the family think, Bret Harte was much indebted for the perfection of his style. Henry Hart had accumulated a library surprisingly large for a man of his small means, and the whole household was given to the reading not simply of books, but of the best books, and to talking about them. It was a household in which the literary second-rate was unerringly, and somewhat scornfully, discriminated from the first-rate.

When Bret Harte was only eleven years old he wrote a poem called *Autumnal Musings* which he sent surreptitiously to the "New York Sunday Atlas," and the poem was published in the next issue. This was a wonderful feat for a boy of that age, and he was naturally elated by seeing his verses in print; but the family critics pointed out their defects with such unpleasant frankness that the conceit of the youthful poet was nipped in the bud. Many years afterward, Bret Harte said with a laugh, "I sometimes wonder that I ever wrote a line of poetry again." But the discipline was wholesome, and as he grew older his mother took his literary ambitions more seriously. When he was about sixteen, he wrote a long poem called *The Hudson River*. It was never published, but Mrs. Hart made a careful study of it; and at her son's request, wrote out her criticisms at length.

It will thus be seen that Bret Harte, as an author, far from being an academic, was strictly a home product. He left school at the age of thirteen and went immediately into a lawyer's office where he remained about a year, and thence into the counting-room of a merchant. He was self-supporting before he reached the age of sixteen. In 1851, as has already been mentioned, his older sister was married; and in 1853 his mother went to California with a party of relatives and friends, in order to make her home there with her elder son, Henry. She had intended to take with her the other two children, Margaret and Francis Brett; but as the daughter was in school, she left the two behind for a few months, and they followed in February, 1854. They travelled by the Nicaragua route, and after a long, tiresome, but uneventful journey, landed safely in San Francisco. No mention of their arrival was made in the newspapers; no guns were fired; no band played; but the youth of eighteen who thus slipped unnoticed into California was the one person, out of the many thousands arriving in those early years, whose coming was a fact of importance.

CHAPTER III

BRET HARTE'S WANDERINGS IN CALIFORNIA

Bret Harte and his sister arrived at San Francisco in March, 1854, stayed there one night, and went the next morning to Oakland, across the Bay, where their mother and her second husband, Colonel Andrew Williams, were living. In this house the boy remained about a year, teaching for a while, and afterward serving as clerk in an apothecary's shop. During this year he began his career as a professional writer, contributing some stories and poems to Eastern magazines.

Bret Harte, like Thackeray, was fortunate in his stepfather, and if, according to the accepted story, Thackeray's stepfather was the prototype of Colonel Newcome, the two men must have had much in common. Colonel Williams was born at Cherry Valley in the State of New York, and was graduated at Union College with the Class of 1819. Henry Hart's class was that of 1820, but the two young men were friends in college. Colonel Williams had seen much of the world, having travelled extensively in Europe early in the century, and he was a cultivated, well-read man. But he was chiefly remarkable for his high standard of honor, and his amiable, chivalrous nature. He was a gentleman of the old school in the best sense, grave but sympathetic, courtly but kind. His generosity was unbounded. Such a man might appear to have been somewhat out of place in bustling California, but his qualities were appreciated there. He was the first Mayor of Oakland, in the year 1857, and was re-elected the following year. Colonel Williams built a comfortable house in Oakland, one of the first, if not the very first in that city in which laths and plaster were used; but land titles in California were extremely uncertain, and after a long and stubborn contest in the courts, Colonel Williams was dispossessed, and lost the house upon which he had expended much time and money. He then took up his residence in San Francisco, where he lived until his return to the East in the year 1871. His wife, Bret Harte's mother, died at Morristown, New Jersey, April 4, 1875, and was buried in the family lot at Greenwood, New York. The following year he went back to California for a visit to Bret Harte's sister, Mrs. Wyman, but soon after his arrival died of pneumonia at the age of seventy-six.

The San Francisco and Oakland papers spoke very highly of Colonel Williams after his death, and one of them closed an account of his life with the following words: "Colonel Williams had that indefinable sweetness of manner which indicates innate refinement and nobility of soul. There was a touch of the antique about him. He seemed a little out of time and place in this hurried age of ours. He belonged to and typified the calmer temper of a former generation. A gentler spirit never walked the earth. He personified all the sweet charities of life. His heart was great, warm and tender, and he died leaving no man in the world his enemy. Colonel Williams was the stepfather of Bret Harte, between whom and himself there existed the most affectionate relations."

It was during his first year in California that Bret Harte had that gambling experience which he has related in his *Bohemian Days in San Francisco*, and which throws so much light on his character that it should be quoted here in part at least:—

"I was watching roulette one evening, intensely absorbed in the mere movement of the players. Either they were so preoccupied with the game, or I was really older looking than my actual years, but a bystander laid his hand familiarly on my shoulder, and said, as to an ordinary *habitué*, 'Ef you're not chippin' in yourself, pardner, s'pose you give *me* a show.' Now, I honestly believe that up to that moment I had no intention, nor even a desire, to try my own fortune. But in the embarrassment of the sudden address I put my hand in my pocket, drew out a coin and laid it, with an attempt at carelessness, but a vivid consciousness that I was blushing, upon a vacant number. To my horror I saw that I had put down a large coin—the bulk of my possessions! I did not flinch, however; I think any boy who reads this will understand my feeling; it was not only my coin but my manhood at stake.... I even affected to be listening to the music. The wheel spun again; the game was declared, the rake was busy, but I did not move. At last the man I had displaced touched me on the arm and whispered, 'Better make a straddle and divide your stake this time.' I did not understand him, but as I saw he was looking at the board, I was obliged to look, too. I drew back dazed and bewildered! Where my coin had lain a moment before was a glittering heap of gold.

"... 'Make your game, gentlemen,' said the croupier monotonously. I thought he looked at me—indeed, everybody seemed to be looking at me—and my companion repeated his warning. But here I must again appeal to the boyish reader in defence of my idiotic obstinacy. To have taken advice would have shown my youth. I shook my head—I could not trust my voice. I smiled, but with a sinking heart, and let my stake remain. The ball again sped round the wheel, and stopped. There was a pause. The croupier indolently advanced his rake and swept my whole pile with others into the bank! I had lost it all. Perhaps it may be difficult for me to explain why I actually felt relieved, and even to some extent triumphant, but I seemed to have asserted my grown-up independence—possibly at the cost of reducing the number of my meals for days; but what of that!... The man who had spoken to me, I think, suddenly realized, at the moment of my disastrous *coup*, the fact of my extreme youth. He moved toward the banker, and leaning over him whispered a few words. The banker looked up, half impatiently, half kindly,—his hand straying tentatively toward the pile of coin. I instinctively knew what he meant, and, summoning my determination, met his eyes with all the indifference I could assume, and walked away."

In 1856, being then twenty years old, young Harte left Colonel Williams's house, and thenceforth shifted for himself. His first engagement was as tutor in a private family at Alamo in the San Ramon Valley. There were several sons in the family, and one or two of them were older than their tutor. The next year he went to Humboldt Bay in Humboldt County, on the upper coast of California, about two hundred and fifty miles north of San Francisco. Thence he made numerous trips as express messenger on stages running eastward to Trinity County, and northward to Del Norte, which, as the name implies, is the extreme upper county in the State. The experience was a valuable one, and it was concerning this period of Bret Harte's career that his friend, Charles Warren Stoddard, wrote: "He bore a charmed life. Probably his youth was his salvation, for he ran a thousand risks, yet seemed only to gain in health and spirits."

The post of express messenger was especially dangerous. Bret Harte's predecessor was shot through the arm by a highwayman; his successor was killed. The safe containing the treasure carried by Wells, Fargo and Company, who did practically all the express business in California, was always heavily chained to the box of the coach, and sometimes, when a particularly large amount of gold had to be conveyed, armed guards were carried inside of the coach. For the stage to be "held up" by highwaymen was a common occurrence, and the danger from breakdowns and floods was not small. In the course of a few months between the towns of Visalia and Kern River the overland stage broke the legs of three several drivers. It was a frequent thing for the stage to cross a stream, suddenly become a river, with the horses swimming, a strong current running through the coach itself, and the passengers perched on the seats to escape being swept away.

With these dangers of flood and field to encounter, with precipices to skirt, with six half-broken horses to control, and with the ever-present possibility of serving as a target for "road-agents," it may be imagined that the California stage-driver was no common man, and the type is preserved in the character of Yuba Bill. He can be compared only with Colonel Starbottle and Jack Hamlin, and Jack Hamlin was one of the few men whom Yuba Bill condescended to treat as an equal. Their meeting in *Gabriel Convoy* is historic: "'Barkeep—hist that pizen over to Jack. Here's to ye agin, ole man. But I'm glad to see ye!' The crowd hung breathless over the two men—awestruck and respectful. It was a meeting of the gods. None dared speak."

"Yuba Bill," writes Mr. Chesterton, "is not convivial; it might almost be said that he is too great even to be sociable. A circle of quiescence and solitude, such as that which might ring a saint or a hermit, rings this majestic and profound humorist. His jokes do not flow from him, like those of Mr. Weller, sparkling and continual like the play of a fountain in a pleasure garden; they fall suddenly and capriciously, like a crash of avalanche from a great mountain. Tony Weller has the noisy humor of London. Yuba Bill has the silent humor of the earth." Then the critic quotes Yuba Bill's rebuke to the passenger who has expressed a too-confident opinion as to the absence of the expected highwaymen: "'You ain't puttin' any price on that opinion, air ye?' inquired Bill politely.

"'No.'

"'Cos thar's a comic paper in 'Frisco pays for them things, and I've seen worse things in it.'"

Even better, perhaps, is Yuba Bill's reply to Judge Beeswinger, who rashly betrayed some over-consciousness of his importance as a member of the State Assembly. "'Any political news from below, Bill?' he asked, as the latter slowly descended from his lofty perch, without, however, any perceptible coming down of mien or manner. 'Not much,' said Bill, with deliberate gravity. 'The President o' the United States hezn't bin hisself sens you refoosed that seat in the Cabinet. The gin'ral feelin' in perlitical circles is one o' regret.'"

"To be rebuked thus," Mr. Chesterton continues, "is like being rebuked by the pyramids or by the starry heavens. There is about Yuba Bill this air of a pugnacious calm, a stepping back to get his distance for a shattering blow, which is like that of Dr. Johnson at his best. And the effect is inexpressibly increased by the background and the whole picture which Bret Harte paints so powerfully,—the stormy skies, the sombre gorge, the rocking and spinning coach, and high above the feverish passengers the huge, dark form of Yuba Bill, a silent mountain of humor."

After his service as expressman, Bret Harte went to a town called Union, about three hundred miles north of San Francisco, where he learned the printer's trade in the office of the "Humboldt Times." He also taught school again in Union, and for the second time acted as clerk in a drug store. Speaking of his experience in this capacity, Mr. Pemberton, his English biographer, gravely says, "I have heard English physicians express wonder at his grasp of the subject." One wonders, in turn, if Bret Harte did not do a little hoaxing in this line. "To the end of his days," writes Mr. Pemberton, "he could speak with authority as to the virtues and properties of medicines." Young Harte had a wonderful faculty of picking up information, and no doubt his two short terms of service as a compounder of medicines were not thrown away upon him. But Bret Harte was the last person in the world to pose as an expert, and it seems probable that the extent of his knowledge was fairly described in the story *How Reuben Allen Saw Life in San Francisco*. That part of this story which deals with the drug clerk is so plainly autobiographical, and so characteristic of the author, that a quotation from it will not be out of place:—

"It was near midnight, the hour of closing, and the junior partner was alone in the shop. He felt drowsy; the mysterious incense of the shop, that combined essence of drugs, spice, scented soap, and orris root—which always reminded him of the Arabian nights—was affecting him. He yawned, and then, turning away, passed behind the counter, took down a jar labelled 'Glycyrr. Glabra,' selected a piece of Spanish licorice, and meditatively sucked it....

"He was just nineteen, he had early joined the emigration to California, and after one or two previous light-hearted essays at other occupations, for which he was singularly unfitted, he had saved enough to embark on his present venture, still less suited to his temperament.... A slight knowledge of Latin as a written language, an American schoolboy's acquaintance with chemistry and natural philosophy, were deemed sufficient by his partner, a regular physician, for practical cooperation in the vending of drugs and putting up of prescriptions. He knew the difference between acids and alkalis and the peculiar results which attended their incautious combination. But he was excessively deliberate, painstaking and cautious. There was no danger of his poisoning anybody through haste or carelessness, but it was possible that an urgent 'case' might have succumbed to the disease while he was putting up the remedy.... In those days the 'heroic' practice of medicine was in keeping with the abnormal development of the country; there were 'record' doses of calomel and quinine, and he had once or twice incurred the fury of local practitioners by sending back their prescriptions with a modest query."

SAN FRANCISCO, NOVEMBER, 1844
J. C. Ward, del.

It was doubtless Bret Harte's experience in the drug store which suggested the story of Liberty Jones, whose discovery of an arsenical spring in the forest was the means of transforming that well-made, but bony and sallow Missouri girl into a beautiful woman, with well-rounded limbs, rosy cheeks, lustrous eyes and glossy hair.

It has been a matter of some discussion whether Bret Harte ever worked as a miner or not; and the evidence upon the point is not conclusive. But it is hard to believe that he did not try his luck at gold-seeking, when everybody else was trying, and his narrative *How I Went to the Mines* seems to have the ear-marks of an autobiographical sketch. It is regarded as such by his sisters; and the modest, deprecating manner in which the storyteller's adventures are related, serves to confirm that impression.

Of all his experiences in California, those which gave him the most pleasure seem to have been his several short but fruitful terms of service as schoolmaster and tutor. His knowledge of children, being based upon sympathy, became both acute and profound. How many thousand million times have children gone to school of a morning and found the master awaiting them, and yet who but Bret Harte has ever described the exact manner of their approach!

"They came in their usual desultory fashion—the fashion of country school-children the world over—irregularly, spasmodically, and always as if accidentally; a few hand-in-hand, others driven ahead of or dragged behind their elders; some in straggling groups more or less coherent and at times only connected by far-off intermediate voices scattered over a space of half a mile, but never quite alone; always preoccupied by something else than the actual business in hand; appearing suddenly from ditches, behind trunks, and between fence-rails; cropping up in unexpected places along the road after vague and purposeless détours—seemingly going anywhere and everywhere but to school!"

Bret Harte realized the essential truth that children are not little, immature men and women, but rather infantile barbarians, creatures of an archaic type, representing a period in the development of the human race which does not survive in adult life. Hence the reserve, the aloofness of children, their remoteness from grown people. There are certain things which the boy most deeply feels that he must not do, and certain other things that he must do; as, for example, to bear without telling any pains that may be inflicted upon him by his mates or by older boys. For a thousand years or more fathers and mothers have held a different code upon these points, but with how little effect upon their children! Johnny Filgee illustrated upon a truly Californian scale these boyish qualities of reticence and endurance. When he had accidentally been shot in the duel between the Master and Cressy's father (the child being perched in a tree), he refrained from making the least sound, although a word or an outcry would have brought the men to his assistance. "A certain respect to himself and his brother kept him from uttering even a whimper of weakness." Left alone in the dark woods, unable to move, Johnny became convinced that his end was near, and he pleased himself by thinking that "they would all feel exceedingly sorry and alarmed, and would regret having made him wash himself on Saturday night." And so, having composed himself, "he turned on his side to die, as became the scion of an heroic race!"

Then follows a sentence in which the artist, with one bold sweep of his brush, paints in Nature herself as a witness of the scene; and yet her material immensity does not dwarf or belittle the spiritual superiority of the wounded youngster in the foreground: "The free woods, touched by an upspringing wind, waved their dark arms above him, and higher yet a few patient stars silently ranged themselves around his pillow."

That other Johnny, for whom *Santa Claus Came to Simpson's Bar*, Richelieu Sharpe in *A Phyllis of the Sierras*, John Milton Harcourt in the *First Family of Tasajara*, Leonidas Boone, the *Mercury of the Foot-Hills*, and John Bunyan Medliker, the *Youngest Prospector in Calaveras,*—all illustrate the same type, with many individual variations.

Another phase of the archaic nature of children is their extreme sensitiveness to impressions. Just as a squirrel hears more acutely than a man, and the dog's sense of smell is keener, so a child, within the comparatively small range of his mental activity, is more open to subtle indications. Bret Harte often touches upon this quality of childhood, as in the following passage: "It was not strange, therefore, that the little people of the Indian Spring School knew perhaps more of the real relations of Cressy McKinstry to her admirers than the admirers themselves. Not that the knowledge was outspoken—for children rarely gossip in the grown-up sense, or even communicate by words intelligent to the matured intellect. A whisper, a laugh that often seemed vague and unmeaning, conveyed to each other a world of secret significance, and an apparently senseless burst of merriment in which the whole class joined—and that the adult critic set down to 'animal spirits'—a quality much more rare with children than is generally supposed—was only a sympathetic expression of some discovery happily oblivious to older perceptions."

This acuteness of perception, seen also in some men of a simple, archaic type, puts children in close relationship with the lower animals, unless, indeed, it is counteracted by that cruelty which is also a quality of childhood. When Richelieu Sharpe retired to rest, it was in company with a whole retinue of dependents. "On the pillow near him an indistinguishable mass of golden fur—the helpless bulk of a squirrel chained to the leg of his cot; at his feet a wall-eyed cat, who had followed his tyrannous caprices with the long-suffering devotion of her sex; on the shelf above him a loathsome collection of flies and tarantulas in dull green bottles, a slab of gingerbread for light nocturnal refreshment, and his sister's pot of bear's grease.... The sleeper stirred slightly and awoke. At the same moment, by some mysterious sympathy, a pair of beady bright eyes appeared in the bulk of fur near his curls, the cat stretched herself, and even a vague agitation was heard in the bottles on the shelf."

That last touch, intimating some community of feeling between Richelieu and his insects, is, as the Reader will grant, the touch of genius. Bridging the gulf impassable for an ordinary mind, it assumes a fact which, like the shape of Donatello's ears, is true to the imagination, and not so manifestly impossible as to shock the reason.

It is sometimes said that California in the Fifties represented the American character in its most extreme form,—the quintessence, as it were, of energy and democracy. This statement would certainly apply to the California children, in whom the ordinary forwardness of the American child became a sort of elfish precocity. Such a boy was Richelieu Sharpe. His gallantries, his independence, his self-reliance, his adult ambitions,—these qualities, oddly assorted with the primeval, imaginative nature of the true child, made Richelieu such a youngster as was never seen outside of the United States, and perhaps never seen outside of California.

The English child of the upper classes, as Bret Harte knew him in after years, made a strange contrast to the Richelieu Sharpes and John Bunyan Medlikers that he had learned to love in California. In a letter to his wife written from the house of James Anthony Froude, in 1878, he said: "The eldest girl is not unlike a highly-educated Boston girl, and the conversation sometimes reminds me of Boston. The youngest daughter, only ten years old, told her sister, in reference to some conversation Froude and I had, that 'she feared' (this child) 'that Mr. Bret Harte was inclined to be sceptical!' Doesn't this exceed any English story of the precocity of American children? The boy, scarcely fourteen, acts like a boy of eight (an American boy of eight) and talks like a man of thirty, so far as pure English and facility of expression go. His manners are perfect, yet he is perfectly simple and boy-like. The culture and breeding of some English children are really marvellous. But somehow—and here comes one of my 'buts'—there's always a suggestion of some repression, some discipline that I don't like."

Bret Harte's last employment during this wandering life was that of compositor, printer's devil, and assistant editor of the "Northern California," published at Eureka, a seacoast town in Humboldt County. Here he met Mr. Charles A. Murdock, who gives this interesting account of him: "He was fond of whist, genial, witty, but quiet and reserved, something of a 'tease'" (the Reader will remember that Mr. Howells speaks of this trait) "and a practical joker; not especially popular, as he was thought to be fastidious, and to hold himself aloof from 'the general'; but he was simply a self-respecting, gentlemanly fellow, with quiet tastes, and a keen insight into character. He was no roisterer, and his habits were clean. He was too independent and indifferent to curry favor, or to counterfeit a liking."

During a temporary absence of the editor Bret Harte was entrusted with the conduct of the paper, and about that time a cowardly massacre of Indians was perpetrated by some Americans in the vicinity. This was no uncommon event, and the usual attitude of the Pioneers toward the Indians may be gathered from the following passage in a letter written to a newspaper in August, 1851, from Rogue River: "During this period we have been searching about in the mountains, disturbing villages, destroying all the males we could find, and capturing women and children. We have killed about thirty altogether, and have about twenty-eight now in camp." At the Stanislaus Diggings, in 1851, a miner called to an Indian boy to help him catch a loose horse. The boy, not understanding English, and being frightened by the man's gestures, ran away, whereupon the miner raised his gun and shot the boy dead.

Nobody hated injustice or cruelty more than Bret Harte, and in his editorial capacity he scathingly condemned the murder of Indians which occurred in the neighborhood of Eureka. The article excited the anger of the community, and a mob was collected for the avowed purpose of wrecking the newspaper office and hanging or otherwise maltreating the youthful writer. Bret Harte, armed with two pistols, awaited their coming during an evening which was probably the longest of his life. But the timely arrival of a few United States cavalrymen, sent for by some peace-lovers in the town, averted the danger; and the young journalist suffered no harm beyond an abrupt dismissal upon the hasty return of the editor.

This event ended his life as a wanderer, and he went back to San Francisco. There is not the slightest reason to think that during this period Bret Harte had any notion of describing California life in fiction or otherwise; and yet, if that had been his object, he could not have ordered his movements more wisely. He had lived on the seacoast and in the interior; he had seen cities, ranches, villages, and mines; he had been tutor, school-teacher, drug clerk, express messenger, printer, and editor. The period was less than two years, and yet he had accumulated a store of facts, impressions and images sufficient to last him a lifetime. He was of a most receptive nature; he was at a receptive age; the world was new to him, and he lived in it and observed it with all the zest of youth, of inexperience, of health and genius.

CHAPTER IV

BRET HARTE IN SAN FRANCISCO

Bret Harte returned to San Francisco in 1857, and his first occupation was that of setting type in the office of the "Golden Era." To this paper his sister, Mrs. Wyman, had been a contributor for some time, and it was through her that Bret Harte obtained employment on it as a printer.

The "Golden Era" had been established by young men. "It was," writes Mr. Stoddard, "the cradle and the grave of many a high hope. There was nothing to be compared with it on that side of the Mississippi; and though it could point with pride—it never failed to do so—to a somewhat notable list of contributors, it had always the fine air of the amateur, and was most complacently patronizing. The very pattern of paternal patronage was amiable Joe Lawrence, its Editor. He was an inveterate pipe-smoker, a pillar of cloud, as he sat in his editorial chair, an air of literary mystery enveloping him. He spoke as an oracle, and I remember his calling my attention to a certain anonymous contribution just received, and nodding his head prophetically, for he already had his eye on the fledgling author, a young compositor on the floor above. It was Bret Harte's first appearance in the 'Golden Era,' and doubtless Lawrence encouraged him as he had encouraged me when, out of the mist about him, he handed me secretly, and with a glance of caution—for his business partner, the marble-hearted, sat at his ledger not far away—he handed me a folded paper on which he had written this startling legend! 'Write some prose for the "Golden Era," and I will give you a dollar a column.'"

BRET HARTE IN 1861

What looks like a "little bill" in the hands, is a glove. The painter, once assumed uncommonly in expostulating with the artist who wished me to have as a background the Pyramids of Cheops — with, of course, "140 Centuries looking down on me."

It was not long before Bret Harte was promoted from the compositor's stand to the editorial room of the paper, and thus began his literary career. Among the sketches which he wrote a few years later, and which have been preserved in the complete edition of his works, are *In a Balcony*, *A Boy's Dog*, and *Sidewalkings*. Except for a slight restraint and stiffness of style, as if the author had not quite attained the full use of his wings, they show no indications of youth or crudity. *M'liss* also appeared in the "Golden Era," illustrated by a specially designed woodcut; and some persons think that this, the first, is also the best of Bret Harte's stories. At all events, the early *M'liss* is far superior to the author's lengthened and rewritten *M'liss* which was included in the collected edition of his works.

When it is added that the *Condensed Novels*, or at least the first of them, were also published in the "Golden Era," it will be seen with what astonishing quickness his literary style matured. He wrote at first anonymously; afterward, gaining a little self-confidence, he signed his stories "B," and then "Bret."

It was while engaged in writing for the "Golden Era," namely, on August 11, 1862, that Bret Harte was married to Miss Anna Griswold, daughter of Daniel S. and Mary Dunham Griswold of the city of New York. The marriage took place at San Raphael.

In 1864 he was appointed Secretary of the California Mint, an office which he held for six years and until he left California. For this position he was indebted to Mr. R. B. Swain, Superintendent of the Mint, a friend and parishioner of the Reverend Mr. King, who in that way became a friend of Bret Harte. Mr. Swain had a great liking for the young author, and made the official path easy for him. In fact, the position seems to have been one of those sinecures—or nearly that—which are the traditional reward of men of letters, but which a reforming and materialistic age has diverted to less noble uses.

In San Francisco, both before and after his marriage, Bret Harte lived a quiet, studious life, going very little into society. Of the time during which he was Secretary of the Mint, Mr. Stoddard writes: "He was now a man with a family; the resources derived from literature were uncertain and unsatisfactory. His influential friends paid him cheering visits in the gloomy office at the Mint where he leavened his daily loaves; and at his desk, between the exacting pages of the too literal ledger, many a couplet cropped out, and the outlines of now famous sketches were faintly limned. His friends were few, but notable. Society he ignored in those days. He used to accuse me of wasting my substance in riotous visitations, and thought me a spendthrift of time. He had the precious companionship of books, and the lives of those about him were as an open volume wherein he read 'curiously and to his profit.'"

Of the notable friends alluded to by Mr. Stoddard, the most important were the Reverend Thomas Starr King, and Mrs. Jessie Benton Frémont, daughter of Senator Benton, and wife of that Captain, afterward General Frémont, who became the first United States Senator from California, and Republican candidate for the Presidency in 1856, but who is best known as The Pathfinder. His adventures and narratives form an important part of California history.

Mrs. Frémont was an extremely clever, kind-hearted woman, who assisted Bret Harte greatly by her advice and criticism, still more by her sympathy and encouragement. Bret Harte was always inclined to underrate his own powers, and to be despondent as to his literary future. On one occasion when, as not seldom happened, he was cast down by his troubles and anxieties, and almost in despair as to his prospects, Mrs. Frémont sent him some cheering news, and he wrote to her: "I shall no longer disquiet myself about changes in residence or anything else, for I believe that if I were cast upon a desolate island, a savage would come to me next morning and hand me a three-cornered note to say that I had been appointed Governor at Mrs. Frémont's request, at a salary of $2400 a year."

How much twenty-four hundred a year seemed to him then, and how little a few years later! A Pioneer who knew them both writes: "Mrs. Frémont helped Bret Harte in many ways. In turn he marvelled at her worldly wisdom,—being able to tell one how to make a living. He named her daughter's pony 'Chiquita,' after the equine heroine of his poem." It was by Mrs. Frémont's intervention that Bret Harte first appeared in the "Atlantic Monthly," for, some years before he achieved fame, namely in 1863, *The Legend of Monte del Diablo* was published in that magazine. The story was gracefully, even beautifully written, but both in style and treatment it was a reflection of Washington Irving, who at that time rivalled Dickens as a popular author.

Many interesting letters were received by Mrs. Frémont from Bret Harte,—letters, her daughter thinks, almost as entertaining as his published writings; but unfortunately these treasures were destroyed by a fire in the city of New York.

Starr King, Bret Harte's other friend, was by far the most notable of the Protestant ministers in California. The son of a Universalist minister, he was born in the city of New York, but was brought up mainly in Charlestown, now a part of Boston. Upon leaving school he became first a clerk, then a school-teacher, and finally a Unitarian minister, preaching first at his father's old church in Charlestown, and afterward at the Hollis Street Unitarian Church in Boston. He obtained a wide reputation as preacher and lecturer, and as author of "The White Hills," still the best book upon the mountains of New England. In 1860, at the very time when his services were needed there, he became the pastor of a church in San Francisco, and to him is largely ascribed the credit of saving California to the Union. He was a man of deep moral convictions, and his addresses stirred the heart and moved the conscience of California.

The Southern element was very strong on the Pacific Slope, and it made itself felt in politics especially. Nearly one third of the delegates to the Constitutional Convention, held in September, 1849, were Southern men, and they acted as a unit under the leadership of W. M. Gwinn, afterward a member of the United States Senate. The ultimate design of the Southern delegates was the division of California into two States, the more southern of which should be a slave State. Slavery in California was openly advocated. But the Southern party was a minority, and the State Constitution declared that "neither slavery nor involuntary servitude, unless for the punishment of crime, shall ever be tolerated in this State." The Constitution did, however, exclude the testimony of colored persons from the courts; and when, in 1852, the negroes in San Francisco presented a petition to the House of Representatives asking for this right or privilege, the House refused to receive the petition, a majority of the members taking it as an insult. One member seriously proposed that it should be thrown out of the window.

In May, 1852, the "San Francisco Daily Herald" declared that the delay in admitting California as a State was due to Northern Abolitionists, of whom it said, with characteristic mildness: "Take the vile crowd of Abolitionists from the Canadian frontier to the banks of the Delaware, and you cannot find one in ten thousand of them who from philanthropy cares the amount of a dollar what becomes of the colored race. What they want is office." It does not seem to have occurred to the writer that in espousing the smallest and most hated political party in the whole country, the Abolitionists had not taken a very promising step in the direction of office-holding.

There was even talk of turning California into a "Pacific Republic," in the event of a dissolution of the Union. And that event was longed for by at least one California paper on the ground that "it would shut down on the immigration of these vermin," *i. e.* the Chinese. How far Southern effrontery went may be gathered from the fact that even the sacred institution of Thanksgiving Day was ridiculed by another California paper as an absurd Yankee notion.

From 1851 until the period of the Civil War the Democratic Party ruled the State of California under the leadership of Gwinn. Northern men constituted a majority of the party, but they submitted to the dictation of the Southerners, just as the Democratic Party in the North submitted to the dictation of the Southern leaders. The only California politician who could cope with Gwinn was Broderick,—a typical Irishman, trained by Tammany Hall.

Not without difficulty was California saved to the Union; in fact, until the rebels fired upon Fort Sumter, the real sentiment of the State was unknown. Bret Harte has touched upon this episode. In *Mrs. Bunker's Conspiracy*, the attempt of the extreme Southern element to seize and fortify a bluff commanding the city of San Francisco is foiled by a Northern woman; and in *Clarence* we have a glimpse of the city as it appeared after news came of the first act of open rebellion: "From every public building and hotel, from the roofs of private houses and even the windows of lonely dwellings, flapped and waved the striped and starry banner. The steady breath of the sea carried it out from masts and yards of ships at their wharves, from the battlements of the forts, Alcatraz and Yerba Buena.... Clarence looked down upon it with haggard, bewildered eyes, and then a strange gasp and fulness of the throat. For afar a solitary bugle had blown the reveille at Fort Alcatraz."

At this critical time, a mass meeting was held in San Francisco, and, at the suggestion of Starr King, Bret Harte wrote a poem to be read at the meeting. The poem was called *The Reveille*, but is better known as *The Drum*. The first and last stanzas are as follows:—

Hark! I hear the tramp of thousands,
And of armèd men the hum;
Lo! a nation's hosts have gathered
Round the quick alarming drum,—
Saying, "Come,
Freemen, Come!
Ere your heritage be wasted," said the quick alarming drum.
………

Thus they answered,—hoping, fearing,
Some in faith, and doubting some,
Till a trumpet-voice, proclaiming,
Said, "My chosen people, come!"
Then the drum
Lo! was dumb,
For the great heart of the nation, throbbing, answered, "Lord, we come!"

As these last words were read, the great audience rose to its feet, and with a mighty shout proclaimed the loyalty of California. Emerson, as Mr. John Jay Chapman has finely said, sent a thousand sons to the war; and it is not unreasonable to suppose that Bret Harte's noble poem fired many a manly heart in San Francisco.

When the war began, Starr King was active in establishing the California branch of the Sanitary Commission. He died of diphtheria in March, 1864, just as the tide of battle was turning in favor of the North. It will thus be seen that his career in California exactly covered, and only just covered, that short period in the history of the State when the services of such a man were, humanly speaking, indispensable.

The Reveille was followed by other patriotic poems, and after Mr. King's death Bret Harte wrote in memory of him the poem called *Relieving Guard*, which indicates, one may safely say, the high-water mark of the author's poetic talent. In the year following Mr. King's death Bret Harte's second son was born, and received the name of Francis King.

On May 25, 1864, the first number of "The Californian" appeared. This was the famous weekly edited and published by the late Charles Henry Webb, and written mainly by Bret Harte, Mark Twain, Webb himself, Prentice Mulford, and Mr. Stoddard. It was of "The Californian" that Mr. Howells wittily said: "These ingenuous young men, with the fatuity of gifted people, had established a literary newspaper in San Francisco, and they brilliantly coöperated to its early extinction."

It is an interesting coincidence that Bret Harte and Mark Twain both began their literary careers in San Francisco, and at almost the same time. Bret Harte was engaged upon "The Californian," and Mark Twain was a reporter for the "Morning Call," when they were introduced to each other by a common friend, Mr. George Barnes. Bret Harte thus describes his first impression of the new acquaintance:—

"His head was striking. He had the curly hair, the aquiline nose, and even the aquiline eye—an eye so eagle-like that a second lid would not have surprised me—of an unusual and dominant nature. His eyebrows were very thick and bushy. His dress was careless, and his general manner one of supreme indifference to surroundings and circumstances. Barnes introduced him as Mr. Sam Clemens, and remarked that he had shown a very unusual talent in a number of newspaper articles contributed under the signature of 'Mark Twain.' We talked on different topics, and about a month afterward Clemens dropped in upon me again. He had been away in the mining districts on some newspaper assignment in the mean time. In the course of conversation he remarked that the unearthly laziness that prevailed in the town he had been visiting was beyond anything in his previous experience. He said the men did nothing all day long but sit around the bar-room stove, spit, and 'swop lies.' He spoke in a slow, rather satirical drawl, which was in itself irresistible. He went on to tell one of those extravagant stories, and half unconsciously dropped into the lazy tone and manner of the original narrator. I asked him to tell it again to a friend who came in, and then asked him to write it out for 'The Californian.' He did so, and when published it was an emphatic success. It was the first work of his that had attracted general attention, and it crossed the Sierras for an Eastern reading. The story was 'The Jumping Frog of Calaveras.' It is now known and laughed over, I suppose, wherever the English language is spoken; but it will never be as funny to any one in print as it was to me, told for the first time by the unknown Twain himself on that morning in the San Francisco Mint."

The first article that appeared in "The Californian" was Bret Harte's *Neighborhoods I have Moved From*, and next his *Ballad of the Emeu*, but neither was signed. Both of these are in the collected edition of his works. The *Condensed Novels* were continued in "The Californian," and Bret Harte also contributed to it many poems, sketches, essays, editorial articles and book reviews. Some of these were unsigned; some were signed "B" or "Bret," and occasionally the signature was his full name.

STORESHIP APOLLO
Old Ship used as a Saloon
Copyright, Century Co.

No reader who appreciates the finished workmanship of Bret Harte will be surprised to learn that he was a slow and intensely self-critical writer. There is much interesting testimony on this point. Mr. Howells says: "His talent was not a facile gift; he owned that he often went day after day to his desk, and sat down before that yellow post-office paper on which he liked to write his literature, in that exquisitely refined script of his, without being able to inscribe a line.... When it came to literature, all the gay improvidence of life forsook him, and he became a stern, rigorous, exacting self-master, who spared himself nothing to achieve the perfection at which he aimed. He was of the order of literary men like Goldsmith and De Quincey and Sterne and Steele, in his relations with the outer world, but in his relations with the inner world, he was one of the most duteous and exemplary citizens."

Noah Brooks wrote as follows: "Scores of writers have become known to me in the course of a long life, but I have never known another so fastidious and so laborious as Bret Harte. His writing materials, the light and heat, and even the adjustment of the furniture of the writing-room, must be as he desired; otherwise he could not go on with his work. Even when his environment was all that he could wish, there were times when the divine afflatus would not come and the day's work must be abandoned. My editorial rooms in San Francisco were not far from his secluded den, and often, if he opened my door late in the afternoon, with a peculiar cloud on his face, I knew that he had come to wait for me to go to dinner with him, having given up the impossible task of writing when the mood was not on him. 'It's no use, Brooks,' he would say. 'Everything goes wrong; I cannot write a line. Let's have an early dinner at Martini's.' As soon as I was ready we would go merrily off to dine together, and, having recovered his equanimity, he would stick to his desk through the later hours of the night, slowly forging those masterpieces which cost him so dearly.

"Harte was reticent concerning his work while it was in progress. He never let the air in upon his story or his verses. Once, indeed, he asked me to help him in a calculation to ascertain how long a half-sack of flour and six pounds of side-meat would last a given number of persons. This was the amount of provision he had allowed his outcasts of Poker Flat, and he wanted to know just how long the snow-bound scapegoats could live on that supply. I used to save for him the Eastern and English newspaper notices of his work, and once, when he had looked through a goodly lot of these laudatory notes, he said: 'These fellows see a heap of things in my stories that I never put there.'"

Mr. Stoddard recalls this incident: "One day I found him pacing the floor of his office in the United States Mint; he was knitting his brows and staring at vacancy,—I wondered why. He was watching and waiting for a word, the right word, the one word of all others to fit into a line of recently written prose. I suggested one; it would not answer; it must be a word of two syllables, or the natural rhythm of the sentence would suffer. Thus he perfected his prose."

In the sketch entitled *My First Book*, printed in volume ten of his works, Bret Harte has given some amusing reminiscences concerning the volume of California poems edited by him, and published in 1866. His selection as Editor, he says, "was chiefly owing to the circumstance that I had from the outset, with precocious foresight, confided to the publisher my intention of not putting any of my own verses in the volume. Publishers are appreciative; and a self-abnegation so sublime, to say nothing of its security, was not without its effect." After narrating his extreme difficulty in reducing the number of his selections from the numerous poets of California, he goes on to describe the reception of the volume. It sold well, the purchasers apparently being amateur poets who were anxious to discover whether they were represented in the book. "People would lounge into the shop, turn over the leaves of other volumes, say carelessly 'Got a new book of California poetry out, haven't you?' purchase it, and quietly depart."

"There were as yet," the Editor continues, "no notices from the press; the big dailies were silent; there was something ominous in this calm. Out of it the bolt fell;" and he quotes the following notice from a country paper: "'The Hogwash and "purp" stuff ladled out from the slop-bucket of Messrs. —— and Co., of 'Frisco, by some lop-eared Eastern apprentice, and called "A Compilation of Californian Verse," might be passed over, so far as criticism goes. A club in the hands of any able-bodied citizen of Red Dog, and a steamboat ticket to the Bay, cheerfully contributed from this office, would be all-sufficient. But when an imported greenhorn dares to call his flapdoodle mixture "Californian," it is an insult to the State that has produced the gifted "Yellowhammer," whose lofty flights have from time to time dazzled our readers in the columns of the "Jay Hawk." That this complacent editorial jackass, browsing among the docks and thistles which he has served up in this volume, should make no allusion to California's greatest bard is rather a confession of his idiocy than a slur upon the genius of our esteemed contributor.'"

Other criticisms, inspired by like omissions, followed, each one rivalling its predecessor in severity. "The big dailies collected the criticisms and published them in their own columns with the grim irony of exaggerated head-lines. The book sold tremendously on account of this abuse, but I am afraid that the public was disappointed. The fun and interest lay in the criticisms, and not in any pointedly ludicrous quality in the rather commonplace collection ... and I have long since been convinced that my most remorseless critics were not in earnest, but were obeying some sudden impulse, started by the first attacking journal.... It was a large, contagious joke, passed from journal to journal in a peculiar cyclonic Western fashion."

A year later, not, as Bret Harte himself states, in 1865, but in 1867, the first collection of his own poems was published. The volume was a thin twelvemo, bound in green cloth, with a gilt design of a sail on the cover, the title-page reading as follows: "The Lost Galleon and Other Tales. By Fr. Bret Harte, San Francisco. Tame and Bacon, Printers, 1867." Most of these poems are contained in the standard edition of his works.

In the same year were published the *Condensed Novels* and the *Bohemian Papers*, reprinted from "The Bulletin" and "The Californian," and making, as the author himself said, "a single, not very plethoric volume, the writer's first book of prose." He adds that "during this period," *i. e.* from 1862 to 1867, he produced "*The Society upon the Stanislaus*, and *The Story of M'liss*,—the first a dialectical poem, the second a Californian romance,—his first efforts toward indicating a peculiarly characteristic Western American literature. He would like to offer these facts as evidence of his very early, half-boyish, but very enthusiastic belief in such a possibility,—a belief which never deserted him, and which, a few years later, from the better known pages of the 'Overland Monthly,' he was able to demonstrate to a larger and more cosmopolitan audience in the story of *The Luck of Roaring Camp*, and the poem of the *Heathen Chinee*."

The "Overland Monthly" was founded in July, 1868, by Anton Roman, a bookseller on Montgomery Street, and later on Clay Street. Mr. Roman was possessed of that enthusiasm which every new enterprise demands. "He had thought and talked about the Magazine," he declared, "until it was in his bones." Bret Harte became the first Editor, and it was he who selected the name. The "Overland" was well printed, on good paper, and the cover was adorned by that historic grizzly bear who, standing on the ties of the newly-laid railroad track, with half-turned body and lowered head, seems prepared to dispute the right of way with the locomotive which might shortly be expected to come screaming down the track.

There was originally no railroad track in the picture, simply the bear; and how the deficiency was supplied is thus explained by Mark Twain in a letter to Thomas Bailey Aldrich: "Do you know the prettiest fancy and the neatest that ever shot through Harte's brain? It was this: When they were trying to decide upon a vignette for the cover of the 'Overland,' a grizzly bear (of the arms of the State of California) was chosen. Nahl Bros. carved him and the page was printed, with him in it, looking thus:

"As a bear, he was a success—he was a good bear.—But then, it was objected, that he was an *objectless* bear—a bear that *meant* nothing in particular, signified nothing,—simply stood there snarling over his shoulder at nothing—and was painfully and manifestly a boorish and ill-natured intruder upon the fair page. All hands said that—none were satisfied. They hated badly to give him up, and yet they hated as much to have him there when there was no *point* to him. But presently Harte took a pencil and drew these two simple lines under his feet and behold he was a magnificent success!—the ancient symbol of Californian savagery snarling at the approaching type of high and progressive Civilization, the first Overland locomotive!

"I think that was nothing less than inspiration itself."

In the same letter Mark Twain pays the following magnanimous tribute to his old friend: "Bret Harte trimmed and trained and schooled me patiently until he changed me from an awkward utterer of coarse grotesqueness to a writer of paragraphs and chapters that have found a certain favor in the eyes of even some of the very decentest people in the land,—and this grateful remembrance of mine ought to be worth its face, seeing that Bret broke our long friendship a year ago without any cause or provocation that I am aware of."

The Editor had no prose article of his own in the first number of the "Overland," but he contributed two poems, the noble lines about San Francisco, which, with characteristic modesty he placed in the middle of the number, and the poem entitled *Returned* in the "Etc." column at the end.

And now we come to the publication which first made Bret Harte known upon the Atlantic as well as upon the Pacific coast. The opening number of the "Overland" had contained no "distinctive Californian romance," as Bret Harte expressed it, and none such being offered for the second number, the Editor supplied the omission with *The Luck of Roaring Camp*. But the printer, instead of sending the proof-sheets to the writer of the story, as would have been the ordinary course, submitted them to the publisher, with a statement that the matter was so "indecent, irreligious and improper" that his proofreader, a young lady, had with difficulty been induced to read it. Then followed many consultations between author, publisher, and various high literary authorities whose judgment had been invoked. Opinions differed, but the weight of opinion was against the tale, and the expediency of printing it. Nevertheless, the author—conceiving that his fitness as Editor was now in question—stood to his guns; the publisher, though fearful of the result, stood by him; and the tale was published without the alteration of a word. It was received very coldly by the secular press in California, its "singularity" being especially pointed out; and it was bitterly denounced by the religious press as being immoral and unchristian. But there was a wider public to hear from. The return mail from the East brought newspapers and reviews "welcoming the little foundling of Californian literature with an enthusiasm that half frightened its author." The mail brought also a letter from the Editor of the "Atlantic Monthly" with a request "upon the most flattering terms" that he would write a story for the "Atlantic," similar to the *Luck*.

It should be recorded, as an interesting contrast to the impression made by the *Luck* upon the San Francisco young woman, that it was also a girl, Miss Susan M. Francis, a literary assistant with the publishers of the "Atlantic Monthly," who, struck by the freshness and beauty of the tale, brought it to the attention of Mr. James T. Fields, then the Editor of the magazine, with the result which Bret Harte has described.

Nor should the attitude of the California young person, and of San Francisco in general, excite surprise. The Pioneers could not be expected to see the moral beauty that lay beneath the rough outward aspect of affairs on the Pacific Slope. The poetry of their own existence was hidden from them. But California, though crude, was self-distrustful, and it bowed to the decision of the East. Bret Harte was honored, even if not understood or appreciated.

The "Overland" was well received, and the high character of the first two numbers was long maintained. Aside from Bret Harte's work, many volumes of prose and verse have been republished from the magazine, and most of them deserved the honor. In the early Fifties the proportion of really educated men to the whole population was greater in California than in any other State, and probably this was true even of the period when the "Overland" was founded. Scholarship and cultivation were concealed in rough mining towns, in lumber camps, and on remote ranches. Among the women, especially, were many who, like the Sappho of Green Springs, gathered from their lonely, primitive lives a freshness and originality which perhaps they never would have shown in more conventional surroundings. This class furnished numerous readers and a few writers. Officers of the Army and Navy stationed in California contributed some interesting scientific and literary articles to the early numbers of the "Overland."

Notwithstanding the success of his first story, Bret Harte was in no haste to rush into print with another. He had none of that disposition to make hay while the sun shines which has spoiled many a story-writer. Six months elapsed before the *Luck* was followed by *The Outcasts of Poker Flat*. Meanwhile he was carefully and patiently discharging his duties as Editor. Mr. Stoddard has thus described him in that capacity: "Fortunately for me he took an interest in me at a time when I was most in need of advice, and to his criticism and his encouragement I feel that I owe all that is best in my literary efforts. He was not afraid to speak his mind, and I know well enough what occasion I gave him: yet he did not judge me more severely than I judged myself.... I am sure that the majority of the contributors to the 'Overland Monthly' profited as I did by his careful and judicious criticism. Fastidious to a degree, he could not overlook a lack of finish in the manuscript offered to him. He had a special taste in the choice of titles, and I have known him to alter the name of an article two or three times in order that the table of contents might read handsomely and harmoniously."

One of the most frequent contributors to the "Overland" was Miss Ina B. Coolbrith, author of many polished and imaginative poems and stories. In a recent letter Miss Coolbrith thus speaks of Bret Harte as an Editor: "To me he was unfailingly kind and generous, looking out for my interests as one of his contributors with as much care as he accorded to his own. I can only speak of him in terms of unqualified praise as author, friend and man."

The poem entitled *Plain Language from Truthful James*, or the *Heathen Chinee*, as it is popularly known, and as Bret Harte himself afterward called it, first appeared in the "Overland" for September, 1870. Within a few weeks it had spread over the English-speaking world. *The Luck of Roaring Camp* gave Bret Harte a literary reputation, but this poem made him famous. It was copied by the newspapers almost universally, both here and in England; and it increased the circulation of the "Overland" so much that, two months after its appearance, a single news company in New York was selling twelve hundred copies of the magazine. Almost everybody had a clipping of these verses tucked into his waistcoat pocket or carried in his purse. Quotations from it were on every lip, and some of its most significant lines were recited with applause in the National House of Representatives.

It came at a fortunate moment when the people of this country were just awaking to the fact that there was a "Chinese problem," and when interest in the race was becoming universal in the East as well as in the West. Says that acute critic, Mr. James Douglas: "There is an element of chance in the fabrication of great poems. The concatenation comes, the artist puts the pieces into their places, and the result is permanent wonder. The *Heathen Chinee* in its happy felicity is quite as unique as 'The Blessed Damozel.'"

The *Heathen Chinee* is remarkable for the absolutely impartial attitude of the writer. He observes the Chinaman neither from the locally prejudiced, California point of view, nor from an ethical or reforming point of view. His part is neither to approve nor condemn, but simply to state the fact as it is, not indeed with the coldness of an historian but with the sympathy and insight of a poet. But this is not all, in fact, as need hardly be said, it is not enough to make the poem endure. It endures because it has a beauty of form which approaches perfection. It is hackneyed, and yet as fresh as on the day when it was written.

Truthful James himself who tells the story was a real character,—nay is, for, at the writing of these pages, he still lived in the same little shanty where he was to be found when Bret Harte knew him. At that time, in 1856, or thereabout, Bret Harte was teaching school at Tuttletown, a few miles north of Sonora, and Truthful James, Mr. James W. Gillis, lived over the hill from Tuttletown, at a place called Jackass Flat. Mr. Gillis was well known and highly respected in all that neighborhood, and he figures not only in Bret Harte's poetry, but also in Mark Twain's works, where he is described as "The Sage of Jackass Hill."

It is a proof both of Bret Harte's remarkable freedom from vanity, and of the keen criticism which he bestowed upon his own writings, that he never set much value upon the *Heathen Chinee*, even after its immense popularity had been attained. When he wrote it, he thought it unworthy of a place in the "Overland" and handed it over to Mr. Ambrose Bierce, then Editor of the "News Letter," a weekly paper, for publication there. Mr. Bierce, however, recognizing its value, unselfishly advised Bret Harte to give it a place in the "Overland," and this was finally done. "Nevertheless," says Mr. Bierce, "it was several months before he overcame his prejudice against the verses and printed them. Indeed he never cared for the thing, and was greatly amused by the meanings that so many read into it. He said he meant nothing whatever by it."

We have Mark Twain's word to the same effect. "In 1866," he writes, "I went to the Sandwich Islands, and when I returned, after several years, Harte was famous as the author of the *Heathen Chinee*. He said that the *Heathen Chinee* was an accident, and that he had higher literary ambitions than the fame that could come from an extravaganza of that sort." "*The Luck of Roaring Camp*," Mr. Clemens goes on to say, "was the salvation of his literary career. It placed him securely on a literary road which was more to his taste."

Bret Harte, indeed, frequently held back for weeks poems which he had completed, but with which he was not content. As one of his fellow-workers declared, "He was never fully satisfied with what he finally allowed to go to the printer."

His position in San Francisco was now assured. He had been made professor of recent literature in the University of California; he retained his place at the Mint, he was the successful Editor of the "Overland," and he was happy in his home life. One who knew him well at this period speaks of him as "always referring to his wife in affectionate terms, and quoting her clever speeches, and relating with fond enjoyment the funny sayings and doings of his children."

Let us, for the moment, leave Bret Harte thus happily situated, and glance at that Pioneer life which he was now engaged in portraying. Said a San Francisco paper in 1851, "The world will never know, and no one could imagine the heart-rending scenes, or the instances of courage and heroic self-sacrifice which have occurred among the California Pioneers during the last three years!"

And yet when these words were penned there was growing up in the East a stripling destined to preserve for posterity some part, at least, of those very occurrences which otherwise would have remained "unrecorded and forgot."

CHAPTER V

THE PIONEER MEN AND WOMEN

When Bret Harte first became famous he was accused of misrepresenting Pioneer society. A California writer of great ability—no less a person than Professor Royce, the eminent philosopher—once spoke of the "perverse romanticism" of his tales; and after Mr. Harte's death these accusations, if they may be called such, were renewed in San Francisco with some bitterness. It is strange that Californians themselves should have been so anxious to strip from their State the distinction which Bret Harte conferred upon it,—so anxious to prove that its heroic age never existed, that life in California has always been just as commonplace, respectable and uninteresting as it is anywhere else in the world.

But, be this as it may, the diaries, letters and narratives written by Pioneers themselves, and, most important of all, the daily newspapers published in San Francisco and elsewhere from 1849 to 1855, fully corroborate Bret Harte's assertion that he described only what actually occurred. "The author has frequently been asked," he wrote, "if such and such incidents were real,—if he had ever met such and such characters. To this he must return the one answer, that in only a single instance was he conscious of drawing purely from his imagination and fancy for a character and a logical succession of incidents drawn therefrom. A few weeks after his story was published, he received a letter, authentically signed, *correcting some of the minor details of his facts*, and inclosing as corroborative evidence a slip from an old newspaper, wherein the main incident of his supposed fanciful creation was recorded with a largeness of statement that far transcended his powers of imagination." Even that bizarre character, the old Frenchman in *A Ship of '49*, was taken absolutely from the life, except that the real man was of English birth. His peculiarities, mental and physical, his dress, his wig, his residence in the old ship were all just as they are described by Bret Harte.

This is not to say that everybody in California was a romantic person, or that life there was simply a succession of startling incidents. Ordinary people were doing ordinary things on the Pacific Slope, just as they did during the worst horrors of the French Revolution. But the exceptional persons that Bret Harte described really existed; and, moreover, they existed in such proportion as to give character and tone to the whole community.

20

The fact is that Bret Harte only skimmed the cream from the surface. To use his own words again, "The faith, courage, vigor, youth, and capacity for adventure necessary to this emigration produced a body of men as strongly distinctive as were the companions of Jason."

They were picked men placed in extraordinary circumstances, and how could that combination fail to result in extraordinary characters, deeds, events, and situations! The Forty-Niners, and those who came in the early Fifties, were such men as enlist in the first years of a war. They were young men. Never, since Mediæval days when men began life at twenty and commonly ended it long before sixty, was there so youthful a society. A man of fifty with a gray beard was pointed out in the streets of San Francisco as a curiosity. In the convention to organize the State which met at Monterey, in September, 1849, there were forty-eight delegates, of whom only four were fifty years or more; fifteen were under thirty years of age; twenty-three were between thirty and forty. These were the venerable men of the community, selected to make the laws of the new commonwealth. A company of California emigrants that left Virginia in 1852 consisted wholly of boys under twenty.

The Pioneers were far above the average in vigor and enterprise, and in education as well. One ship, the "Edward Everett," sailed from Boston in January, 1849, with one hundred and fifty young men on board who owned both ship and cargo; and the distinguished gentleman for whom they had named their ship gave them a case full of books to beguile the tedium of the voyage around Cape Horn. William Grey, who wrote an interesting account of California life, sailed from New York with a ship-load of emigrants. He describes them as a "fine-looking and well-educated body of men,—all young"; and he gives a similar description of the passengers on three other ships that came into the port of Rio Janeiro while he was there. He adds that on his ship there were only three bad characters, a butcher from Washington Market and his two sons. They all perished within a year of their arrival in California. The father died while drunk, one of the sons was hanged, and the other was killed in a street row.

The Pioneers were handsome men. They were tall men. Of the two hundred grown men in the town of Suisun, twenty-one stood over six feet high. Many of the Pioneers were persons for whom a career is not easily found in a conservative, sophisticated society; who, in such a society, fail to be successful as much because of their virtues as of their defects; men who lack that combination of cunning and ferocity which leads most directly to the acquisition of wealth; magnanimous, free-handed, and brave, but unthrifty and incapable of monotonous toil; archaic men, not quite broken in to the modern ideal of drudging at one task for six days in the week and fifty weeks in the year. Who does not know the type! The hero of novels, the idol of mothers, the alternate hope and despair of fathers, the truest of friends, the most ideal and romantic, but perhaps not the most constant of lovers.

From the Western and Southwestern States there came across the Plains a different type. These men were Pioneers already by inheritance and tradition, somewhat ignorant, slow and rough, but of boundless courage and industry, stoical as Indians, independent and self-reliant. Most of Bret Harte's tragic characters, such as Tennessee's Partner, Madison Wayne, and the Bell-Ringer of Angel's, were of this class.

Many of these emigrants, especially those who crossed the Mountains before the discovery of gold, were trappers and hunters,—stalwart, bearded men, clad in coats of buffalo hide, with faces deeply tanned and wrinkled by long exposure to wind and weather. Perhaps the best known among them was "old Greenwood," a tall, raw-boned, muscular man, who at the age of eighty-three was still vigorous and active. For thirty years he made his home among the Crow Indians, and he had taken to wife a squaw who bore him four handsome sons. His dress was of tanned buckskin, and one observer, more squeamish than the ordinary Pioneer, noted the seeming fact that it had never been removed since first he put it on. His heroic calibre may be estimated from the fact that he was capable of eating ten pounds of meat a day. This man used to boast that he had killed more than a hundred Indians with his own hand. But all that killing had been done in fair fight; and when a cowardly massacre of seven Indians, captured in a raid led by Greenwood's sons, took place near Sacramento in 1849,—one of many such acts,—the Greenwood family did their best to save the victims. After the deed had been done, "Old Greenwood," an eye-witness relates, "raved around his cabin, tossed his arms aloft with violent denunciation, and, stooping down, gathered the dust in his palms, and sprinkled it on his head, swearing that he was innocent of their blood."

Another hero of the Pacific Slope in those large, early days was Peg-leg Smith. He derived his nickname from a remarkable incident. While out on the Plains with a wagon-load of supplies, Smith—plain Smith at that time—was accidentally thrown from his seat, and the heavy wheel passed over his leg below the knee, crushing it so that amputation became necessary. There was no surgeon within hundreds of miles; but if the amputation were not performed, it was plain that mortification and death would soon result. In this emergency, Smith hacked out a rude saw from a butcher's knife which he had with him, built a fire and heated an iron bolt that he took from the wagon, and then, with his hunting knife and his improvised saw, cut off his own leg. This done, he drew the flesh down over the wound, and seared it with the hot iron to prevent bleeding. He recovered, procured a wooden leg, and lived to take part in many succeeding adventures.

We owe California primarily to these hunters, trappers and adventurous farmers who crossed the Mountains on their own account, or, later, as members of Frémont's band:

Stern men, with empires in their brains.

They firmly believed that it was the "manifest destiny" of the United States to spread over the Continent; and this conviction was not only a patriotic, but in some sense a religious one. They were mainly descendants of the Puritans, and as such had imbibed Old Testament ideas which justified and sanctioned their dreams of conquest. We have seen how the venerable Greenwood covered his head with dust as a symbolic act. The Reverend Mr. Colton records a significant remark made to him by a Pioneer, seventy-six years old, who had four sons in Frémont's company, and who himself joined the Volunteers raised in California. "I asked him if he had no compunction in taking up arms against the native inhabitants, the moment of his arrival. He said he had Scripture example for it. The Israelites took the promised land of the East by arms, and the Americans must take the promised land of the West in the same way."

And Mr. Colton adds: "I find this kind of parallel running in the imagination of all the emigrants. They seem to look upon this beautiful land as their own Canaan, and the motley race around them as the Hittites, the Hivites and Jebusites whom they are to drive out."

But, it need hardly be said, the Biblical argument upon which they relied was in the nature of an afterthought—the justification, rather than the cause of their actions. What really moved them, although they did not know it, was that primeval instinct of expansion, based upon conscious superiority of race, to which have been due all the great empires of the past.

Many of these people were deeply religious in a Gothic manner, and Bret Harte has touched lightly upon this aspect of their natures, especially in the case of Mr. Joshua Rylands. "Mr. Joshua Rylands had, according to the vocabulary of his class, 'found grace' at the age of sixteen, while still in the spiritual state of 'original sin,' and the political one of Missouri.... When, after the Western fashion, the time came for him to forsake his father's farm, and seek a new 'quarter section' on some more remote frontier, he carried into the secluded, lonely, half-monkish celibacy of pioneer life—which has been the foundation of so much strong Western character—more than the usual religious feeling."

Exactly the same kind of man is described in that once famous story, Mr. Eggleston's "Circuit-Rider"; and it is still found in the mountains of Kentucky, where the maintenance of ferocious feuds and a constant readiness to kill one's enemies at sight are regarded as not inconsistent with a sincere profession of the Christian religion.

The reader of Bret Harte's stories will remember how often the expression "Pike County" or "Piker" occurs; and this use is strictly historical. As a very intelligent Pioneer expressed it, "We recognize in California but two types of the Republican character, the Yankee and the Missourian. The latter term was first used to represent the entire population of the West; but Pike County superseded, first the name of the State, and soon that of the whole West."

How did this come about? Pike County, Missouri, was named for Lieutenant Zebulon Montgomery Pike, the discoverer of Pike's Peak, and the officer who was sent by the United States Government to explore the upper part of the Mississippi River. He was killed in the War of 1812. The territory was first settled in 1811 by emigrants from Virginia, Kentucky and Louisiana; and it was incorporated as a county in 1818. It borders on the Mississippi River, about forty miles north of St. Louis; and its whole area is only sixty square miles. It was and is an agricultural county, and in 1850 the population amounted to only thirteen thousand, six hundred and nine persons, of whom about half were negroes, mostly slaves. The climate is healthy, and the soil, especially on the prairies, is very fertile, being a rich, deep loam.

Pike County, it will thus be seen, is but a small part, both numerically and geographically, of that vast Western territory which contributed to the California emigration; and it owes its prominence among the Pioneers chiefly to a copy of doggerel verses. In 1849, Captain McPike, a leading resident of the County, organized a band of two hundred Argonauts who crossed the Plains. Among them was an ox-driver named Joe Bowers, who soon made a reputation in the company as a humorist, as an "original," as a "greenhorn," and as a "good fellow" generally. Joe Bowers was poor, he was in love, he was seeking a fortune in order that he might lay it at the feet of his sweetheart; and the whole company became his confidants and sympathizers.

Another member of the party was a certain Frank Swift, who afterward attained some reputation as a journalist; and one evening, as they were all sitting around the camp-fire, Swift recited, or rather sang to a popular air, several stanzas of a poem about Joe Bowers, which he had composed during the day's journey. It caught the fancy of the company at once, and soon every member was singing it. The poem grew night by night, and long before they reached their destination it had become a ballad of exasperating length. The poet, looking forward in a fine frenzy, describes the girl as proving faithless to Joe Bowers and marrying a red-haired butcher. This bad news comes from Joe's brother Ike in a letter which also states the culminating fact of the tragedy, as the following lines reveal:—

It told me more than that,
Oh! it's enough to make me swear.
It said Sally had a baby,
And the baby had red hair!

GRAND PLAZA, SAN FRANCISCO, 1852

Upon their arrival in California, the two hundred men who composed this party dispersed in all directions, and carried the ballad with them. It was heard everywhere in the mines, and in 1856 it was printed in a cheap form in San Francisco, and was sung by Johnson's minstrels at a hall known as the Old Melodeon. Joe Bowers thus became the type of the unsophisticated Western miner, and Pike County became the symbol of the West. Crude as the verses are they are sung to this day in the County which gave them birth, and "Joe Bowers" is still a familiar name in Missouri, if not in the West generally.

This ballad which came across the Plains had its counterpart in a much better song produced by Jonathan Nichols, a Pioneer who sailed on the bark "Eliza" from Salem, Massachusetts, in December, 1848. The first stanza is as follows:—

Tune, *Oh! Susanna.* (Key of G.)

I came from Salem city,
With my washbowl on my knee,
I'm going to California,

The gold dust for to see.
It rained all night the day I left,
The weather, it was dry,
The sun so hot I froze to death,
Oh! brothers, don't you cry,
Oh! California,
That's the land for me!
I'm going to Sacramento
With my washbowl on my knee.

Under the title of the "California Song" these verses soon became the common property of every ship sailing from Atlantic ports for San Francisco, and later they were heard in the mines almost as frequently as "Joe Bowers." But, as hope diminished and homesickness increased, both ballads—so an old miner relates—gave place to "Home, Sweet Home," "Ole Virginny," and other sad ditties.

Pike County seems to have had a natural tendency to burst into poetry. In the story called *Devil's Ford*, Bret Harte gives us two lines from a poem otherwise unknown to fame,—

"'Oh, my name it is Johnny from Pike,
I'm hell on a spree or a strike.'"

In the story of *The New Assistant at Pine Clearing School*, three big boys from Pike County explained to the schoolmistress their ideas upon the subject of education, as follows: "'We ain't hankerin' much for grammar and dictionary hogwash, and we don't want no Boston parts o' speech rung in on us the first thing in the mo'nin'. We reckon to do our sums and our figgerin', and our sale and barter, and our interest tables and weights and measures when the time comes, and our geograffy when it's on, and our readin' and writin' and the American Constitution in regular hours, and then we calkillate to git up and git afore the po'try and the Boston airs and graces come round.'"

The "Sacramento Transcript," of June 11, 1850, tells a story about a minister from Pike County which has a similar ring. "A miner took sick and died at a bar that was turning out very rich washings. As he happened to be a favorite in the camp, it was determined to have a general turn-out at his burial. An old Pike County preacher was engaged to officiate, but he thought it proper to moisten his clay a little before his solemn duty. The parson being a favorite, and the grocery near by, he partook with one and another before the services began, until his underpinning became quite unsteady. Presently it was announced that the last sad rites were about to be concluded, and our clerical friend advanced rather unsteadily to perform the functions of his office. After an exordium worthy of his best days, the crowd knelt around the grave, but as he was praying with fervency one of the party discovered some of the shining metal in the dirt thrown from the grave, and up he jumped and started for his pan, followed by the crowd. The minister, opening his eyes in wonder and seeing the game, cried out for a share; his claim was recognized and reserved for him until he should get sober. In the mean time, another hole was dug for the dead man, that did not furnish a like temptation to disturb his grave, and he was hurriedly deposited without further ceremony."

Bret Harte's best and noblest character, Tennessee's Partner, might have been from Pike County,—he was of that kind; and Morse, the hero of the story called *In the Tules*, certainly was:—

"The stranger stared curiously at him. After a pause he said with a half-pitying, half-humorous smile:—

"'Pike—aren't you?'

"Whether Morse did or did not know that this current California slang for a denizen of the bucolic West implied a certain contempt, he replied simply:—

"'I'm from Pike County, Mizzouri.'"

To the same effect is the historian: "To be catalogued as from Pike County seems to express a little more churlishness, a little more rudeness, a greater reserve when courtesy or hospitality is called for than I ever found in the Western character at home."

The type thus indicated was a very marked one, and was often spoken of with astonishment by more sophisticated Pioneers. Some of these Missouri men had never seen two houses together, until they came to California, so that even a little village in the mines appeared to them as a marvel of civilization and luxury. Their dress was home-made and by no means new or clean. Over their shoulders they wore strips of cotton or cloth as suspenders, and their coats were tight-waisted, long-tailed surtouts such as were fashionable in the eighteenth century. Their inseparable companion was a long-barrelled rifle, with which they could "draw a bead" on a deer or a squirrel or the white of an Indian's eye with equal coolness and certainty of killing.

Bayard Taylor describes the same type as he met it in the ship which carried him from New Orleans to Panama in '49. "Long, loosely-jointed men, with large hands, and awkward feet and limbs; their faces long and sallow; their hair long, straight and black; their expression one of settled melancholy. The corners of their mouths curved downward, and their upper lips were drawn tightly over their lower ones, thus giving to their faces that look of ferocity which is peculiar to Indians. These men chewed tobacco incessantly, drank copiously, were heavily armed with knives and pistols, and breathed defiance to all foreigners."

These long, sallow-faced men were probably sufferers from that fever and ague, or malaria, as we now call it, which was rife in all the "bottom lands" of the Western States; and the greater part of Pike County was included in that category. Much, indeed, of the emigration from Missouri and Illinois to California was inspired less by the love of gold than by the desire to escape from disease. Bret Harte, in many places, speaks of these fever-ridden Westerners, especially in *An Apostle of the Tules*, where he describes a camp-meeting, attended chiefly by "the rheumatic Parkinsons, from Green Springs; the ophthalmic Filgees, from Alder Creek; the ague-stricken Harveys, from Martinez Bend; and the feeble-limbed Steptons, from Sugar Mill." "These," he adds, "might in their combined families have suggested a hospital, rather than any other social assemblage."

But these sickly or ague-smitten people formed only a small part of the Pioneers. The greater number represented the youth and strength of both the Western and Eastern States. In 1852, an interior newspaper called the "San Andreas Independent" declared, "We have a population made up from the most energetic of the civilized earth's population"; and the boast was true.

Moreover, the Pioneers who reached California had been winnowed and sifted by the hardships and privations which beset both the land and the sea route. Thousands of the weaker among them had succumbed to starvation or disease, and their bones were whitening the Plains or lying in the vast depths of the Pacific Ocean. There was scarcely a village in the West or South, or even in New England, which did not mourn the loss of some brave young gold-seeker whose unknown fate was a matter of speculation for years afterward.

The length of the voyage from Atlantic ports to San Francisco was from four to five months, but most of the Pioneers who came by sea avoided the passage around Cape Horn, and crossed the Isthmus of Nicaragua, or, more commonly, of Panama. This, in either case, was a much shorter route; but it added the horrors of pestilence and fever, and of possible robbery and murder, to the ordinary dangers of the sea. All the blacklegs, it was noticed, took the shorter route, deeming themselves, no doubt, incapable of sustaining the prolonged ennui of a voyage around the Cape. Passengers who crossed the Isthmus of Panama disembarked at Chagres, a port so unhealthy that policies of life insurance contained a clause to the effect that if the insured remained there more than one night, his policy would be void. Chagres enjoyed the distinction of being the dirtiest place in the world. The inhabitants were almost all negroes, and one Pioneer declared that a flock of buzzards would present a favorable comparison with them.

From Chagres there was, first, a voyage of seventy-five miles up the river of the same name to Gorgona, or to Cruces, five miles farther. This was accomplished in dugouts propelled by the native Indians. Thence to Panama the Pioneers travelled on foot, or on mule-back, over a narrow, winding bridle-path through the mountains, so overhung by trees and dense tropical growths that in many places it was dark even at mid-day.

This was the opportunity of the Indian muleteer, and more than one gold-seeker never emerged from the gloomy depths of that winding trail. Originally, it was the work of the Indians; but the Spaniards who used the path in the sixteenth century had improved it, and in many places had secured the banks with stones. Now, however, the trail had fallen into decay, and in spots was almost impassable. But the tracks worn in the soft, calcareous rock by the many iron-shod hoofs which had passed over it, still remained; and the mule that bore the American seeking gold in California placed his feet in the very holes which had been made by his predecessors, painfully bearing the silver of Peru on its way to enrich the grandees of Spain.

Bad as the journey across the Isthmus was or might be, the enforced delay at Panama was worse. The number of passengers far exceeded the capacity of the vessels sailing from that port to San Francisco, and those who waited at Panama were in constant danger of cholera, of the equally dreaded Panama fever, and sometimes of smallpox. The heat was almost unbearable, and the blacks were a source of annoyance, and even of danger. "There is not in the whole world," remarked a contemporary San Francisco paper, "a more infamous collection of villains than the Jamaica negroes who are congregated at Panama and Chagres."

In their eagerness to get away from Panama, some Pioneers paid in advance for transportation in old rotten hulks which were never expected or intended to reach San Francisco, but which, springing a leak or being otherwise disabled, would put into some port in Lower California where the passengers would be left without the means of continuing their journey, and frequently without money.

Both on the voyage from Panama and also on the long route around Cape Horn, ship-captains often saved their good provisions for the California market, and fed their passengers on nauseous "lobscouse" and "dunderfunk." Scurvy and other diseases resulted. An appeal to the United States consul at Rio Janeiro, when the ship touched there, was sometimes effectual, and in other cases the passengers took matters into their own hands and disciplined a rapacious captain or deposed a drunken one. In view of these uprisings, some New York skippers declined to take command of ships about to sail for California, supposing that passengers who could do such an unheard-of thing as to rebel against the master of a vessel must be a race of pirates. Great pains were taken to secure a crew of determined men for these ships, and a plentiful supply of muskets, handcuffs and shackles was always put on board. But such precautions proved to be ridiculously unnecessary. There was no case in which the Pioneers usurped authority on shipboard without sufficient cause; and in no case was an emigrant brought to trial on reaching San Francisco.

In the various ports at which they stopped much was to be seen of foreign peoples and customs; and not infrequently the Pioneers had an opportunity to show their mettle. At Santa Catharina, for example, a port on the lower coast of Brazil, a young American was murdered by a Spaniard. The authorities were inclined to treat the matter with great indifference; but there happened to be in the harbor two ship-loads of passengers en route for San Francisco, and these men threatened to seize the fortress and demolish it if justice was not done. Thereupon the murderer was tried and hung. Many South Americans in the various ports along the coast got their first correct notion of the people of the United States from these chance encounters with sea-going Pioneers.

Still more, of course, was the overland journey an education in self-reliance, in that resourcefulness which distinguishes the American, and in that courage which was so often needed and so abundantly displayed in the early mining days. Independence in the State of Missouri was a favorite starting-point, and from this place there were two routes, the southern one being by way of Santa Fé, and the northern route following the Oregon Trail to Fort Hall, and thence ascending the course of the Humboldt River to its rise in the Sierra Nevadas.

At Fort Hall some large companies which had travelled from the Mississippi River, and even from States east of that, separated, one half going to Oregon, the other turning westward to California; and thus were broken many ties of love and friendship which had been formed in the close intimacy of the long journey, especially between the younger members of the company. Old diaries and letters reveal suggestions of romance if not of tragedy in these separations, and in the choice which the emigrant maiden was sometimes forced to make between the conflicting claims of her lover and her parents.

In the year 1850 fifty thousand crossed the Plains. In 1851 immigration fell off because even at that early date there was a business "depression," almost a "panic" in California, but in 1852 it increased again, and the Plains became a thoroughfare, dotted so far as the eye could see with long trains of white-covered wagons, moving slowly through the dust. In one day a party from Virginia passed thirty-two wagons, and during a stop in the afternoon five hundred overtook them. In after years the course of these wagons could easily be traced by the alien vegetation which marked it. Wherever the heavy wheels had broken the tough prairie sod there sprang up, from the Missouri to the Sierras, a narrow belt of flowering plants and familiar door-yard weeds,—silent witnesses of the great migration which had passed that way. Multitudes of horsemen accompanied the wagons, and other multitudes plodded along on foot. Banners were flying here and there, and the whole appearance was that of an army on the march. At night camp-fires gleamed for miles through the darkness, and if the company were not exhausted the music of a violin or a banjo floated out on the still air of the prairies. But the fatigue of the march, supplemented by the arduous labors of camping out, was usually sufficient to send the travellers to bed at the earliest possible moment.

The food consisted chiefly of salt pork or bacon,—varied when that was possible with buffalo meat or venison,—beans, baked dough called bread, and flapjacks. The last, always associated with mining life in California, were made by mixing flour and water into a sort of batter, seasoning with salt, adding a little saleratus or cooking soda, and frying the mixture in a pan greased with fat. Men ate enormously on these journeys. Four hundred pounds of sugar lasted four Pioneers only ninety days. This inordinate appetite and the quantity of salt meat eaten frequently resulted in scurvy, from which there were some deaths. Another cause of illness was the use of milk from cows driven along with the wagon-trains, and made feverish by heat and fatigue.

Many of the emigrants, especially those who undertook the journey in '49 or '50, were insufficiently equipped, and little aware of the difficulties and dangers which awaited them. Death in many forms hovered over those heavy, creaking, canvas-covered wagons—the "prairie-schooners," which, drawn sometimes by horses, sometimes by oxen, sometimes by mules, jolted slowly and laboriously over two thousand miles and more of plain and mountain,—death from disease, from want of water, from starvation, from Indians, and, in crossing the Sierras, from raging snow-storms and intense cold. Rivers had to be forded, deserts crossed and a thousand accidents and annoyances encountered.

Some men made the long journey on foot, even from points east of the Mississippi River. One gray-haired Pioneer walked all the way from Michigan with a pack on his back. Another enthusiast obtained some notoriety among the emigrants of 1850 by trundling a wheelbarrow, laden with his goods, from Illinois to Salt Lake City.

Bret Harte, as we have seen, reached California by sea, and there is no record of any journey by ox-cart that he made; and yet in *A Waif of the Plains* he describes such a journey with a particularity which seems almost impossible for one who knew it only by hearsay. Thus, among many other details, he speaks of "a chalky taste of dust on the mouth and lips, a gritty sense of earth on the fingers, and an all-pervading heat and smell of cattle." And in the same description occurs one of those minute touches for which he is remarkable: "The hoofs of the draught-oxen, occasionally striking in the dust with a dull report, sent little puffs like smoke on either side of the track."

Often the cattle would break loose at night and disappear on the vast Plains, and men in search of them were sometimes lost, and died of starvation or were killed by Indians. Simply for the sake of better grazing oxen have been known to retrace their steps at night for twenty-five miles.

The opportunities for selfishness, for petulance, for obstinacy, for resentment were almost innumerable. Cooking and washing were the labors which, in the absence of women, proved most vexatious to the emigrants. "Of all miserable work," said one, "washing is the worst, and no man who crossed the Plains will ever find fault again with his wife for scolding on a washing day." All the Pioneers who have related their experiences on the overland journey speak of the bad effect on men's tempers. "The perpetual vexations and hardships keep the nerves in a state of great irritability. The trip is a sort of magic mirror, exposing every man's qualities of heart, vicious or amiable."

The shooting affairs which occurred among the emigrants were usually the result of some sudden provocation, following upon a long course of irritation between the persons concerned. Those who crossed the Plains in the summer of 1853, or afterward, might have passed a grave with this inscription:

BEAL SHOT BY BOLSBY, JUNE 15, 1853.

And, a day's journey further, they would have noticed another grave thus inscribed:

BOLSBY SHOT FOR THE MURDER OF BEAL, JUNE 16, 1853.

This murder, to call it such, was the consequence of some insult offered to Bolsby by the other. Bolsby was forthwith tried by the company, and condemned to be shot the next morning at sunrise. He had been married only about a year before, and had left his wife and child at their home in Kentucky. For the remainder of the day he travelled with the others, and the short hours of the summer night which followed were spent by him in writing to his wife and to his father and mother. Of all the great multitude, scattered over the wide earth, who passed that particular night in sleepless agony of mind, perhaps none was more to be pitied. When morning came he dressed himself neatly in his wedding suit, and was led out to execution. With rare magnanimity, he acknowledged that his sentence was a just one, and said that he had so written to his family, and that he had been treated with consideration; but he declared that if the thing were to happen again, he would kill Beal as before. He then knelt on his blanket, gave the signal for shooting, and fell dead, pierced by six bullets.

The misfortunes of the Donner party began with a homicide. This is the party whose sufferings are described by Bret Harte without exaggeration in *Gabriel Conroy*. It included robbers, cannibals, murderers and heroes; and one interesting aspect of its experience is the superior endurance, both moral and physical, shown by the women. In the small detachment which, as a forlorn hope, tried to cross the Mountains in winter without provisions, and succeeded, there were twelve men and five women. Of the twelve men five died, of the five women none died!

Indians were often encountered on the Great Plains and in the valleys of the Colorado and Rio Grande. They were well-disposed, at first, and soon acquired some familiarity with the ordinary forms of speech used by the Pioneers. Thus one traveller reports the following friendly salutation from a member of the Snake Tribe:

"How de do—Whoa haw! G—d d—n you!"

On another occasion when a party of Pioneers were inquiring of some Indians about a certain camping-ground ahead of them, they were assured that there would be "plenty of grass there for the whoa haws, but no water for the g—d d—ns."

Later, however, owing chiefly to unprovoked attacks by emigrants, the Indians became hostile and dangerous. Many Pioneers were robbed and some were killed by them. The Western Indian was a figure at once grotesque and terrible; and Bret Harte's description of him,

25

as he appeared to the emigrant boy lost on the Plains, gives the reader such a pleasant thrill of horror as he may not have experienced since Robinson Crusoe made his awful discovery of a human footprint in the sand.

"He awoke with a start. A moving figure had suddenly uplifted itself between him and the horizon!... A human figure, but so dishevelled, so fantastic, and yet so mean and puerile in its extravagance that it seemed the outcome of a childish dream. It was a mounted figure, yet so ludicrously disproportionate to the pony it bestrode, whose slim legs were stiffly buried in the dust in a breathless halt, that it might have been a straggler from some vulgar wandering circus. A tall hat, crownless and brimless, a castaway of civilization, surmounted by a turkey's feather, was on its head; over its shoulders hung a dirty tattered blanket that scarcely covered the two painted legs which seemed clothed in soiled yellow hose. In one hand it held a gun; the other was bent above its eyes in eager scrutiny of some distant point.... Presently, with a dozen quick noiseless strides of the pony's legs, the apparition moved to the right, its gaze still fixed on that mysterious part of the horizon. There was no mistaking it now! The painted Hebraic face, the large curved nose, the bony cheek, the broad mouth, the shadowed eyes, the straight long matted locks! It was an Indian!"

There were some cases of captivity among the Indians the details of which recall the similar occurrences in New England in the seventeenth century. Perhaps the most remarkable case was that of Olive Oatman, a young girl from Illinois, who was carried off by one tribe of Indians, was sold later to another, nearly died of starvation, and, finally, after a lapse of six years, was recovered safe and sound. Her brother, a boy of twelve, was beaten with clubs by the Indians, and left for dead with the bodies of his father and mother; but he revived, and succeeded in making his way back for a distance of seventy miles, when he met a party of Pima Indians, who treated him with kindness. Forty-five miles of that lonely journey lay through a desert where no water could be obtained.

Abner Nott's daughter, Rosey, the attractive heiress of the Pontiac, was made of the same heroic stuff. "The Rosey ez I knows," said her father, "is a little gal whose voice was as steady with Injuns yellin' round her nest in the leaves on Sweetwater ez in her purty cabin up yonder." Lanty Foster, too, was of "that same pioneer blood that had never nourished cravens or degenerates, ... whose father's rifle had been levelled across her cradle, to cover the stealthy Indian who prowled outside."

It was from these Western and Southwestern emigrants that Bret Harte's nobler kind of woman, and, in most cases, of man also was drawn. The "great West" furnished his heroic characters,—California was only their accidental and temporary abiding-place. These people were of the muscular, farm type, with such health and such nerves as result from an out-door life, from simple, even coarse food, from early hours and abundant sleep.

The Pioneer women did indeed lack education and inherited refinement, as Bret Harte himself occasionally points out. "She brushed the green moss from his sleeve with some towelling, and although this operation brought her so near to him that her breath—as soft and warm as the Southwest trades—stirred his hair, it was evident that this contiguity was only frontier familiarity, as far removed from conscious coquetry as it was perhaps from educated delicacy."

And yet it is very easy to exaggerate this defect. In most respects the wholesomeness, the democratic sincerity and dignity of Bret Harte's women, and of his men as well, give them the substantial benefits of gentle blood. Thus he says of one of his characters, "He had that innate respect for the secrets of others which is as inseparable from simplicity as it is from high breeding;" and this remark might have been put in a much more general form. In fact, the essential similarity between simplicity and high breeding runs through the whole nature of Bret Harte's Pioneers, and perhaps, moreover, explains some obscure points in his own life.

Be this as it may, the defects of Bret Harte's heroines relate rather to the ornamental than to the indispensable part of life, whereas the qualities in which they excel are those fundamental feminine qualities upon which, in the last analysis, is founded the greatness of nations. A sophisticated reader would be almost sure to underestimate them. Even that English critic who was perhaps his greatest admirer, makes the remark, literally true, but nevertheless misleading, that Bret Harte "did not create a perfectly noble, superior, commanding woman." No, but he created, or at least sketched, more than one woman of a very noble type. What type of woman is most valuable to the world? Surely that which is fitted to become the mother of heroes; and to that type Bret Harte's best women belong. They have courage, tenderness, sympathy, the power of self-sacrifice; they have even that strain of fierceness which seems to be inseparable in man or beast from the capacity for deep affection. They have the independence, the innocent audacity, the clear common-sense, the resourcefulness, typical of the American woman, and they have, besides, a depth of feeling which is rather primeval than American, which certainly is not a part of the typical American woman as we know her in the Eastern States.

Perhaps the final test of nobility in man or woman is the capacity to value *something*, be it honor, affection, or what you will, be it almost anything, but to value something more than life itself; and this is the characteristic of Bret Harte's heroines. They are as ready to die for love as Juliet was, and along with this *abandon* they have the coolness, the independence, the practical faculty, which belong to their time and race, but which were not a part of woman's nature in the age that produced Shakspere's "unlessoned girl."

Bret Harte's heroines have a strong family resemblance to those of both Tourgueneff and Thomas Hardy. In each case the women obey the instinct of love as unreservedly as men of an archaic type obey the instinct of fighting. There is no question with them of material advantage, of wealth, position, or even reputation. Such considerations, so familiar to women of the world, never enter their minds. They love as nature prompts, and having once given their love, they give themselves and everything that they have along with it. There is a magnificent forgetfulness of self about them. This is the way of nature. Nature never counts the cost, never hoards her treasures, but pours them out, to live or die as the case may be, with a profusion which makes the human by-stander—economical, poverty-stricken man— stand aghast. In Russia this type of woman is frequently found, as Tourgueneff, and to a lesser degree Tolstoi, found her among the upper classes, which have retained a pristine quality long since bred out of the corresponding classes in England and in the United States. For women of the same type in England, Thomas Hardy is forced to look lower down in the social scale; and this probably accounts for the fact that his heroines are seldom drawn from the upper classes.

Women of this kind sometimes fail in point of chastity, but it is a failure due to impulse and affection, not to mere frivolity or sensuality. After all, chastity is only one of the virtues that women owe to themselves and to the race. The chaste woman who coldly marries for money is, as a rule, morally inferior to the unchaste woman who gives up everything for love.

26

It is to be observed, however, that Bret Harte's women do not need this defence, for his heroines, with the single exception of the faithful Miggles, are virtuous. The only loose women in Bret Harte's stories are the obviously bad women, the female "villains" of the play, and they are by no means numerous. Joan, in *The Argonauts of North Liberty*, the wives of Brown of Calaveras and The Bell-Ringer of Angel's, respectively, the cold-blooded Mrs. Decker, and Mrs. Burroughs, the pretty, murderous, feline little woman in *A Mercury of the Foot-Hills*—these very nearly exhaust the list. On the other hand, in Thomas Hardy and Tourgueneff, to say nothing of lesser novelists, it is often the heroine herself who falls from virtue. Too much can hardly be made of the moral superiority of Bret Harte's stories in this respect. It is due, not simply to his own taste and preference, but to the actual state of society in California, which, in this respect as in all others, he faithfully portrayed. The city of San Francisco might have told a different story; but in the mining and agricultural parts of the State the standard of feminine virtue was high. Perhaps this was due, in part at least, to the chivalry of the men reacting upon the women,—to that feeling which Bret Harte himself called "the Western-American fetich of the sanctity of sex," and, again, "the innate Far-Western reverence for women."

In all European societies, and now, to a lesser degree, in the cities of the United States, every man is, generally speaking, the enemy of every young and good-looking woman, as much as the hunter is the enemy of his game. How vast is the difference between this attitude of men to women and that which Bret Harte describes! The California men, as he says somewhere, "thought it dishonorable and a proof of incompetency to rise by their wives' superior fortune." They married for love and nothing else, and their love took the form of reverence.

The complement of this feeling, on the woman's side, is a maternal, protecting affection, perhaps the noblest passion of which women are capable; and this is the kind of love that Bret Harte's heroines invariably show. No mother could have watched over her child more tenderly than Cressy over her sweetheart. The cry that came from the lips of the Rose of Tuolumne when she flew to the rescue of her bleeding lover was "the cry of a mother over her stricken babe, of a tigress over her mangled cub."

Bret Harte's heroines are almost all of the robust type. A companion picture to the Rose is that of Jinny in the story *When the Waters Were Up at "Jules'."* "Certainly she was graceful! Her tall, lithe, but beautifully moulded figure, even in its characteristic Southwestern indolence, fell into poses as picturesque as they were unconscious. She lifted the big molasses can from its shelf on the rafters with the attitude of a Greek water-bearer. She upheaved the heavy flour sack to the same secure shelf with the upraised palm of an Egyptian caryatid."

Trinidad Joe's daughter, too, was large-limbed, with blue eyes, black brows and white teeth. It was of her that the Doctor said, "If she spoke rustic Greek instead of bad English, and wore a cestus instead of an ill-fitting corset, you'd swear she was a goddess."

Something more, however, goes to the making of a handsome woman than mere health and muscle. Bret Harte often speaks of the sudden appearance of beauty and refinement among the Western and Southwestern people. Kitty, for example, as the Reader will remember, "was slight, graceful, and self-contained, and moved beside her stumpy commonplace father and her faded commonplace mother, in the dining-room of the Boomville hotel, like some distinguished alien." In *A Vision of the Fountain*, Bret Harte, half humorously, suggested an explanation. He speaks of the hero as "a singularly handsome young fellow with one of those ideal faces and figures sometimes seen in Western frontier villages, attributable to no ancestor, but evolved possibly from novels and books devoured by ancestresses in the long, solitary winter evenings of their lonely cabins on the frontier."

It seems more likely, however, that a fortunate environment is the main cause of beauty, a life free from care or annoyance; a deep sense of security; that feeling of self-respect which is produced by the respect of others, and, finally, surroundings which have either the beauty of art or the beauty of nature. These are the very advantages which, with many superficial differences, no doubt, are enjoyed alike by the daughters of frontiersmen and by the daughters of a nobility. On the other hand, they are the very advantages with which the middle class in cities, the cockney class, is almost always obliged to dispense, and that class is conspicuously deficient in beauty. Perhaps no one thing is more conducive to beauty than the absence of those hideous creations known as "social superiors." Imagine a society in which it would be impossible to make anybody understand what is meant by the word "snob"! And yet such was, and to a considerable extent still is, the society of the Far West and of rural New England.

Bret Harte himself glanced at this subject in describing the Blue-Grass Penelope. "Beautiful she was, but the power of that beauty was limited by being equally shared with her few neighbors. There were small, narrow, arched feet besides her own that trod the uncarpeted floors of outlying cabins with equal grace and dignity; bright, clearly opened eyes that were equally capable of looking unabashed upon princes and potentates, as a few later did, and the heiress of the County judge read her own beauty without envy in the frank glances and unlowered crest of the blacksmith's daughter."

No less obvious is the connection of repose with beauty. Beauty springs up naturally among people who know the luxury of repose, and yet are vigorous enough to escape the dangers of sloth. Salomy Jane was lazy as well as handsome, and when we first catch a glimpse of her she is leaning against a door-post, engaged in the restful occupation of chewing gum. The same repose, amounting indeed to indolence, formed the chief charm of Mr. MacGlowrie's Widow.

Whether or not the landscape plays a part in the production of womanly beauty is a question more open to dispute. Not many persons feel this influence, but, as experience will show, the proportion of country people who feel it is greater than that of city people, although they have considerably less to say upon the subject. The wide, open spaces, the distant horizon, the gathering of storms, the changing green of Spring and Summer, the scarlet and gold of Autumn, the vast expanse of spotless snow glistening in Midwinter,—these things must be seen by the countryman, his eyes cannot escape them, and in some cases they will be felt as well as seen. Whoever has travelled a New England country road upon a frosty, moonless night in late October, and has observed the Northern Lights casting a pale, cold radiance through the leafless trees, will surely detect some difference between that method of illumination and a kerosene lantern.

A New England farmer whose home commanded a noble view of mountain, lake and forest was blessed with two daughters noted for their beauty. They grew up and married, but both died young; and many years afterward he was heard to say, as he looked dreamily out from his doorway, "I have often thought that the reason why my girls became beautiful women was that from their earliest childhood they always had this scene before their eyes." And yet he had never read Wordsworth or Ruskin!

Bret Harte's heroines enjoyed all the advantages just enumerated as being conducive to beauty, and they escaped contamination from civilization. They were close to nature, and as primitive in their love-affairs as the heroines of Shakspere. "Who ever loved that loved not at first sight!" John Ashe's betrothed and Ridgeway Dent had known each other a matter of two hours or so, before they exchanged that immortal kiss which nearly cost the lives of both. Two brief meetings, and one of those in the dark, sufficed to win for the brave and clever young deputy sheriff the affections of Lanty Foster. In *A Jack and Jill of the Sierras*, a handsome girl from the East tumbles over a precipice, and falls upon the recumbent hero, part way down, with such violence as to stun him. This is hardly romantic, but the dangerous and difficult ascent which they make together furnishes the required opportunity. Ten minutes of contiguity suffice, and so well is the girl's character indicated by a few masterly strokes, that the reader feels no surprise at the result.

And yet there is nothing that savors of coarseness, much less of levity, in these abrupt romances. When Bret Harte's heroes and heroines meet, it is the coming together of two souls that recognize and attract each other. It is like a stroke of lightning, and is accepted with a primeval simplicity and un-selfconsciousness. The impression is as deep as it is sudden.

What said Juliet of the anonymous young man whom she had known something less than an hour?

"Go, ask his name: if he be marrièd
My grave is like to be my wedding bed."

So felt Liberty Jones when she exclaimed to Dr. Ruysdael, "I'll go with you or I'll die!"

It is this sincerity that sanctifies the rapidity and frankness of Bret Harte's love-affairs. Genuine passion takes no account of time, and supplies by one instinctive rush of feeling the experience of years. Given the right persons, time becomes as long and as short as eternity. Thus it was with the two lovers who met and parted at midnight on the hilltop. "There they stood alone. There was no sound or motion in earth or woods or heaven. They might have been the one man and woman for whom this goodly earth that lay at their feet, rimmed with the deepest azure, was created. And seeing this they turned toward each other with a sudden instinct, and their hands met, and then their lips in one long kiss."

But this same perfect understanding may be arrived at in a crowd as well as in solitude. Cressy and the Schoolmaster were mutually aware of each other's presence at the dance before they had exchanged a look, and when their eyes met it was in "an isolation as supreme as if they had been alone."

Could any country in the world except our own produce a Cressy! She has all the beauty, much of the refinement, and all the subtle perceptions of a girl belonging to the most sophisticated race and class; and underneath she has the strong, primordial, spontaneous qualities, the wholesome instincts, the courage, the steadfastness of that Pioneer people, that religious, fighting, much-enduring people to whom she belonged.

Cressy is the true child of her father; and there is nothing finer in all Bret Harte than his description of this rough backwoodsman, ferocious in his boundary warfare, and yet full of vague aspirations for his daughter, conscious of his own deficiencies, and oppressed with that melancholy which haunts the man who has outgrown the ideals and conventions of his youth. Hiram McKinstry, compared with the masterful Yuba Bill, the picturesque Hamlin, or the majestic Starbottle, is not an imposing figure; but to have divined him was a greater feat of sympathetic imagination than to have created the others.

It is characteristic, too, of Bret Harte that it is Cressy's father who is represented as acutely conscious of his own defects in education; whereas her mother remains true to the ancestral type, deeply distrusting her husband's and her daughter's innovations. Mrs. McKinstry, as the Reader will remember, "looked upon her daughter's studies and her husband's interest in them as weaknesses that might in course of time produce infirmity of homicidal purpose and become enervating of eye and trigger finger.... 'The old man's worrits hev sorter shook out a little of his sand,' she had explained."

Mr. McKinstry, on the other hand, had almost as much devotion to "Kam" as Matthew Arnold had to Culture, and meant very nearly the same thing by it. Thus he said to the Schoolmaster: "'I should be a powerful sight more kam if I knowed that when I was away huntin' stock or fightin' stakes with them Harrisons that she was a-settin' in school with the other children and the birds and the bees, listenin' to them and to you. Mebbe there's been a little too many scrimmages goin' on round the ranch sence she's been a child; mebbe she orter know sunthin' more of a man than a feller who sparks her and fights for her.'

"The master was silent. Had this selfish, savage, and literally red-handed frontier brawler been moved by some dumb instinct of the power of gentleness to understand his daughter's needs better than he?"

Alas that no genius has arisen to write the epic of the West, as Hawthorne and Mary Wilkins and Miss Jewett have written the epic of New England! Bret Harte's stories of the Western people are true and striking, but his limitations prevented him from giving much more than sketches of them. They are not presented with that fullness which is necessary to make a figure in fiction impress itself upon the popular imagination, and become familiar even to people who have never read the book in which it is contained. Cressy, like the other heroines of Bret Harte, flits across the scene a few times, and we see her no more. Mrs. McKinstry is drawn only in outline; and yet she is a strong, tragic figure, of a type now extinct, or nearly so, as powerful and more sane than Meg Merrilies, and far more worthy of a permanent place in literature.

CHAPTER VI

To be successful and popular among the Pioneers was something really to a man's credit. Men were thrown upon their own resources, and, as in Mediæval times, were their own police and watchmen, their own firemen, and in most cases their own judge and jury. There was no distribution of the inhabitants into separate classes: they constituted a single class, the only distinction being that between individuals. There was not even the broad distinction between those who worked with their heads and those who worked with their hands. Everybody, except the gamblers, performed manual labor; and although this condition could not long prevail in San Francisco or Sacramento, it continued in the mines for many months. In fact, any one who did not live by actual physical toil was regarded by the miners as a social excrescence, a parasite.

An old miner, after spending a night in a San Francisco lodging house, paid the proprietor with gold dust. While waiting for his change he seemed to be studying the keeper of the house as a novel and not over-admirable specimen of humanity. Finally he inquired of him as follows: "Say, now, stranger, do you do nothing else but just sit there and take a dollar from every man that sleeps in these beds?" "Yes," was the reply, "that is my business." "Well, then," said the miner after a little further reflection, "it's a damned mean way of making your living; that's all I can say."

Even those who were not democratic by nature became so in California. All men felt that they were, at last, free and equal. Social distinctions were rubbed out. A man was judged by his conduct, not by his bank account, nor by the set, the family, the club, or the church to which he belonged. All former records were wiped from the slate; and nobody inquired whether, in order to reach California, a man had resigned public office or position, or had escaped from a jail.

"Some of the best men," says Bret Harte, "had the worst antecedents, some of the worst rejoiced in a spotless, Puritan pedigree. 'The boys seem to have taken a fresh deal all round,' said Mr. John Oakhurst one day to me, with the easy confidence of a man who was conscious of his ability to win my money, 'and there is no knowing whether a man will turn out knave or king.'"

This, perhaps, sounds a little improbable, and yet here, as always, Bret Harte has merely stated the fact as it was. One of the most accurate contemporary historians says: "The man esteemed virtuous at home becomes profligate here, the honest man dishonest, and the clergyman sometimes a profane gambler; while, on the contrary, the cases are not few of those who were idle or profligate at home, who came here to be reformed."

"It was a republic of incognitos. No one knew who any one else was, and only the more ill-mannered and uneasy even desired to know. Gentlemen took more trouble to conceal their gentility than thieves living in South Kensington would take to conceal their blackguardism."

THE FIRST HOTEL AT SAN FRANCISCO
Copyright, Century Co.

"Have you a letter of introduction?" wrote a Pioneer to a friend in the East about to sail for California. "If you have, never present it. No one here has time to read such things. No one cares even to know your name. If you are the right sort of a man, everything goes smoothly here." "What is your partner's last name?" asked one San Francisco merchant of another in 1850. "Really, I don't know," was the reply; "we have only been acquainted three or four weeks." A miner at Maryville once offered to wager his old blind mule against a plug of tobacco that the company, although they had been acquainted for some years, could not tell one another's names; and this was found upon trial to be the case.

Men were usually known, as Bret Harte relates, by the State or other place from which they came,—with some prefix or affix to denote a salient characteristic. Thus one miner, in a home letter, speaks of his friends, "Big Pike, Little Pike, Old Kentuck, Little York, Big York, Sandy, and Scotty." Men originally from the East, and long supposed to be dead, turned up in California, seeking a new career. In fact, there seems to have been a general inclination among the Pioneers to strike out in new directions. "To find a man here engaged in his own trade or profession," wrote a Forty-Niner, "is a rare thing. The merchant of to-day is to-morrow a doctor; lawyers turn bankers, and bankers lawyers. The miners are almost continually on the move, passing from one claim to another, and from the Southern to the Northern mines, or *vice versa.*"

Bret Harte was startled by meeting an old acquaintance in a strange situation. "At my first breakfast in a restaurant on Long Wharf I was haunted during the meal by a shadowy resemblance which the waiter who took my order bore to a gentleman to whom in my boyhood I had looked up as to a mirror of elegance, urbanity, and social accomplishment. Fearful lest I should insult the waiter—who carried a revolver—by this reminiscence, I said nothing to him; but a later inquiry of the proprietor proved that my suspicions were correct. 'He's mighty handy,' said this man, 'and can talk elegant to a customer as is waiting for his cakes, and make him kinder forget he ain't sarved.'"

Bret Harte relates another case. "An Argonaut just arriving was amazed at recognizing in the boatman who pulled him ashore, and who charged him the modest sum of fifty dollars for the performance, a classmate at Oxford. 'Were you not,' he asked eagerly, 'Senior Wrangler in '43?' 'Yes,' said the other significantly, 'but I also pulled stroke against Cambridge.'"

A Yale College professor was hauling freight with a yoke of oxen; a Yale graduate was selling peanuts on the Plaza at San Francisco; an ex-governor was playing the fiddle in a bar-room; a physician was washing dishes in a hotel; a minister was acting as waiter in a restaurant; a lawyer was paring potatoes in the same place. Lawyers, indeed, were doing a great deal of useful work in California. One kept a mush and milk stand; another sold pies at a crossing of the American River; a third drove a team of mules.

John A. McGlynn, one of the best known and most successful Forty-Niners, began by hitching two half-broken mustangs to an express wagon, and acting as teamster. He was soon chosen to enforce the rules regulating the unloading of vessels and the cartage of goods. All the drivers obeyed him, except one, a native of Chili, a big, powerful man, with a team of six American mules. McGlynn ordered him into line; he refused; and McGlynn struck him with his whip. In an instant both men had leaped from their wagon-seats to the ground. The Chileno rushed at McGlynn, with his bowie-knife in his hand; but the American was left-handed, for which the Chileno was not prepared; and with his first blow McGlynn stretched his antagonist on the ground. There he held him until the fellow promised good behavior. On regaining his feet the defeated man invited all hands to drink, and became thenceforth a warm friend of the victor.

The judge of the Court for Santa Cruz County kept a hotel, and after court adjourned, he would take off his coat and wait on the table, serving jurors, attorneys, criminals and sheriffs with the same impartiality which he exhibited on the bench. A brief term of service as waiter in a San Francisco restaurant laid the foundation of the highly successful career of another lawyer, a very young man. One day a merchant upon whom he was waiting remarked to a companion: "If I only had a lawyer who was worth a damn, I could win that suit." "I am a lawyer," interposed the waiter, "and I am looking for a chance to get into business. Try me." The merchant did so; the suit was won; and the former waiter was soon in full legal practice.

Acquaintances were formed, and the beginning of a fortune was often made, by chance meetings and incidents. Men got at one another more quickly than is possible in an old and conservative society. One who became a distinguished citizen of California began his career by accepting an offer of humble employment when he stepped into the street on his first morning in San Francisco. "Look here, my friend," said a merchant to him, "if you won't get mad about it, I'll offer you a dollar to fill this box with sand." "Thank you," said the young fellow, "I'll fill it all day long on those terms, and never become angry in the least." He filled the box, and received payment. "Now," he said, "we'll go and take a drink with this dollar." The merchant acquiesced with a laugh, and thus began a life-long connection between the two men.

There were some recognitions of old acquaintances as remarkable as the making of new friends. Two brothers, Englishmen from the Society Islands, met in a mining town, and were not aware of their relationship until a chance conversation between them disclosed it. A merchant from Cincinnati arrived in San Francisco with the intention of settling there. One of the first persons whom he met was a prosperous business man who had absconded some years before with ten thousand dollars of his money. He recovered the ten thousand dollars and interest, without making the matter public, and went back to Ohio well satisfied.

A lawyer of note in San Francisco remarked, in 1850, that the last time he saw Ned McGowan, previous to his arrival in California, McGowan stood in the criminal dock of a Philadelphia court where he was receiving a sentence to the State prison for robbery. Subsequently he was pardoned by the Governor of Pennsylvania, on condition that he should leave the State. When this lawyer settled in San Francisco, he was employed to defend some persons who had been arrested for drunkenness; and upon entering the court room he was thunderstruck by the appearance of the magistrate upon the bench. After a careful survey of the magistrate and a pinch of the flesh to make sure that he was not dreaming, he exclaimed:—

"Ned McGowan, is that you?"

"It is," was the cool reply.

"Well, gentlemen," said the lawyer, turning to his clients, "you had better toll down heavy, for I can do you no good with such a judge." Tolling down heavy was probably a practice which the judge encouraged, for, a year later, upon the organization of the Vigilance Committee, Ned McGowan fled from San Francisco, if not from California.

California, from 1849 to 1858, was a meeting ground for all the nations of the earth. One of the first acts of the Legislature was to appoint an official translator. The confusion of languages resulted in many misunderstandings and some murders. A Frenchman and a German at Moquelumne Hill had a controversy about a water-privilege, and being unable to understand each other, they resorted first to pantomime, and then to firearms, with the unfortunate result that the German was killed.

A trial which occurred at San José illustrates the multiplicity of tongues in California. A Spaniard accused a Tartar of assaulting him, but as the Tartar and his witnesses could not speak English the proceedings were delayed. At last another Tartar, called Arghat, was found who could speak Chinese, and then a Chinaman, called Alab, who could speak Spanish; and with these as interpreters the trial began. Another difficulty then arose, namely, the swearing of the witnesses. The court, having ascertained that the Tartar mode of swearing is by lifting a lighted candle toward the sun, adopted that form. The judge administered the ordinary oath to the English and Spanish interpreters; the latter then swore Arghat as Tartar and Chinese interpreter, and he, in turn, swore Alab, by the burning candle and the sun, as Chinese and Spanish interpreter; and the trial then proceeded in four languages.

The first newspaper was printed half in English, half in Spanish. Sermons were preached by Catholic priests both in English and in Spanish. The Fourth of July was celebrated at San José in 1850 by one oration in English and another in Spanish. German and Italian weekly papers were published in San Francisco. The French population of the city was especially large. They made *rouge-et-noir* the fashion. "Where there are Frenchmen," remarks a Pioneer, "you will find music, singing and gayety." A French benevolent society was established at San Francisco in 1851.

Many of the best citizens of California were Englishmen. There was a famous ale-house in San Francisco, called the Boomerang, where sirloins of beef could be washed down with English ale, and followed by Stilton cheese; where the London "Times," "Punch" and "Bell's Life" were taken in.

Australia and New South Wales contributed a considerable and by no means the best part of the population. The "Sydney Ducks" who infested the dark lanes and alleys of San Francisco, and lurked about the wharves at night, lived mainly by robbery; and they often murdered in order to rob. An English traveller said of them: "I have seen vice in almost every form, and under almost every condition in the Old World, but never did it appear to me in so repulsive and disgusting a shape as it exists among the lower orders of Sydney, and generally in New South Wales."

But not all of the immigrants from English colonies were of this character. Many were respectable men, and succeeded well in California. An Australian cabman, for example, brought a barouche, a fine pair of horses, a tall hat and a livery coat all the way across the Pacific, and made a fortune by hiring out at the rate of twenty dollars an hour.

There were many Jews in San Francisco, but none in the mines;—they alone of all the nations gathered in California kept to their ordinary occupations, chiefly the selling of clothes, and never looked for gold. Even their dress did not change. "They are," writes a Pioneer, "exactly the same unwashed-looking, slobbery, slipshod individuals that one sees in every seaport town." But the Jew prospered, and was a good citizen. Another Pioneer, who could look beneath the surface, said, "The Jew does honor to his name here. The pressure which elsewhere bows him to the earth is removed."

The variety and mixture of races in California were without precedent, and San Francisco especially prided itself upon the barbaric aspect of its streets. Perhaps the Chinese were the most striking figures. The low-caste Chinamen wore full jackets and breeches of blue calico, and on their heads a huge wicker-work hat that would have made a good family clothes-basket. The aristocratic Chinaman displayed a jacket of gay-colored silk, yellow satin breeches, a scarlet skull-cap with a gold knob on top, and, in cold weather, a short coat of Astrakhan fur.

There was, of course, a Chinese quarter, and a district known as little Chili, where South Americans of every country could be found, with a mixture of Kanakas from the Sandwich Islands, and negroes from the South Seas. In July, 1850, there arrived a ship-load of Hungarian exiles, and somewhat later a company of Bayonnais from the south of France, the men wild and excitable in appearance, the women dark-skinned, large-eyed, and graceful in their movements.

There was a Spanish quarter where, as Bret Harte said, "three centuries of quaint customs, speech and dress were still preserved; where the proverbs of Sancho Panza were still spoken in the language of Cervantes, and the high-flown allusions of the La Manchian knight still a part of the Spanish Californian hidalgo's dream."

The Spanish women were usually attended by Indian girls, and their dress was coquettish and becoming. Their petticoats, short enough to display a well-turned ankle, were richly laced and embroidered, and striped and flounced with gaudy colors, of which scarlet was the most common. Their tresses fell in luxuriant plaits down their backs; and, in all the little accessories of dress, such as earrings, and necklaces, their costume was very rich. Its chief feature, the *reboso*, was a sort of scarf, like the mantilla of old Spain. This was sometimes twined around the waist and shoulders, and at other times hung in pretty festoons about the figure.

It was only in respect to their diversions that the Spanish had any influence upon the Americans. The gambling houses and theatres were largely in Spanish hands at first, and the *fandango* was the national amusement in which the American miners soon learned to join.

And yet the fundamental gravity of the Spanish nature, a gravity which is epitomized and immortally fixed in the famous portrait of Admiral Pareja by Velasquez, was as marked in California as at home. It is thus that Bret Harte describes Don José Sepulvida, the Knight Errant of the Foot-Hills: "The fading glow of the western sky through the deep, embrasured windows lit up his rapt and meditative face. He was a young man of apparently twenty-five, with a colorless, satin complexion, dark eyes, alternating between melancholy and restless energy, a narrow, high forehead, long straight hair, and a lightly pencilled mustache."

One is struck by the resemblance between Don José Sepulvida, and Culpeper Starbottle, the Colonel's nephew, whose tragic death the Reader will remember. Bret Harte thus depicts him: "The face was not an unprepossessing one, albeit a trifle too thin and lank and bilious to be altogether pleasant. The cheek-bones were prominent, and the black eyes sunken in their orbits. Straight black hair fell slantwise off a high but narrow forehead, and swept part of a hollow cheek. A long, black mustache followed the perpendicular curves of his mouth. It was on the whole a serious, even quixotic face, but at times it was relieved by a rare smile of such tender and even pathetic sweetness, that Miss Jo is reported to have said that, if it would only last through the ceremony, she would have married the possessor on the spot. 'I once told him so,' added that shameless young woman; 'but the man instantly fell into a settled melancholy, and has not laughed since.'"

MINERS' BALL
A. Castaigne, del.

There were, in fact, many things in common between the Southerner and the Spaniard. They lived in similar climates, and the fundamental ideas of their respective communities were very much the same. The Southerner was almost as deeply imbued as the Spaniard with extreme, aristocratic notions of government and society; and he, like the Spaniard, was conservative, religious, dignified, courteous, chivalrous to women, brave, narrow-minded and indolent.

In *The Secret of Sobriente's Well*, this resemblance suddenly occurs to Larry Hawkins, who, in describing to Colonel Wilson, from Virginia, the character of his Spanish predecessor, the former owner of the *posada* in which the Colonel lived, said: "He was that kind o' fool that he took no stock in mining. When the boys were whoopin' up the place and finding the color everywhere, he was either ridin' round lookin' up the wild horses he owned, or sittin' with two or three lazy peons and Injuns that was fed and looked after by the priests. Gosh! Now I think of it, it was mighty like you when you first kem here with your niggers. That's curous, too, ain't it?"

The hospitality of the Spanish Californian was boundless. "There is no need of an orphan asylum in California," wrote the American Alcalde at Monterey. "The question is not who shall be burdened with the care of an orphan, but who shall have the privilege of rearing it. An industrious man of rather limited means applied to me to-day for the care of *six* orphan children. He had fifteen of his own;" and when the Alcalde questioned the prudence of his offer, the Spaniard replied, "The hen that has twenty chickens scratches no harder than the hen that has one."

A Pioneer, speaking from his own experience, said: "If you are sick there is nothing which sympathy can divine which is not done for you. This is as true of the lady whose hand has only figured her embroidery or swept her guitar, as of the cottage-girl wringing from her laundry the foam of the mountain stream; and all this from the heart!"

Generosity and pride are Spanish traits. "The worst and weakest of them," remarks an English Pioneer, "has that indefinable something about him that lifts so immeasurably the beggar of Murillo above the beggar of Hogarth." The Reader will remember how cheerfully and punctiliously Don José Sepulvida paid the wagers of his friend and servant, Bucking Bob. A gambling debt was regarded by the Spaniards in so sacred a light that if he who incurred it was unable to pay, then, for the honor of the family, any relative, a godfather, or even one who had the misfortune to be connected by marriage with the debtor, was bound to discharge the obligation. Some Americans basely took advantage of this sentiment; and, in one case, an old Spanish lady was deprived of a vineyard, her only means of support, in order to preserve the reputation of a scapegrace nephew who had lost to an American at faro a greater sum than he possessed.

Some convenient and becoming articles of Spanish dress were adopted by the Americans, notably the sombrero and the serapé, or horseman's cloak. Jack Hamlin, as the Reader will remember, sometimes went a little further. Thus, when he started on his search for the Sappho of Green Springs, he "modified his usual correct conventional attire by a tasteful combination of a roquero's costume, and in loose white bullion-fringed trousers, red sash, jacket and sombrero, looked infinitely more dashing and picturesque than his original."

The profuse wearing of jewelry, even by men, was another foreign fashion which Americans adopted in the early years; so much so, in fact, that to appear in a plain and unadorned state was to be conspicuous. The jewelry thus worn was not of the conventional kind, but a sort of miner's jewelry, significant of the place and time. Ornaments were made from the gold in its native state by soldering into one mass many small nuggets, without any polish or other embellishment. Everybody carried a gold watch, and watch-chains were constructed upon a massive plan, the links sometimes representing dogs in pursuit of deer, horses at full speed, birds in the act of flight, or serpents coiled and hissing. Scarf-pins were made from lumps of gold retaining their natural form and mixed with quartz, rose-colored, blue-gray, or white, according to the rock from which they were taken. The big "specimen ring" worn by the hero of *A Night on the Divide* was an example.

Some Americans adhered to their usual dress which, in the Eastern States, was a sober suit of black; but usually the Pioneers discarded all conventional clothes, and appeared in a rough and picturesque costume much like that of a stage pirate. Indeed, it was impossible for any man in '49 to make his dress sufficiently bizarre to attract attention. The prevailing fashion included a red or blue flannel shirt, a "wide-awake" hat of every conceivable shape and color, trousers stuffed into a huge pair of boots coming up above the knee, and a belt decorated with pistols and knives. More than one Pioneer landed in San Francisco with a rifle slung on his back, a sword-cane in his hand, two six-shooters and a bowie-knife in his belt, and a couple of small pistols protruding from his waistcoat pockets.

In the rainy season of '49, long boots were so scarce, and so desirable on account of the mud, that they sold for forty dollars a pair in San Francisco, and higher yet in Stockton. Learning of this, Eastern merchants flooded the market with top-boots a year later; but by that time the streets had been planked, the miner's costume was passing out of fashion, and long boots were no longer in demand. These changes were greatly regretted by unconventional Pioneers, and even so early as 1850 they were lamenting "the good old times,"—just one year back,—before the tailor and the barber were abroad in the land.

Local celebrations were marked by more color and display than are usually indulged in by Americans. In 1851, on Washington's Birthday, there was a procession in San Francisco headed by the Mayor in a barouche drawn by four white horses. Next came the fire engines of the city, each with a team of eight gray horses, and followed by a long train of firemen in white shirts and black trousers. Then came a company of teamsters mounted on their draught horses, and carrying gay banners; and finally a delegation of Chinamen, preceded by a Chinese band and bearing aloft a huge flag of yellow silk.

Horsemen, more or less intoxicated, and shouting like wild Indians, charged up and down the streets at all hours of the day and night, to the great discomfort of many and the fatal injury of some pedestrians. "On Sundays especially, one would imagine," a local newspaper remarks, "that a horde of Cossacks or Tartars had taken possession of the city."

"The Spaniard," Bret Harte says, "taught the Americans horsemanship, and they rode off with his cattle." The Americans usually adopted the Spanish equipment, consisting of a huge saddle, with cumbrous leather saddle-flaps, stirrups carved from solid oak, heavy metal spurs, a bridle jingling with ornaments, and a cruel curb bit,—the whole paraphernalia being designed to serve the convenience and vanity of the rider without the least regard to the comfort of his beast. The Spanish manner of abrupt stopping, made possible by the severe bit, was also taken up by young Americans who loved to charge down upon a friend, halting at the last possible moment, in a cloud of dust, with the horse almost upon his haunches. This was Jack Hamlin's habit.

A popular figure in the streets of San Francisco was a black pony, the property of a constable, that stood most of the day, saddled and bridled, in front of his master's office. The pony's favorite diversion was to have his hoofs blacked and polished, and whenever a coin was placed between his lips, he would carry it to a neighboring boot-black, put, first, one fore-foot, and then the other, on the foot-rest, and, after receiving a satisfactory "shine," would walk gravely back to his usual station. Even the dumb animals felt that something unusual was expected of them in California.

There were no harness horses or carriages in San Francisco in the early part of '49; and when they were introduced toward the end of that year, a touch of barbaric splendor marked the fashionable equipage of the hour. A pair of white horses with gilt trappings, drawing a light, yellow-wheeled buggy, was once a familiar sight in the streets of the city. The *demi-monde* rode on horseback, in parties of two or three, and even of six or more, and the pace which they set corresponded with that of California life in general. The appearance of one of the most noted of these women is thus described by a Pioneer, the wife of a sea-captain: "I have seen her mounted on a glossy, lithe-limbed race-horse, one that had won for her many thousands on the race-course, habited in a close-fitting riding-dress of black velvet, ornamented with one hundred and fifty gold buttons, a hat from which depended magnificent sable plumes, and over her face a short, white lace veil of the richest texture, so gossamer-like one could almost see the fire of passion flashing from the depths of her dark, lustrous eyes."

Even the climate, the dry, bracing air, the cool nights, the aromatic fragrance of the woods, tended to quicken the pulse of the Argonauts, and to heighten the general exuberance of feeling.

Central California, the scene of Bret Harte's stories, is a great valley bounded on the west by the Coast Range of hills or mountains, which rise from two thousand to four thousand, and in a few places to five thousand feet, and on the east by the Foot-Hills. After the immigration, this valley furnished immense crops of wheat, vegetables and fruit; but in '49 it was a vast, uncultivated plain, free from underbrush or other small growth, and studded by massive, spreading oaks, by tall plane trees, and occasionally by a gigantic redwood, sending its topmost branches two and even three hundred feet into the air. In the dry season, the surface was brown and parched, but as soon as the rains began, the wild grasses and wild oats gave it a rich carpet of green, sparkling with countless field flowers. The resemblance of the valley, in the rainy season at least, to an English park, was often spoken of by Pioneers who found in it a reminder of home.

On the eastern side this great central valley gradually merges into the Foot-Hills, the vanguards of the lofty mountain range which separates central California from Nevada. The Foot-Hills form what is perhaps the most picturesque part of the State, watered in the rainy season by numerous rocky, swift-flowing streams, the tributaries of the Sacramento and the San Joaquin, and broken into those deep, narrow glens so often described in Bret Harte's poetry and prose. This was the principal gold-bearing region. The Foot-Hills extend over a space about five hundred miles long and fifty wide, and from them arise, sometimes abruptly, and sometimes gradually, the snow-crowned Sierras.

Such is central California. A region extending from latitude 32° 30′ in the South to 42° in the North, and rising from the level of the Pacific Ocean to mountain peaks fifteen thousand feet high, must needs present many varieties of weather; but on the whole the State may be said to have a mild, dry, breezy, healthy climate. Except in the mountains and in the extreme northeast, snow never lies long, the earth does not freeze, and Winter is like a wet Spring during which the cattle fare much better than they do in Summer. The passing of one season into the other was thus described by Bret Harte: "The eternal smile of the California Summer had begun to waver and grow fixed; dust lay thick on leaf and blade; the dry hills were clothed in russet leather; the trade winds were shifting to the south with an ominous warm humidity; a few days longer, and the rains would be here."

San Francisco has a climate of its own. Ice never forms there, and geraniums bloom throughout the Winter; but during the dry season, which lasts from May or June until September or October, a strong, cold wind blows in every afternoon from the ocean, dying down at sunset. The mercury falls with the coming of the wind, the rays of the sun seem to have no more warmth than moonbeams, the sand blows up in clouds, doors and windows rattle, and the city is swept and scourged. But fifty miles inland the air is still and balmy, and residents of San Francisco leave the city in Summer not to escape unpleasant heat, but to enjoy the relaxation of a milder and less stimulating climate. "In the interior one bright, still day follows another, as calm, as dreamy, as disconnected from time and space as was the air which lulled the lotus-eaters to rest." This evenness of temperature was amazing and delightful to the weather-beaten Pioneers from New England.

The Midsummer days are often intensely hot in the interior, but the nights are cool, and the atmosphere is so dry that the heat is not enervating. Men have been seen hard at work digging a cellar with the thermometer at 125° F. in the shade; and sunstrokes, though not unknown, are extremely rare. Nothing decays or becomes offensive. Fresh meat hung in the shade does not spoil. Dead animal or vegetable matter simply dries up and wastes away.

In 1849 the rains were uncommonly severe, to the great discomfort of the Pioneers; and Alvarado, the former Spanish governor, explained the fact in all sincerity by saying that the Yankees had been accompanied to California by the devil himself. This explanation was accepted by the natives generally, without doubt or qualification. The streets of San Francisco, in that year, were like the beds of rivers. It was no uncommon thing to see, at the same time, a mule stalled in the middle of the highway, with only his head showing above the road, and an unfortunate pedestrian, who had slipped off the plank sidewalk, in process of being fished out by a companion. At the corner of Clay and Kearney Streets there once stood a sign, erected by some joker, inscribed as follows,—

This street is impassable,
Not even jackassable!

But the rainy season is usually neither long nor constant. The fall of rain on the Pacific Slope is only about one third of the rainfall in the Atlantic States; and, before water was supplied artificially, the miner was often obliged to suspend operations for want of it. Frequently a day's rain would have been cheaply bought at the price of a million dollars; and even a good shower gave an impetus to business which was felt by the merchants and gamblers of San Francisco and Sacramento. It was observed that after a long drought dimes took the place of gold slugs upon the roulette and faro tables. Thus, even the weather was a speculation in Pioneer times.

And yet, notwithstanding the general mildness of the climate, extremes of cold, at high levels, are close at hand. Snow often falls to a depth of one or two feet within fifty miles of San Francisco. Near the head-waters of the Feather River the snow is sometimes twelve and even fifteen feet deep; and in December, 1850, eighteen men out of a party of nineteen, and sixty-eight of their seventy mules froze to death in one night. A snow-storm came up so suddenly, and fell with such fury, that their firewood became inaccessible, and they were obliged to burn their cabin; but even that did not save them.

Bret Harte has described a California snow-storm not only in *The Outcasts of Poker Flat*, but in several other stories, notably in *Gabriel Conroy, Snow-Bound at Eagle's*, and *A Night on the Divide*. It is interesting to know, as Mr. Pemberton tells us, that the description of the snow-storm in *Gabriel Conroy* was written on a hot day in August.

Poker Flat was in Sierra County, and in March, 1860, the snow was so deep in that county that tunnels were dug through it as a picturesque and convenient means of access to local saloons. The storm which overwhelmed the Outcasts was no uncommon event. But when these storms clear off, the cold, though often intense, is not disagreeable, owing to the dryness of the air. "We are now working every fair day," wrote a miner in January, 1860, "and have been all the Winter without inconvenience. The long, sled-runner Norwegian snow-shoes are used here by nearly everybody. I have seen the ladies floating about, wheeling and soaring, with as much grace and ease of motion as swans on the bosom of a placid lake or eagles in the sun-lit air."

On the summit of the mountains the snow is perpetual, and on the easterly slopes it often attains the almost incredible depth, or height, of fifty feet. In *A Tale of Three Truants*, Bret Harte has described an avalanche of snow, carrying the Three Truants along with it, in the course of which they "seemed to be going through a thicket of underbrush, but Provy Smith knew that they were the tops of pine trees."

On the whole, the climate of California justified the enthusiasm which it aroused in the Pioneers, and which sometimes found an amusing expression. The birth of twins to an immigrant and his wife, who had been childless for fifteen years, was triumphantly recorded by a San José paper as the natural result of even a short residence on the Pacific Slope. Large families and long life marked not only the Spaniards, but also the Mexicans and Indians. Families of fifteen, twenty, and even twenty-five children excited no surprise and procured no rewards of merit for the parents. In 1849 there was a woman living at Monterey whose children, all alive and in good health, numbered twenty-eight.

We read of an Indian, blind but still active at the age of one hundred and forty; and of a squaw "very active" at one hundred and twenty-six. Mr. Charles Dudley Warner a speaks of "Don Antonio Serrano, a tall, spare man, who rides with grace and vigor at ninety-three," and of an Indian servant "who was a grown man, breaking horses, when Don Antonio was an infant. This man is still strong enough to mount his horse and canter about the country. He is supposed to be about one hundred and eighteen." This wonderful longevity was ascribed by Mr. Warner to the equable climate and a simple diet.

Ancient Mexicans and Indians figure occasionally in Bret Harte's stories. There is, for example, Concepcion, "a wrinkled Indian woman, brown and veined like a tobacco leaf," who acts as servant to the Convert of the Mission; and, at the Mission of San Carmel, Sanchicha, in the form of a bundle, is brought in and deposited in a corner of the room. "Father Pedro bent over the heap, and distinguished in its midst the glowing black eyes of Sanchicha, the Indian centenarian of the Mission. Only her eyes lived. Helpless, boneless, and jelly-like, old age had overtaken her with a mild form of deliquescence."

But it was not length of days,—it was feverish energy that the climate produced in the new race which had come under its influence. The amount of labor performed by the Pioneers was prodigious. "There is as much difference," wrote the Methodist preacher, Father Taylor, "between the muscular action of the California miner and a man hired to work on a farm, as between the aimless movements of a sloth and the pounce of the panther."

"We have," declared a San Francisco paper, "the most exhilarating atmosphere in the world. In it a man can do more work than anywhere else, and he feels under a constant pressure of excitement. With a sun like that of Italy, a coast wind as cool as an Atlantic breeze in Spring, an air as crisp and dry as that of the high Alps, people work on without let or relaxation, until the vital cord suddenly snaps. Few Americans die gradually here or of old age; they fall off without warning."

So late as 1860 it was often said that there were busy men in San Francisco who had never taken a day's vacation, or even left the city to cross the Bay, from the hour of their arrival in 1849 until that moment. Even this record has been eclipsed. A Pioneer of German birth, named Henry Miller, who accumulated a fortune of six million dollars, is said to have lived, or at least to have existed, in San Francisco for thirty-five years without taking a single day's vacation.

It was even asserted at first that the climate neutralized the effect of intoxicating liquor, and that it was difficult, if not impossible, to get really drunk in California. Possibly a somewhat lax definition of drunkenness accounted in part for this theory. A witness once testified in a San Francisco court that he did not consider a man to be drunk so long as he could move. But the crowning excellence of the California climate remains to be stated. It was observed by the Pioneers,—and they had ample opportunity to make observations upon the subject,—that in that benign atmosphere gunshot wounds healed rapidly.

With a climate exhilarating and curative; with youth, health, courage, and the prospect of almost immediate wealth; with new and exciting surroundings, it is no wonder that the Pioneers enjoyed their hour. In San Francisco, especially, a kind of pleasant madness seized upon every newcomer. "As each man steps his foot on shore," writes one adventurer, "he seems to have entered a magic circle in which he is under the influence of new impulses." And another, in a letter to a friend says, "As soon as you reach California you will think every one is crazy; and without great caution, you will be crazy yourself."

Still another Pioneer wrote home even more emphatically on this point: "You can form no conception of the state of affairs here. I do believe, in my soul, everybody has gone mad,—stark, staring mad."

To the same effect is the narrative of Stephen J. Field, afterward, and for many years, a Justice of the Supreme Court of the United States. Mr. Field, who arrived in San Francisco as a very young man, thus describes his first experience:—

"As I walked along the streets, I met a great many persons whom I had known in New York, and they all seemed to be in the highest spirits. Every one in greeting me said, 'It is a glorious country!' or 'Isn't it a glorious country?' or 'Did you ever see a more glorious country?' In every case the word 'glorious' was sure to come out.... I caught the infection, and though I had but a single dollar in my pocket, no business whatever, and did not know where I was to get my next meal, I found myself saying to everybody I met, 'It is a glorious country!'"

"The exuberance of my spirits," Judge Field continues, "was marvellous"; and the readers of his interesting reminiscences will not be inclined to dispute the fact when they learn that four days after his arrival, having made the sum of twenty dollars by selling a few New York newspapers, he forthwith put down his name for sixty-five thousand dollars' worth of town lots, and received the consideration due to a capitalist bent upon developing the resources of a new country.

The most extravagant acts appeared reasonable under the new dispensation. Nobody was surprised when an enthusiastic miner offered to bet a friend that the latter could not hit him with a shotgun at the distance of seventy-eight yards. As a result the miner received five shots, causing severe wounds, beside losing the bet, which amounted to four drinks. After the first State election, a magistrate holding an important office fulfilled a wager by carrying the winner a distance of three miles in a wheelbarrow.

A characteristic scene in a Chinese restaurant is described as follows in the "Sacramento Transcript" of October 8, 1850:—

"One young man called for a plate of mutton chops, and the waiter, not understanding, asked for a repetition of the order.

"'Mutton chops, you chuckle head,' said the young gentleman.

"'Mutton chops, you chuckle head,' shouted the Chinaman to the kitchen.

"The joke took among the customers, and presently one of them called out, 'A glass of pigeon milk, you long-tailed Asiatic.'

"'A glass of pigeon milk, you long-tailed satic,' echoed the waiter.

"'A barrel of homœopathic soup, old smooth head,' shouted another.

"'Arrel homepatty soup, you old smooth head,' echoed the waiter.

"'A hatful of bricks,' shouted a fourth.

"'Hatter bricks,' repeated the waiter.

"By this time the kitchen was in a perfect state of confusion, and the proprietor in a stew of perplexity rushed into the dining-room. 'What you mean by pigeon milk, homepatty soup, and de brick? How you cooking, gentlemen?'

"A roar burst from the tables, and the shrewd Asiatic saw in a moment that they were hoaxing his subordinates. 'The gentlemen make you all dam fools,' said he, rushing again into the smoky recess of the kitchen."

At a dinner given in San Francisco a local orator thus discoursed upon the glories of California: "Look at its forest trees, varying from three hundred to one thousand feet in height, with their trunks so close together that you can't stick this bowie-knife between them; and the lordly elk, with antlers from seventeen to twenty feet spread, with their heads and tails up, ambling through these grand forests. It's a sight, gentlemen"—

"Stop," cried a newcomer who had not yet been inoculated with the atmosphere. "My friend, if the trees are so close together, how does the elk get through the woods with his wide-branching horns?"

The Californian turned on the stranger with a look of thorough contempt and replied, "That's the elk's business"; and continued his unvarnished tale, no more embarrassed than the sun at noonday.

"There was a spirit of off-hand, jolly fun in those days, a sort of universal free and easy cheerfulness.... The California Pioneer that could not give and take a joke was just no Californian at all. It was this spirit that gives the memory of those days an indescribable fascination and charm."

The very names first given to places and situations show the same exuberant spirit; such, for example, as Murderer's Alley, Dead Man's Bar, Mad Mule Cañon, Skunk Flat, Whiskey Gulch, Port Wine Diggins, Shirt-Tail Hollow, Bloody Bend, Death Pass, Jackass Flat, and Hell's Half Acre.

Even crime took on a bold and original form. A scapegrace in Sacramento stole a horse while the owner still held the bridle. The owner had stepped into a shop to ask a question, but kept the end of the reins in his hand, when the thief gently slipped the bridle from the horse's head, hung it on a post, and rode off with steed and saddle.

Bizarre characters from all parts of the world, drawn as by a magnet, took ship for California in '49 and '50 and became wealthy, or landed in the Police Court, as fate would have it. The latter was the destination of one Murphy, an Irishman presumably, and certainly a man of imagination, who described himself as a teacher of mathematics, and acknowledged that he had been drunk for the preceding six years. He added, for the benefit of the Court, that he had been at the breaking of every pane of glass from Vera Cruz to San Francisco, that he had smoked a dozen cigars in the halls of the Montezumas, and that there were as many persons contending for his name as there were cities for the birth of Homer. The Court gave him six months.

Two residents of San Francisco, one a Frenchman, the other a Dutchman, were so enthusiastic over their new and republican surroundings that they slept every night under the Liberty Pole on the Plaza; and seldom did they fail to turn in patriotically drunk, shouting for freedom and equality. Prize-fighters, as a matter of course, were attracted to a place where sporting blood ran so high. In June, 1850, news came that Tom Hyer (of whose celebrity the Reader is doubtless aware) was shortly expected with "his lady" at Panama; and he must have arrived in due course, for in August, Tom Hyer was tried in the Police Court of San Francisco for entering several saloons on horseback, in one case performing the classic feat of riding up a flight of steps. The defence set up that this was not an uncommon method of entering saloons in San Francisco, and the Court took "judicial notice" of the fact, his honor having witnessed the same thing himself on more than one occasion. However, as Mr. Hyer was somewhat intoxicated, and as the alleged offence was committed on a Sunday, the Judge imposed a small fine.

In the same year, Mr. T. Belcher Kay, another famous prize-fighter from the East, narrowly escaped being murdered while returning from a ball before daylight one Sunday morning; and subsequently Mr. Kay was tried, but acquitted, on a charge of burglary.

In that strange collection of human beings drawn from all parts of the earth, for the most part unknown to one another, but almost all having this fundamental trait in common, namely, that they were close to nature, it was inevitable that incidents of pathos and tragedy, deeds of rascality and cruelty, and still more deeds of unselfishness and heroism, should continually occur.

Some Pioneers met good fortune or disaster at the very threshold. One young man, upon landing in San Francisco, borrowed ten dollars, went immediately to a gambling saloon, won seven thousand dollars, and with rare good sense took the next steamer for home. Another newcomer, who brought a few hundred dollars with him, wandered into the gambling rooms of the Parker House soon after his arrival, won twenty thousand dollars there, and went home two days later.

A Pioneer who had just crossed the Plains fell into a strange experience upon his arrival at Placerville. He was a poor man, his only property being a yoke of oxen which he sold almost immediately for one hundred dollars in gold dust. Shortly before that a purse containing the same quantity of gold had been stolen; and when, a few hours later, the newly-arrived teamster took out his pocket-book to pay for a small purchase, a man immediately stepped forward and accused him of the robbery. He was, of course, arrested, and a jury to try him was impanelled on the spot. The quality of the gold in his purse corresponded exactly with the quality of the stolen gold. It was known that he had only just arrived from the Plains and could not have obtained the gold dust by mining. The man to whom he sold his cattle had gone, and he was unable to prove how he had come by the treasure. Under these circumstances, the jury found him guilty, and sentenced him to receive thirty lashes on the bare back, which were thereupon administered, the unfortunate man all the time protesting his innocence.

After he was whipped, he procured a pistol, walked deliberately up to the person who first accused him, placed the pistol at his head, and declared that he believed him to be the guilty man, and that if he did not then and there confess that he had stolen the money he would blow his brains out. The fellow could not stand the power of injured innocence. He became frightened, acknowledged that he was the thief, and drew the identical stolen money out of his pocket. The enraged crowd instantly set upon him, bore him to the nearest tree, and hung him. A subscription was then started, and about eighteen hundred dollars were raised in a few minutes for the sagacious teamster, who departed forthwith for his home in the East.

Of the many thousand Pioneers at work in the mines very few reaped a reward at all commensurate with their toils, privations and sufferings,—much less with their expectations. The wild ideas which prevailed in some quarters as to the abundance of the gold may be gathered from the advice given to one young Argonaut by his father, on the eve of his departure from Illinois. The venerable man urged his son not to work too hard, but to buy a low chair and a small iron rake, and, taking his seat comfortably, to rake over the sand, pick up the nuggets as they came to view, and place them in a convenient box.

In reality, the miners' earnings, after deducting necessary living expenses, are computed to have averaged only about three times the wages of an unskilled day-laborer in the East. Few of them saved anything, for there was every temptation to squander their gains in dissipation; and men whose income is subject to wide fluctuations are notoriously unthrifty. The following is a typical experience: "Our diet consists of hard bread, flour which we eat half-cooked, and salt pork, with occasionally a salmon which we purchase of the Indians. Vegetables are not to be procured. Our feet are wet all day, while a hot sun shines down upon our heads, and the very air parches the skin like the hot air of an oven. Our drinking water comes down to us thoroughly impregnated with the mineral substances washed through the thousand cradles above us. The hands and feet of the novice become painfully blistered and the limbs are stiff. Besides all these causes of sickness, many men who have left their wives and children in far-distant States are homesick, anxious and despondent."

Many a family in the East was desolated and reduced to poverty by the untimely death of a husband and father; and in other cases long absence was as effectual in this respect as death itself. The once-common expression "California widow" is significant. Some Eastern men took informal wives on the Pacific Slope; others, who had succeeded, put off their home-coming from month to month, and even from year to year, hoping for still greater success; others yet, who had failed, were ashamed to go home in poverty, and lingered in California until death overtook them. This phase of Pioneer life is treated by Bret Harte in the stories *How Old Man Plunkett went Home*, and *Jimmy's Big Brother from California*. Of those who were lucky enough to find gold in large quantities, many were robbed, and some of these unfortunates went home, or died, broken-hearted.

But as a rule, the Pioneers rose superior to every blow that fate could deal them. Men met misfortune, danger, even death with composure, and yet without bravado. A traveller being told that a man was about to be lynched, proceeded to the spot and found a large gathering of miners standing around in groups under the trees, and quietly talking. Seeing no apparent criminal there, he stepped up to one person who stood a little apart from the others, and asked him which was the man about to be hung. The person addressed replied, without the slightest change of countenance, "I believe, Sir, it's me." Half an hour later he was dead.

There was a battle at Sacramento in 1850 between a party of "Squatters" on one side, and city officials and citizens on the other. Among the latter was one J. F. Hooper from Independence in Missouri. Hooper, armed only with a pistol, discharged all his cartridges, then threw the weapon at his advancing opponents, and calmly faced them, crossing his hands over his breast as a protection. They fired at him, notwithstanding his defenceless situation, and one ball piercing his right hand inflicted a wound, but not a mortal one, in his side. Four men were killed and several others badly wounded in this fight.

When a father and son were arrested by a vigilance committee at Santa Clara for horse-stealing, and were sentenced to receive thirty-six lashes apiece, the son begged that he might take his father's share as well as his own.

Men died well in California. In November, 1851, two horse-thieves were hung by a vigilance committee at Stockton. One of them, who was very young, smoked a cigar up to the last moment, and made a little speech in which he explained that the act was not dictated by irreverence, but that he desired to die like a man. When Stuart, a noted robber and horse-thief was being tried for his life by the Vigilance Committee in San Francisco, he complained that the proceedings were "tiresome," and asked for a chew of tobacco.

THE TWO OPPONENTS CAME NEARER
From "The Iliad of Sandy Bar"
Frederic Remington, del.

The death of this man was one of the most impressive scenes ever witnessed upon this blood-stained earth. Sentence having been passed upon the prisoner the Committee, numbering one thousand men, came down from the hall where they met and formed in the street, three abreast. They comprised, with some exceptions, the best, the most substantial, the most public-spirited citizens of San Francisco. In the centre was Stuart, handcuffed and pinioned, but perfectly self-possessed and cool. A gallows had been erected some distance off, and the procession moved up Battery Street, followed by a great throng of men. There was no confusion, no outcry, no apparent excitement,—not a sound, indeed, except the tread of many feet upon the planked streets, every footfall sounding the prisoner's knell.

It was of this event that Bret Harte wrote in his *Bohemian Days in San Francisco*: "Under the reign of the Committee the lawless and vicious class were more appalled by the moral spectacle of several thousand black-coated, serious-minded business men in embattled procession than by mere force of arms."

When they reached the gallows, a rope was placed around the prisoner's neck, and even then, except for a slight paleness, there was no change in his appearance. Amid the breathless silence of the whole assemblage Stuart, standing under the gallows, said, "I die reconciled. My sentence is just." His crimes had been many, and he seemed to accept his death as the proper and almost welcome result of his deeds. He was a man of intellect, and, hardened criminal though he was, the instinct of expiation asserted itself in his breast.

In July, 1851, a Spanish woman was tried and condemned by an impromptu vigilance committee for killing an American who, she declared, had insulted her. Being sentenced to be hanged forthwith, she carefully arranged her dress, neatly coiled her hair, and walked quietly and firmly to the gallows. There she made a short speech, saying that she would do the same thing again if she were permitted to live, and were insulted in the same way. Then she bade the crowd farewell, adjusted the noose with her own hands, and so passed bravely away.

A few years later at Moquelumne Hill, a young Welshman, scarcely more than a boy, met death in a very similar manner, and for a similar offence. On the scaffold he turned to one of the by-standers, and said, "Did you ever know anything bad of me before this affair occurred?" The answer was, "No, Jack." "Well," said the youth, "tell those Camp Saco fellows that I would do the same thing again and be hung rather than put up with an insult." Men like these died for a point of honor, as much as did Alexander Hamilton.

But far higher was the heroism of those who suffered or died for others, and not for themselves. No event, not even the discovery of gold, stirred California more profoundly than did the death of James King. In 1856, King, the editor of the "Bulletin," was waging single-handed a vigorous warfare against the political corruption then rife in California, and especially against the supineness of the city officials in respect to gambling and prostitution. He had given out that he would not accept a challenge to a duel, but he was well aware of the risk that he ran. San Francisco, even at that time, indulged in an easy toleration of vice, and only some striking, some terrible event could have aroused the conscience of the public.

Among the city officials whose hatred Mr. King had incurred was James Casey, a typical New York politician, and a former convict, yet not wholly a bad man. The two men, King and Casey, really represented two stages of morality, two kinds of government. Their personal conflict was in a condensed form the clashing of the higher and the lower ideals. Casey, meeting King on the street, called upon him to "draw and defend himself"; but King, being without a weapon, calmly folded his arms and faced his enemy. Casey fired, and King fell to the ground, mortally wounded.

"It was expedient that one man should die for the people"; and the death of King did far more than his life could have done to purify the political and social atmosphere of California. On the day following the murder, a Vigilance Committee was organized, and an Executive Committee, consisting chiefly of those who had managed the first Vigilance Committee in 1851, was chosen as the practical ruler of the city. It was supported by a band of three thousand men, distributed in companies, armed, officered and well drilled. For two months and a half the Executive Committee remained in office, exercising its power with marked judgment and moderation. Four men were hung, many more were banished, and the city was purged. Having accomplished its work the Committee disbanded, but its members and sympathizers secured control of the municipal government through the ordinary legal channels, and for twenty years administered the affairs of the city with honesty and economy.

The task in 1851 had been mainly to rid the city of Australian convicts; in 1856 it was to correct the political abuses introduced by professional politicians from the East, especially from New York; and in each case the task was successfully accomplished, without unnecessary bloodshed, and even with mercy.

Nor was Casey's end without pathos, and even dignity. On the scaffold he was thinking not of himself, but of the old mother whom he had left in New York. "Gentlemen," he said, "I stand before you as a man about to come into the presence of God, and I declare before Him that I am no murderer! I have an aged mother whom I wish not to hear that I am guilty of murder. I am not. My early education taught me to repay an injury, and I have done nothing more. The 'Alta California,' 'Chronicle,' 'Globe,' and other papers in the city connect my name with murder and assassination. I am no murderer. Let no newspaper in its weekly or monthly editions dare publish to the world that I am one. Let it not get to the ears of my mother that I am. O God, I appeal for mercy for my past sins, which are many. O Lord Jesus, unto thee I resign my spirit. O mother, mother, mother!"

The sinking of the steamer, "Central America," off the coast of Georgia, in 1857, is an event now almost forgotten, and yet it deserves to be remembered forever. The steamer was on her way from Aspinwall to New York, with passengers and gold from San Francisco, when she sprang a leak and began to sink. The women and children, fifty-three in all, were taken off to a small brig which happened to come in sight, leaving on board, without boats or rafts, five hundred men, all of whom went down, and of whom all but eighty were drowned. Though many were armed, and nearly all were rough in appearance, they were content that the women and children should be saved first; and if here and there a grumble was heard, it received little encouragement. Never did so many men face death near at hand more quietly or decorously.

And yet the critic tells us about the "perverse romanticism" of Mr. Bret Harte's California tales!

One incident more, and this brief record of California heroism, which might be extended indefinitely, shall close. Charles Fairfax, the tenth Baron of that name, whose family have lived for many years in Virginia, was attacked without warning by a cowardly assassin, named Lee. This man stabbed Fairfax twice, and he was raising his arm for a third thrust when his victim covered him with a pistol. Lee, seeing the pistol, dropped his knife, stepped back, and threw up his hands, exclaiming, "I am unarmed!"

"Shoot the damned scoundrel!" cried a friend of Fairfax who stood by.

Fairfax, holding the pistol, with the blood streaming from his wounds, said: "You are an assassin! You have murdered me! Your life is in my hands!" And then, after a moment, gazing on him, he added, "But for the sake of your poor sick wife and of your children, I will spare you." He then uncocked the pistol, and fell fainting in the arms of his friend.

All California rang with the nobility of the deed.

CHAPTER VII

PIONEER LAW AND LAWLESSNESS

California certainly contained what Borthwick describes as "the élite of the most desperate and consummate scoundrels from every part of the world"; but they were in a very small minority, and the rather common idea that the miners were a mass of brutal and ignorant men is a wild misconception. An English writer once remarked, somewhat hysterically, "Bret Harte had to deal with countries and communities of an almost unexampled laxity, a laxity passing the laxity of savages, the laxity of civilized men grown savage."

Far more accurate is the observation of that eminent critic, Mr. Watts-Dunton: "Bret Harte's characters are amenable to no laws except the improvised laws of the camp, and the final arbiter is either the six-shooter or the rope of Judge Lynch. And yet underlying this apparent lawlessness there is that deep law-abiding-ness which the late Grant Allen despised as being the Anglo-Saxon characteristic."

The almost spontaneous manner in which mining laws came into existence, and the ready obedience which the miners yielded to them, show how correct is the view taken by Mr. Watts-Dunton. What constituted ownership of a claim; how it must be proved; how many square feet a claim might include; how long and by what means title to a claim could be preserved without working it; when a "find" should become the property of the individual discoverer, and when it should accrue to the partnership of which he was a member,—all these matters and many more were regulated by a code quickly formed, and universally respected. Thus a lump of gold weighing half an ounce or more, if observed before it was thrown into the cradle, belonged to the finder, and not to the partnership.

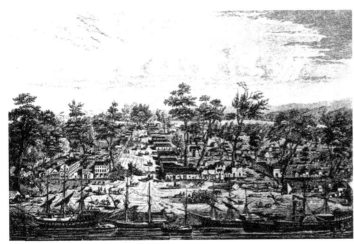

SACRAMENTO CITY IN 1852

In the main, mining rules were the same throughout the State, but they varied somewhat according to the peculiar circumstances of each "diggings"; and the custom was for the miners to hold a meeting, when they became sufficiently numerous at any point, and make such laws as they deemed expedient. If any controversy arose under them it was settled by the Alcalde.

In respect to this office, again, the miners showed the same instinct for law and order, and the same practical readiness to make use of such means as were at hand. The Alcalde (Al Cadi) was originally a Spanish official, corresponding in many respects with our Justice of the Peace. But in the mining camps, the Alcalde, usually an American, was often given, by a kind of tacit agreement, very full, almost despotic powers, combining the authority of a Magistrate with that of a Selectman and Chief of Police.

The first Alcalde of Marysville was the young lawyer already mentioned, Stephen J. Field, and he administered affairs with such firmness that the town, although harboring many desperate persons,—this was in 1850,—gamblers, thieves and cut-throats, was as orderly as a New England village. He caused the streets and sidewalks to be kept clean and in repair; he employed men to grade the banks of the river so as to facilitate landing, and he did many other things for the good of the community, but really with no authority except that of common consent. Sitting as a judge, he did not hesitate to sentence some criminals to be flogged. There was no law for it; but it was the only punishment that was both adequate and practicable, for the town contained no prison or "lock-up."

And yet, so far as was possible, Alcalde Field observed the ancient forms with true Anglo-Saxon scrupulosity. "In civil cases," he relates, "I always called a jury if the parties desired one; and in criminal cases when the offence was of a high grade I went through the form of calling a grand jury, and having an indictment found; and in all cases I appointed an attorney to represent the people, and also one to represent the accused, when that was necessary."

Spanish and Mexicans, as well as Americans, reaped the benefit of the change in government. Property, real estate especially, rose in value at once, and justice was administered as it never had been administered before. An entry in the diary of the Reverend Walter Colton, Chaplain in the United States Navy, and Alcalde of Monterey, whose book has already been cited, runs as follows:—

"*September 4, 1849.* I empanelled to-day the first jury ever summoned in California. One third were Californians, one third Mexicans, one third Americans. The trial was conducted in three languages and lasted six hours. The result was very satisfactory. The inhabitants who witnessed the trial said it was what they liked,—that there could be no bribery in it,—that the opinion of twelve honest men should set the case forever at rest. And so it did.... If there is anything on earth for which I would die, beside religion, it is the right of trial by jury."

At first no one quite knew what laws were in force in California. The territory became a part of the United States by means of the treaty with Mexico which was proclaimed on July 4, 1848, but California was not admitted as a State until 1850, and in the mean time it was a question whether the laws of Mexico still prevailed, or the common law, or what. In this situation the Alcaldes usually fell back upon common sense and the laws of the State from which they happened to come.

Others had recourse to an older dispensation. Thus, on one occasion the Alcalde of Santa Cruz had before him a man who was found guilty of shaving the hair from the tail of a fine American horse, and the sentence of the court was that the criminal should have his own head shaved. The young attorney who represented the defendant thereupon sprang to his feet, and, with great indignation, demanded to be told what law or authority there was for so unusual a punishment. "I base that judgment," said the Alcalde with solemnity, "on the oldest law in the world, on the law of Moses. Go home, young man, and read your Bible."

In another case a Spaniard was suing for a divorce from his wife on the ground of infidelity; but the Alcalde, an American, refused it, inasmuch as the man was unable to swear that he had been faithful himself. "Is that United States law?" asked the suitor in naïve amazement. "I don't know about that," replied the Alcalde; "but it is the law by which I am governed,—the law of the Bible, and a good law too."

The Alcalde of Placerville very properly refused to marry a certain man and woman, because the woman was already married to a man who had been absent for three months. But another Alcalde who happened to be present intervened. "Any man in California," he declared, "who has a wife, and so fine looking a wife as I see here before me, and who remains absent from her for three months, must be insane, Mr. Alcalde, or dead; and in either case the lady is free to marry again. I am Alcalde of Santa Cruz, and will with great pleasure make you man and wife. Step forward, madam, step forward; I feel sure you will get through this trying occasion without fainting, if you make the effort, and do not give way to your natural shyness. Step forward, my dear sir, by the side of your blushing bride, and I will make you a happy man."

One other case that was tried in an Alcalde's court is so illustrative of California life that the Reader will perhaps pardon its insertion at length.

"Bill Liddle, conductor of a mule train of eight large American mules, had just started from Sacramento for a mining camp far in the interior. He was obliged to pass a dangerous trail about two miles long, cut in the side of a steep cliff overhanging the river. The trail was only wide enough for a loaded mule to walk on. In the lead was 'Old Kate,' a heavy, square-built, bay mule. Bill always said that she understood English, and he always spoke to her as if that were the fact, and we were often forced to laugh at the wonderful intelligence she showed in understanding and obeying him. Sometimes she broke into the stable, unlatching the door, went to the bin where the barley was kept in sacks, raised the cover, took out a sack, set it up on one end, ripped the sewing as neatly as Bill could, and then helped herself to the contents. On such occasions Bill would shake his head, and exclaim, 'I wonder who Kate is! Oh, I wish I knew, for of course she is some famous woman condemned to live on earth as a mule!'

"The train had advanced about a quarter of a mile on the trail just described, Bill riding behind, when he was startled by hearing a loud bray from Kate, and all the mules stopped. Ahead was a return train of fifteen Californian mules, approaching on a jog trot. The two trains could not pass, and there was not space for Bill's large and loaded mules to turn around. Bill raised himself in his saddle and furiously called on the other conductor to stop. He did so, but refused to turn his mules around, although Bill explained to him the necessity. At last, after much talk, the other conductor started up his mules, shouting and cracking his whip and urging them on. Meanwhile Old Kate stood in the centre of the trail, her fore-legs well apart, her nose dropped lower than usual, and her long, heavy ears thrown forward as if aimed at the head mule of the other train, while her large bright eyes were fixed on his motions. Seeing the danger, Bill called out, 'Kate, old girl, go for them; pitch them all, and the driver with them, to hell!' Thereupon Kate gave an unearthly bray, dropped on her knees with her head stretched out close along the rocks, her neck and lower jaw rubbing the trail, and received the leading mule across her neck. In a second more that mule was thrown into the air, and fell into the river far below.

"Two or three times the conductor of the other train made a similar attempt, urging his mules forward, and did not stop until five of his mules had gone into the river. Then he said, 'Well, I will go back, but when we get out of this trail you and I will settle accounts.' Bill drew his revolver and his knife, made sure that they were all right, and as soon as they emerged from the cliff rode up to the other conductor with his revolver in his hand, and said, 'Shall we settle this business here, or shall we go before the Alcalde of the next diggings?' The man looked at him for a moment in silence, and then said, 'Damn me if you don't look like that she-devil of a mule of yours that threw my mules down the cliff. Are you and she any blood relation that you know of?' Not at all offended, Bill answered, 'I can't say positively that we are, but one thing I can say: I would rather be full brother to a mule that would act as Kate did to-day, than a forty-second cousin to a man that would act as you did.' 'Well,' said the other, 'put up your revolver, and let us settle matters before the Alcalde.'

"The mule-drivers found the Alcalde working in the bottom of a shaft which he was sinking. They asked him to come up, but he said that was unnecessary, as he could hear and settle the case where he was. Accordingly, he turned a bucket upside down, sat down on it, and lit a cigar, leaning his back against the wall of the shaft. The two conductors then kissed a Bible which the Alcalde had sent for, and swore to tell the truth; and they gave their testimony from the top of the shaft, the driver of the unloaded mules asking for six hundred dollars damages, five hundred dollars for his mules and one hundred dollars for the pack saddles lost with them. When they had finished, the Alcalde said, 'I know the trail well, and I find for the defendant, and order the plaintiff to pay the costs of court, which are only one ounce.' Thereupon the Alcalde arose, turned up his bucket and began to shovel the earth into it. As he worked on, he told the plaintiff to go to the store kept by one Meyer not far off, and weigh out the ounce of dust and leave it there for him. This was done without hesitation. Bill went along, treated the plaintiff to a drink, and paid for a bottle of the best brandy that Meyer had, to be given in the evening to the Alcalde and his partner as they returned from work."

California magistrates were somewhat informal for several years. On one occasion, during a long argument by counsel, the Alcalde interrupted with the remark that the point in question was a difficult one, and he would like to consult an authority; whereupon, the clerk, understanding what was meant, produced a demijohn and glasses from a receptacle beneath the bench, and judge and counsel refreshed themselves. A characteristic story is told of Judge Searls, a San Francisco magistrate who had several times fined for contempt of court a lawyer named Francis J. Dunn. Dunn was a very able but dissipated and eccentric man, and apt to be late, and on one such occasion the judge fined him fifty dollars. "I did not know that I was late, your Honor," said Mr. Dunn, with mock contrition; "I have no watch, and I shall never be able to get one if I have to pay the fines which your Honor imposes upon me." Then, after a pause of reflection, he looked up and said: "Will your Honor *lend* me fifty dollars so that I can pay this last fine?" "Mr. Clerk," said the judge, leaning over the bench, "remit that fine: the State can afford to lose the money better than I can."

But informality is not inconsistent with justice. The Pioneers did not like to have men, though they were judges, take themselves too seriously; but the great majority of them were law-abiding, intelligent, industrious and kind-hearted. It was, as has been said already, a picked and sifted population. The number of professional men and of well-educated men was extraordinary. They were a magnanimous people. As the Reverend Dr. Bushnell remarked, "With all the violence and savage wrongs and dark vices that have heretofore abounded among the Pioneers, they seldom do a mean thing."

An example of this magnanimity was the action of California in regard to the State debt amounting to five million dollars. It was illegal, having been contracted in violation of the State Constitution, and the money had been spent chiefly in enriching those corrupt politicians and their friends who obtained possession of the California government in the first years. But the Pioneers were too generous and too proud of the good name of their State to stand upon their legal rights. They were as anxious to pay this unjust debt as Pennsylvania and Mississippi had been in former years to repudiate their just debts. The matter was put to popular vote, and the bonds were paid.

Stephen J. Field remarked in his old age, "I shall never forget the noble and generous people that I found in California, in all ranks of life." Another Pioneer, Dr. J. D. B. Stillman, wrote, "There are more intelligence and generous good feeling here than in any other country that I have ever seen." "The finest body of men ever gathered together in the world's history," is the declaration of another Pioneer, and even this extreme statement is borne out by the contemporary records.

That there was a minority equally remarkable for its bad qualities, is also unquestionable. Moreover, many men who at home would have been classed as good citizens gave way in California to their avarice or other bad passions. Whatever depravity there was in a man's heart showed itself without fear and without restraint. The very Pioneer, Dr. Stillman, who has just been quoted to the effect that California had, on the whole, the best population in the world, gives us also the other side of the picture: "Last night I saw a man lying on the wet ground, unknown, unconscious, uncared for, and dying. Money is the all-absorbing object. There are men who would hang their heads at home at the mention of their heartless avarice. What can be expected from strangers when a man's own friends abandon him because he sickens and becomes an encumbrance!"

Mrs. Bates, whose account of California is never exaggerated, tells us of a miner who, night after night, deserted his dying brother for a gambling house, leaving him unattended and piteously crying for water until, at last, he expired alone.

It must be remembered, also, that the moral complexion of California changed greatly from year to year. The first condition was almost an idyllic one. It was a period of honesty and good-will such as never existed before, except in the imagination of Rousseau. There were few doors, and no locks. Gold was left for days at a time unguarded and untouched. "A year ago," said the "Sacramento Transcript," in October, 1850, "a miner could have left his bag of dust exhibited to full view, and absent himself a week. His tools might have remained unmolested in any ravine for months, and his goods and chattels, bed and bedding might have remained along the highway for an indefinite period without being stolen."

There was much drinking, much gambling, and some murders were committed in the heat of passion; but nowhere else in the world, except perhaps in the smaller villages of the United States, was property so safe as it was in California.

"I have not heard," wrote Dr. Stillman in 1849, "of a theft or crime of any sort. Firearms are thrown aside as useless, and are given away on the road." Grave disputes involving the title to vast wealth were settled by arbitration without the raising of a voice in anger or controversy. Even in Sacramento and San Francisco, merchants left their goods in their canvas houses and tents, open to any who might choose to enter, while they went to church or walked over the hills on Sundays. Their gold was equally unguarded, and equally safe.

"It was wonderful," said a Pioneer early in the Fifties, "how well we got on in '49 without any sort of government beyond the universally sanctioned action of the people, and I have often since questioned in my own mind if we might not have got on just the same ever since, and saved all the money we have paid out for thieving legislation and selfish office-holders."

The change came in the late Summer and early Autumn of 1850, and was chiefly owing to the influx of convicts from Australia and elsewhere,—"low-browed, heavy-featured men, with cold, steel-gray eyes." In a less degree the change was also due to the deterioration of a small minority of Americans and Europeans, whose moral stamina was not equal to life in a lawless community, although at first that community was lawless only in the strict sense of the word;—it had no laws and needed none. As one Pioneer wrote, "There is no law regarded here but the natural law of justice."

Beginning with the Autumn of 1850, things went from bad to worse until February, 1851, when robbery and murder in San Francisco were stopped by the first Vigilance Committee; and in the mines the same drastic remedy was applied, but not always with the same moderation. A Sacramento paper said in December, 1850: "It is an undeniable fact that crime of almost every description is on the increase in California, especially horse-stealing, robbery, arson and murder. In the city of Sacramento alone, since last April, we should judge there have been at least twenty murders committed, and we are not aware that any murderer has suffered capital punishment, or any other kind of punishment. We have got used to these things, and look upon it as a matter of course that somebody will be killed and robbed as often as once a week at least; and yet notwithstanding all this our people generally are composed of the most orderly, respectable citizens of the United States. The laws furnish us no protection because they are not enforced."

But the Reader may ask, why were the laws not enforced? The answer is that the Pioneers were too busy to concern themselves with their political duties or to provide the necessary machinery for the enforcement of the laws. State officers, municipal officers, sheriffs, constables and even judges were chosen, not because they were fit men, but because they wanted the job, and no better candidates offered themselves. Moreover, the Pioneers did not expect to become permanent residents of California; they expected to get rich, off-hand, and then to go home, and why should they bother themselves about elections or laws? In short, an attempt was made to do without law, and, as we have seen, it succeeded for a year or so, but broke down when criminals became numerous.

A letter from the town of Sonora, written in July, 1850, said: "The people are leaving here fast. This place is much deeper in guilt than Sodom or Gomorrah. We have no society, no harmony. Gambling and drunkenness are the order of the day."

In four years there were one thousand two hundred homicides in California. Almost every mile of the travelled road from Monterey, in the southern part of the State, to San Francisco, was the scene of some foul murder in those eventful years. There was more crime in the southern mines than in the northern, because the Mexicans were more numerous there.

In Sonora County, in 1850, there were twenty-five murders in a single month, committed mainly by Mexicans, Chilians, and British convicts from the penal colonies. A night patrol was organized. Every American tent had a guard around it, and mining almost ceased.

Murder and robbery had reached the stage at which they seriously interfered with business. This was not to be endured; and at a mass meeting held at Sonora on August 3, the following resolution was passed: "Resolved: That for the safety of the lives and property of the citizens of this portion of the country, notice shall be given immediately ordering all Mexicans and South Americans to remove from township No. 2 in one week from this date."

The consequence was a melancholy exodus of men, women and children, which included the just and the unjust. Many of them were destitute, and, as respects the Mexicans, many were being banished from the place of their birth. "We fear," remarked a contemporary citizen, "that the money-making, merry old times in Sonora are gone forever."

This was a characteristic Pioneer remark. The "old times" meant were somewhat less than a year back; and their "merry" quality was, as we have seen, considerably modified by robbery and murder. The point of view is much like that of the landlord of a hotel in Virginia City, where Bret Harte was once a guest. After a night disturbed by sounds of shouting, scuffling and pistol shots, Mr. Harte found his host behind the counter in the bar-room "with a bruised eye, a piece of court-plaster extending from his cheek to his forehead, yet withal a pleasant smile upon his face. Taking my cue from this, I said to him, 'Well, landlord, you had rather a lively time here last night.' 'Yes,' he replied, pleasantly, 'it *was* rather a lively time.' 'Do you often have such lively times in Virginia City?' I added, emboldened by his cheerfulness. 'Well, no,' he said reflectively; 'the fact is we've only just opened yer, and last night was about the first time that the boys seemed to be gettin' really *acquainted!*'"

The absence of police, and, to a great extent, of law, led to deeds of violence, and to duelling; but it also tended to make men polite. The civility with which cases were conducted in court, and the restraint shown by lawyers in their comments upon one another and upon the witnesses were often spoken of in California. The experience of Alcalde Field in this regard is interesting:—"I came to California with all those notions in respect to acts of violence which are instilled into New England youth; if a man were rude, I would turn away from him. But I soon found that men in California were likely to take very great liberties with a person who acted in such a manner, and that the only way to get along was to hold every man responsible, and resent every trespass upon one's rights."

Accordingly, young Field bought a brace of pistols, had a sack-coat made with pockets appropriate to contain them, and practised the useful art of firing the pistols with his hands in his pockets. Subsequently he added a bowie-knife to his private arsenal, and he carried these weapons until the Summer of 1854. "I found," he says, "that the knowledge that pistols were generally worn created a wholesome courtesy of manner and language."

Even the members of the State Legislature were armed. It was a thing of every-day occurrence for a member, when he entered the House, to take off his pistols and lay them in the drawer of his desk. Such an act excited neither surprise nor comment.

At one time Mr. Field sent a challenge to a certain Judge Barbour who had grossly insulted him. Barbour accepted the challenge, but demanded that the duel should be fought with Colt's revolvers and bowie-knives, that it should take place in a room only twenty feet square, and that the fight should continue until at least one of the principals was dead. Mr. Field's second, horrified by these savage proposals, was for rejecting them; but Field himself insisted that they should be accepted, and the result was what he had anticipated. Judge Barbour, of his own motion, waived, first the knives, then the small room, and finally declined the meeting altogether. But the very next day, when Field had stepped out of his office, and was picking up an armful of wood for his stove, Barbour crept up behind him, and putting a pistol to his head, called upon Field to draw and defend himself. Field did not turn or move, but spoke somewhat as follows: "You infernal scoundrel, you cowardly assassin,—you come behind my back, and put your revolver to my head, and tell me to draw! You haven't the courage to shoot,—shoot and be damned!" And Barbour slunk away.

Shooting at sight, especially in San Francisco and the larger towns, was as common as it is represented by Bret Harte. For the few years, beginning with and succeeding 1850, the newspapers were full of such events. On November 25, 1851, the "Alta California" said: "Another case of the influenza now in fashion occurred yesterday. We allude to a mere shooting-match in which only one of the near by-standers was shot down in his tracks."

Even so late as August, 1855, the "San Francisco Call" was able to refer in a modest way to the "two or three shooting encounters per week" which enlivened its columns.

Duels were common, and in most cases very serious affairs, the battle being waged with destructive weapons and at close range. As a rule, they took place in public. Thus, at a meeting between D. C. Broderick, leader of the Democratic Party in the State, and one J. Cabot Smith, seventy or eighty persons were present. Broderick was wounded, and would have been killed had not the bullet first struck and shattered his watch.

These California duels must be ascribed mainly to the Southern element, which was strong numerically, and which, moreover, exerted an influence greater than its numbers warranted. One reason, perhaps the main reason, for this predominance of the Southerners was that the aristocratic, semi-feudal system which they represented had a more dignified, more dashing aspect than the plain democratic views in which the Northern and Western men had been educated. It made the individual of more importance. Upon this point Professor Royce makes an acute remark: "The type of the Northern man who has assumed Southern fashions, and not always the best Southern fashions, has often been observed in California life. The Northern man frequently felt commonplace, simple-minded, undignified, beside his brother from the border or the plantation.... The Northern man admired his fluency, his vigor, his invective, his ostentatious courage, his absolute confidence about all matters of morals, of politics, of propriety, and the inscrutable union in his public discourse of sweet reasonableness with ferocious intolerance."

The extreme type of Southerner, as he appeared in California, is immortalized in Colonel Starbottle. The moment when this strange planet first swam into Bret Harte's ken seems to have been seized and recorded with accuracy by his friend, Mr. Noah Brooks. "In Sacramento he and I met Colonel Starbottle, who had, of course, another name. He wore a tall silk hat and loosely-fitting clothes, and he carried on his left arm by its crooked handle a stout walking-stick. The Colonel was a dignified and benignant figure; in politics he was everybody's friend. A gubernatorial election was pending, and with the friends of Haight he stood at the hotel bar, and as they raised their glasses to their lips he said, 'Here's to the Coming Event!' Nobody asked at that stage of the canvass what the coming event would be, and when the good Colonel stood in the same place with the friends of Gorham, he gave the same toast, 'The Coming Event!'"

This may have been a certain Dr. Ruskin, a Southern politician, who is described by a Pioneer as wearing "a white fur plug hat, a blue coat with brass buttons, a buff-colored vest, white trousers, varnished boots, a black satin stock, and, on state occasions, a frilled shirt front. He always carried a cane with a curved handle." This, the Reader need not be reminded, is the exact costume of Colonel Starbottle,—the "low Byronic collar," which Bret Harte mentions, being the only item omitted.

From this person Bret Harte undoubtedly derived an idea as to the appearance and carriage of Colonel Starbottle, and it is not unlikely that in drawing the character he had also in mind the notorious Judge David S. Terry. Terry, a native of Texas, was a fierce, fighting Southerner, a brave and honest man, but narrow, prejudiced, abusive, and ferocious. He was a leading Democrat, a judge of the Supreme Court of the State, and a bitter opponent of the San Francisco Vigilance Committee. He nearly killed an agent of the Committee who attempted to arrest one of his companions, and was himself in some danger of being hung by the Committee on that account. Later, Terry killed Senator Broderick, of whom mention has just been made, in a duel which seems to have had the essential qualities of a murder, and which was forced upon Broderick in much the same way that the fatal duel was forced upon Alexander Hamilton.

Later still, Terry became involved in the affairs of one of his clients, a somewhat notorious woman, whom he married,—clearly showing that mixture of chivalrous respect for women, combined with a capacity for misunderstanding them, and of being deluded by them, which was so remarkable in Colonel Starbottle. In the course of litigation on behalf of his wife, Terry bitterly resented certain action taken by Mr. Justice Field of the Supreme Court of the United States,—the same Field who began his judicial career as Alcalde of Marysville. Terry's threats against the Justice, then an old man, were so open and violent, and his character was so well known, that, at the request of the court officials in San Francisco, a deputy marshal was assigned as a guard to the Justice while he should be hearing cases on the California circuit. At a railroad station, one day, Terry and the Justice met; and as Terry was, apparently, in the act of drawing a weapon, the deputy marshal shot and killed him.

It was Judge Terry who remarked of the San Francisco Vigilance Committee, which was mainly composed of business men,—the lawyers holding aloof,—that they were "a set of damned pork-merchants,"—a remark so characteristic of Colonel Starbottle that it is difficult to attribute it to anybody else.

Colonel Starbottle was as much the product of slavery as Uncle Tom himself, and he exemplified both its good and its bad effects. His fat white hand and pudgy fingers indicated the man who despised manual labor and those who performed it. His short, stubby feet, and tight-fitting, high-heeled boots conveyed him sufficiently well from office to bar-room, but were never intended for anything in the nature of a "constitutional." His own immorality did not prevent him from cherishing a high ideal of feminine purity; but his conversation was gross. He was a purveyor, Bret Harte relates, "of sprightly stories such as Gentlemen of the Old School are in the habit of telling, but which, from deference to the prejudices of gentlemen of a more recent school, I refrain from transcribing here."

He had that keen sense of honor, and the determination to defend it, even, if need be, at the expense of his life, which the Southern slave-holder possessed, and he had also the ferocity which belonged to the same character. One can hardly recall without a shudder of disgust the "small, beady black eyes" of Colonel Starbottle, especially when they "shone with that fire which a pretty woman or an affair of honor could alone kindle."

The Reader will remember that the Colonel was always ready to hold himself "personally responsible" for any consequences of a hostile nature, and that by some irreverent persons he was dubbed "Old Personal Responsibility." The phrase was not invented by Bret Harte. On the contrary, it was almost a catchword in California society; it was a Southern phrase, and indicated the Southerner's attitude. In a leading article published in the "San Francisco Bulletin" in 1856, it is said, "The basis of many of the outrages which have disgraced our State during the past four years has been the 'personal responsibility' system,—a relic of barbarism."

Colonel Starbottle's lack of humor was also a Southern characteristic. The only humorists in the South were the slaves; and the reason is not far to seek. The Southerner's political and social creed was that of an aristocrat; and an aristocrat is too dignified and too self-absorbed to enter curiously into other men's feelings, and too self-satisfied to question his own. Dandies are notoriously grave men. The aristocratic, non-humorous man always takes himself seriously; and this trait in Colonel Starbottle is what makes him so interesting. "It is my invariable custom to take brandy—a wineglass-full in a cup of strong coffee—immediately on rising. It stimulates the functions, sir, without producing any blank derangement of the nerves."

There is another trait, exemplified in Colonel Starbottle, which often accompanies want of humor, namely, a tendency to be theatrical. It would seem as if the ordinary course of human events was either too painful or too monotonous to be endured. We find ourselves obliged to throw upon it an aspect of comedy or of tragedy, by way of relief. The man of humor sees the incongruity,—in other words, the jest in human existence; and the non-humorous, having no such perception, represents it to himself and to others in an exaggerated or theatrical form. The one relies upon understatement; the other upon overstatement. Colonel Starbottle was always theatrical; his walk was a strut, and "his colloquial speech was apt to be fragmentary incoherencies of his larger oratorical utterances."

But we cannot help feeling sorry for the Colonel as his career draws to a close, and especially when, after his discomfiture in the breach of promise case, he returns to his lonely chambers, and the negro servant finds him there silent and unoccupied before his desk. "'Fo' God! Kernel, I hope dey ain't nuffin de matter, but you's lookin' mighty solemn! I ain't seen you look dat way, Kernel, since de day pooh Massa Stryker was fetched home shot froo de head.' 'Hand me down the whiskey, Jim,' said the Colonel, rising slowly. The negro flew to the closet joyfully, and brought out the bottle. The Colonel poured out a glass of the spirit, and drank it with his old deliberation. 'You're quite right, Jim,' he said, putting down his glass, 'but I'm—er—getting old—and—somehow—I am missing poor Stryker damnably.'"

This is the last appearance of Colonel Starbottle. He represents that element of the moral picturesque,—that compromise with perfection which, in this imperfect and transitory world, is universally craved. Even Emerson, best and most respectable of men, admitted, in his private diary, that the irregular characters who frequented the rum-selling tavern in his own village were indispensable elements, forming what he called "the fringe to every one's tapestry of life." Such men as he had in mind mitigate the solemnity and tragedy of human existence; and in them the virtuous are able to relax, vicariously, the moral tension under which they suffer. This is the part which Colonel Starbottle plays in literature.

43

CHAPTER VIII

WOMEN AND CHILDREN AMONG THE PIONEERS

The chief source of demoralization among the Pioneers was the absence of women and children, and therefore of any real home. "Ours is a bachelor community," remarked the "Alta California," "but nevertheless possessing strong domestic propensities." Most significant and pathetic, indeed, is the strain of homesickness which underlies the wild symphony of Pioneer life. "I well remember," writes a Forty-Niner, "the loneliness and dreariness amid all the excitement of the time." The unsuccessful miner often lost his strength by hard work, exposure, and bad food; and then fell a prey to that disease which has slain so many a wanderer—homesickness. At the San Francisco hospital it was a rule not to give letters from the East to patients, unless they were safely convalescent. More than once the nurses had seen a sick man, after reading a letter from home, turn on his side and die.

In the big gambling saloons of San Francisco, when the band played "Home, Sweet Home," hundreds of homeless wanderers stood still, and listened as if entranced. The newspapers of '49 and '50 are full of lamentations, in prose and in verse, over the absence of women and children. In 1851 the "Alta California" exclaimed, "Who will devise a plan to bring out a few cargoes of respectable women to California?"

On those rare occasions when children appeared in the streets, they were followed by admiring crowds of bearded men, eager to kiss them, to shake their hands, to hear their voices, and humbly begging permission to make them presents of gold nuggets and miners' curiosities. In the autumn of 1849 a beautiful flaxen-haired little girl, about three years old, was frequently seen playing upon the veranda of a house near the business centre of San Francisco, and at such times there was always on the opposite side of the street a group of miners gazing reverently at the child, and often with tears running down their bronzed cheeks. The cry of a baby at the theatre brought down a tumultuous encore from the whole house. The chief attraction of every theatrical troupe was a child, usually called the "California Pet," whose appearance on the stage was always greeted with a shower of coins. Next to the Pet, the most popular part of the entertainment was the singing of ballads and songs relating to domestic subjects.

In '49 a woman in the streets of San Francisco created more excitement than would have been caused by the appearance of an elephant or a giraffe. Once at a crowded sale in an auction room some one cried out, "Two ladies going along the sidewalk!" and forthwith everybody rushed pell-mell into the street, as if there had been a fire or an earthquake. A young miner, in a remote mountain camp, borrowed a mule and rode forty miles in order to make a call upon a married woman who had recently arrived. He had a few minutes' conversation with her, and returned the next day well satisfied with his trip. At another diggings, when the first woman resident appeared, she and the mule upon which she rode, were raised from the ground by a group of strong-armed, enthusiastic miners, and carried triumphantly to the house which her husband had prepared for her.

When the town where Stephen J. Field purchased his corner lots was organized, the first necessity was of course a name. Various titles, suggested by the situation, or by the imagination of hopeful miners, were proposed, such as Yubaville and Circumdoro; but finally a substantial, middle-aged man arose and remarked that there was an American lady in the place, the wife of one of the proprietors, that her name was Mary, and that in his opinion, the town should be called Marysville, as a compliment to her. No sooner had he made this suggestion than the meeting broke out in loud huzzahs; every hat made a circle around its owner's head, and the new town was christened Marysville without a dissenting voice. The lady, Mrs. Coullard, was one of the survivors of the Donner party, and the honor was therefore especially fitting.

Doubts have been cast upon the story of the bar surmounted by a woman's sunbonnet, to which every customer respectfully lifted his glass before tossing off its contents; but the fact is substantiated by the eminent engraver, Mr. A. V. S. Anthony, who, as a young man, drank a glass of whiskey at that very bar, in the early Fifties, and joined in the homage to the sunbonnet. There is really nothing unnatural in this incident, or in that other story of some youthful miners coming by chance upon a woman's cast-off skirt or hat, spontaneously forming a ring and dancing around it. In both cases, the motive, no doubt, was partly humorous, partly amorous, and partly a vague but intense longing for the gentle and refining influence of women's society.

This feeling of the miners, roughly expressed in the incidents of the sunbonnet and skirt, was poetically treated by Bret Harte in the story called *The Goddess of Excelsior*,—another example of that "perverse romanticism" which has been discovered in his California tales.

Said the "Sacramento Transcript," in April, 1850, "May we not hope soon to see around us thousands of happy homes whose genial influences will awaken the noble qualities that many a wanderer has allowed to slumber in his heart while absent from the objects of his affection!"

In the same strain, but in the more florid style which was common in the California newspapers, another writer thus anticipated the coming of women and children: "No longer will the desolate heart seek to drown its loneliness in the accursed bowl. But the bright smiles of love will shed sunshine where were dark clouds and fierce tornadoes, and the lofty spire, pointing heavenward, will remind us in our pilgrimage here of the high destiny we were created to fulfil." This has the ring of sincerity, and yet, as we read it, we cannot help thinking that when the writer laid down his pen, he went out and took one more drink from the "accursed bowl"; and who could blame him!

A loaf of home-made cake sent all the way around Cape Horn from Brooklyn to San José was reverently eaten, a portion being given to the local editor who duly returned thanks for the same.

The arrival of the fortnightly mail steamer was always the most important event of those early years; and Bret Harte thus described it: "Perhaps it is the gilded drinking saloon into which some one rushes with arms extended at right angles, and conveys in that one pantomimic action the signal of the semaphore telegraph on Telegraph Hill that a side-wheel steamer has arrived, and that there are letters from home. Perhaps it is the long queue that afterward winds and stretches from the Post Office half a mile away. Perhaps it is the eager men who, following it rapidly down, bid fifty, a hundred, two hundred, three hundred, and even five hundred dollars for favored places in the line. Perhaps it is the haggard man who nervously tears open his letter, and falls senseless beside his comrade."

Thus far Bret Harte. In precisely the same vein, and with a literary finish almost equal, is the following paragraph from a contemporary newspaper: "This other face is well known. It is that of one who has always been at his post on the arrival of each steamer for the past six months, certain at each time that he will get a letter. His eye brightens for a moment as the clerk pauses in running over the yellow-covered documents, but the clerk goes on again hastily, and then shakes his head, and says 'No letter.' The brightened eye looks sad again, the face pales, and the poor fellow goes off with a feeling in his heart that he is forgotten by those who knew and loved him at home."

Anxious men sometimes camped out on the steps of the Post Office, the night before a mail steamer was due, in order that they might receive the longed-for letter at the earliest possible moment.

The coming of three women on a steamer from New York in 1850 was mentioned by all the newspapers as a notable event. In May of that year the "Sacramento Transcript" contained an advertisement, novel for California, being that of a "*Few* fashionably-trimmed, Florence braid velvet and silk bonnets." A month later a Sydney ship arrived at San Francisco, having on board two hundred and sixty passengers, of whom seventy were women. As soon as this vessel had anchored, there was a rush of bachelors to the Bay, and boat-loads of them climbed the ship's side, trying to engage housekeepers.

In 1851 women began to arrive in somewhat larger numbers, and the coming of wives from the East gave rise to many amusing, many pathetic and some tragic scenes. "You could always tell a month beforehand," said a Pioneer, "when a man was expecting the arrival of his real or intended wife. The old slouch hat, checked shirt and coarse outer garments disappeared, and the gentleman could be seen on Sunday going to church, newly rigged from head to foot, with fine beaver hat, white linen, nice and clean, good broadcloth coat, velvet vest, patent-leather boots, his long beard shaven or neatly shorn,—he looked like a new man. As the time drew near many of his hours were spent about the wharves or on Telegraph Hill, and every five minutes he was looking for the signal to announce the coming of the steamer. If, owing to some breakdown or wreck, there was a delay of a week or two, the suspense was awful beyond description."

THE POST-OFFICE, SAN FRANCISCO, 1849-50
A. Castaigne, del.
Copyright by the Century Co.

The great beards grown in California were sometimes a source of embarrassment. When a steamer arrived fathers might be seen caressing little ones whom they now saw for the first time, while the children, in their turn, were frightened at finding themselves in the arms of such fierce-looking men. Wives almost shared the consternation of the children. "Why don't you kiss me, Bessie?" said a Pioneer to his newly arrived wife. She stood gazing at the hirsute imitation of her husband in utter astonishment. At last she timidly ejaculated, "I can't find any place."

In March, 1852, forty four women and thirty-six children arrived on one steamer. The proportion of women Pioneers in that year was one to ten. By 1853, women were one in five of the population, and children one in ten. Even so late as 1860, however, marriageable women were very scarce. In November of that year the "Calaveras Chronicle" declared: "No sooner does a girl emerge from her pantalettes than she is taken possession of by one of our bachelors, and assigned a seat at the head of his table. We hear that girls are plenty in the cities below, but such is not the case here."

The same paper gives an account of the first meeting between a heroine of the Plains, and a Calaveras bachelor. "One day this week a party of immigrants came down the ridge, and the advance-wagon was driven by a young and pretty woman—one of General Allen's maidens. When near town the train was met by a butcher's cart, and the cart was driven by a young 'bach.' He, staring at the lovely features of the lady, neglected to rein his horse to one side of the road, and the two wagons were about to come in collision, when a man in the train, noticing the danger, cried out to the female driver, 'Gee, Kate, Gee!' Said Kate, 'Ain't I a-tryin', but the dog-gone horses won't gee!'"

45

Mrs. Bates speaks of two emigrant wagons passing through Marysville one day in 1850, "each with three yoke of oxen driven by a beautiful girl. In their hands they carried one of those tremendous, long ox-whips which, by great exertion, they flourished to the admiration of all beholders. Within two weeks each one was married."

But it was seldom that a woman who had crossed the Plains presented a comely appearance upon her arrival. The sunken eyes and worn features of the newcomers, both men and women, gave some hint of what they had endured.

A letter from Placerville, written in September, 1850, describes a female Pioneer who had not quite reached the goal. "On Tuesday last an old lady was seen leading a thin, jaded horse laden with her scanty stores. The heat of the sun was almost unbearable, and the sand ankle deep, yet she said that she had travelled in the same way for the last two hundred miles."

And then comes a figure which recalls that of Liberty Jones on her arrival in California: "By the side of one wagon there walked a little girl about thirteen years old, and from her appearance she must have walked many hundreds of miles. She was bare-footed and haggard, and she strode on with steps longer than her years would warrant, as though in the tiresome journey she had thrown off all grace, and had accustomed herself to a gait which would on the long marches enable her with most ease to keep up with the wagon."

The long journey across the Plains without the comforts and conveniences, and sometimes without even the decencies of life, the contact with rough men, the shock of hardships and fatigues under which human nature is apt to lose respect for itself and consideration for others,—these things inevitably had a coarsening effect upon the Pioneer women. Only those who possessed exceptional strength and sweetness of character could pass through them unscathed. As one traveller graphically puts it: "A woman in whose virtue you might have the same confidence as in the existence of the stars above would suddenly horrify you by letting a huge oath escape from her lips, or by speaking to her children as an ungentle hostler would to his cattle, and perhaps listening undisturbed to the same style of address in reply." The callousness which Liberty Jones showed at the death of her father was not in the least exaggerated by Bret Harte.

And yet these defects shrink almost to nothing when we contrast them with the deeds of love and affection silently performed by women upon those terrible journeys, and often spoken of with emotion by the Pioneers who witnessed them. A few of those deeds are chronicled in this book, many more may be found in the narratives and newspapers of the day, but by far the greater number were long since buried in oblivion. They are preserved, if preserved at all, only in the characters of those descended from the women who performed them.

Upon one thing the Pioneer women could rely,—the universal respect shown them by the men. In the roughest mining camp in California an unprotected girl would not only have been safe, she would have been treated with the utmost consideration and courtesy. Such was the society of which the English critic declared that "its laxity surpassed the laxity of savages!"

In this respect, if in no other, the Pioneers insisted that foreigners should comply with their notions. Nothing, indeed, gave more surprise to the "Greasers" and Chilenos than the fact that they were haled into court and punished for beating their wives.

As to the Mexican and Chilean women themselves, it must be admitted that they contributed more to the gaiety than to the morality or peacefulness of California life. "Rowdyism and crime," remarked the "Alta California" in October, 1851, "increase in proportion to the increase in the number of Señoritas. This is true in the mines as well as in the city."

At a horse-race that came off that year in San Francisco, we hear of the Señoritas as freely backing their favorite nags with United States money, though how it came into their possession, as a contemporary satirist remarked, "is matter of surmise only." This species of woman is portrayed by Bret Harte in the passionate Teresa, who met her fate, in a double sense, in *The Carquinez Woods*, finding there both a lover and her death. The Spanish woman of good family is represented by Doña Rosita in *The Argonauts of North Liberty*, by Enriquez Saltello's charming sister, Consuelo, and by Concepcion, the beautiful daughter of the Commandante, who, after the death of her lover, the Russian Envoy, took the veil, and died a nun at Benicia.

Even before the discovery of gold a few Americans had married into leading Spanish families of Los Angeles, Santa Barbara, Monterey and Sonoma. The first house erected on the spot which afterward became San Francisco was built in 1836 by Jacob P. Leese, an American who had married a sister of General Vallejo. It was finished July 3, and on the following day was "dedicated to the cause of freedom."

There is something of great interest in the union of races so diverse, and Bret Harte has touched upon this aspect of California life in the character of that unique heroine, Maruja. "'Hush, she's looking.' She had indeed lifted her eyes toward the window. They were beautiful eyes, and charged with something more than their own beauty. With a deep, brunette setting, even to the darkened cornea, the pupils were blue as the sky above them. But they were lit with another intelligence. The soul of the Salem whaler looked out of the passion-darkened orbits of the mother, and was resistless."

Chapter and verse can always be given to confirm Bret Harte's account of California life, and even Maruja can be authenticated. A Lieutenant in the United States Navy, who visited the Coast in 1846, gave this description of the reigning belle of California: "Her father was an Englishman, her mother a Spanish lady. She was brunette, with an oval face, magnificent grey eyes, the corners of her mouth slightly curved downward, so as to give a proud and haughty expression to the face. She was tall, graceful, well-shaped, with small feet and hands, a dead shot, an accomplished rider, and amiable withal. I never saw a more patrician style of beauty and native elegance."

California was always the land of romance, and Bret Harte in his poems and stories touched upon its whole history from the beginning. Even the visit of Sir Francis Drake in 1578 was not overlooked. In *The Mermaid of Light-House Point*, Bret Harte quotes a footnote, perhaps imaginary, from an account of Drake's travels, as follows: "The admiral seems to have lost several of his crew by desertion, who were supposed to have perished miserably by starvation in the inhospitable interior or by the hands of savages. But later voyagers have suggested that the deserters married Indian wives, and there is a legend that a hundred years later a singular race of half-breeds, bearing unmistakable Anglo-Saxon characteristics, was found in that locality."

This was the origin of the blue-eyed and light-haired mermaid of the story; and it is only fair to add that the tradition of which the author speaks was current among the Nicasio Indians who inhabited the valley of that name, about fifteen miles eastward of Drake's Bay.

Among the women who first arrived from the East by sea, there were many of easy virtue; but even these women—and here is disclosed a wonderful compliment to the sex—were held by observing Pioneers to have an elevating influence upon the men. "The bad women," says one careful historian, "have improved the morals of the community. They have banished much barbarism, softened many hard hearts, and given a gentleness to the men which they did not have before."

If this was the effect of the bad, what must have been the influence of the good women! Let the same writer tell us: "Soon after their arrival, schools and churches began to spring up; social circles were formed; refinement dawned upon a debauched and reckless community; decorum took the place of obscenity; kind and gentle words were heard to fall from the lips of those who before had been accustomed to taint every phrase with an oath; and smiles displayed themselves upon countenances to which they had long been strangers."

And then the author pays a tribute to woman which could hardly be surpassed: "Had I received no other benefit from my trip to California than the knowledge I have gained, inadequate as it may be, of woman's many virtues and perfections, I should account myself well repaid." In a ship-load of Pioneers which sailed from New York around Cape Horn to San Francisco in 1850 there was just one woman; and yet her influence upon the men was so marked and so salutary that it was often spoken of by the Captain.

The effect of their peculiar situation upon the married women was not good. They were apt to be demoralized by the attentions of their men friends, and they were too few in number to inflict upon improper females that rigid ostracism from society, which, some cynics think, is the strongest safeguard of feminine virtue. Women in California were released from their accustomed restraints, they were much noticed and flattered; and, then, as a San Francisco belle exclaimed, "The gentlemen are so rich and so handsome, and have such superb whiskers!"

In a single issue of the "Sacramento Transcript," in July, 1850, are the following two items: "A certain madam now in this town buried her husband, and seventy-four hours afterward she married another." "One of our fair and lovely damsels had a quarrel with her husband. He took the stage for Stockton, and the same day she married another man."

Even those Pioneers who were fortunate enough to have their wives with them did not always appreciate the blessing. Being absorbed in business they often felt hampered by obligations from which their bachelor rivals were free, or perhaps, they chafed at the wholesome restraint imposed upon a married man in a community of unmarried persons. There was a dangerous tendency among California husbands to permit their friends to look after their wives. On this subject Professor Royce very acutely remarks: "The family grows best in a garden with its kind. When family life does not involve healthy friendship with other families, it is likely to be injured by unhealthy if well-meaning friendships with wanderers." This is a sentiment which Brown of Calaveras would have echoed.

Men with attractive wives were apt to be uncomfortably situated in California. It is matter of history how The Bell-Ringer of Angel's protected his young and pretty spouse from dangerous communications: "When I married my wife and brought her down here, knowin' this yer camp, I sez: 'No flirtin', no foolin', no philanderin' here, my dear! You're young and don't know the ways o' men. The first man I see you talking with, I shoot.'"

In 1851, there was a man named Crockett whose predicament was something like that of the Bell-Ringer, and still more like that of Brown of Calaveras, for he not only had a very handsome wife, but it was his additional misfortune to keep a tavern on the road between Sacramento and Salmon Falls. It was not unusual for a dozen or more bearded miners to be gazing at Mrs. Crockett or watching for an opportunity to speak with her. This kept Crockett in a continual state of jealous irritation. He was a very small man, and he carried ostentatiously a very large pistol, which he would often draw and exhibit. A guest who stopped at the tavern for breakfast at a time when miners along the road had been more numerous than usual, found Crockett "charging around like a madman, and foaming at the mouth." However, he received the guest with hospitality, informed him that "he (Crockett) was a devilish good fellow when he was right side up," and finally set before him an excellent meal. Mrs. Crockett presided at the table, "but in a very nervous manner, as if she were in expectation of being at almost any minute made a target of."

If life in California during the earlier years was bad for women, it was still worse for children. In San Francisco there was no public school until the autumn of 1851. Before that time there had been several small private schools, and one free school supported by charity, but in 1851 this was given up for want of funds. In the cities and towns outside of San Francisco there was even greater delay in establishing public schools. In 1852 there were many children at Marysville who were receiving no instruction, and others, fourteen years old and even older, were only just learning to read. Horace Greeley visited California in the year 1859, and he wrote, "There ought to be two thousand good common schools in operation this winter, but I fear there will not be six hundred."

Partly in consequence of this lack of schools, partly on account of the general demoralization and ultra freedom of California society, boys grew up in the streets, and were remarkable for their precocious depravity. Even the climate contributed to this result, for, except in the rainy season, the shelter of a house could easily be dispensed with by night as well as by day. "It was the voice of a small boy, its weak treble broken by that preternatural hoarseness which only vagabondage and the habit of premature self-assertion can give. It was the face of a small boy, a face that might have been pretty and even refined but that it was darkened by evil knowledge from within, and by dirt and hard experience from without."

It was no uncommon thing, in San Francisco especially, to see small boys drinking and gambling in public places.

A Pioneer describes "boys from six upward swaggering through the streets, begirt with scarlet sashes, cigar in mouth, uttering huge oaths, and occasionally treating men and boys at the bar." Miners not more than ten years old were washing for gold on their own account, and obtaining five or ten dollars a week, which they spent chiefly on drinks and cigars. Bret Harte's Youngest Prospector in Calaveras was not an uncommon child.

An instance of precocity was the attempted abduction in May, 1851, of a girl of thirteen by two boys a little older. They were all the children of Sydney parents, and the girl declared that she loved those boys, and had begged them to take her away, and she thought it very hard to be compelled to return to her home. This incident may recall to the Reader the precocious love affairs of Richelieu Sharpe, whose father thus explained his absence from supper: "'Like ez not, he's gone over to see that fammerly at the summit. There's a little girl there that he's sparkin', about his own age.'

"'His own age!' said Minty indignantly, 'why, she's double that, if she's a day. Well—if he ain't the triflinest, conceitedest little limb that ever grew!'"

The son of a tavern-keeper at Sacramento, a boy only eight years old, was described as a finished gambler. Upon an occasion when he was acting as dealer, all the other players being men, one of them accused him of cheating. The consequence was a general fight: two men were shot, one fatally, and the man who killed him was hung the next day by a vigilance committee. Even Bret Harte's "perverse romanticism" never carried him quite so far in delineation of the California child. The word "hoodlum," meaning a youthful, semi-criminal rough, originated in San Francisco.

But there is another side to this picture of childhood on the Pacific Slope, and we obtain a glimpse of it occasionally. There was a Sunday-school procession at Sacramento in July, 1850, upon which the "Sacramento Transcript" remarked, "We have seen no sight here which called home so forcibly to our minds with all its endearments." Three years later in San Francisco, there was a May-Day procession of a thousand children, each one carrying a flower.

Even Bret Harte's story of the adoption of a child by the city of San Francisco had a solid foundation in fact, though perhaps he was not aware of it. In July, 1851, the City Fathers charged themselves with the support and protection of an orphan girl, and on the thirteenth of that month a measure providing for her maintenance was introduced in the Board of Aldermen.

The scarcity, or rather, as we have seen, the almost total absence at first of women and children, of wives and sweethearts, led to the adoption by the Pioneers of a great number and variety of pet animals. Dogs and cats from all quarters, parrots from over-seas, canaries brought from the East, bears from the Sierras, wolves from the Plains, foxes and raccoons from the Foot-Hills,—all these were found in miners' cabins, in gambling saloons and in restaurants. They occupied the waste places in the hearts of the Argonauts, and furnished an object, if an inadequate one, for those affections which might otherwise have withered at the root. One miner was accompanied in all his wanderings by a family consisting of a bay horse, two dogs, two sheep and two goats.

These California pets had their little day, perished, and are forgotten,—all save one. Who can forget the bear cub that Bret Harte immortalized under the name of Baby Sylvester! "He was as free from angles as one of Leda's offspring. Your caressing hand sank away in his fur with dreamy languor. To look at him long was an intoxication of the senses; to pat him was a wild delirium; to embrace him an utter demoralization of the intellectual faculties.... He takes the only milk that comes to the settlement—brought up by Adams' Express at seven o'clock every morning."

CHAPTER IX

FRIENDSHIP AMONG THE PIONEERS

In Bret Harte's stories woman is subordinated to man, and love is subordinated to friendship. This is a strange reversal of modern notions, but it was the reflection of his California experience,—reinforced, possibly, by some predilection of his own. There is a significant remark in a letter written by him from a town in Kansas where he once delivered a lecture: "Of course, as in all such places, the women contrast poorly with the men—even in feminine qualities. Somehow, a man here may wear fustian and glaring colors, and paper collars, and yet keep his gentleness and delicacy, but a woman in glaring 'Dolly-Vardens,' and artificial flowers, changes natures with him at once."

Friendship between one man and another would seem to be the most unselfish feeling of which a human being is capable. The only sentiment that can be compared with it in this respect is that of patriotism, and even in patriotism there is an instinct of self-preservation, or at least of race-preservation. In modern times the place which the friend held in classic times is taken by the wife; but in California, owing to the absence of women and the exigencies of mining, friendship for a brief and brilliant period, never probably to recur, became once more an heroic passion.

That there was no exaggeration in Bret Harte's pictures of Pioneer friendship might be shown by many extracts from contemporary observers, but one such will suffice:—"Two men who lived together, slept in the same cabin, ate together, took turns cooking and washing, tended on each other in sickness, and toiled day in and day out side by side, and made an equal division of their losses and gains, were regarded and generally regarded themselves as having entered into a very intimate tie, a sort of band of brotherhood, almost as sacred as that of marriage. The word 'partner,' or 'pard' as it was usually contracted, became the most intimate and confidential term that could be used."

Even in the cities friendship between men assumed a character which it had nowhere except in California. Partners in business were partners in all social and often in all domestic matters. They took their meals and their pleasures together, and showed that interest in each other's welfare which, at home, they would have expended upon wives and children. The withdrawal of one member from a firm seemed like the breaking up of a family. The citizens of San Francisco and Sacramento were all newcomers, they were mostly strangers to one another; and every partnership, though established primarily for business purposes, became a union of persons bound together by a sense of almost feudal loyalty, confident of one another's sympathy and support under all circumstances, and forming a coherent group in a chaotic community.

In the mines the partnership relation was even more idyllic. Gold was sought at first by the primitive method of pan-mining. The miners travelled singly sometimes, but much more often in pairs, with knapsacks, guns and frying-pans; and they used a wooden bowl, or a metal pan, and sometimes an Indian wicker basket for washing the gravel or sand which was supposed to contain gold. Even a family bread-pan might be made to serve this purpose, and that was the article which the youthful miner, Jack Fleming, borrowed from beautiful Tinka Gallinger, and so became possessed in the end, not indeed of gold, but of something infinitely more valuable,—Tinka herself, the Treasure of the Redwoods.

The operation of washing was thus described by a Pioneer: "The bowl is held in both hands, whirled violently back and forth through a half circle, and pitched this way and that sufficiently to throw off the earth and water, while the gold mixed with black sand settles to the bottom. The process is extremely tiresome, and involves all the muscles of the frame. In its effect it is more like swinging a scythe than any other labor I ever attempted."

This work was much less laborious when the miner had access to a current of water, and in later times it was assisted by the use of a magnet to draw away the iron of which the black sand was largely composed.

The bowl or pan stage was the first stage, and its tendency was to arrange the miners in couples like that of Tennessee and his Partner. Next came the use of the rocker or cradle,—the "golden canoe," as the Indians called it. The rocker was an oblong box, open at the lower end, the upper end being protected by a screen or grating. The screen intercepted all pebbles and gravel, and the finer material, earth and sand, was swept through the screen by the action of water thrown or directed against it. The same water carried the earth through the box, and out at the lower end; but the heavy sand, containing the gold, sank and was intercepted by cleats nailed across the inside of the box. A rough cradle, formed from a hollow log, would sell at one time for two hundred dollars.

This process required the services of four or five men, and in pursuing it the miner ceased to be a vagrant. He acquired a habitation, more or less permanent, and entered into various relationships with his fellows, which finally included the lynching of a small portion of them. This is the life described by Bret Harte in *The Luck of Roaring Camp*, *Left Out on Lone Star Mountain*, and many other stories.

The rocker period lasted only about a year, and was succeeded by that of the sluice, a sort of magnified rocker, fifty or even a hundred feet long. The necessary stream of water was diverted from some river, or was supplied by an artificial reservoir. It was the bursting of such a reservoir, as the Reader may remember, that precipitated the romance in the life of the Youngest Miss Piper.

But the evolution of the industry was not yet complete. The next step was to explore the bed of a river by laboriously turning the stream aside. This was accomplished by constructing a dam across the river, and directing the water into a canal or flume prepared for it, thus leaving the bed of the river bare, perhaps for miles. These operations required the labor of many hands, and were extremely arduous and difficult. The dam could be built, of course, only in the dry season, and the first autumnal rains would be sure to send the stream back to its old channel. The coming of the rainy season in California is extremely uncertain, and river-bed mining was correspondingly precarious. Sometimes, great perseverance in these attempts was rewarded by great success. In November, 1849, the Swett's Bar Company, composed of seventy miners, succeeded in damming and diverting the Sonora River after fifteen days of extreme exertion. Five hours later the dam was swept away by a flood. The following summer the same company, reduced to sixty members, constructed a second and larger dam, which required sixty-nine days' labor. This also was swept away on the very day of its completion. But the miners did not give up. The next morning they began anew, the directors leading the way into the now ice-cold water, and the rest of the company following, some fairly shrieking with the contact. The dam was rebuilt as quickly as possible,—and, again, the river brushed it aside. The third year, a remnant of the company, some twenty-seven stubborn souls, for the fourth time completed a dam. This time it stood fast, and before the rains set in the persevering miners had obtained gold enough to make them all rich.

Men who had struggled, side by side, through such difficulties and disappointments were bound by no common tie,—and the tie was a still closer one when, as in the first idyllic days, the partnership consisted of two members only.

Bret Harte has devoted to friendship four of his best stories, namely, *Tennessee's Partner*, *Captain Jim's Friend*, *In the Tules*, *Uncle Jim and Uncle Billy*. The subject is touched upon also in the story called *Under the Eaves*.

Unquestionably the best of these stories is the first one, and if we should also set this down as the best of all Bret Harte's stories, we could not go far wrong. The author himself is said to have preferred it. It is a complete tale and a dramatic one, and yet it has the simplicity of an incident. There is not, one makes bold to say, a superfluous word in it, and perhaps only one word which an exacting reader could wish to change. The background of scenery that the story requires is touched in with that deep but restrained feeling for nature, with that realization of its awful beauty, when contrasted with the life of man, which is a peculiar trait of modern literature. The Reader will remember that rough, mean, kerosene-lighted, upper room in which the trial took place. "And above all this, etched on the dark firmament, rose the Sierra, remote and passionless, crowned with remoter, passionless stars."

The pathos of *Tennessee's Partner* consists chiefly in the fact that Tennessee, so far as we can judge him, was unworthy of his partner's devotion. He was courageous and good-humored, to be sure, but he was a robber, something of a drunkard, and inconsiderate enough to have run off with his partner's wife. Had Tennessee been a model of all the virtues, his partner's affection for him would have been a bestowal only of what was due. It would not have been, as it was in fact, the spontaneous outpouring of a generous and affectionate character. Whether we consider that the partner saw in Tennessee something which was really there, some divine spark or quality, known only to the God who created and to the friend who loved him, or that in Tennessee he beheld an ideal of his own creation, something different from the real man,—in either case his affection is equally disinterested and noble.

Those who do not give the first place to *Tennessee's Partner* would probably assign it either to *The Luck of Roaring Camp* or *The Outcasts of Poker Flat*; but in both of those stories the element of accident is utilized, though not improbably. It was more or less an accident that the Luck was swept away by a flood; it was an accident that the Outcasts were banished on the eve of a storm. But in *Tennessee's Partner*, there is no accident. Given the characters, all the rest followed inevitably.

An acute, if somewhat degenerate critic, Mr. James Douglas, writing in the "Bookman," presents the case against the *Luck* and the *Outcasts* in its most extreme form: "There is no doubt that we have outgrown the art which relies on picturesque lay figures grouped against a romantic background.... In Bret Harte's best stories the presence of the scene painter, the stage carpenter and the stage manager jars on our consciousness.... Bret Harte takes Cherokee Sal, an Indian prostitute, puts her in a degraded mining settlement, and sanctifies her by motherhood. That is good art. He lets her die, while her child survives. That is not so good. It is the pathos of accident. He sends the

49

miners in to see the child. That is good art. He makes the presence of the child work a revolution in the camp. Strong men wash their faces and wear clean shirts in order to be worthy of the child. That is not good art."

But here let us interrupt Mr. Douglas for a moment. It should be remembered that the clean faces and clean shirts were not spontaneous improvements. "Stumpy imposed a kind of quarantine upon those who aspired to the honor and privilege of holding the Luck." Moreover, the miners of Roaring Camp, like the miners generally in California, were no strangers to clean shirts or clean faces. With few exceptions, they had been brought up to observe the decencies of life, and if, in the wild freedom of the mining camp, some of those decencies had been cast off, it was not difficult to reclaim them.

However, let us hear Mr. Douglas out: "Finally he drowns the child and his readers in a deluge of melodramatic sentiment. That is bad art.... The *Outcasts* might be analyzed in the same way. The whole tableau is arranged with a barefaced resolution to draw your tears. You feel that there is nothing inevitable in the isolation of the Outcasts, in the snow-storm, in the suicide of the card-sharper, or in the in-death-they-were-not-divided pathos of vice and virtue. And even Miggles, I fear, will hardly bear a close examination. The assault and battery on our emotions is too direct, too deliberate. We like to be outflanked nowadays, and the old-fashioned frontal attack melts away before our indulgent smiles with their high velocity and flat trajectory. M'liss, alas! no longer moves us. We prefer 'What Maisie Knew' to what M'liss didn't know."

But at this point the Reader may become a little impatient. What attention should be paid to a critic who prefers the effeminate subtleties of Henry James to the wholesome pathos of Bret Harte! And the man himself seems to be conscious of his degeneracy, for he concludes by saying, with admirable frankness, "Perhaps, after all, the fault is ours, not Bret Harte's, and we ought to apologize for the sophisticated insidiousness of our nerves."

One or two obvious remarks are suggested by Mr. Douglas's canon of romance against realism. If it were adopted without qualification, sad havoc would be made with established reputations. All the great tragedians from Æschylus to Shakspere, and almost all the great story-tellers from Haroun al Raschid to Daniel Defoe would suffer. Antigone, Juliet and Robinson Crusoe were all the victims of accident. Moreover, without the element of accident, or romance as Mr. Douglas calls it, life could not truly be represented. What might conceivably happen, and what occasionally does happen, are as much a part of life as is the thing which always happens. Many a "Kentuck" was swept away by floods in California. To perish in a snow-storm was by no means an unheard-of event. It was on the twenty-third of November, 1850, that the Outcasts were exiled, and on that very day, as the newspapers recorded soon afterward, a young man was frozen to death in the snow while endeavoring to walk from Poor Man's Creek to Grass Valley. One week later a miner from Virginia was frozen to death a few miles north of Downieville; and Poker Flat and Downieville are in the same county.

To know a man, we must know how he acts in the face of death as well as how he appears in his shop or parlor; and therefore, unusual and tragic events, as well as commonplace events, have their place in good art.

But the substratum of truth in Mr. Douglas's view seems to be this, that a tragedy which results from the character of the hero or heroine is, other things being equal, a higher form of art than the tragedy which results wholly, or in part, from accident. If human passion can work out the destiny desired by the author, without the intervention of fire, flood or disease, without the help of any catastrophe quaintly known in the common law as "the act of God," why so much the better. From this point of view, we may fairly place *Tennessee's Partner* even above *The Luck of Roaring Camp* and *The Outcasts of Poker Flat*.

It only remains to add that like most of Bret Harte's stories, as we have seen, *Tennessee's Partner* was suggested by a real incident, which, however, ended happily; and the last chapter of the true story may be gathered from a paragraph which appeared in the California newspapers in June, 1903:—

"J. A. Chaffee, famous as the original of *Tennessee's Partner*, has been brought to an Oakland Sanatorium. He has been living since 1849 in a small Tuolumne county mining camp with his partner, Chamberlain. In the early days he saved Chamberlain from the vigilance committee by a plea to Judge Lynch when the vigilantes had a rope around the victim's throat. It was the only instance on record in the county where the vigilantes gave way in such a case. Chamberlain was accused of stealing the miners' gold, but Chaffee cleared him, as every one believed Chaffee. The two men settled down to live where they have remained ever since, washing out enough placer gold to maintain them. Professor Magee of the University of California found Chaffee sick in his cabin last week, and induced him to come to Oakland for treatment. Chamberlain was left behind. Both men are over eighty."

One who witnessed Chaffee's rescue of his partner gives some details of the affair, which show how closely Bret Harte kept to the facts until he saw occasion to depart from them. Chaffee had a donkey and a cart—the only vehicle in the settlement, and he is described as standing before the vigilance committee, "hat in hand, his bald head bare, his big bandanna handkerchief hanging loosely about his neck."

Of the four stories especially devoted to friendship, the second is *Captain Jim's Friend*, published in the year 1887. This is almost a *reductio ad absurdum* of *Tennessee's Partner*, for Captain Jim's friend, Lacy Bassett, is a coward, a liar, and an impostor. In the end, Captain Jim discovers this, and he endeavors to wipe out the disgrace which, he thinks, Bassett has brought upon him by forcing the latter, at the point of his pistol, to a more manly course of conduct. And yet, when Bassett commits the dastardly act of firing at his life-long friend and benefactor, the heroic Captain Jim feels not only that his own reputation for "foolishness" is redeemed, but also, in his dying moments, he recurs to his old affection for the man who shot him; and thus the tinge of cynicism which the story would otherwise wear is removed.

The third story, *In the Tules*, is a recurrence to the theme of *Tennessee's Partner*, the two leading characters being almost a repetition of those in the earlier story. *In the Tules* has not the spontaneousness of its predecessor, not quite the same tragic reality; but it is a noble story, nevertheless, and the climax forms one of those rare episodes which raise one's idea of human nature.

In the fourth story, *Uncle Jim and Uncle Billy*, published much later, Bret Harte takes the subject in a lighter vein. The sacrifice made to friendship is not of life, but of fortune; and though, unquestionably, some men would lay down their lives more easily than they would give up their property, yet the sacrifice does not wear so tragic an aspect.

In *Left Out on Lone Star Mountain*, among the very best of the later stories, we have a little group of miners held together, inspired, and redeemed from selfishness by the youngest of their number, affectionately spoken of as "The Old Man," one of those brilliant, fine, lovable natures, rare but not unknown in real life, to which all the virtues seem to come as easily as vice and weakness come to the generality of men.

HE LOOKED CURIOUSLY AT HIS REFLECTION
From "Left Out on Lone Star Mountain"
E. Boyd Smith, del.

The hero of this story plays a part much resembling that of the late James G. Fair, United States Senator from California, and a leading man in the State. Mr. Fair, who was of Scotch-Irish descent, crossed the Plains in 1850 with a company of men who were demoralized by their privations and misfortunes. Though the youngest of the party, being but eighteen years old, Fair, by mere force of natural fitness, became their leader; and it was owing to his determined good nature, energy and high spirits that they finally reached the Pacific Slope. A member of the band afterward wrote: "My comrades became so peevish from the wear upon the system, and ... the absence of accustomed comforts, that they were more like children than men, and at times it was as much as the boy could do to keep them from killing one another."

The moral of Bret Harte's stories, it has often been said, is that even bad men have a good side, and are frequently capable of performing noble acts. But this, surely, is only a small part of the lesson, or rather of the inspiration to be derived from his works. In fact most of his heroes are not bad men, but good men. Would it not be far more true to say that the moral of Bret Harte's stories is very nearly the same as the moral of the New Testament, namely, that the best thing a man can do with his life or anything else that he has, is to give it up,—for love, for honor, for a child, for a friend!

CHAPTER X

GAMBLING IN PIONEER TIMES

Doubts have sometimes been cast upon Bret Harte's description of the gambling element in California life, but contemporary accounts fully sustain the picture which he drew. One reason for the comparative respectability of gambling among the Pioneers was that most of the California gamblers came from the West and South, especially from States bordering upon the Mississippi River, and in those quarters the status of the gambler was far higher than in the Eastern or Middle parts of the country. Early in 1850 a whole ship-load of gamblers arrived from New Orleans. They stopped, *en route*, at Monterey, went ashore for a few hours, and, as a kind of first-fruits of their long journey, relieved the Spaniards and Mexicans resident there of what loose silver and gold they happened to have on hand. These citizens of Monterey, like all the native Californians, were inveterate gamblers; but an American who was there at the time relates that they were like children in the hands of the men from New Orleans;—and thus we have one more proof of Anglo-Saxon superiority.

Nor does Bret Harte's account lack direct confirmation. "The gamblers," says a contemporary historian, "were usually from New Orleans, Louisville, Memphis, Richmond, or St. Louis. Not infrequently they were well-born and well-educated, and among them were as many good, honest, square-dealing men as could be found in any other business; and they were, as a rule, more charitable and more ready to help those in distress."

A certain William Thornton, a gambler from St. Louis, known as "Lucky Bill," had many of the traits associated with Bret Harte's gamblers. He was noted for his generosity, and, though finally hanged by a vigilance committee, he made a "good end," for, on the scaffold, he exhorted his son who was among the spectators, to avoid bad company, to keep away from saloons, and to lead an industrious and honest life.

No surprise need be felt, therefore, that in California a gambler like Jack Hamlin should have the qualities and perform the deeds of a knight-errant. Bret Harte himself records the fact that it was the generous gift of a San Francisco gambler which started the Sanitary Commission in the Civil War, so far at least as California was concerned. The following incident occurred in the town of Coloma in the summer of 1849. Two ministers, a Mr. Roberts and a Mr. Dawson, preached there one Sunday to a company of miners, and one of them held forth especially against the sin of gambling. When the collection had been made, a twenty dollar and a ten dollar gold piece were found, carefully wrapped in paper, and on the paper was written: "I design the twenty dollars for Mr. Roberts because he fearlessly dealt out the truth against the gamblers. The ten dollars are for Mr. Dawson." The paper was signed by the leading gambler in the town.

The principal building in the new city, the Parker House, a two-story, wooden affair, with a piazza in front, was erected in 1849 at a cost of thirty thousand dollars, and was rented almost immediately at fifteen hundred dollars a month for games of chance. Almost everybody played, and in '49 and '50 the gambling houses served as clubs for business and professional men. As Bret Harte wrote in the Introduction to the second volume of his works:—"The most respectable citizens, though they might not play, are to be seen here of an evening. Old friends who, perhaps, parted at the church door in the States, meet here without fear and without reproach. Even among the players are represented all classes and conditions of men. One night at a faro table a player suddenly slipped from his seat to the floor, a dead man. Three doctors, also players, after a brief examination, pronounced it disease of the heart. The coroner, sitting at the right of the dealer, instantly impanelled the rest of the players, who, laying down their cards, briefly gave a verdict in accordance with the facts, and then went on with their game!"

A similar but much worse scene is recorded as occurring in a Sacramento gambling house. A quarrel arose in the course of which a man was shot three times, each wound being a mortal one. The victim was placed in a dying condition on one of the tables; but the orchestra continued to play, and the gambling went on as before in the greater part of the room. A notorious woman, staggering drunk, assailed the ears of the dying man with profane and obscene remarks, while another by-stander endeavored to create laughter by mimicking the contortions that appeared in his face, as he lay there gasping in his death agony upon a gambler's table.

In San Francisco the principal gambling houses were situated in the very heart of the city, and they were kept open throughout the whole twenty-four hours. At night, the brilliantly lighted rooms, the shifting crowd of men, diverse and often picturesque in costume and appearance, the wild music which arose now and then, and which, except for the jingling of gold and silver, was almost the only sound,—all this, as a youthful spectator recalled in after years, "was a rapturous and fearful thing." The rooms were gorgeously furnished, with a superabundance of gilt frames, sparkling chandeliers, and ornaments of silver.

Behind the long bar were more mirrors, gold clocks, ornamental bottles and decanters, china vases, bouquets of flowers, and glasses of many colors and fantastic shapes.

The atmosphere was often hazy with tobacco smoke and redolent of the fumes of brandy; but perfect order prevailed, and in the pauses of the music not a sound could be heard except the subdued murmur of voices, and the ceaseless chink of gold and silver. It was the fashion for those who stood at the tables to have their hands full of coins which they shuffled backward and forward, like so many cards. The noise of a cane falling upon the marble floor would cause everybody to look up. If a voice were raised in hilarity or altercation, the by-standers would frown upon the offender with a stare of virtuous indignation. Every gambling house, even the most squalid resort on Long Wharf, had its music, which might be that of a single piano-player or fiddler, or an orchestra of five or six performers. In the large gambling halls the music was often very good. Two thousand dollars a month for a nightly performance was the sum once offered to a violin-player by a San Francisco gambler; and, to the honor of the artist be it said, the offer was declined.

All California, sooner or later, was seen in the gambling rooms of San Francisco: Mexicans wrapped in their blankets, smoking cigarettes, and watching the game intently from under their broad-brimmed hats; Frenchmen in their blouses, puffing at black pipes; countrymen fresh from the mines, wearing flannel shirts and high boots, with pistols and knives in their belts; boys of ten or twelve years, smoking big cigars, and losing hundreds of dollars at a play, with the nonchalance of veterans; low-browed, villainous-looking convicts from Australia; thin, glassy-eyed men, in the last stages of a misspent life, clad in the greasy black of a former gentility. The professional gamblers usually had a pale, careworn look, not uncommon, by the way, in California; but no danger or excitement could disturb their equanimity. In this respect the players strove hard to imitate them, though not always with success. The most popular games were *monte*, usually conducted by Mexicans, and faro, an American game. The French introduced *rouge-et-noir*, *roulette*, *lansquenet*, and *vingt-et-un*.

In the larger halls the custom was to rent different parts of the room to different proprietors, each of whom carried on his own game independently. Most of the proprietors were foreigners, and many of them were women. These women included some of great beauty, and they were all magnificently attired, their rustling silks, elaborately dressed hair and glittering diamonds contrasting strangely with the hairy faces, slouch hats and flannel shirts of the miners.

That gambling was looked upon at first as a legitimate industry is plain from the surprising fact that the local courts in Sacramento upheld gambling debts as valid, and authorized their collection by process of law. But these decisions—almost sufficient to make Blackstone rise from his grave—were reversed the following year.

Indeed, a healthy public opinion against gambling developed very soon. Even in 1850, the grand jury sitting at San Francisco condemned the practice; and in 1851 gambling on Sunday was forbidden in that city by an ordinance which the authorities enforced in so far that open gambling on that day was no longer permitted. In December, 1850, an ordinance against gaming in the streets was passed by the city council of Sacramento. By the end of 1851 there was a perceptible decrease in both gaming and drinking in all the larger towns of California. "Gambling with all the attractions of fine saloons and tastefully dressed women is on the wane in Marysville," a local observer reported; and the same thing was noticed in San Francisco. The gambling house, as a general *rendez-vous*, was succeeded by the saloon, and that, in turn, by the club.

Gambling houses continued to be licensed in San Francisco until 1856, but public opinion against them steadily grew. "They are tolerated," said the "San Francisco Herald," "for no other reason that we know of except that they are charged heavily for licenses. Almost all of them are owned by foreigners." By the end of the year 1855, the "Bulletin" was condemning the gamblers as among the worst elements of society; and the death of the "Bulletin's" heroic Editor in the following year marked the close of the gambling era in San Francisco. When Bret Harte's first stories were written the type represented by John Oakhurst and Jack Hamlin had begun to pass away, and those worthies would soon have been forgotten.

But who can forget them now! "Bret Harte," said the "Academy," after his death, "was the Homer of Gamblers. Gamblers there had been before, but they were of the old sullen type." In making his gamblers good-looking, Bret Harte only followed tradition, and the tradition is founded on fact. The one essential trait of the gambler is good nerves. These are largely a matter of good health and physique, and good looks have much the same origin. It follows that gamblers having good nerves should also have good looks. It is natural, too, that they should have excellent manners. The habit of easy shooting and of being shot at is universally recognized as conducive to politeness, and, moreover, a certain persuasiveness of manner, a mingling of suavity and authority, is part of the gambler's stock-in-trade. An American of wide experience once declared that he had met but one fellow-countryman whose manners could fairly be described as "courtly," and he was a professional gambler of Irish birth. Good looks and good manners, the former especially, were very common among the California Pioneers, and it is but natural that Oakhurst and Hamlin should have had an unusual share of these attractions.

Mr. Oakhurst appears in only a few of the stories, but there is a certain intensity in the description of him which makes one almost certain that he, like most of Bret Harte's characters, was drawn from life. "There was something in his carriage, something in the pose of his beautiful head, something in the strong and fine manliness of his presence, something in the perfect and utter control and discipline of his muscles, something in the high repose of his nature—a repose not so much a matter of intellectual ruling as of his very nature,—that go where he would and with whom, he was always a notable man in ten thousand."

In this description one cannot help perceiving the Author's effort, not quite successful perhaps, to lay his finger upon the essential trait of a real and striking personality.

In two stories only does he play the part of hero, these being *A Passage in the Life of Mr. John Oakhurst*, and the immortal *Outcasts of Poker Flat*. The former story closes with a characteristic remark. Two weeks after the duel in which his right arm was disabled, Mr. Oakhurst "walked into his rooms at Sacramento, and in his old manner took his seat at the faro table. 'How's your arm, Jack?' asked an incautious player. There was a smile following the question, which, however, ceased as Jack looked up quietly at the speaker. 'It bothers my dealing a little, but I can shoot as well with my left.' The game was continued in that decorous silence which usually distinguished the table at which Mr. John Oakhurst presided."

It has been objected by one critic that Oakhurst and Jack Hamlin are too much alike; but if we imagine one of these characters as placed in the situation of the other, we cannot help seeing how very different they are. Jack Hamlin could never have been infatuated, as Oakhurst was, by Mrs. Decker,—or indeed by any woman. Oakhurst was too simple, too solid, too grave a person to understand women. He lacked the humor, the sympathy, the cynicism, and the acute perceptive powers of Hamlin.

One of the best scenes in all Bret Harte is that in which Oakhurst bursts in upon Mrs. Decker, recounts her guilt and treachery, and declares his intention to kill her and then himself. "She did not faint, she did not cry out. She sat quietly down again, folded her hands in her lap, and said calmly,—

"'And why should you not?'

"Had she recoiled, had she shown any fear or contrition, had she essayed an explanation or apology, Mr. Oakhurst would have looked upon it as an evidence of guilt. But there is no quality that courage recognizes so quickly as courage, there is no condition that desperation bows before but desperation; and Mr. Oakhurst's power of analysis was not so keen as to prevent him from confounding her courage with a moral quality. Even in his fury he could not help admiring this dauntless invalid."

Jack Hamlin's power of analysis was far more keen; and Mrs. Decker would never have deceived him.

The two men were equally brave, equally desperate, but perhaps Oakhurst was the more heroic. The simplicity of his nature was more akin to heroism than was the dashing, mercurial, laughter-loving temperament of Jack Hamlin. Hamlin is almost always represented with companions, male or female, but Oakhurst was a solitary man in life as in death. His dignity, his reserve, even his want of humor tended to isolate him. Bret Harte, it will be noticed, almost always speaks of him as "Mr." Oakhurst. Though he was numbered among the outcasts of Poker Flat, he was far from being one of them.

There is a classic simplicity, not only in Bret Harte's account of Oakhurst, but in the whole telling of the story, and a depth of feeling which is more than classic. Every line of that marvellous tale seems to thrill with anticipation of the tragedy in which it closes; and every incident is described in the tense language of real emotion. "Mr. Oakhurst was a light sleeper. Toward morning he awoke benumbed and cold. As he stirred the dying fire, the wind, which was now blowing strongly, brought to his cheek that which caused the blood to leave it,—snow!"

Then comes the catastrophe of the snow-storm. We may condemn Oakhurst, on this or that ground, for his act of self-destruction, but we cannot regard it as weak or cowardly. To be capable of real despair is the mark of a strong character. A weaker man will shuffle, disguise the truth in his own mind, and hope not only against hope but against reason. Oakhurst, when he saw that the cards were absolutely against him, having done all that he could do for his helpless companions, decorously withdrew, and, in the awful solitude of the forest and the storm, forever renounced that game of life which he had played with so much courage and skill, and yet with so little success.

Jack Hamlin figures much more extensively than Oakhurst in the stories, and he would probably be regarded by most readers of Bret Harte as the Author's best creation, surpassing even Colonel Starbottle;—and, as Mr. Chesterton exclaims, "How terrible it is to speak of any character as surpassing Colonel Starbottle!" His traits are now almost as familiar as those of George Washington; but the type was a new one, and it completely revolutionized the ideal of the gambler which had long obtained both in fiction and on the stage. As a London critic very neatly said, "With this dainty and delicate California desperado, Bret Harte vanquished forever the turgid villains of Ainsworth and Lytton."

In his *Bohemian Days in San Francisco* Bret Harte gives an account of the real person who was undoubtedly Jack Hamlin's prototype. He speaks of his handsome face, his pale Southern look, his slight figure, the scrupulous elegance and neatness of his dress,—his genial manner, and the nonchalance with which he set out for the duel that ended in his death.

In the representation of Jack Hamlin there are some seeming discrepancies. Such, for instance, is Hamlin's arrogant treatment of the ostler in *Brown of Calaveras*, and still more his conduct toward Jenkinson, the tavern-keeper, whom Don José Sepulvida, with contrasting Spanish courtesy, described as "our good Jenkinson, our host, our father." The barkeeper in *A Sappho of Green Springs* fares no better at his hands; and in *Gabriel Conroy*, Bret Harte, falling into the manner of Dickens at his very worst, represents Jack Hamlin as concluding a tirade against a servant by "intimating that he would forcibly dislodge certain vital and necessary organs from the porter's body." Even less excusable is his retort to the country youth in *The Convalescence of Jack Hamlin*; and in one story he is actually guilty of rudeness to a woman, the unfortunate Heiress of Red Dog.

In these passages Bret Harte might be accused of admiring Jack Hamlin in the wrong place. But was he not rather consciously depicting the bad points of what would seem to have been his favorite character? Hamlin had several imperfections. Bret Harte does not even represent him as a gentleman, but only as an approach to one. In the story which first brings us face to face with him, the gambler is described as lounging up and down "with that listless and grave indifference of his class which was perhaps the next thing to good breeding."

That there should be any doubt as to the author's attitude upon this point shows how carefully Bret Harte keeps his own personality in the background. He does not sit in judgment upon his characters; he seldom says even a word of praise or blame in regard to them. All that he leaves to the reader. Moreover, he has a rare power of perceiving the defects of his own heroes and heroines. Occasionally, in fact, the reader of Bret Harte is a little shocked by his admission of some moral or intellectual blemish in the person whom he is sketching; and yet, after a moment's reflection, one is always forced to agree that the blemish is really there, and that without it the portrait would be incomplete and misleading.

A fine example of this subtlety of art is found in *Maruja*, where the author frankly declares that his heroine could not quite appreciate the delicacy shown by Captain Carroll when he abstained from any display of affection, lest he should presume upon the fact that he had just undertaken a difficult service at her request. "Maruja stretched out her hand. The young man bent over it respectfully, and moved toward the door. She had expected him to make some protestation—perhaps even to claim some reward. But the instinct which made him forbear even in thought to take advantage of the duty laid upon him, which dominated even his miserable passion for her, and made it subservient to his exaltation of honor, ... all this, I grieve to say, was partly unintelligible to Maruja, and not entirely satisfactory.... He might have kissed her! He did not."

Bret Harte did not describe perfect characters or mere types, destitute of individual peculiarities, but real men and women. Let us, therefore, be thankful for Maruja's lack of delicacy and for Jack Hamlin's petulance and arrogance. His failings in this respect were a part of the piquancy of his character, and in part, also, they resulted from his discontent with himself.

DENNISON'S EXCHANGE, AND PARKER HOUSE, DECEMBER, 1849, BEFORE THE FIRE
Copyright, Century Co.

This discontent is hidden by his more obvious traits, his love of music and of children, the facile manner in which he charmed and subdued horses, dogs, servants, women, and all the other inferior animals, as Bret Harte somewhere puts it; his scorn of all meanness, his chivalrous defence of all weakness; his iron nerve; his self-confidence and easy, graceful assurance; his appreciation of the refinements and niceties of existence. These are his obvious qualities; but behind them all was something more important and more original, namely, an undertone of self-condemnation which ran through his life, and gave the last touch of recklessness and *abandon* to his character. We never quite realize what Jack Hamlin was until we come to that scene in the story of his protegée where, grasping by the shoulders the two blackguards who had discovered his secret and were attempting to take advantage of it, he forced them beyond the rail, above the grinding paddle-wheel of the flying steamer, and threatened to throw himself and them beneath it.

"'No,' said the gambler, slipping into the open space with a white and rigid face in which nothing seemed living but the eyes,—'No; but it's telling you how two d—d fools who didn't know when to shut their mouths might get them shut once and forever. It's telling you what might happen to two men who tried to "play" a man who didn't care to be "played,"—a man who didn't care much what he did, when he did it, or how he did it, but would do what he'd set out to do—even if in doing it he went to hell with the men he sent there.' He had stepped out on the guards, beside the two men, closing the rail behind him. He had placed his hands on their shoulders; they had both gripped his arms; yet, viewed from the deck above, they seemed at that moment an amicable, even fraternal group, albeit the faces of the three men were dead white in the moonlight."

One might draw a parallel, not altogether fanciful, between those three figures standing in apparent quietude on the verge of what was worse than a precipice, and those other three that compose the immortal group of the Laocoön.

The tragedy of Jack Hamlin's life, that which formed a dark background to his gay and adventurous career, was his own deep dissatisfaction with his lawless and predatory manner of existence. In this respect, his experience was the universal experience intensified; and that is why one can find in Hamlin something of that representative character which readers of many different races and kinds have found in Hamlet. Who that has passed the first flush of youth, and has ever taken a single glance at his own heart will fail to sympathize with Jack Hamlin's self-disgust! It is this feeling that goes as far as anything can go to reconcile a man to death, for death ends the struggle. There is no remorse in the grave.

CHAPTER XI

OTHER FORMS OF BUSINESS

"Two years ago," said the "Alta California" in 1851, "trade was a wild unorganized whirl." Staple goods went furiously up and down in price like wild-cat mining stocks. There was no telegraph by which supplies could be ordered from the East or inquiries could be answered, and several months must elapse before an order sent by mail to New York could be filled. A merchant at Valparaiso once paid twenty thousand dollars for the information contained in a single letter from San Francisco.

Consignors in the East were almost wholly ignorant as to what people needed in California, and how goods should be stowed for the long voyage around the Cape. Great quantities of preserved food—it was before the days of canning—were spoiled *en route*. Coal was shipped in bulk without any ventilating appliances, and it often took fire and destroyed the vessels in which it was carried. One unfortunate woman, the wife of a Cape Cod sea-captain, was wrecked thrice in this way, having been transferred from one coal-laden schooner to another, and later to a third, all of which were set on fire by the heating of the coal, and burned to the water's edge. In one of these adventures she was lashed to a chair on deck, where she spent five days, in a rough sea, with smoke and gas pouring from the ship at every seam. Her final escape was made in a row-boat which landed at a desolate spot on the coast of Peru.

Elaborate gold-washing machines which proved to be useless and ready-made houses that nobody wanted were among the articles shipped to San Francisco. The rate of interest was very high, capital being scarce, and storage in warehouses was both insecure, from the great danger of fire, and extremely expensive. It was, therefore, nearly impossible for the merchants to hold their goods for a more favorable market.

In July, 1849, lumber sold at the enormous rate of five hundred dollars a thousand feet,—fifty times the New England price; but in the following Spring, immense shipments having arrived, it brought scarcely enough to pay the freight bills. Tobacco, which at first sold for two dollars a pound, became so plentiful afterward that boxes of it were used for stepping stones, and in one case, as Bret Harte has related, tobacco actually supplied the foundation for a wooden house.

Holes in the sidewalk were stopped with bags of rice or beans, with sacks of coffee, and, on one occasion, with three barrels of revolvers, the supply far exceeding even the California demand for that article. Potatoes brought sixty dollars a bushel at wholesale in 1849, but were raised so extensively in California the next year that the price fell to nothing, and whole cargoes of these useful vegetables, just arrived from the East, were dumped into the Bay. In some places near San Francisco it was really feared that a pestilence would result from huge piles of superfluous potatoes that lay rotting on the ground. Saleratus, worth in New York four cents a pound, sold at San Francisco in 1848 for fifteen dollars a pound. The menu of a breakfast for two at Sacramento in the same year was as follows:—

1	box of sardines,	$16.00
1	pound of hard bread,	2.00
1	pound of butter,	6.00
½	pound of cheese,	3.00
2	bottles of ale,	16.00
	Total,	$43.00

Flour in the mining camps cost four and even five dollars a pound, and eggs were two dollars apiece. A chicken brought sixteen dollars; a revolver, one hundred and fifty dollars; a stove, four hundred dollars; a shovel, one hundred dollars. Laudanum was one dollar a drop, brandy twenty dollars a bottle; and dried apples fluctuated from five cents to seventy-five cents a pound. It is matter of history that a bilious miner once gave fifteen dollars for a small box of Seidlitz powders, and at the Stanislaus Diggings a jar of raisins, regarded as a cure for the scurvy then prevailing, sold for their weight in gold, amounting to four thousand dollars. As showing the dependence of California upon the East for supplies, it is significant that even so late as 1853 six thousand tons of hard bread were imported annually from New York.

Wages and prices were high, but nobody complained of them. There was in fact a disdain of all attempts to cheapen or haggle. Gold dust poured into San Francisco from the launches and schooners which plied on the Sacramento River, and almost everybody in California seemed to have it in plenty. "Money," said a Pioneer in a letter written at the end of '49, "is about the most valueless article that a man can have in his possession here."

As an illustration of the lavish manner in which business was transacted, it may be mentioned that the stamp box in the express office of Wells, Fargo and Company was a sort of common treasury. Clerks, messengers and drivers dipped into it for change whenever they wanted a lunch or a drink. There was nothing secret about this practice, and if not sanctioned it was at least winked at by the superior officers. Huge lumps of gold were exhibited in hotels and gambling houses, and the jingling of coins rivalled the scraping of the fiddle as the characteristic music of San Francisco.

The first deposit in the United States Mint of gold from California was made on December 8, 1848, and between that date and May 1, 1850, there were presented for coinage gold dust and nuggets valued at eleven million four hundred and twenty thousand dollars. A lot of land in San Francisco rose from fifteen dollars in price to forty thousand dollars. In September, 1850, bricklayers receiving twelve dollars a day struck for fourteen dollars, and obtained the increase. The wages of carpenters varied from twelve dollars to twenty dollars a day. Those who did best in California were, as a rule, the small traders, the mechanics and skilled workmen, and the professional men who, resisting the temptation to hunt for gold, made money by being useful to the community. "It may truly be said," remarked the "San Francisco Daily Herald" in 1852, "that California is the only spot in the world where labor is not only on an equality with capital, but to a certain extent is superior to it."

Women cooks received one hundred dollars a month, and chambermaids and nurses almost as much. Washerwomen made fortunes and founded families. A resident of San Francisco went to the mines for four weeks, and came back with a bag of gold dust which, he thought, would astonish his wife, who had remained in the city; but meanwhile she had been "taking in washing," at the rate of twelve dollars a dozen; and he was crestfallen to find that her gains were twice as much as his. It was cheaper to have one's clothes sent to China or the Sandwich Islands to be laundered, and some thrifty and patient persons took that course. A valuable trade sprang up between China and San Francisco. The solitude became a village, and the village a city, with startling rapidity. In less than a year, twelve thousand people gathered at Sacramento where there had not been a single soul.

Events and changes followed one another so rapidly that each year formed an epoch by itself. In 1853 men spoke of 1849 as of a romantic and half-forgotten past. An old citizen was one who had been on the ground a year. When Stephen J. Field offered himself as a candidate for the newly-created office of Alcalde at Marysville, the supporters of a rival candidate objected to Field as being a newcomer. He had been there only three days. His opponent had been there six days.

56

But in 1851 the material progress of California received a great, though only a temporary, check. As commerce adjusted itself to the needs of the community prices and wages fell. A drink cost fifteen cents (the half of "two bits"), instead of fifty cents, which had been the usual price, and the wages of day laborers shrank to five dollars a day. The change was thus humorously described by an editor, obviously of Southern extraction: "About this time the Yankees began to pour into San Francisco, to invest in corner lots, and speculate in wooden gingerbread, framed houses and the like. Prices gradually came down, and money which was once thrown about so recklessly has now come to be regarded as an article of considerable importance."

In San Francisco there was almost a commercial panic. The city was heavily in debt, many private fortunes were swept away, property was insecure, and robbery and murder were common events. Delano relates that a young man of his acquaintance, a wild and daring fellow, was offered at this time a salary of seven hundred dollars a month, to steal horses and mules in a large, systematic and business-like manner.

The tone of the San Francisco papers in 1851 was by no means cheerful. The following is the description which the "Alta California" gave of the city in December of that year: "Our city is certainly an unfortunate one in the matter of public accommodation. Her wharves are exposed to tempestuous northers and to the ravages of the worm; the piles that are driven into the mud for houses to rest upon are forced out of their perpendicular and crowded over by pressure of sand used in filling in other water lots against them; a most valuable portion of the city survey is converted into a filthy lake or salt water *laguna* filled with garbage, dead animals and refuse matter from the streets; the streets are narrow and are constructed with sidewalks so irregular, miserable, and behampered as to drive off passengers into the middle of the street to take the chance of being ridden over and trampled under foot by scores of recklessly driven mules and horses; with drays, wagons and carriages without number to deafen, confuse and endanger the unfortunate pedestrian. A few thin strips of boards, pieces of dry-goods boxes or barrel staves constitute the sidewalks in some of our most important thoroughfares, and even this material is so irregularly and insecurely laid that the walks are shunned as stumbling places full of man-traps; more than all this, the sidewalks of the principal streets in the city are strewn and obstructed with shop wares."

The first Vigilance Committee of 1851 checked crime and restored order for a short period, and the second Vigilance Committee of 1856, together with the election which followed it, effected a most decided and lasting improvement in the government of San Francisco, and especially in the management of its police. In the brief account already given of James King and his career, this episode in California life has been touched upon.

The fires which successively overran the cities of California, and especially San Francisco, were another source of disaster to the business world. There were many small fires in San Francisco and six conflagrations, all within two years. The first of these occurred in December, '49, the loss being about one million dollars. A characteristic act at this fire was that of a merchant whose shop had been burned, but who had saved several hundred suits of black clothes. Having no place for storing them, and seeing that they would be stolen or ruined, he gave them away to the bystanders. "Help yourselves, gentlemen!" he cried. The invitation was accepted, and the next day an unusual proportion of the citizens of San Francisco were observed to be in mourning.

In May, and again in June, 1850, there were large fires, and it was after these disasters that the use of cloth for the sides and roofs of buildings was prohibited by law. Up to that time the shops of the city had been constructed very commonly of that highly inflammable material.

In September, 1850, there was another but less destructive fire, and on May 4, 1851, occurred the "great fire," in which the loss of property was at least seven million dollars. It was estimated at the time at fifteen million dollars. This conflagration produced a night of horror such as even California had not seen before. The fire started at eleven P. M., and the flames were fanned by a strong, westerly breeze. The glow in the sky was seen at Monterey,—one hundred miles distant. So rapidly did the flames spread that merchants in some cases removed their stock of goods four or five times, and yet had them overtaken and destroyed in the end. Since the burning of Moscow no other city had suffered so much from fire. Delicate women, driven from their homes at midnight, were wandering through the streets, with no protection from the raw wind except their nightclothes. A sick man was carried from his bed in a burning house, and placed in the street, where, amid all the turmoil of the scene, the roaring of the flames, the shouts, cries and imprecations of men, amid falling sparks and cinders, and jostled by the half-frenzied passers-by, he breathed his last.

Among the brave acts performed at this fire was that of a clerk who picked up a burning box which contained canisters of powder, carried it a block on his shoulder, and threw it into a pool of water. It was during this fire, also, that an American flag, released by the burning of the cord which held it, soared away, above the flames and smoke, while a cry that was half a cheer and half a sob, burst from the throats of the crowd beneath it.

But, great as this disaster was, the merchants rallied from it with true California courage. "One year here," wrote the Reverend Mr. Colton, "will do more for your philosophy than a lifetime elsewhere. I have seen a man sit and quietly smoke his cigar while his house went heavenward in a column of flame." This was exemplified in the great fire. Men began to fence in their lots although the smouldering ruins still emitted an almost suffocating heat. Contracts for new stores were made while the old ones were yet burning; and in many cases the ground was cleared, and temporary buildings went up before the ashes of the burned buildings had cooled. Lumber, fortunately, was abundant, and the morning after the fire every street and lane leading to the ruined district was crowded with wagons full of building tools and material. The city resembled a hive of bees after it has been rifled of its honey.

The smaller cities suffered almost as severely from fire. Sacramento was burned twice and flooded three times before the year 1854. In *The Reincarnation of Smith*, Bret Harte describes the appearance of the city when the river upon which it is situated suddenly burst its banks and "a great undulation of yellow water" swept through the streets of the city. Two other stories, *In the Tules* and *When the Waters Were Up at "Jules',"* deal with the floods of 1854 and of 1860, and in the first of these the escape of Martin Morse, the solitary inhabitant of the river-bank, is described. "But one night he awakened with a start. His hand, which was hanging out of his bunk, was dabbling idly in water. He had barely time to spring to his middle in what seemed to be a slowly filling tank before the door fell out as from inward pressure, and his whole shanty collapsed like a pack of cards. But it fell outwards, the roof sliding from over his head like a withdrawn canopy; and he was swept from his feet against it, and thence out into what might have been another world! For the rain had ceased, and the full moon revealed only one vast, illimitable expanse of water! As his frail raft swept under a cottonwood he caught at one of the overhanging limbs, and, working his way desperately along the bough, at last reached a secure position in the fork of the tree."

Martin Morse was saved eventually; but another victim of the same flood, and not a fictitious one, was found dead from exposure and exhaustion in the tree which he had reached by swimming. So close, even in small incidents, are Bret Harte's stories to the reality of California life!

During this freshet a man and his wife, who occupied a ranch on the Feather River, had an experience more remarkable than that of Martin Morse. They took refuge, first, on the roof of their house, and then, when the house floated off, they clung to a piece of timber, and so drifted to a small island. But here they found a prior occupant in the person of a grizzly bear, and to escape him they climbed a tree, whence they were rescued the next morning.

What with fire and flood added to the uncertainties and vicissitudes of trade carried on thousands of miles from the base of supplies, with no telegraphic communication and only a fortnightly mail; what with land values rising and falling; with cities and towns springing up like mushrooms and often withering as quickly:—under these circumstances, and in a stimulating climate, it is no wonder that the Californians lived a feverish, and often a reckless life. The Pioneers could recount more instances of misfortune and more triumphs over misfortune than any other people in the world. But suicides were frequent,—they numbered twenty-nine in San Francisco in a single year,—and one of the first public buildings erected by the State was an Insane Asylum at Stockton. It was quickly filled.

Nevertheless, contemporary with the feverish life of the mining camp and the city was the life of the farm and the vineyard; and this, too, was not neglected by Bret Harte. The agricultural resources of California were beginning to be known even before the discovery of gold, and many of those who crossed the Plains in '49 and '50 were bent not upon mining but upon farming. Others, who failed as miners, or who were thrown out of business by the hard times of '51 and '56, turned to the fertile valleys and hillsides for support. Monterey, on the lower coast of central California, was the sheep county; and flocks of ten thousand from Ohio and of one hundred thousand from Mexico were grazing there before 1860. In that year it was said to contain more sheep than could be found in any other county in the United States. Tasajara was known as a "cow county."

An immigrant from New Jersey, in 1850, brought thirty thousand fruit trees; and by 1859 the Foot-Hills in the counties of Yuba, Nevada, El Dorado and Sacramento were covered with vineyards, interspersed with vine-clad cottages, where, a few years before, there had been only the rough and scattered huts of a few miners.

Immense quantities of wheat were raised, especially in Humboldt County on the northern coast of the State, where we hear of crops averaging sixty bushels to the acre. In 1860 the surplus of wheat, the quantity, that is, available for exportation, exceeded three million bushels; and the barley crop was still larger. The Stanislaus and Santa Clara Valleys, not far from San Francisco, and southeast of the city, were also grain-growing districts, as is recorded in Bret Harte's story *Through the Santa Clara Wheat*.

He describes his heroine as following her guide between endless rows of stalks, rising ten and even twelve feet high, like "a long, pillared conservatory of greenish glass." "She also discovered that the close air above her head was continually freshened by the interchange of lower temperature from below,—as if the whole vast field had a circulation of its own,—and that the adobe beneath her feet was gratefully cool to her tread. There was no dust; what had at first half suffocated her seemed to be some stimulating aroma of creation that filled the narrow green aisles, and now imparted a strange vigor and excitement to her as she walked along."

So early as 1851 the newspapers began to publish articles about the opportunities for farming, and soon afterward the "California Farmer," an excellent weekly, was started at Sacramento, and supplied the community with news in general as well as with agricultural information. One can imagine the relief with which in those strenuous days the reader of the "Farmer" turned from accounts of robbery, murder, suicide and lynching to gentle disquisitions upon the rearing of calves, the merits of Durham steers, and the most approved method of fattening sheep in winter. The Hubbard squash, then a novelty, was treated by the "Farmer" as seriously as the Constitutional Convention, or the expulsion of foreigners from the mines. Practical subjects, as for instance, subsoil ploughs, remedies for smut, and recipes for rhubarb wine, were carefully discussed by this Pioneer agriculturist; and not infrequently he rose to higher themes, such as "The Age of the Earth," and "The Influence of Females on Society."

CHAPTER XII

LITERATURE, JOURNALISM AND RELIGION

Most of the newspaper men in the early days of California were Southerners or under Southern influence, as is plain from many indications. For example, duelling and shooting at sight were common editorial functions.

Bret Harte, in *An Episode of Fiddletown*, gives an instance: "An unfortunate *rencontre* took place on Monday last between the Honorable Jackson Flash, of the 'Dutch Flat Intelligencer,' and the well-known Colonel Starbottle of this place, in front of the Eureka Saloon. Two shots were fired by the parties without injury to either, although it is said that a passing Chinaman received fifteen buckshot in the calves of his legs from the Colonel's double-barrelled shotgun which were not intended for him. John will learn to keep out of the way of Melican man's firearms hereafter."

This fictitious incident can be paralleled almost exactly from the California papers of the day. In July, 1851, a certain Colonel Johnston pulled the nose of the Editor of the "Marysville Times," whereupon the Editor drew a pistol, and the Colonel ran away. In September of the same year the "Alta California" announced that a duel between one of the proprietors of that paper and a brother to the Governor of the State had been prevented by the police. In March, 1851, two Sacramento Editors had a dispute in the course of which one endeavored to shoot the other. In May of the same year, the Editor of the "Calaveras Chronicle" fought a duel with another citizen of that town, and was dangerously wounded. In November, 1860, the Editor of the "Visalia Delta" was killed in a street affray. In San Francisco a duel took place between ex-Governor McDougall and the Editor of "The Picayune," "A. C. Russell, Esq."

This use of "Esquire," by the way, was an English custom imported to California by way of the South, and many humorous examples of it may be found in Bret Harte. Thus, in the "Star's" account of "Uncle Ben" Dabney's sudden elevation to wealth and to a more aristocratic name, we read: "Benjamin Daubigny, Esq., who left town for Sacramento on important business, not entirely unconnected with his new interests in Indian Springs, will, it is rumored, be shortly joined by his wife, who has been enabled by his recent good fortune to leave her old home in the States, and take her proper proud position by his side.... Mr. Daubigny was accompanied by his private secretary, Rupert, the eldest son of H. G. Filgee, Esq.,"—"H. G. Filgee, Esq." being a species of bar-room loafer.

Another indication of the Southern origin of Californian Editors is the Starbottlian lack of humor which they often display. In August, 1850, the junior Editor of the "Alta California" published an extremely long letter in that paper describing his personal difficulties with two acquaintances, and concluding as follows: "I had simply intended in our interview to pronounce Messrs. Crane and Rice poltroons and cowards, and spit in their faces; and had they seen fit to resent it on the spot, I was prepared for them."—Nothing more. The "Sacramento Transcript" concluded the account of a funeral as follows: "She was buried in a neat mahogany coffin, furnished by Mr. Earle Youmans at one half the established price." The "San Francisco Daily Herald" of June 21, 1852, contains a very long, minute, and extremely technical account of a prize-fight, written with evident relish, but concluding with a wholly unexpected comment as follows: "Thus ended this brutal exhibition!"

The editorial tone, especially in San Francisco, was distinguished by great solemnity, but it was the assumed solemnity of youth, for the Editors, like everybody else in California, were young. None but a youthful journalist could have written a leading article, published one Monday in a San Francisco paper, describing a sermon which the writer had heard on the preceding Sunday, giving the name of the preacher, and complaining bitterly, not that he was heterodox or bigoted, but that he was stupid and uninteresting!

In fact, the California Editors, despite the solemnity of their tone, showed a decided inclination to deal with the amusing, rather than with the serious, aspects of life. The "Sacramento Transcript" in August, 1850, contained a column letter, in large type, minutely describing "an alleged difficulty" which occurred at the American Fork House, between Mr. Gelston of Sacramento, and Mr. Drake, "who has been stopping at this place for his health,"—with poor results, it is to be feared. In another issue of the same paper two columns are devoted to an account of a practical joke played upon a French barber in San Francisco.

Most of all, however, did the California journalists betray their youth, and their Southern origin as well, by the ornate style and the hyperbole in which the early papers indulged, and which are often satirized by Bret Harte. An editorial article dealing with the prospects of California began as follows: "When the eagle, emblem of model Republican liberty, winged its final flight westward from its home where Atlantic surges chafe our shores, and sought the sunny clime of the mild Pacific Strand, it bore in its strong talons," and so forth for a sentence of one hundred and twenty words.

But the California newspapers, though often crude and provincial, were almost wholly free from vulgarity. In this respect they far excelled the average newspaper of to-day. There was nothing of the Philistine about them. They give the impression of having been written "by gentlemen and for gentlemen." These California writers were, indeed, very young gentlemen, as we have seen, and they often lacked breadth of view, self-restraint, and knowledge of the world, but they were essentially men of honor, and in public matters they took high ground. The important part played by the "Bulletin" and its Editor, James King, has already been described. Nor did they lack literary skill, as is sufficiently shown by some of the passages from San Francisco papers already quoted. A correspondent of the "Sacramento Transcript," writing in July, 1850, from the northern mines, gives an account of the destruction by fire of a store and restaurant owned by a Mr. Cook, concluding as follows: "With the recuperative energy so peculiar to American character, Mr. Cook has already gone down to your city to purchase a new stock, having reëstablished his boarding-house before leaving. The son of Ethiopia who conducts the culinary department is not the darker for 'the cloud which has lowered o'er our house,' and deprived him of many of the instruments of his office."

The delicate humor of the last sentence does not seem out of place in the "Sacramento Transcript" of that date. The same paper published on the fourth of July, 1850, a patriotic leader which closed with these words,—they appear far from extravagant now, but at that time they must have sounded like a rash and audacious prophecy: "'God Save the Queen' and 'Yankee Doodle' will blend in unison around the world."

The first newspaper published in California was a small sheet called "The Californian," started at Monterey in the Fall of 1846, and printed half in English, half in Spanish. Needless to say, its conductors were Americans. They had discovered in the ruins of the Mission, and used for this purpose, an old press which the Spaniards had imported in the day of their rule for printing the edicts of the Governor. In the following year "The Californian" was removed to San Francisco. Many other newspapers sprang into existence after the discovery of gold, especially the "Alta California," which became the leading journal on the Pacific Slope. By the end of 1850 there were fifteen newspapers in the State, including six daily papers in San Francisco, and that excellent home and farm weekly, the "California Farmer."

As for the buoyant, confident tone of these Pioneer papers, exaggerated though it was, it only reflected the general feeling. So early as November, 1851, a meeting was held in San Francisco to advocate the building of a railroad which should connect the Atlantic with the Pacific. In June, 1850, the "Sacramento Transcript" warned Europe as follows: "The present is the most remarkable period the world has ever been called upon to pass through.... The nations are centering hitherward. Europe is poor, California is rich, and equilibrium is inevitable. Four years will pass, and ours will be the most popular State in the Union. She is putting in the Keystone of Commerce, and concentrating the trade of the world."

Moreover, busy as the Pioneers were, their reading was not confined to newspapers. Bret Harte said of them: "Eastern magazines and current Eastern literature formed their literary recreation, and the sale of the better class of periodicals was singularly great. Nor was their taste confined to American literature. The illustrated and satirical English journals were as frequently seen in California as in Massachusetts; and the author records that he has experienced more difficulty in procuring a copy of 'Punch' in an English provincial town than was his fortune at 'Red Dog' or 'One-Horse Gulch.'"

MAIN STREET, NEVADA CITY, 1852
From a photograph in the possession of Colonel Thomas L. Livermore

This statement has been questioned, but it is borne out by the contemporary records and publications. The "Atlantic Monthly," for example, was regularly advertised in the California papers, and the "Atlantic" at that time was essentially a literary magazine. In the list of its contributors published in the "California Farmer" are the names of Emerson, Longfellow, Lowell, Holmes, Parsons, Whittier, Prescott, Mrs. Stowe, Motley, Herman Melville, C. C. Felton, F. J. Child, Edmund Quincy, J. T. Trowbridge, and G. W. Curtis. The London "Illustrated News" had a particularly large sale among the Pioneers, although the California price was a dollar a copy.

The shifting character of the population, and the fact, already mentioned, that, almost to a man, the Pioneers expected to return to the East within a few months, or, at the latest, within a year or two,—these reasons discouraged the founding of permanent institutions such as libraries and colleges; but even in this direction something was done at an early date. The rush of immigration began in the Spring of 1849, and within less than a year a meeting had been held at San Francisco to establish a State college; a State library had been founded at San José; mercantile library associations had been started both in San Francisco and Sacramento, and an auction sale of books had been held in the latter city.

In September, 1850, an audience gathered at Stockton to hear a lecture upon so recondite a subject as the "State of Learning from the Fall of Rome to the Fall of Constantinople." In June, 1851, a San Francisco firm advertised the receipt by the latest steamer of ten thousand new books, including the complete works of Dickens and Washington Irving. In November, 1851, a literary society called The California Institute was organized in San Francisco, and in April, 1856, some one entertained a hall full of people by giving an account of a lecture which Cardinal Wiseman had delivered in London upon the Perception of Natural Beauty by the Ancients and Moderns.

Before the close of 1856 numerous boarding-schools had been established, such as the Alameda Collegiate Institute for Young Ladies and Gentlemen, the Stockton Female Seminary, the Female Institute at Santa Clara, the Collegiate Institute at Benicia, the Academy of Notre Dame at San José.

The "legitimate drama," and even Shakspere, flourished in California. In the Summer of 1850 Charles R. Thorne was playing at Sacramento, and in the Autumn "Richard III" and "Macbeth" were on the boards there. In the Fall of 1851 two theatres were open in San Francisco, "Othello" being the play at one, "Ernest Maltravers" at the other. In 1852 "The Hunchback" was performed in the same city with Miss Baker, the once-famous Philadelphia actress, in the leading part. There was no exaggeration in the remark made by the "Sacramento Transcript" in May, 1850: "Nowhere have we seen more critical theatrical audiences than those which meet nightly in Sacramento.... Every mind is wide awake, and the discriminating eye of an impartial public easily selects pure worth from its counterfeit."

An amusing incident, which would have delighted Charles Lamb, and which shows the youthfulness, the humor, and, equally, the decorum of the California audience, is thus related by an eye-witness: "One night at the theatre a countryman from Pike, sitting in the 'orchestra' near the stage, and becoming uncomfortably warm, took off his coat. Thereupon the gallery-gods roared and hissed,—stopping the play until the garment should be resumed. Some one touched the man on the shoulder and explained the situation. The hydra watched and waited. Shirt-sleeves appeared to be refractory, and a terrific roar came from the hydra. Shirt-sleeves, quailing at the sound, and at the angry looks and gestures of those who sat near him, started up with an air of coerced innocence, and resumed his *toga virilis*. The yell of triumph that arose from the 'gods' in their joyful sense of victory was beyond the description of tongue or pen."

It was remarked at an early date that nothing really satisfied the Pioneers unless it was the best of its kind that could be obtained, whether that kind were good or bad. Thus San Francisco, as many travellers observed, had the prettiest courtesans, the truest guns and pistols, the purest cigars and the finest wines and brandies to be found in the United States. The neatness and good style which marked the best hotels and restaurants prove the natural refinement of the people. Bret Harte has spoken of the old family silver which figured at a certain coffeehouse in San Francisco; and the Rev. Dr. Bushnell, who, being a minister, may perhaps be cited as an expert on this subject, was impressed by the good food and the excellent service which the traveller in California enjoyed:—

"Passing hither and thither on the little steamers to Marysville, to Stockton, to the towns north of the Bay, where often the number of passengers did not exceed thirty, we have seen again and again a table most neatly set, the silver bright and clean, the meals well prepared and good, without any nonsense of show dishes, the servants tidy, quiet and respectful,—the whole entertainment more rational and better than we have ever seen on Mississippi steamboats, or on those of the Atlantic Coast."

The steamers that plied up and down the Sacramento were "fast, elegant, commodious." In July, 1851, some one gave an aristocratic evening party in the heart of the mountains, fifty miles from Marysville. A long artificial bower had been constructed under which were spread tables ornamented with flowers, and loaded with delicious viands, turkeys at twenty dollars apiece, pigs as costly, jellies, East India preserves, and ice cream. Some of the guests came from a great distance, ten, twenty, and even thirty miles. "No gamblers were present," said the local paper which gave an account of the affair, thus showing how quickly the social line was drawn.

But even if we regard the beginnings of education and literature in California as somewhat meagre, it is otherwise with religion. Those who have looked upon the early California society as essentially lawless and immoral will be surprised to find how large and how potent was the religious element. Churches sprang up almost as quickly as gambling houses. The Baptists have the credit of erecting, in the Summer of '49, the first church building; but Father William Taylor, the Methodist, was a close second. Father Taylor set out to build a church with his own hands. Every morning he crossed the Bay from San Francisco to San Antonio Creek and toiled with his axe in a grove of redwoods until he had cut down and hewn into shape the needed timber. This he transported in a sloop to the city, and then, with the aid of his congregation, constructed the church which was finished in October, '49. By September, 1850, the following congregations had been formed in San Francisco: one Catholic, four Methodist (one being for negroes), one Presbyterian, one Congregational, one Baptist, one Episcopal, one Union Church. Three separate services were held at the Catholic Church, which was the largest, one in English, one in Spanish, one in French. Two years later a Jewish synagogue was established.

In July, 1850, five Episcopal clergymen met at San Francisco to create the diocese of California, and in the following month Dr. Horatio Southgate was elected Bishop. In the same year the San Francisco Bible Society was formed, and the next year, the "California Christian Advocate," a Methodist paper, began publication.

At Sacramento, in the Spring of 1850, the Episcopalians, Methodists, Baptists, Congregationalists and Presbyterians were holding regular services, and church building had begun. In July, 1851, a Methodist College at San José was incorporated; and in the same month the San Francisco papers have a long and enthusiastic account of a concert given by the children of the Baptist church there. "It was like an oasis in the desert for weary travellers," remarked one of them. A Sacramento paper speaking of a school festival in that city said: "No bull-fight, horse-race or card-table ever gave so much pleasure to the spectators."

A miner, writing from Stockton on a Sunday morning in October, 1851, says, "The church bell is tolling, and gayly-dressed ladies are passing by the window."

The congregations at the early religious meetings were extremely impressive, being composed almost wholly of men, and of men young, vigorous and sincere. As Professor Royce remarks: "Nobody gained anything by hypocrisy in California, and consequently there were few hypocrites. The religious coldness of a larger number who at home would have seemed to be devout did not make the progress of the churches in California less sure." And he speaks of the impression which these early congregations of men made upon his mother. "She saw in their countenances an intensity of earnestness that made her involuntarily thank God for making so grand a being as man."

It has often been remarked that in times of unbelief and lax morality there is always found a small element in the community which maintains the standard of faith and conduct with a strictness wholly alien to the period. Such was the case in the Roman Empire just before and just after the advent of the Christian religion. So, in the English Church, in its most idle, most worldly, most unspiritual days, as before the Evangelical movement, and again before the Tractarian movement, there was a small body of priests and laymen, chiefly, as in the Roman Empire, isolated persons living in the country, who preserved the torch of faith, humility and self-denial, and served as a nucleus for the new party which was to revive and reform the Church. Extremes can be met only by extremes. Intense worldliness can be vanquished only by intense unworldliness; unbelief fosters faith among a few; and the more loose the habits of the majority, the more severe will be the practice of the minority.

This was abundantly seen in California. As Bret Harte himself said: "Strangely enough, this grave materialism flourished side by side with—and was even sustained by—a narrow religious strictness more characteristic of the Pilgrim Fathers of a past century than the Western Pioneers of the present. San Francisco was early a city of churches and church organizations to which the leading men and merchants belonged. The lax Sundays of the dying Spanish race seemed only to provoke a revival of the rigors of the Puritan Sabbath. With the Spaniard and his Sunday afternoon bull-fight scarcely an hour distant, the San Francisco pulpit thundered against Sunday picnics. One of the popular preachers, declaiming upon the practice of Sunday dinner-giving, averred that when he saw a guest in his best Sunday clothes standing shamelessly upon the doorstep of his host, he felt like seizing him by the shoulder and dragging him from that threshold of perdition."

An example of this narrow, not to say Pharisaic point of view was commented upon as follows by the "San Francisco Daily Herald" of February 3, 1852: "Of all countries in the world California is the least favorable to cant and bigotry.... It is not surprising that a general feeling of loathing should have been created by an article which recently appeared in a so-called religious newspaper having the title of the 'Christian Advocate,' commenting in terms of invidious and slanderous malignity on the fact of Miss Coad, recently attached to the American Theatre, being engaged to sing in the choir of the Pacific Church."

This is well enough, though put in an extravagant and rather boyish way; but the writer then goes on in the true Colonel Starbottle manner as follows: "With the conductors of a clerical press it is difficult to deal. Under the cloak of piety they do not hesitate to libel and malign, and at the same time not recognizing the responsibility of gentlemen , and being therefore not fit subjects of attack in retort, one feels almost ashamed in checking their stupidity or reproving their falsehood." And so on at great length.

Nevertheless, the Puritan minority, reinforced by the good sense of a majority of the Pioneers, very quickly succeeded in modifying the free and easy life of San Francisco, and later of the mining regions. Gamblers of the better sort, and business men in general, welcomed and supported the churches as tending to the peace and prosperity even of the Pacific Slope. "I have known five men," wrote the Reverend Mr. Colton, "who never contributed a dollar in the States for the support of a clergyman, subscribe here five hundred dollars each per annum, merely to encourage, as they termed it, 'a good sort of a thing in a community.'"

The steps taken in 1850 and 1851 to prohibit or restrain gambling have already been noticed. In August, 1850, the Grand Jury condemned bull-baiting and prize-fighting at any time, and theatrical and like exhibitions on Sunday. In September of the same year, the "Sacramento Transcript" said, "The bull-fights we have had in this city have been barbarous and disgusting in the extreme, and their toleration on any occasion is disgraceful."

This sentiment prevailed, and shortly afterward bull-fights in Sacramento were forbidden by city ordinance. A year later gambling houses and theatres, both in San Francisco and Sacramento, were closed on Sunday, and we find the "Alta California" remarking on a Monday morning in May, "Yesterday all was like Sunday in the East, as quiet as the fury of the winds would allow. Two years ago under similar circumstances many hundreds of men would have forgotten the day, and the busy hum of business would have rung throughout the land."

In the mines Sunday, at first, was almost wholly disregarded; but abstention from work on that day was soon found to be a physical necessity. Thus an English miner wrote home, "We have all of us given over working on Sundays, as we found the toil on six successive days quite hard enough."

Men who stood by their principles in California never lost anything by that course. A merchant from Salem, Massachusetts, came up the Sacramento River with a cargo of goods in December, 1848. Early on the morning after his arrival three men with three mules appeared on the bank of the river to purchase supplies for the mines. It being Sunday, however, the man from Salem refused to do business on that day, but, after the New England fashion, accommodated his intending customers with a little good advice. This they resented in a really violent manner, and went off in a rage, swearing that they would never trade with such a Puritanical hypocrite. Yet they came back the next morning, purchased goods then, and on various later occasions, and finally made the Sabbath-keeper their banker, depositing in his safe many thousands of dollars.

Even a matter so unpopular as that of temperance reform was not neglected by the religious people. A temperance society was organized at Sacramento in June, 1850, addresses were made in the Methodist chapel, and numerous persons, including some city officials, signed a total abstinence pledge. "The subject is an old one," the "Sacramento Transcript" naïvely remarked; "but this is a new country. Temperance is rather a new idea here, and its introduction among us seems almost like a novel movement." In the same month and year a similar society was formed in San Francisco, and arrangements were made to celebrate the Fourth of July "on temperance principles."

The most genuine, the most thorough-going kind of religion found in California was that of the Western Pioneers, who were mainly Methodists and Baptists of a rude, primitive sort. Nothing could be further from Bret Harte's manner of thinking, and yet he has depicted the type with his usual insight, though perhaps not quite with his usual sympathy. Joshua Rylands, in *Mr. Jack Hamlin's Mediation* (a story already mentioned), is one example of it, and Madison Wayne, in *The Bell-Ringer of Angel's*, is another. Of all Bret Harte's stories this is the most tragic, a terrible fate overtaking every one of the four characters who figure in it. Madison Wayne is a Calvinistic Puritan,—a New Englander such as has not been seen in New England for a hundred years, but only in that Far West to which New England men penetrated, and in which New England ideas and beliefs, protected by the isolation of prairie and forest, survived the scientific and religious changes of two centuries.

In *A Night at Hays'* we have the same character under a more morose aspect. "Always a severe Presbyterian and an uncompromising deacon, he grew more rigid, sectarian, and narrow day by day…. A grim landlord, hard creditor, close-fisted patron, and a smileless neighbor who neither gambled nor drank, old Hays, as he was called, while yet scarce fifty, had few acquaintants and fewer friends."

In *An Apostle of the Tules* Bret Harte has described a camp-meeting of Calvinistic families whose gloom was heightened by malaria contracted from the Stockton marshes. "One might have smiled at the idea of the vendetta-following Ferguses praying for 'justification by faith'; but the actual spectacle of old Simon Fergus, whose shotgun was still in his wagon, offering up that appeal with streaming eyes and agonized features, was painful beyond a doubt."

As for Bret Harte's own religious views, it can scarcely be said that he had any. He was indeed brought up with some strictness as an Episcopalian, his mother being of that faith; and when he returned from her funeral with his sisters, he seemed deeply moved by the beauty of the Episcopal burial service, and expressed the hope that it would be read at his own grave. His friends in this country remember that he declined to take part in certain amusements on Sunday, remarking that, though he saw no harm in them, he could not shake off the more strict notions of Sunday observance in which he had been trained as a child. Through life he had a horror of gambling, and always refused even to play cards for money. In San Francisco he used to attend the church where his friend Starr King preached, and in New York he was often present at another Unitarian church, that of the Reverend O. B. Frothingham; but this seems to have been the extent of his church-going, and of his connection, external or internal, with any form of Christianity.

Nor, so far as one can judge from his writings, and from such of his letters as have been published, was he one who thought much or cared much about those mysteries of human existence with which religion is supposed to deal. Even as a child, Bret Harte had no sense of sin,—no sense of that hideous discrepancy between character and ideals, between conduct and duty, which ought to oppress all men, and which, at some period of their lives, does oppress most men. Everybody, from the Digger Indian up, has a standard of right and wrong; everybody is aware that he continually falls below that standard; and from these two facts of consciousness arise the sense of sin, remorse, repentance, and the instinct of expiation. Perhaps this is religion, or the fundamental feeling upon which religion is based.

To be deficient in this feeling is a great defect in any man, most of all in a man of powerful intellect. In a letter, Bret Harte, speaking of "Pilgrim's Progress," says that he read it as a boy, but that the book made no impression upon him, except that the characters seemed so ridiculous that he could not help laughing at them. This statement gives a rather painful shock even to the irreligious reader. The truth is,

Bret Harte had the moral indifference, the spiritual serenity of a Pagan, and, as a necessary concomitant, that superficial conception of human life and destiny which belongs to Paganism.

Benjamin Jowett, speaking of the Mediæval hymns, said, "We seem to catch from them echoes of deeper feelings than we are capable of." That Mediæval, Gothic depth of feeling, that consciousness of sin and mystery hanging over and enveloping man's career on earth, survives even in some modern writers, as in Hawthorne, George Eliot, Tolstoi, and, by a kind of negation, in Thomas Hardy; and it gives to their stories a sombre and imposing background which is lacking in the tales of Bret Harte and of Kipling.

It is owing partly to this defect, and partly to the unfortunate character of most of the ministers who reached California before 1860, that the clerical element fares but ill in Bret Harte's stories. His most frequent type is the smooth, oily, self-seeking hypocrite. Such is the Reverend Joshua McSnagley whose little affair with Deacon Parnell's "darter" is sarcastically mentioned in *Roger Catron's Friend*, and who comes to a violent end in *M'liss*. The Reverend Mr. Staples who meanly persecutes the Youngest Prospector in Calaveras, is McSnagley under another name; and the same type briefly appears again in the Reverend Mr. Peasley, who greets the New Assistant at Pine Clearing School "with a chilling Christian smile"; in the Reverend Mr. Belcher, who attempts the reform of Johnnyboy; and still again in Parson Greenwood, who profits by the Convalescence of Jack Hamlin to learn the mysteries of poker, and of whom the gambler said that, when he had successfully "bluffed" his fellow-players, "there was a smile of humble self-righteousness on his face that was worth double the money."

A much less conventional and more interesting type is that of the jovial, loud-voiced hypocrite who conceals a cold heart and a selfish nature with an affectation of frankness and geniality. Such are the Reverend Mr. Windibrook in *A Belle of Cañada City*, and Father Wynn, described in *The Carquinez Woods*. It was Father Wynn who thus addressed the newly-converted expressman, to the great disgust and embarrassment of that youth: "'Good-by, good-by, Charley, my boy, and keep in the right path; not up or down, or round the gulch, you know, ha, ha! but straight across lots to the shining gate.'

"He had raised his voice under the stimulus of a few admiring spectators, and backed his convert playfully against the wall. 'You see! We're goin' in to win, you bet. Good-by! I'd ask you to step in and have a chat, but I've got my work to do, and so have you. The gospel mustn't keep us from that, must it, Charley? Ha, ha!'"

James Seabright, the amphibious minister who is responsible for the Episode of West Woodlands, is rather good than bad, and so is Stephen Masterton, the ignorant, fanatical, but conscientious Pike County revivalist who, yielding to the combined charms of a pretty Spanish girl and the Catholic Church, becomes a Convert of the Mission.

Of another Protestant minister, the Reverend Mr. Daws, it is briefly mentioned in *The Iliad of Sandy Bar* that "with quiet fearlessness" he endeavored to reconcile those bitter enemies, York and Scott. "When he had concluded, Scott looked at him, not unkindly, over the glasses of his bar, and said, less irreverently than the words might convey, 'Young man, I rather like your style; but when you know York and me as well as you do God Almighty, it'll be time enough to talk.'"

But of all Bret Harte's Protestant ministers the only one who figures in the least as a hero is Gideon Deane, the Apostle of the Tules. Gideon Deane, it will be remembered, first ventures his own life in an effort to save that of a gambler about to be lynched, and then, making perhaps a still greater sacrifice, declines the church and the parsonage and the fifteen hundred dollars a year offered to him by Jack Hamlin and his friends, and returning to the lonely farmhouse and the poverty-stricken, unattractive widow Hiler, becomes her husband, and a father to her children.

The story is not altogether satisfactory, for Gideon Deane is in love with a young girl who loves him, and it is not perfectly clear why her happiness, as well as that of the preacher himself, should be sacrificed to the domestic necessities of the widow and her children. Nor is the hero himself made quite so real as are Bret Harte's characters in general. We admire and respect him, but he does not excite our enthusiasm, and this is probably because the author failed to get that imaginative, sympathetic grasp of his nature which, as a rule, makes Bret Harte's personages seem like living men and women.

There is a rather striking resemblance in the matter of ministers between Bret Harte and Rhoda Broughton. Both have the same instinctive antipathy to a parson that boys have to a policeman; both have the same general notion that ministers are mainly canting hypocrites; both, being struck apparently by the idea of doing full justice to the cloth, have set themselves to describe one really good and even heroic minister, and in each case the type evolved is the same, and not convincing. Gideon Deane has the slender physique, the humility, the courage, the self-sacrificing spirit, the melancholy temperament of the Reverend James Stanley, and, it may be added, the same unreality, the same inability to stamp his image upon the mind of the reader.

Bret Harte's treatment of the Spanish priest in California is very different. He pokes a little fun at his Reverence, now and then. He shows us Father Felipe entering the *estudio* of Don José Sepulvida "with that air of furtive and minute inspection common to his order"; and in the interview with Colonel Parker, Don José's lawyer, there is a beautiful description of what might be called an ecclesiastical wink. "The Padre and Colonel Parker gazed long and gravely into each other's eyes. It may have been an innocent touch of the sunlight through the window, but a faint gleam seemed to steal into the pupil of the affable lawyer at the same moment that, probably from the like cause, there was a slight nervous contraction of the left eyelid of the pious father."

Father Sobriente, again, "was a polished, cultivated man; yet in the characteristic, material criticism of youth, I am afraid that Clarence chiefly identified him as a priest with large hands whose soft palms seemed to be cushioned with kindness, and whose equally large feet, encased in extraordinary shapeless shoes of undyed leather, seemed to tread down noiselessly—rather than to ostentatiously crush—the obstacles that beset the path of the young student.... In the midnight silence of the dormitory, he was often conscious of the soft, browsing tread and snuffy, muffled breathing of his elephantine-footed mentor."

But the simplicity, the unaffected piety, and the sweet disposition of the Spanish priest are clearly shown in Bret Harte's stories. The ecclesiastic with whom he has made us best acquainted is Padre Esteban of the Mission of Todos Santos, that remote and dreamy port in which the Crusade of the Excelsior ended. And yet even there the good priest had learned how to deal with the human heart, as appeared when he became the confidant of the unfortunate Hurlstone.

63

"'A woman,' said the priest softly. 'So! We will sit down, my son.' He lifted his hand with a soothing gesture—the movement of a physician who has just arrived at an easy diagnosis of certain uneasy symptoms. There was also a slight suggestion of an habitual toleration, as if even the seclusion of Todos Santos had not been entirely free from the invasion of the primal passion."

The Reader need not be reminded how often Bret Harte speaks of Junipéro Serra, the Franciscan Friar who founded the Spanish Missions in California. Father Junipéro was a typical Spaniard of the religious sort, austere, ascetic,—a Commissioner of the Inquisition. He ate little, avoiding all meat and wine. He scourged himself in the pulpit with a chain, after the manner of St. Francis, and he was accustomed, while reciting the confession, to hold aloft the Crucifix in his left hand, and to strike his naked breast with a heavy stone held in his right hand. To this self-punishment, indeed, was attributed the disease of the lungs which ultimately caused his death.

THE BELLS, SAN GABRIEL MISSION
Copyright, Detroit Photographic Co.

Each Mission had its garrison, for the intention was to overcome the natives by arms, if they should offer resistance to Holy Church. But the California Indians were a mild, inoffensive people, lacking the character and courage of the Indians who inhabited the Plains, and they quickly succumbed to that combination of spiritual authority and military force which the Padres wielded. At the end of the eighteenth century there were eighteen Missions in California, with forty Padres, and a neophyte Indian population of about thirteen thousand. But all this melted away when the Missions were secularized. In 1822 Mexico became independent of Spain, and thenceforth California was an outlying, neglected Mexican province. From that time the office-holding class of Mexicans were intriguing to get possession of the Mission lands, flocks and herds; and in 1833 they succeeded. The Missions were broken up, the Friars were deprived of all support; and many of the Christian Indians were reduced to a cruel slavery in which their labor was recompensed chiefly by intoxicating liquors. Little better was the fate of the others. Released from the strict discipline in which they had been held by the priests, they scattered in all directions, and quickly sank into a state of barbarism worse than their original state.

But the Missions were not absolutely deserted. In some cases a small monastic brotherhood still inhabited the buildings once thronged by soldiers and neophytes; and these men were of great service. They ministered to the spiritual needs of Spanish and Mexicans; they instructed the sons and daughters of the ranch-owners; they kept alive religion, and to some extent learning in the community; and, finally,—if one may say so without irreverence,—they contributed that Mediæval element which, otherwise, would have been the one thing lacking to complete the picturesque contrasts of Pioneer life. The Missions had been the last expression of the instinct of conquest upon the part of a decaying nation; and the Angelus that nightly rang from some fast-crumbling tower sounded the knell of Spanish rule in America.

CHAPTER XIII

BRET HARTE'S DEPARTURE FROM CALIFORNIA

Bret Harte, as we have seen, was, for a few years at least, well placed in San Francisco, but, as time went on, he had many causes of unhappiness. There were heavy demands upon his purse from persons not of his immediate family, which he was too generous to refuse, although they distressed, harassed and discouraged him. His own constitutional improvidence added to the difficulties thus created.

Mr. Noah Brooks, who knew Bret Harte well, has very truly described this aspect of his life: "It would be grossly unjust to say that Harte was a species of Harold Skimpole, deliberately making debts that he did not intend to pay. He sincerely intended and expected to meet every financial obligation that he contracted. But he was utterly destitute of what is sometimes called the money sense. He could not drive a bargain, and he was an easy mark for any man who could. Consequently he was continually involved in troubles that he might have escaped with a little more financial shrewdness."

The theory, thus stated by Mr. Brooks, is supported by an unsolicited letter, now first published, but written shortly after Mr. Harte's death:—

... After going abroad, Mr. Harte from time to time—whenever able to do so—sent through the business house of my husband and son money in payment of bills he was yet owing,—and this when three thousand miles removed from the pressure of payment,—which too many would have left unpaid. Life was often hard for him, yet he met it uncomplainingly, unflinchingly and bravely. A kindly, sweet soul, one without gall, bitterness or envy, has gone beyond the reach of our finite voices, leaving the world to us who knew and loved him darker and poorer in his absence.

Mrs. Charles Watrous

Hague, N. Y.

May 26, 1902.

Moreover, there was much friction between Bret Harte and the new publisher of the "Overland," who had succeeded Mr. Roman; and finally, the moral and intellectual atmosphere of San Francisco was uncongenial to him. The early, generous, reckless days of California had passed, and now, especially in San Francisco, a commercial type of man was coming to the front. In *The Argonauts of North Liberty*, Bret Harte has depicted "Ezekiel Corwin, ... a shrewd, practical, self-sufficient and self-asserting unit of the more cautious later California emigration."

More than once Bret Harte had run counter to California sentiment. As we have seen already, he was dismissed from his place as assistant Editor of a country newspaper because he had chivalrously espoused the cause of the friendless Indian. His first contribution to the "Overland," as also we have seen, was that beautiful poem in which he laments the shortcomings of the city. Had the same thing been said in prose, the business community would certainly have resented it.

I know thy cunning and thy greed,
Thy hard, high lust, and wilful deed,

And all thy Glory loves to tell
Of specious gifts material.

Drop down, O Fleecy Fog, and hide
Her sceptic sneer and all her pride!

And yet, with characteristic optimism, the poet looks forward to a time—

When Art shall raise and Culture lift
The sensual joys and meaner thrift.

Later, but in the same year, Bret Harte incurred the enmity of some leading men in San Francisco by his gentle ridicule of their attempts to explain away—for the sake of Eastern capitalists—the destructive earthquake which shook the city in October, 1868. An old Californian thus relates the story: "As soon as the first panic at this disturbance had subsided, and while lesser shocks were still shaking the earth, some of the leading business men of San Francisco organized themselves into a sort of vigilance committee, and visited all the newspaper offices. They strictly enjoined that the story of the earthquake be treated with conservatism and understatement;—it would injure California if Eastern people were frightened away by exaggerated reports of *el temblor*; and a similar censorship was exercised over the press despatches sent out from San Francisco at that time.

"This greatly amused Bret Harte, and in his 'Etc.' in the November number of the 'Overland,' he treated the topic jocularly, saying that, according to the daily papers, the earthquake would have suffered serious damage if the people had only known it was coming. Harte's pleasantry excited the wrath of some of the solid men of San Francisco, and when, not long after that, it was proposed to establish a chair of recent literature in the University of California and invite Bret Harte to occupy it, one of the board of regents, whose word was a power in the land, temporarily defeated the scheme by swearing roundly that a man who had derided the dispute between the earthquake and the newspapers should never have his support for a professorship. Subsequently, however, this difficulty was overcome, and Harte received his appointment."

San Francisco was then a crude, commercial, restless town, caring little for art or literature, religious in a narrow way, confident of its own ideals, and as content with the stage through which it was passing as if human history had known, and human imagination could conceive, nothing higher or better.

In *A Jack and Jill of the Sierras* Bret Harte makes the youthful hero reproach himself by saying, or rather thinking, "He had forgotten them for those lazy, snobbish, purse-proud San Franciscans—for Bray had the miner's supreme contempt for the moneyed trading classes."

Bret Harte, whose view of life was mainly derived from eighteenth-century literature, shared that contempt, and expressed his own feeling, no doubt, in the sentiment which he attributes to the two girls in *Devil's Ford*. "It seemed to them that the five millionaires of Devil's Ford, in their radical simplicity and thoroughness, were perhaps nearer the type of true gentlemanhood than the citizens who imitated a civilization which they were unable yet to reach."

No wonder, then, that, with tempting offers from the East, harassed with debts, disputes, cares and anxieties, disgusted with the atmosphere in which he was living,—no wonder Bret Harte felt that the hour for his departure had struck. Had he remained longer, his art would probably have suffered. A nature so impressionable as Bret Harte's, so responsive, would insensibly have been affected by his surroundings, and the more so because he had in himself no strong, intellectual basis. His life was ruled by taste, rather than by conviction; and taste is a harder matter than conviction to preserve unimpaired. Of all the criticisms passed upon Bret Harte there has been nothing more true than Madame Van de Velde's observations upon this point: "It was decidedly fortunate that he left California when he did, never to return to it; for his quick instinctive perceptions would have assimilated the new order of things to the detriment of his talent. As it was, his singularly retentive memory remained unbiassed by the transformation of the centres whence he drew his inspiration. California remained to him the Mecca of the Argonauts."

Bret Harte left many warm friends in California, and they were much hurt, in some cases much angered, because they never had a word from him afterward. And yet it is extremely doubtful if he expected any such result. Certainly it was not intended. Kind and friendly feelings may still exist, although they are not expressed in letters. Bret Harte was indolent and procrastinating about everything except the real business of his life, and into that all his energy was poured. And there was another reason for the failure to communicate with his old friends, which has probably occurred to the Reader, and which is suggested in a private letter from one of the very persons who were aggrieved by his silence. "He went away with a sore heart. He had cares, difficulties, hurts here, *many*, and they may have embittered him against all thoughts of the past."

This, no doubt, is true. The California chapter in Bret Harte's life was closed, and it would have been painful for him to reopen it even by the writing of a letter. To say this, however, is not to acquit him of all blame in the matter.

The night before he left California a few of his more intimate friends gave him a farewell dinner which, in the light of all that followed, now wears an almost tragic aspect. It is thus described by one of the company: "A little party of us, eight, all working writers, met for a last symposium. It was one of the veritable *noctes ambrosianae*; the talk was intimate, heart-to-heart, and altogether of the shop. Naturally Harte was the centre of the little company, and he was never more fascinating and companionable. Day was breaking when the party dispersed, and the ties that bound our friend to California were sundered forever."

Bret Harte left San Francisco in February, 1871.

Seventeen years before he had landed there, a mere boy, without money or prospects, without trade or profession. Now he was the most distinguished person in California, and his departure marked the close of an epoch for that State. Who can imagine the mingled feelings, half-triumphant, half-bitter, with which he must have looked back upon the slow-receding, white-capped Sierras that had bounded his horizon for those seventeen eventful years!

CHAPTER XIV

BRET HARTE IN THE EAST

Before Bret Harte left California he had been in correspondence with some persons in Chicago who proposed to make him Editor and part proprietor of a magazine called the "Lakeside Monthly." A dinner was arranged to take place soon after his arrival in Chicago at which Mr. Harte might meet the men who were to furnish the capital for this purpose. But the guest of the evening did not appear. Many stories were told in explanation of his absence; and Bret Harte's own account is thus stated by Mr. Noah Brooks:—"When I met Harte in New York I asked him about the incident, and he said: 'In Chicago I stayed with relations of my wife's, who lived on the North Side, or the East Side, or the Northeast Side, or the Lord knows where, and when I accepted an invitation to dinner in a hotel in the centre of the city, I expected that a guide would be sent me. I was a stranger in a strange city; a carriage was not easily to be obtained in the neighborhood where I was, and, in utter ignorance of the way I should take to reach the hotel, I waited for a guide until the hour for dinner had passed, and then sat down, as your friend S. P. D. said to you in California "*en famille*, with my family." That's all there was to it.'"

Mr. Pemberton, commenting on this explanation says, "I can readily picture Bret Harte, as the unwelcome dinner hour approached, making excuses to himself for himself and conjuring up that hitherto unsuggested 'guide.'"

That Mr. Pemberton was right as to the "guide" being an afterthought, is proved by the following account, for which the author of this book is indebted to Mr. Francis F. Browne, at that time editor of the "Lakeside Monthly": "I remember quite clearly Mr. Harte's visit to my office,—a small, rather youthful looking but alert young man of pleasing manners and conversation. We talked of the literary situation, and he seemed impressed with the opportunity offered by Chicago for a high-class literary enterprise. A day or two after his arrival here Mr. Harte was invited to a dinner at the house of a prominent citizen, to meet the gentlemen who were expected to become interested in the magazine project with him. Mr. Harte accepted the invitation. There is no doubt that he intended going, for he was in my office the afternoon of the dinner, and left about five o'clock, saying he was going home to dress for the occasion. But he did not appear at the dinner; nor did he send any explanation whatever. There being then no telephones, no explanation was given until the next day, and it was then to the effect that he had supposed a carriage would be sent for him, and had waited for it until too late to start. A friend of the author tells me that he had previously asked Mr. Harte whether he should call for him and take him to the dinner; but Harte assured him that this was not at all necessary, that he knew perfectly well how to find the place. The other members of the party, however, were on hand, and after waiting, with no little surprise, for the chief guest to appear, they proceeded to eat their dinner and disperse; but Mr. Harte and the project of a literary connection with him in Chicago no longer interested them."

It is evident that for some reason, unknown outside of his own family, Bret Harte could not or would not attend the dinner, and simply remained away. The result was thus stated by the author himself in a letter to a friend in California: "I presume you have heard through the public press how nearly I became editor and part owner of the 'Lakeside,' and how the childishness and provincial character of a few of the principal citizens of Chicago spoiled the project."

Bret Harte, therefore, continued Eastward, leaving Chicago on February 11, "stopping over" a few days in Syracuse, and reaching New York on February 20. His stories and poems—especially the *Heathen Chinee*—had lifted him to such a pinnacle of renown that his progress from the Pacific to the Atlantic was detailed by the newspapers with almost as much particularity as were the movements of Admiral Dewey upon his return to the United States after the capture of Manila. The commotion thus caused extended even to England, and a London paper spoke humorously, but kindly, of the "Bret Harte circular," which recorded the daily events of the author's life.

"The fame of Bret Harte," remarked the "New York Tribune," as the railroad bore him toward that city, "has so brilliantly shot to the zenith as to render any comments on his poems a superfluous task. The verdict of the popular mind has only anticipated the voice of sound criticism."

In New York Mr. Harte and his family went immediately to the house of his sister, Mrs. F. F. Knaufft, at number 16 Fifth Avenue; and with her they spent the greater part of the next two years. Three days after their arrival in New York the whole family went to Boston, Mr. Harte being engaged to dine with the famous Saturday Club, and being desirous of seeing his publishers. He arrived in Boston February 25, his coming having duly been announced by telegrams published in all the papers. Upon the morning of his arrival the "Boston Advertiser" had the following pleasant notice of the event. "He will have a hearty welcome from many warm friends to whom his face is yet strange; and after a journey across the continent, in which his modesty must have been tried almost as severely as his endurance by the praises showered upon him, we hope that he will find Boston so pleasant, even in the soberest dress which she wears during the year, that he may tarry long among us."

In Boston, or rather at Cambridge, just across Charles River, Bret Harte was to be the guest of Mr. Howells, then the assistant Editor of the "Atlantic Monthly," James Russell Lowell being the Editor-in-Chief. Mr. Howells' account of this visit is so interesting, and throws so much light upon Bret Harte's character, that it is impossible to refrain from quoting it here:—

"When the adventurous young Editor who had proposed being his host for Boston, while Harte was still in San Francisco, and had not yet begun his princely progress Eastward, read of the honors that attended his coming from point to point, his courage fell, as if he perhaps had committed himself in too great an enterprise. Who was he, indeed, that he should think of making this dear son of memory, great heir of fame, his guest, especially when he heard that in Chicago Harte failed of attending a banquet of honor because the givers of it had not sent a carriage to fetch him to it, as the alleged use was in San Francisco? Whether true or not, and it was probably not true in just that form, it must have been this rumor which determined his host to drive into Boston for him with the handsomest hack which the livery of Cambridge afforded, and not trust to the horse-car and the express to get him and his baggage out, as he would have done with a less portentous guest.

"However it was, he instantly lost all fear when they met at the station, and Harte pressed forward with his cordial hand-clasp, as if he were not even a fairy prince, and with that voice and laugh which were surely the most winning in the world. The drive out from Boston was not too long for getting on terms of personal friendship with the family which just filled the hack, the two boys intensely interested in the novelties of a New England city and suburb, and the father and mother continually exchanging admiration of such aspects of nature as presented themselves in the leafless sidewalk trees, and patches of park and lawn. They found everything so fine, so refined, after the gigantic coarseness of California, where the natural forms were so vast that one could not get on companionable terms with them. Their host heard them with misgiving for the world of romance which Harte had built up among those huge forms, and with a subtle perception that this was no excursion of theirs to the East, but a lifelong exodus from the exile which he presently understood they must always have felt California to be. It is different now, when people are every day being born in California, and must begin to feel it home from the first breath, but it is notable that none of the Californians of that great early day have gone back to live amidst the scenes which inspired and prospered them.

"Before they came in sight of the Editor's humble roof he had mocked himself to his guest at his trepidations, and Harte with burlesque magnanimity had consented to be for that occasion only something less formidable than he had loomed afar. He accepted with joy the theory of passing a week in the home of virtuous poverty, and the week began as delightfully as it went on. From first to last Cambridge amused him as much as it charmed him by that air of academic distinction which was stranger to him even than the refined trees and grass. It has already been told how, after a list of the local celebrities had been recited to him, he said, 'Why, you couldn't stand on your front porch and fire off your revolver without bringing down a two-volumer,' and no doubt the pleasure he had in it was the effect of its contrast with the wild California he had known, and perhaps, when he had not altogether known it, had invented.

"Cambridge began very promptly to show him those hospitalities which he could value, and continued the fable of his fairy princeliness in the curiosity of those humbler admirers who could not hope to be his hosts or fellow-guests at dinner or luncheon. Pretty presences in the tie-backs of the period were seen to flit before the home of virtuous poverty, hungering for any chance sight of him which his outgoings or incomings might give. The chances were better with the outgoings than with the incomings, for these were apt to be so hurried, in the final result of his constitutional delays, as to have the rapidity of the homing pigeon's flight, and to afford hardly a glimpse to the quickest eye.

"It cannot harm him, or any one now, to own that Harte was nearly always late for those luncheons and dinners which he was always going out to, and it needed the anxieties and energies of both families to get him into his clothes, and then into the carriage, where a good deal of final buttoning must have been done, in order that he might not arrive so very late. He was the only one concerned who was quite unconcerned; his patience with his delays was inexhaustible; he arrived smiling, serenely jovial, radiating a bland gayety from his whole person, and ready to ignore any discomfort he might have occasioned.

"Of course, people were glad to have him on his own terms, and it may be said that it was worth while to have him on any terms. There was never a more charming companion, an easier or more delightful guest. It was not from what he said, for he was not much of a talker, and almost nothing of a story-teller; but he could now and then drop the fittest word, and with a glance or smile of friendly intelligence express the appreciation of another's word which goes far to establish for a man the character of born humorist.

"It must be said of him that if he took the honors easily that were paid him, he took them modestly, and never by word or look invited them, or implied that he expected them. It was fine to see him humorously accepting the humorous attribution of scientific sympathies from Agassiz, in compliment of his famous epic describing the incidents that 'broke up the Society upon the Stanislaus.'"

Of his personal appearance at this time Mr. Howells says: "He was then, as always, a child of extreme fashion as to his clothes and the cut of his beard, which he wore in a mustache and the drooping side-whiskers of the day, and his jovial physiognomy was as winning as his voice, with its straight nose and fascinating forward thrust of the under-lip, its fine eyes and good forehead, then thickly covered with black hair which grew early white, while his mustache remained dark, the most enviable and consoling effect possible in the universal mortal necessity of either aging or dyeing."

It can easily be imagined, although Mr. Howells does not say so, that the atmosphere of Cambridge was far from being congenial to Bret Harte. University towns are notorious for taking narrow, academic views of life; and in Cambridge, at least during the period in question, the college circle was complicated by some remnants of colonial aristocracy that looked with suspicion upon any person or idea originating outside of England—Old or New. Bret Harte, as may be imagined, was not awed by his new and highly respectable surroundings. "It was a little fearsome," writes Mr. Howells, "to hear him frankly owning to Lowell his dislike for something over-literary in the phrasing of certain verses of 'The Cathedral.' But Lowell could stand that sort of thing from a man who could say the sort of things that Harte said to him of that delicious line picturing the bobolink as he

Runs down a brook of laughter in the air.

That, Bret Harte told him, was the line he liked best of all his lines, and Lowell smoked, well content with the phrase. Yet they were not men to get on well together, Lowell having limitations in directions where Harte had none. Afterward, in London, they did not meet often or willingly."

Bret Harte was taken to see Emerson at Concord, but probably without much profit on either side, though with some entertainment for the younger man. "Emerson's smoking," Mr. Howells relates, "amused Bret Harte as a Jovian self-indulgence divinely out of character with so supreme a god, and he shamelessly burlesqued it, telling how Emerson proposed having a 'wet night' with him, over a glass of sherry, and urged the wine upon his young friend with a hospitable gesture of his cigar."

"Longfellow, alone," Mr. Howells adds, "escaped the corrosive touch of his subtle irreverence, or, more strictly speaking, had only the effect of his reverence. That gentle and exquisitely modest dignity of Longfellow's he honored with as much veneration as it was in him to bestow, and he had that sense of Longfellow's beautiful and perfected art which is almost a test of a critic's own fineness."

Bret Harte and Longfellow met at an evening party in Cambridge, and walked home together afterward; and when Longfellow died, in 1882, Bret Harte wrote down at some length his impressions of the poet. It had been a characteristic New England day in early Spring, with rain followed by snow, and finally clearing off cold and still.

"I like to recall him at that moment, as he stood in the sharp moonlight of the snow-covered road; a dark mantle-like cloak hiding his evening dress, and a slouched felt hat covering his full silver-like locks. The conventional gibus or chimney-pot would have been as intolerable on that wonderful brow as it would be on a Greek statue, and I was thankful there was nothing to interrupt the artistic harmony of the most impressive vignette I ever beheld.... I think I was at first moved by his voice. It was a very deep baritone without a trace of harshness, but veiled and reserved as if he never parted entirely from it, and with the abstraction of a soliloquy even in his most earnest moments. It was not melancholy, yet it suggested one of his own fancies as it fell from his silver-fringed lips

'Like the water's flow
Under December's snow.'

Yet no one had a quicker appreciation of humour, and his wonderful skill as a *raconteur*, and his opulence of memory, justified the saying of his friends that 'no one ever heard him tell an old story or repeat a new one.'... Speaking of the spiritual suggestions in material things, I remember saying that I thought there must first be some actual resemblance, which unimaginative people must see before the poet could successfully use them. I instanced the case of his own description of a camel as being 'weary' and 'baring his teeth,' and added that I had seen them throw such infinite weariness into that action after a day's journey as to set spectators yawning. He seemed surprised, so much so that I asked him if he had seen many—fully believing he had travelled in the desert. He replied simply, 'No,' that he had 'only seen one once in the *Jardin des Plantes*.' Yet in that brief moment he had noticed a distinctive fact, which the larger experience of others fully corroborated."

Mr. Pemberton also contributes this interesting reminiscence: "With his intimate friends Bret Harte ever delighted to talk enthusiastically of Longfellow, and would declare that his poems had greatly influenced his thoughts and life. Hiawatha he declared to be 'not only a wonderful poem, but a marvellously true descriptive narrative of Indian life and lore.' I think he knew it all by heart."

Bret Harte and his family stayed a week with Mr. Howells, and one event was the Saturday Club dinner which Mr. Howells has described. "Harte was the life of a time which was perhaps less a feast of reason than a flow of soul. The truth is, there was nothing but careless stories, carelessly told, and jokes and laughing, and a great deal of mere laughing without the jokes, the whole as unlike the ideal of a literary symposium as well might be."

One of the guests, unused to the society of literary men, Mr. Howells says, had looked forward with some awe to the occasion, and Bret Harte was amused at the result. "'Look at him!' he said from time to time. '*This is the dream of his life*'; and then shouted and choked with fun at the difference between the occasion, and the expectation he would have imagined in his commensal's mind." The "commensal," as appears from a subsequent essay by Mr. Howells, was Mark Twain, who, like Bret Harte, had recently arrived from the West. Somehow, the account of this dinner as given by Mr. Howells leaves an unpleasant impression.

The atmosphere of Boston was hardly more congenial to Bret Harte than that of Cambridge. Boston was almost as provincial as San Francisco, though in a different way. The leaders of society were men and women who had grown up with the bourgeois traditions of a rich, isolated commercial and colonial town; and they had the same feeling of horror for a man from the West that they had for a Methodist. The best part of Boston was the serious, well-educated, conscientious element, typified by the Garrison family; but this element was much less conspicuous in 1871 than it had been earlier. The feeling for art and literature, also, was neither so widespread nor so deep as it had been in the thirty-five years preceding the Civil War. Moreover, the peculiar faults of the Boston man, his worship of respectability, his self-satisfied narrowness, his want of charity and sympathy,—these were the very faults that especially jarred upon Bret Harte, and it is no wonder that the man from Boston makes a poor appearance in his stories.

"It was a certain Boston lawyer, replete with principle, honesty, self-discipline, statistics, authorities, and a perfect consciousness of possessing all these virtues, and a full recognition of their market values. I think he tolerated me as a kind of foreigner, gently waiving all argument on any topic, frequently distrusting my facts, generally my deductions, and always my ideas. In conversation he always appeared to descend only halfway down a long moral and intellectual staircase, and always delivered his conclusions over the balusters."

And yet, with characteristic fairness, Bret Harte does not fail to portray the good qualities of the Boston man. The Reader will remember the sense of honor, the courage and energy, and even—under peculiar circumstances—the capacity to receive new ideas, shown by John Hale, the Boston man who figures in *Snow-Bound at Eagle's*, and who was of the same type as the lawyer just described.

Henry Hart and his family spent a year in Boston when Bret Harte was about the age of four, but, contrary to the general impression, Bret Harte never lived there afterward, although he once spent a few weeks in the city as the guest of the publisher, Mr. J. R. Osgood, then living on Pinckney Street, in the old West End. A small section of the north side of Pinckney Street forms the northern end of Louisburg Square; and this square, as it happens, is the only place in Boston which Bret Harte depicts. Here lived Mr. Adams Rightbody, as appears from the brief but unmistakable description of the place in *The Great Deadwood Mystery*. A telegram to Mr. Rightbody had been sent at night from Tuolumne County, California; and its progress and delivery are thus related: "The message lagged a little at San Francisco, laid over half an hour at Chicago, and fought longitude the whole way, so that it was past midnight when the 'all-night' operator took it from the wires at Boston. But it was freighted with a mandate from the San Francisco office; and a messenger was procured, who sped with it through dark, snow-bound streets, between the high walls of close-shuttered, rayless houses to a certain formal square, ghostly with snow-covered statues. Here he ascended the broad steps of a reserved and solid-looking mansion, and pulled a bronze bell-knob that, somewhere within those chaste recesses, after an apparent reflective pause, coldly communicated the fact that a stranger was waiting without—as he ought."

That Bret Harte made no mistake in selecting Louisburg Square as the residence of that intense Bostonian, Mr. Rightbody, will be seen from Mr. Lindsay Swift's description in his "Literary Landmarks of Boston." "This retired spot is the quintessence of the older Boston. Without positive beauty, its dignity and repose save it from any suggestion of ugliness. Here once bubbled up, it is fondly believed, in the centre of the iron-railed enclosure, that spring of water with which First Settler William Blackstone helped to coax Winthrop and his followers over the river from Charlestown. There is no monument to Blackstone, here or anywhere, but in this significant spot stand two statues, one to Columbus and one to Aristides the Just, both of Italian make, and presented to the city by a Greek merchant of Boston."

After the week's stay in Cambridge, with, of course, frequent excursions to Boston, Bret Harte and his family returned to New York. The proposals made to him by publishing houses in that city were, Mr. Howells reports, "either mortifyingly mean or insultingly vague"; and a few days later Bret Harte accepted the offer of James R. Osgood and Company, then publishers of "The Atlantic," to pay him ten thousand dollars during the ensuing year for whatever he might write in the twelve months, be it much or little. This offer, a munificent one for the time, was made despite the astonishing fact that of the first volume of Bret Harte's stories, issued by the same publishers six months before, only thirty-five hundred copies had then been sold. The arrangement did not, of course, require Mr. Harte's residence in Boston, and for the next two Winters he remained with his sister in New York, spending the first Summer at Newport.

It has often been stated that the rather indefinite contract which the publishers made with Bret Harte turned out badly for them, and that he wrote but a single story, as it is sometimes put, during the whole year. But the slightest investigation will show that these statements do our author great injustice. The year of the contract began with July, 1871, and ended with June, 1872; and the two volumes of the "Atlantic" covering that period, No. 28 and No. 29, contain the following stories by Bret Harte:—

The Poet of Sierra Flat, Princess Bob and Her Friends, The Romance of Madroño Hollow, How Santa Claus Came to Simpson's Bar;

And the following poems: *A Greyport Legend, A Newport Romance, Concepcion de Arguello, Grandmother Tenterden, The Idyl of Battle Hollow*.

Surely, this was giving full measure, and it represents a year of very hard work, unless indeed it was partly done in California. One of the stories, *How Santa Clans Came to Simpson's Bar*, is, as every reader of Bret Harte will admit, among the best of his tales, inferior only to *Tennessee's Partner, The Luck*, and *The Outcasts*.

It is noticeable that all these "Atlantic Monthly" stories deal with California; and an amusing illustration of Bret Harte's literary habits may be gathered from the fact that in every case his story brings up the rear of the magazine, although it would naturally have been given the place of honor. Evidently the manuscript was received by the printers at the last possible moment. One of the poems, the *Newport Romance*, seems to lack those patient, finishing touches which it was his custom to bestow.

For the next seven years of Bret Harte's life there is not much to record. During the greater part of the time New York was his winter home. From his Summer at Newport resulted the poems already mentioned, *A Greyport Legend* and *A Newport Romance*. Hence also a scene or two in *Mrs. Skaggs's Husbands*, published in 1872. But the poems deal with the past, and neither in them nor in any story did the author attempt to describe that luxurious, exotic life, grafted upon the Atlantic Coast, over which other romancers have fondly lingered.

Two or three Summers were spent by Bret Harte and his family in Morristown, New Jersey. Here he wrote *Thankful Blossom*, a pretty story of Revolutionary times, describing events which occurred at the very spot where he was living, but lacking the strength and originality of his California tales. "Thankful Blossom" was not an imaginary name, but the real name of one of his mother's ancestors, a member of the Truesdale family; and it should be mentioned that before writing this story Bret Harte, with characteristic thoroughness, made a careful study of the place where Washington had his headquarters at Morristown, and of the surrounding country.

One other Summer the Harte family spent at New London, in Connecticut, and still another at Cohasset, a seashore town about twenty miles south of Boston. Here he became the neighbor and friend of the actors, Lawrence Barrett and Stuart Robson, for the latter of whom he wrote the play called *Two Men of Sandy Bar*. This was produced in September, 1876, at the Union Square Theatre in New York, but, although not a failure, it did not attain permanent success. The principal characters were Sandy Morton, played by Charles R. Thorne, and Colonel Starbottle, taken by Stuart Robson. John Oakhurst, the Yankee Schoolmistress (from *The Idyl of Red Gulch*), a Chinaman, an Australian convict, and other figures taken from Bret Harte's stories, also appeared in the piece. The part of Hop Sing, the Chinaman, was played by Mr. C. T. Parsloe, and with so much success that afterward, in collaboration with Mark Twain, Bret Harte wrote a melodrama for Mr. Parsloe called *Ah Sin*; but this, too, failed to keep the boards for long.

Mr. Pemberton speaks of another play in respect to which Bret Harte sought the advice of Dion Boucicault; but this appears never to have been finished. It was a cause of annoyance and disgust to Bret Harte after he had left this country, that a version of *M'liss* converting that beautiful story into a vulgar "song and dance" entertainment was produced on the stage and in its way became a great success. Bret Harte was unable to prevent these performances in the United States, but he did succeed, by means of a suit, threatened if not actually begun, in preventing their repetition in England. A very inferior theatrical version of *Gabriel Conroy*, also, was brought out in New York without the author's consent, and much against his will.

Bret Harte had a lifelong desire to write a notable play, and made many attempts in that direction. One of them succeeded. With the help of his friend and biographer, Mr. Pemberton, he dramatized his story, *The Judgment of Bolinas Plain*; and the result, a melodrama in three acts, called *Sue*, was produced in New York in 1896, and was well received both by the critics and the audience. Afterward the play was successfully performed on a tour of the United States; and in 1898 it was brought out in London, and was equally successful there. The heroine's part was taken by Miss Annie Russell, of whom Mr. Pemberton gracefully says, "How much the writers owed to her charming personality and her deft handling of a difficult part they freely and gratefully acknowledged." But even this play has not become a classic.

Of his experience as a fellow-worker with Bret Harte, Mr. Pemberton gives this interesting account. "Infinite painstaking, I soon learned, was the essence of his system. Of altering and re-altering he was never tired, and though it was sometimes a little disappointing to find that what we had considered as finished over-night, had, at his desire, to be reconsidered in the morning, the humorous way in which he would point out how serious situations might, by a twist of the pen, or by incompetent acting, create derisive laughter, compensated for double or even treble work. No one realized more keenly than he did that to most things there is a comic as well as a serious side, and it seemed to make him vastly happy to put his finger on his own vulnerable spots."

Mr. Pemberton speaks of several other plays written by Bret Harte and himself, and of one written by Bret Harte alone for Mr. J. L. Toole. But none of these was ever acted. It is needless to say that Bret Harte loved the theatre and had a keen appreciation of good acting. In a letter to Mr. Pemberton, he spoke of John Hare's "wonderful portrayal of the Duke of St. Olpherts in 'The Notorious Mrs. Ebbsmith.' He is gallantly attempting to relieve Mrs. Thorpe of the tray she is carrying, but of course lacks the quickness, the alertness, and even the actual energy to do it, and so follows her with delightful simulation of assistance all over the stage, while she carries it herself, he pursuing the form and ignoring the performance. It is a wonderful study."

Bret Harte had not been long in the East, probably he had not been there a month, before he began to feel the pressure of those money difficulties from which neither he, nor his father before him, was ever free. Doubtless he would often have been at a loss for ready money, even if he had possessed the wealth of all the Indies. He left debts in California, and very soon had acquired others in New York and Boston.

Mr. Noah Brooks, who was intimate with Bret Harte in New York as well as in San Francisco, wrote, after his death: "I had not been long in the city before I found that Harte had already incurred many debts, chiefly for money borrowed. When I said to Bowles that I was anxious on Harte's account that a scandal should not come from this condition of things, Bowles said, with his good-natured cynicism, 'Well, it does seem to me that there ought to be enough rich men in New York to keep Harte a-going.'

"One rich man, a banker and broker, with an ambition to be considered a patron of the arts and literature, made much of the new literary lion, and from him Harte obtained a considerable sum, $500 perhaps, in small amounts varying from $5 to $50 at a time. One New Year's day Harte, in as much wrath as he was ever capable of showing, spread before me a note from our friend Dives in which the writer, who, by the way, was not reckoned a generous giver, reminded Harte that this was the season of the year when business men endeavored to enter a new era with a clean page in the ledger; and, in order to enable his friend H. to do that, he took the liberty of returning to him sundry I. O. U.'s which his friend H. had given him from time to time. 'Damn his impudence!' exclaimed the angry artist.

"'What are you going to do about it?' I asked, with some amusement. 'Going to do about it!' he answered with much emphasis on the first word. 'Going! I have made a new note for the full amount of these and have sent it to him with an intimation that I never allow pecuniary matters to trespass on the sacred domain of friendship.' Poor Dives was denied the satisfaction of giving away a bad debt."

"Once, while we were waiting on Broadway for a stage to take him down town, he said, as the lumbering vehicle hove in sight, 'Lend me a quarter; I haven't money enough to pay my stage fare.' Two or three weeks later, when I had forgotten the incident, we stood in the same place waiting for the same stage, and Harte, putting a quarter of a dollar in my hand, said: 'I owe you a quarter and there it is. You hear men say that I never pay my debts, but you can deny the slander.' While he lived in Morristown, N. J., it was said that he pocketed postage stamps sent to him for his autographs, and these applications were so numerous that with them he paid his butcher's bill. A bright lady to whom this story was told declared that the tale had been denied, 'on the authority of the butcher.' Nobody laughed more heartily at this sally than Harte did when it came to his ears."

"Never," says Mr. Howells, to the same effect, "was any man less a *poseur*. He made simply and helplessly known what he was at any and every moment, and he would join the witness very cheerfully in enjoying whatever was amusing in the disadvantage to himself." And then Mr. Howells relates the following incident: "In the course of events which in his case were so very human, it came about on a subsequent visit of his to Boston that an impatient creditor decided to right himself out of the proceeds of the lecture which was to be given, and had the law corporeally present at the house of the friend where Harte dined, and in the ante-room at the lecture-hall, and on the platform where the lecture was delivered with beautiful aplomb and untroubled charm. He was indeed the only one privy to the law's presence who was not the least affected by it, so that when his host of an earlier time ventured to suggest, 'Well, Harte, this is the old literary tradition: this is the Fleet business over again,' he joyously smote his thigh and cried out: 'Yes; that's it; we can see it all now,—the Fleet Prison with Goldsmith, Johnson, and all the rest of the old masters in a bunch!'"

It is highly probable that in his own mind, though perhaps half unconsciously, Bret Harte excused himself by the "old literary tradition" for his remissness in paying his debts. And for such a feeling on his part there would be, the present writer makes bold to say, some justification. It is a crude method of collecting from the community a small part of the compensation due to the author for the pleasure which he has conferred upon the world in general. The method, it must be admitted, is imperfectly just. The particular butcher or grocer to whom a particular poet is indebted may have a positive distaste for polite literature, and might naturally object to paying for books which other people read. Nevertheless there is an element of wild justice in the attitude of the poet. The world owes him a living, and if the world does not pay its debt, why, then, the debt may fairly be levied upon the world in such manner as is possible. This at least is to be said: the extravagance or improvidence of a man like Bret Harte stands upon a very different footing from that of an ordinary person. We should be ashamed not to show some consideration, even in money matters, for the soldier who has served his country in time of war; and the romancer who has contributed to the entertainment of the race is entitled to a similar indulgence.

Soon after Bret Harte's arrival in the East his friends urged him to give public lectures on the subject of life in California. The project was extremely distasteful to him, for he had an inborn horror of notoriety,—even of publicity; and this feeling, it may be added, is fully shared by the other members of his family. But his money difficulties were so great, and the prospect held out to him was so flattering that he finally consented. He prepared two lectures; the first, entitled *The Argonauts*, is now printed, with some changes, as the Introduction to the second volume of his collected works. This lecture was delivered at Albany, New York, on December 3, 1872, at Tremont Temple in Boston on the thirteenth of the same month, on December 16 at Steinway Hall in New York, and at Washington on January 7, 1873.

From Washington the lecturer wrote to his wife: "The audience was almost as quick and responsive as the Boston folk, and the committee-men, to my great delight, told me they made money by me.... I called on Charlton at the British Minister's, and had some talk with Sir Edward Thornton, which I have no doubt will materially affect the foreign policy of England. If I have said anything to promote a better feeling between the two countries I am willing he should get the credit of it. I took a carriage and went alone to the Capitol of my country. I had expected to be disappointed, but not agreeably. It is really a noble building,—worthy of the republic,—vast, magnificent, sometimes a little weak in detail, but in intent always high-toned, grand and large principled."

The same lecture was delivered at Pittsburgh, Pennsylvania, on January 9, 1873, and at Ottawa and Montreal in March of that year.

From Montreal he wrote to Mrs. Harte as follows:—

"In Ottawa I lectured twice, but the whole thing was a pecuniary failure. There was scarcely enough money to pay expenses, and of course nothing to pay me with. —— has no money of his own, and although he is blamable for not thoroughly examining the ground before bringing me to Ottawa, he was evidently so completely disappointed and miserable that I could not find it in my heart to upbraid him. So I simply told him that unless the Montreal receipts were sufficient to pay me for my lecture there, and a reasonable part of the money due me from Ottawa, I should throw the whole thing up. To-night will in all probability settle the question. Of course there are those who tell me privately that he is no manager, but I really do not see but that he has done all that he could, and that his only fault is in his sanguine and hopeful nature.

"I did not want to write of this disappointment to you so long as there was some prospect of better things. You can imagine, however, how I feel at this cruel loss of time and money—to say nothing of my health, which is still so poor. I had almost recovered from my cold, but in lecturing at Ottawa at the Skating Rink, a hideous, dismal damp barn, the only available place in town, I caught a fresh cold and have been coughing badly ever since. And you can well imagine that my business annoyances do not add greatly to my sleep or appetite.

"Apart from this, the people of Ottawa have received me very kindly. They have vied with each other in social attention, and if I had been like John Gilpin, 'on pleasure bent,' they would have made my visit a success. The Governor-General of Canada invited me to stay with him at his seat, Rideau Hall, and I spent Sunday and Monday there. Sir John and Lady Macdonald were also most polite and courteous.

"I shall telegraph you to-morrow if I intend to return at once. Don't let this worry you, but kiss the children for me and hope for the best. I would send you some money but *there isn't any to send*, and maybe I shall only bring back myself.—Your affectionate

"Frank.

"P. S.—26th.

"Dear Nan,—I did not send this yesterday, waiting to find the result of last night's lecture. It was a *fair* house and —— this morning paid me one hundred and fifty dollars, of which I send you the greater part. I lecture again to-night, with fair prospects, and he is to pay something on account of the Ottawa engagement besides the fee for that night. I will write again from Ogdensburg.—Always yours,

"Frank."

This lecture trip in the Spring of 1873 was followed in the Autumn by a similar trip in the West, with lectures at St. Louis, Topeka, Atchison, Lawrence, and Kansas City. From St. Louis he wrote to his wife as follows:—

"My dear Anna,—As my engagement is not until the 21st at Topeka, Kansas, I lie over here until to-morrow morning, in preference to spending the extra day in Kansas. I've accepted the invitation of Mr. Hodges, one of the managers of the lecture course, to stay at his house. He is a good fellow, with the usual American small family and experimental housekeeping, and the quiet and change from the hotel are very refreshing to me. They let me stay in my own room—which by the way is hung with the chintz of our 49th Street house—and don't bother me with company. So I was very good to-day and went to church. There was fine singing. The contralto sang your best sentences from the *Te Deum*, 'We believe that Thou shalt come,' &c., &c., to the same minor chant that I used to admire.

"The style of criticism that my lecture—or rather myself as a lecturer—has received, of which I send you a specimen, culminated this morning in an editorial in the 'Republic,' which I shall send you, but have not with me at present. I certainly never expected to be mainly criticised for being *what I am not*, a handsome fop; but this assertion is at the bottom of all the criticism. They may be right—I dare say they are—in asserting that I am no orator, have no special faculty for speaking, no fire, no dramatic earnestness or expression, but when they intimate that I am running on my good looks—save the mark! I confess I get hopelessly furious. You will be amused to hear that my gold studs have again become 'diamonds,' my worn-out shirts 'faultless linen,' my haggard face that of a 'Spanish-looking exquisite,' my habitual quiet and 'used-up' way, 'gentle and eloquent languor.' But you will be a little astonished to know that the hall I spoke in was worse than Springfield, and *notoriously* so—that the people seemed genuinely pleased, that the lecture inaugurated the 'Star' course very handsomely, and that it was the first of the first series of lectures ever delivered in St. Louis."

In a letter dated Lawrence, Kansas, October 23, 1873, he relates an interesting experience.

"My dear Anna,—I left Topeka—which sounds like a name Franky might have invented—early yesterday morning, but did not reach Atchison, only sixty miles distant, until seven o'clock at night—an hour before the lecture. The engine as usual had broken down, and left me at four o'clock fifteen miles from Atchison, on the edge of a bleak prairie with only one house in sight. But I got a saddle-horse—there was no vehicle to be had—and strapping my lecture and blanket to my back I gave my valise to a little yellow boy—who looked like a dirty terra-cotta figure—with orders to follow me on another horse, and so tore off towards Atchison. I got there in time; the boy reached there two hours after.

"I make no comment; you can imagine the half-sick, utterly disgusted man who glared at that audience over his desk that night, and d——d them inwardly in his heart. And yet it was a good audience, thoroughly refined and appreciative, and very glad to see me. I was very anxious about this lecture, for it was a venture of my own, and I had been told that Atchison was a rough place—energetic but coarse. I think I wrote you from St. Louis that I had found there were only three actual engagements in Kansas, and that my list which gave Kansas City twice was a mistake. So I decided to take Atchison. I made a hundred dollars by the lecture, and it is yours, for yourself, Nan, to buy 'Minxes' with, if you want, for it is over and above the amount Eliza and I footed up on my lecture list. I shall send it to you as soon as the bulk of the pressing claims are settled.

"Everything thus far has gone well; besides my lecture of to-night I have one more to close Kansas, and then I go on to St. Joseph. I've been greatly touched with the very honest and sincere liking which these Western people seem to have for me. They seem to have read everything I have written—and appear to appreciate the best. Think of a rough fellow in a bearskin coat and blue shirt repeating to me *Conception de Arguello*! Their strange good taste and refinement under that rough exterior—even their tact—are wonderful to me. They are 'Kentucks' and 'Dick Bullens' with twice the refinement and tenderness of their California brethren....

"I've seen but one that interested me—an old negro wench. She was talking and laughing outside my door the other evening, but her laugh was so sweet and unctuous and musical—so full of breadth and goodness that I went outside and talked to her while she was scrubbing the stones. She laughed as a canary bird sings—because she couldn't help it. It did me a world of good, for it was before the lecture, at twilight, when I am very blue and low-tuned. She had been a slave.

"I expected to have heard from you here. I've nothing from you or Eliza since last Friday, when I got yours of the 12th. I shall direct this to Eliza's care, as I do not even know where you are. Your affectionate

"Frank."

The same lecture was delivered in London, England, in January, 1879, and in June, 1880. Bret Harte's only other lecture had for its subject *American Humor*, and was delivered in Chicago on October 10, 1874, and in New York on January 26, 1875. The money return from these lectures was slight, and the fatigue and exposure of the long journeys in the West had, his relatives think, a permanently bad effect upon Bret Harte's health.

In the Autumn of 1875 we find him at Lenox, in the Berkshire Hills of Western Massachusetts. Lenox has its place in literature, for Hawthorne spent a year there, and in adjoining towns once lived O. W. Holmes, Catherine Sedgwick, Herman Melville, and G. P. R. James.

Gabriel Conroy, Bret Harte's only novel, and on the whole, it must be admitted, a failure, though containing many exquisite passages, was published in "Scribner's Magazine" in 1876.

The poems and stories which Bret Harte wrote during his seven years' residence in the Eastern part of the United States did not deal with the human life of that time and place. They either concerned the past, like *Thankful Blossom* and the Newport poems, or they harked back to California, like *Gabriel Conroy* and the stories published in the "Atlantic." The only exceptions are the short and pathetic tale called *The Office-Seeker*, and the opening chapter of that powerful story, *The Argonauts of North Liberty*. North Liberty is a small town in Connecticut, and the scene is quickly transferred from there to California; but Joan, the Connecticut woman, remains the chief figure in the story.

It is seldom that Bret Harte fails to show some sympathy with the men and women whom he describes, or at least some relenting consciousness that they could not help being what they were. But it is otherwise with Joan. She and her surroundings had a fascination for Bret Harte that was almost morbid. The man or woman whom we hate becomes an object of interest to us nearly as much as the person whom we love. An acute critic declares that Thackeray's wonderful insight into the characters and feelings of servants is due to the fact that he had almost a horror of them, and was abnormally sensitive to their criticisms,—the more felt for being unspoken. So Joan represents what Bret Harte hated more than anything else in the world, namely, a narrow, censorious, hypocritical, cold-blooded Puritanism. Her character is not that of a typical New England woman; its counterpart would much more easily be found among the men; but it is a perfectly consistent character, most accurately worked out. Joan combines a prim, provincial, horsehair-sofa respectability with a lawless and sensual nature,—an odd combination, and yet not an impossible one. She might, perhaps, be called the female of that species which Hawthorne immortalized under the name of Judge Pyncheon.

Joan is a puzzle to the reader, but so she was to those who knew her. Was she a conscious hypocrite, deliberately playing a false part in the world, or was she a monstrous egotist, one in whom the soul of truth had so died out that she thought herself justified in everything that she did, and committed the worst acts from what she supposed to be the most excusable motives? Her intimates did not know. One of the finest strokes in the story is the dawning of suspicion upon the mind of her second husband. "For with all his deep affection for his wife,

Richard Demorest unconsciously feared her. The strong man whose dominance over men and women alike had been his salient characteristic, had begun to feel an indefinable sense of some unrecognized quality in the woman he loved. He had once or twice detected it in a tone of her voice, in a remembered and perhaps even once idolized gesture, or in the accidental lapse of some bewildering word."

New England people at their best did not attract Bret Harte. That Miltonic conception of the universe upon which New England was built seemed to him simply ridiculous, and he did not appreciate the strength of character in which it resulted. Moreover, the crudity of New England offended his æsthetic taste as much as its theology offended his reason and his charity. North Liberty on a cold, stormy Sunday night in March is described with that *gusto*, with that minuteness of detail which could be shown only by one who loved it or by one who hated it.

And yet it would be unjust to say that Bret Harte had no conception of the better type of New England women. The schoolmistress in *The Idyl of Red Gulch*, one of his earliest and best stories, is as pure and noble a maiden, and as characteristic of the soil, as Hilda herself. The Reader will remember the description of Miss Mary as she appeared playing with her pupils in the woods. "The color came faintly into her pale cheeks.... Felinely fastidious and entrenched as she was in the purity of spotless skirts, collars and cuffs, she forgot all else, and ran like a crested quail at the head of her brood, until romping, laughing and panting, with a loosened braid of brown hair, a hat hanging by a knotted ribbon from her throat, she came ..." upon Sandy, the unheroic hero of the tale.

In the culminating scene of this story, the interview between Miss Mary and the mother of Sandy's illegitimate boy, when the teacher consents to take the child with her to her home in the East, although she is still under the shock of the discovery that Sandy is the boy's father,—in this scene the schoolmistress exhibits true New England restraint, and a beautiful absence of heroics. It was just at sunset. "The last red beam crept higher, suffused Miss Mary's eyes with something of its glory, nickered and faded and went out. The sun had set in Red Gulch. In the twilight and silence Miss Mary's voice sounded pleasantly, 'I will take the boy. Send him to me to-night.'"

One can hardly help speculating about Bret Harte's personal taste and preferences in regard to women. Cressy and the Rose of Tuolumne were both blondes; and yet on the whole he certainly preferred brunettes. Even his blue-eyed girls usually have black hair. The Treasure of the Redwoods disclosed from the recesses of her sunbonnet "a pale blue eye and a thin black arch of eyebrow." One associates a contralto voice with a brunette, and Bret Harte's heroines, so far as the subject is mentioned, have contralto voices. Not one is spoken of as having a soprano voice. Even the slight and blue-eyed Tinka Gallinger "sang in a youthful, rather nasal contralto." Bret Harte's wife had a contralto voice and was a good singer.

As to eyes, he seems to have preferred them gray or brown, a "tender gray" and a "reddish brown." Ailsa Callender's hair was "dark with a burnished copper tint at its roots, and her eyes had the same burnished metallic lustre in their brown pupils." Mrs. MacGlowrie was "a fair-faced woman with eyes the color of pale sherry."

A small foot with an arched instep was a *sine qua non* with Bret Harte, and he speaks particularly of the small, well-shod foot of the Southwestern girl. He believed in breeding, and all his heroines were well-bred,—not well-bred in the conventional sense, but in the sense of coming from sound, courageous, self-respecting, self-improving stock. Within these limits his range of heroines is exceedingly wide, including some that are often excluded from that category. He is rather partial to widows, for example, and always looks upon their innocent gayeties with an indulgent eye. Can a woman be a widow and untidy in her dress, and still retain her preëminence as heroine? Yes, Bret Harte's genius is equal even to that. "Mrs. MacGlowrie was looking wearily over some accounts on the desk before her, and absently putting back some tumbled sheaves from the shock of her heavy hair. For the widow had a certain indolent Southern negligence, which in a less pretty woman would have been untidiness, and a characteristic hook-and-eye-less freedom of attire, which on less graceful limbs would have been slovenly. One sleeve-cuff was unbuttoned, but it showed the vein of her delicate wrist; the neck of her dress had lost a hook, but the glimpse of a bit of edging round the white throat made amends. Of all which, however, it should be said that the widow, in her limp abstraction, was really unconscious."

I THOUGHT YOU WERE THAT HORSE-THIEF
From "Lanty Foster's Mistake"
Denman Fink, del.

Red-haired women have been so popular in fiction during recent years that it was perhaps no great feat for Bret Harte in the *Buckeye Hollow Inheritance* to make a heroine out of a red-haired girl, and a bad-tempered one too; but what other romancer has ever dared to represent a young and lovely woman as "hard of hearing"! There can be no question that The Youngest Miss Piper was not quite normal in this respect, although, for purposes of coquetry and sarcasm no doubt, she magnified the defect. In her memorable interview with the clever young grocery clerk (whom she afterward married) she begins by failing to hear distinctly the title of the book which he was reading when she entered the store; and we have this picture: "Miss Delaware, leaning sideways and curling her little fingers around her pink ear: 'Did you say the first principles of geology or politeness? You know I am so deaf; but of course it couldn't be that.'"

The one kind of woman that did not attract Bret Harte as a subject for literature was the conventional woman of the world. He could draw her fairly well, for we have Amy Forester in *A Night on the Divide*, Jessie Mayfield in *Jeff Briggs's Love Story*, Grace Nevil in *A Mæcenas of the Pacific Slope*, Mrs. Ashwood in *A First Family of Tasajara*, and Mrs. Horncastle in *Three Partners*. But these women do not bear the stamp of Bret Harte's genius.

His Army and Navy girls are better, because they are redeemed from commonplaceness by their patriotism. Miss Portfire in *The Princess Bob and her Friends*, and Julia Cantire in *Dick Boyle's Business Card*, represent those American families, more numerous than might be supposed, in which it is almost an hereditary custom for the men to serve in the Army or Navy, and for the women to become the wives and mothers of soldiers and sailors. In such families patriotism is a constant inspiration, to a degree seldom felt except by those who represent their country at home or abroad.

Bret Harte was patriotic, as many of his poems and stories attest, and his long residence in England did not lessen his Americanism. "Apostates" was his name for those American girls who marry titled foreigners, and he often speaks of the susceptibility of American women to considerations of rank and position. In *A Rose of Glenbogie*, after describing the male guests at a Scotch country house, he continues: "There were the usual half-dozen smartly-frocked women who, far from being the females of the foregoing species, were quite indistinctive, with the single exception of an American wife, who was infinitely more Scotch than her Scotch husband." And in *The Heir of the McHulishes* the American Consul is represented as being less chagrined by the bumptiousness of his male compatriots than by "the snobbishness and almost servile adaptability of the women. Or was it possible that it was only a weakness of the sex which no Republican nativity or education could eliminate?"

CHAPTER XV

BRET HARTE AT CREFELD

The sums that Bret Harte received for his stories and lectures did not suffice to free him from debt, and he suffered much anxiety and distress from present difficulties, with no brighter prospects ahead. An additional misfortune was the failure of a new paper called "The Capital," which had been started in Washington by John J. Piatt.

There is an allusion to this in a letter written by Bret Harte to his wife from Washington. "Thank you, dear Nan, for your kind, hopeful letter. I have been very sick, very much disappointed; but I'm better now, and am only waiting for some money to return. I should have, for the work that I have done, more than would help us out of our difficulties. But it doesn't come, and even the money I've expected from the 'Capital' for my story is seized by its creditors. That hope and the expectations I had from the paper and Piatt in the future amount to nothing. I have found that it is bankrupt.

"Can you wonder, Nan, that I have kept this from you? You have so hard a time of it there, and I cannot bear to have you worried if there is the least hope of a change in my affairs as they look, day by day. Piatt has been gone nearly a month, was expected to return every day, and only yesterday did I know positively of his inability to fulfil his promises. —— came here three days ago, and in a very few moments I learned from him that I need expect nothing for the particular service I had done him. I've been vilified and abused in the papers for having received compensation for my services, when really and truly I have only received less than I should have got from any magazine or newspaper for my story. I sent you the fifty dollars by Mr. D——, because I knew you would be in immediate need, and there is no telegraph transfer office on Long Island. It was the only fifty I have made since I've been here.

"I am waiting to hear from Osgood regarding an advance on that wretched story. He writes me he does not quite like it. I shall probably hear from him to-night. When the money comes I shall come with it. God bless you and keep you and the children safe for the sake of

"Frank."

Bret Harte's friends, however, were aware of his situation, and they procured for him an appointment by President Hayes as United States Commercial Agent at Crefeld in Prussia. The late Charles A. Dana was especially active in this behalf. Bret Harte, much as he dreaded the sojourn in a strange country, gladly accepted the appointment, and leaving his family for the present at Sea Cliff, Long Island, he sailed for England in June, 1878, little thinking that he was never to return.

Crefeld is near the river Rhine, about thirty miles north of Cologne. Its chief industry is the manufacture of silks and velvets, in respect to which it is the leading city in Germany, and is surpassed by no other place in Europe except Lyons. This industry was introduced in Crefeld by Protestant refugees who fled thither from Cologne in the seventeenth century in order to obtain the protection of the Prince of Orange. A small suburb of Philadelphia was settled mainly by emigrants from Crefeld, and bears the same name.

The Prussian Crefeld is a clean, spacious place, with wide streets, substantial houses, and all the appearance of a Dutch town. At this time it contained about seventy-five thousand inhabitants. Bret Harte arrived at Crefeld on the morning of July 17, 1878, after a sleepless journey of twelve hours from Paris, and on the same day he wrote to his wife a very homesick letter.

"I have audaciously travelled alone nearly four hundred miles through an utterly foreign country on one or two little French and German phrases, and a very small stock of assurance, and have delivered my letters to my predecessor, and shall take possession of the Consulate to-morrow. Mr. ——, the present incumbent, appears to me—I do not know how I shall modify my impression hereafter—as a very narrow, mean, ill-bred, and not over-bright Puritanical German. It was my intention to appoint him my vice-Consul—an act of courtesy suggested both by my own sense of right and Mr. Leonard's advice, but he does not seem to deserve it, and has even received my suggestion of it with the suspicion of a mean nature. But at present I fear I may have to do it, for I know no one else here. I am to all appearance utterly friendless; I have not received the first act of kindness or courtesy from any one, and I suppose this man sees it. I shall go to Bavaria to-morrow to see the Consul there, who held this place as one of his dependencies, and try to make matters straight."

This letter shows that the craving for sympathy and companionship, which is associated with artistic natures, was intensely felt by Bret Harte, more so, perhaps, than would have been expected in a man of his self-reliant character. His despondent tone is almost child-like. The letter goes on: "It's been up-hill work ever since I left New York, but I shall try to see it through, please God! I don't allow myself to think over it at all, or I should go crazy. I shut my eyes to it, and in doing so perhaps I shut out what is often so pleasant to a traveller's first impressions; but thus far London has only seemed to me a sluggish nightmare through which I have waked, and Paris a confused sort of hysterical experience. I had hoped for a little kindness and rest here.... At least, Nan, be sure I've written now the worst; I think things must be better soon. I shall, please God, make some friends in good time, and will try and be patient. But I shall not think of sending for you until I see clearly that I can stay myself. If the worst comes to the worst I shall try to stand it for a year, and save enough to come home and begin anew there. But I could not stand it to see you break your heart here through disappointment, as I mayhap may do."

The tone of this letter is so exaggerated that it might seem as if Bret Harte had been a little theatrical and insincere,—that he had endeavored to create an impression which was partly false. But such a conjecture would be erroneous, for under the same date, with the addition of the word "midnight," we find him writing a second letter to correct the effect of the first, as follows:—

"My dear Nan,—I wrote and mailed you a letter this afternoon that I fear was rather disconsolate, so I sit down to-night to send another, which I hope will take a little of the blues out of the first. Since I wrote I have had some further conversation with my predecessor, Mr. ———, and I think I can manage matters with him. He has hauled in his horns considerably since I told him that the position I offered him—so far as the honor of it went—was better than the one he held. For the one thing pleasant about my office is that the dignity of it has been raised on my account. It was only a dependence—a Consular Agency—before it was offered to me.

"I feel a little more hopeful, too, for I have been taken out to a 'fest'—or a festival—of one of the vintners, and one or two of the people were a little kind. I forced myself to go; these German festivals are distasteful to me, and I did not care to show my ignorance of their language quite so prominently, but I thought it was the proper thing for me to do. It was a very queer sight. About five hundred people were in an artificial garden beside an artificial lake, looking at artificial fireworks, and yet as thoroughly enjoying it as if they were children. Of course there were beer and wine. Here as in Paris everybody drinks, and all the time, and nobody gets drunk. Beer, beer, beer; and meals, meals, meals. Everywhere the body is worshipped. Beside them we are but unsubstantial spirits. I write this in my hotel, having had to pass through a mysterious gate and so into a side courtyard and up a pair of labyrinthine stairs, to my dim 'Zimmer' or chamber. The whole scene, as I returned to-night, looked as it does on the stage,—the lantern over the iron gate, the inn strutting out into the street with a sidewalk not a foot wide. I know now from my own observation, both here and in Paris and London, where the scene-painters at the theatres get their subjects. Those impossible houses—those unreal silent streets all exist in Europe."

On one of those first, melancholy days at Crefeld, the new Consul, walking listlessly along the main street of the town, happened to throw a passing glance at the window of a bookseller's shop, and there he saw on the back of a neat little volume the familiar words "Bret Harte." It was a German translation of his stories, and it is easy to imagine how the sight refreshed and comforted the homesick exile. After that, he felt that to some extent, at least, he was living among friends. Translations of Bret Harte's poems and stories had appeared before this in German magazines, and later his stories were reproduced in Germany, in book form, as fast as they were published in England. In fact, his books have been printed in every language of Europe, and translations of his stories have appeared in the "Revue des Deux Mondes," in the "Moscow Gazette," and in periodicals of Italy, Spain, Portugal, Denmark and Sweden. In 1878 a translation of six of Bret Harte's tales was published in the Servian language, with an enthusiastic preface in German, by the translator, Ivan B. Popovitch.

The impression that Bret Harte received from Europe,—and it is the one that every uncontaminated American must receive,—may be gathered from a letter written by him to his younger son, then a small boy: "We drove out the other day through a lovely road, bordered with fine poplar trees, and more like a garden walk than a country road, to the Rhine, which is but two miles and a half from this place. The road had been built by Napoleon the First when he was victorious everywhere, and went straight on through everybody's property, and even over their dead bones. Suddenly to the right we saw the ruins of an old castle, vine-clad and crumbling, exactly like a scene on the stage. It was all very wonderful. But Papa thought, after all, he was glad his boys live in a country that is as yet quite *pure*, and *sweet* and *good*; not in one where every field seems to cry out with the remembrance of bloodshed and wrong, and where so many people have lived and suffered, that to-night, under this clear moon, their very ghosts seemed to throng the road and dispute our right of way. Be thankful, my dear boy, that you are an American. Papa was never so fond of his country before, as in this land that has been so great, so powerful, and so very, very hard and wicked."

Bret Harte, though disclaiming any knowledge of music, had a real appreciation of it, and wrote as follows to his wife who was a connoisseur: "I have been several times to the opera at Dusseldorf, and I have been hesitating whether I should slowly prepare you for a great shock or tell you at once that musical Germany is a humbug. My first operatic experience was 'Tannhäuser.' I can see your superior smile, Anna, at this; and I know how you will take my criticism of Wagner, so I don't mind saying plainly, that it was the most diabolically hideous and stupidly monotonous performance I ever heard. I shall say nothing about the orchestral harmonies, for there wasn't anything going on of that kind, unless you call something that seemed like a boiler factory at work in the next street, and the wind whistling through the rigging of a channel steamer, harmony.... But what I wanted to say was that even my poor uneducated ear detected bad instrumentation and worse singing in the choruses. I confided this much to a friend, and he said very frankly that I was probably right, that the best musicians and choruses went to America....

"Then I was awfully disappointed in 'Faust,' or, as it is known here in the playbills, 'Marguerite.' You know how I love that delicious idyl of Gounod's, and I was in my seat that night long before the curtain went up. Before the first act was over I felt like leaving, and yet I was glad I stayed. For although the chorus of villagers was frightful, and Faust and Mephistopheles spouted and declaimed blank verse at each other—whole pages of Goethe, yet the acting was superb. I have never seen such a Marguerite. But think of my coming to Germany to hear opera badly sung, and magnificently acted!"

Having put the affairs of the Consular office upon a proper footing, Bret Harte returned to England about the middle of August for a short vacation, which proved, however, to be a rather long one. His particular object was a visit to James Anthony Froude at his house in Devonshire. Bret Harte had a great admiration for Froude's writings; and when the two men met they formed a friendship which was severed only by death.

From Froude's home Bret Harte wrote to his wife as follows: "Imagine, if you can, something between 'Locksley Hall,' and the High Walled Garden, where Maud used to walk, and you have some idea of this graceful English home. I look from my windows down upon exquisite lawns and terraces, all sloping toward the sea wall, and then down upon the blue sea below.... I walk out in the long, high garden, past walls hanging with netted peaches and apricots, past terraces looking over the ruins of an old feudal castle, and I can scarcely believe I am not reading an English novel or that I am not myself a wandering ghost. To heighten the absurdity, when I return to my room I am confronted by the inscription on the door, 'Lord Devon' (for this is the property of the Earl of Devon, and I occupy his favourite room), and I seem to have died and to be resting under a gilded mausoleum that lies even more than the average tombstone does. Froude is a connection of the Earl's, and has hired the house for the Summer.

"But Froude—dear old noble fellow—is splendid. I love him more than I ever did in America. He is great, broad, manly,—democratic in the best sense of the word, scorning all sycophancy and meanness, accepting all that is around him, yet more proud of his literary profession than of his kinship with these people whom he quietly controls. There are only a few literary men like him here, but they are kings. So far I've avoided seeing any company here; but Froude and I walk and walk, and talk and talk. They let me do as I want, and I have not been well enough yet to do aught but lounge. The doctor is coming to see me to-day, and if I am no better I shall return in a day or two to London, and then to Crefeld."

Bret Harte's health seems at all times to have been easily upset, and he was particularly subject to colds and sore throats. This letter was written in August, but it was the first week in November before he was on his way back to Crefeld. While in London he had arranged for a lecture tour in England during the next January (1879), and in that month a volume of his stories and poems was published in England with the following Introduction by the author:—

"In offering this collection of sketches to the English public, the author is conscious of attaching an importance to them that may not be shared by the general reader, but which he, as an American writer on English soil, cannot fail to feel very sensibly. The collection is made by himself, the letter-press revised by his own hand, and he feels for the first time that these fugitive children of his brain are no longer friendless in a strange land, entrusted to the care of a foster-mother, however discreet, but are his own creations, for whose presentation to the public in this fashion he is alone responsible. Three or four having been born upon English soil may claim the rights of citizenship, but the others he must leave to prove their identity with English literature on their own merits."

The lecture on the Argonauts, delivered the first time at the Crystal Palace, was very well received both by the hearers and the press; but financially it was a disappointment. Bret Harte was in England three weeks, lectured five times, and made only two hundred dollars over and above his expenses.

A second lecture tour, however, carried out in March of the same year, was successful in every way. The audiences were enthusiastic, and the payment was liberal.

It was during this visit to England that Bret Harte became involved in a characteristic tangle. He had received the compliment of being asked to respond for Literature at the Royal Academy banquet in 1879, and, with his constitutional unwillingness to give a point-blank refusal, had promised or half-promised to be present. Meanwhile, he had returned to Crefeld, and the prospect of speaking at the dinner loomed more and more horrific in his imagination, while the uncertainty in which he left the matter was a source of vexation in London. Letters and telegrams from his friends remained unanswered, until finally, Sir Frederic Leighton, the President of the Academy, sent him a message, the reply to which was prepaid, saying, "In despair; cannot do without you. Please telegraph at once if quite impossible."

This at last drew from Bret Harte a telegram stating that the pressure of official business would render it impossible for him to leave Crefeld. But the matter was not quite ended yet. In a day or two Bret Harte received a letter from Froude, good-naturedly reminding him that a note as well as a telegram was due to Sir Frederic Leighton. "The President of the Royal Academy," he wrote, "is a sacred person with the state and honors of a sovereign on these occasions." And after some further delay Bret Harte did write to Sir Frederic, and received in reply the following polite but possibly somewhat ironical note: "Dear Mr. Bret Harte,—It was most kind of you to write to me after your telegram. I fully understand the impossibility of your leaving your post, and sincerely regret my loss."

A year later, however, in 1880, Bret Harte answered the toast to Literature at the Royal Academy dinner, and his brief speech on that occasion is included in the volume of lectures by him recently published.

In October of this year, 1879, Bret Harte wrote to Washington stating that his health had suffered at Crefeld, and requesting leave of absence for sixty days in order that he might follow the advice of his physician, and seek a more favorable climate. He also asked for a reply by telegraph; and in the same letter he made application for a better Consular position, mentioning, as one reason for the exchange, that the business of the Agency at Crefeld had greatly increased during his tenure. His request for leave of absence was immediately granted, and in November he wrote to the State Department acknowledging the receipt of its telegram and letter, but adding, "Neither my affairs nor my health have enabled me yet to avail myself of the courtesy extended to me by the Department. When I shall be able to do so, I shall, agreeably to your instructions, promptly inform you." He took this leave of absence in the following January and April.

So far as can be judged from his communications to the State Department, Bret Harte discharged the duties of the Agency in a very business-like manner. For one thing, he reduced the time consumed in passing upon invoices of goods intended for exportation to the United States from twenty-four hours to three hours, greatly to the convenience of the Crefeld manufacturers. The increase in the value of the silks and velvets shipped to this country during Bret Harte's term amounted to about two hundred thousand dollars quarterly; but perhaps the demands of trade had something to do with this.

Two of the reports to the State Department from our Agent at Crefeld deserve to be rescued from their official oblivion. The first is dated, October 8, 1879, and it accompanies a table showing the rainfall, snowfall, and thunderstorms occurring in the district from July 1, 1878, to June 30, 1879. The Agent states:—

"The table is compiled from the observations of a competent local meteorologist. In mitigation of the fact that it has rained in this district in the ratio of every other day in the year, it may be stated that the general gloom has been diversified and monotony relieved by twenty-nine thunderstorms and one earthquake."

The second communication, dated October 10, 1879, is in response to an official inquiry. "In reference to the Department Circular dated August 27, 1879, I have the honor to report that upon careful inquiry of the local authorities of this district I find that there is not now and never has been any avowed Mormon emigration from Crefeld, nor any emigration of people likely to become converts to that faith. Its name as well as its tenets are unknown to the inhabitants, and only to officials through the Department Circular.

"The artisans and peasants of this district—that class from which the Mormon ranks are supposed to be recruited—are hard-working, thrifty, and home-loving. They are averse to emigration for any purpose, and as Catholics to any new revealed religion. A prolific household with *one* wife seems to exclude any polygamous instinct in the manly breast, while the woman, who works equally with her husband, evinces no desire to share any division of the affections or the profits. The like may be predicated of the manufacturers, with the added suggestion that a duty of 60 per cent *ad valorem* by engaging the fullest powers of the intellect in its evasion, leaves little room for the play of the lower passions. In these circumstances I did not find it necessary to report to the Legation at Berlin."

The literary product of Bret Harte's two years at Crefeld was *A Legend of Sammtstadt*, in which there is a pleasant blending of the romantic and the humorous, *The Indiscretion of Elsbeth*, the *Views from a German Spion*, and *Unser Karl. Unser Karl*, however, was not written, or at least was not published, until several years later.

Perhaps the most valuable impression which Bret Harte carried away from Crefeld was that of the German children. Children always interested him, and in Prussia he found a new variety, which he described in the *Views from a German Spion*: "The picturesqueness of Spanish and Italian childhood has a faint suspicion of the pantomime and the conscious attitudinizing of the Latin races. German children are not exuberant or volatile; they are serious,—a seriousness, however, not to be confounded with the grave reflectiveness of age, but only the abstract wonderment of childhood. These little creatures I meet upon the street—whether in quaint wooden shoes and short woollen petticoats, or neatly booted and furred, with school knapsacks jauntily borne on little square shoulders—all carry likewise in their round chubby faces their profound wonderment and astonishment at the big busy world into which they have so lately strayed. If I stop to speak with this little maid, who scarcely reaches to the top-boots of yonder cavalry officer, there is less of bashful self-consciousness in her sweet little face than of grave wonder at the foreign accent and strange ways of this new figure obtruded upon her limited horizon. She answers honestly, frankly, prettily, but gravely. There is a remote possibility that I might bite; and with this suspicion plainly indicated in her round blue eyes, she quietly slips her little red hand from mine, and moves solemnly away."

The Continental practice of making the dog a beast of burden shocked Bret Harte, as it must shock any lover of the animal. "Perhaps it is because I have the barbarian's fondness for dogs, and for their lawless, gentle, loving uselessness that I rebel against this unnatural servitude. It seems as monstrous as if a child were put between the shafts and made to carry burdens; and I have come to regard those men and women, who in the weakest, perfunctory way affect to aid the poor brute by laying idle hands on the barrow behind, as I would unnatural parents.... I fancy the dog seems to feel the monstrosity of the performance, and, in sheer shame for his master, forgivingly tries to assume it is *play*; and I have seen a little collie running along, barking and endeavoring to leap and gambol in the shafts, before a load that any one out of this locality would have thought the direst cruelty. Nor do the older or more powerful dogs seem to become accustomed to it."

And then comes an example of that extraordinary keenness of observation with which Bret Harte was gifted:—"I have said that the dog was generally sincere in his efforts. I recall but one instance to the contrary. I remember a young collie who first attracted my attention by his persistent barking. Whether he did this, as the plough-boy whistled, 'for want of thought,' or whether it was a running protest against his occupation, I could not determine, until one day I noticed that, in barking, he slightly threw up his neck and shoulders, and that the two-wheeled barrow-like vehicle behind him, having its weight evenly poised on the wheels by the trucks in the hands of its driver, enabled him by this movement to cunningly throw the centre of gravity and the greater weight on the man,—a fact which the less sagacious brute never discerned.... I cannot help thinking that the people who have lost this gentle, sympathetic, characteristic figure from their domestic life and surroundings have not acquired an equal gain through his harsh labors."

Of his Consular experiences at Crefeld the following is the only one which found its way into literature: "The Consul's chief duty was to uphold the flag of his own country by the examination and certification of divers invoices sent to his office by the manufacturers. But, oddly enough, these messengers were chiefly women,—not clerks, but ordinary household servants, and on busy days the Consulate might have been mistaken for a female registry office, so filled and possessed it was by waiting Mädchen. Here it was that Gretchen, Liebchen, and Clarchen, in the cleanest of gowns, and stoutly but smartly shod, brought their invoices in a piece of clean paper, or folded in a blue handkerchief, and laid them, with fingers more or less worn and stubby from hard service, before the Consul for his signature. Once, in the case of a very young Mädchen, that signature was blotted by the sweep of a flaxen braid upon it as the child turned to go; but generally there was a grave, serious business instinct and sense of responsibility in these girls of ordinary peasant origin, which, equally with their sisters of France, were unknown to the English or American woman of any class."

Bret Harte remained nearly two years at Crefeld, but his wife did not join him there, and, so far as the world knows, they never met again. In May, 1880, he was transferred to the much more lucrative and more desirable Consulship at Glasgow. It was one of the last cases in which government bestowed public office as a reward for literary excellence,—a custom so hallowed by age and association that every lover of literature will look back upon it with fond regret.

CHAPTER XVI

BRET HARTE AT GLASGOW

After a month in London, Bret Harte took possession of the Consulate at Glasgow in July, 1880, and remained there five years. His annual salary was three thousand dollars.

In September he wrote to a friend: "As I am trying to get up a good reputation here, I stay at my post pretty regularly, occasionally making a cheap excursion. This is a country for them. The other day I went to Staffa. It was really the only 'sight' in Europe that quite filled all my expectations. But alas! that magnificent, cathedral-like cave was presently filled with a howling party of sandwich-eating tourists, splashing in the water and climbing up the rocks. One should only go there alone, or with some sympathetic spirit."

How far the Consul's good intentions were fulfilled it is difficult to say. London attracted Bret Harte as it attracts everybody of Anglo-Saxon descent. That vast and sombre metropolis may weary the body and vex the soul of the visitor, but, after all, it remains the headquarters of the English-speaking race, and the American, as well as the Canadian or the Australian, returns to it again and again with a vague longing, never satisfied, but never lost.

Another reason for the absenteeism of the Consul was that he lectured now and again in different parts of England, and that he paid frequent visits to country houses. Mr. Pemberton quotes a letter from him which contains an amusing illustration of the English boy's sporting spirit:—

"My Dear Pemberton,—Don't be alarmed if you should hear of my nearly having blown the top of my head off. Last Monday I had my face badly cut by the recoil of an overloaded gun. I do not know yet beneath these bandages whether I shall be permanently marked. At present I am invisible, and have tried to keep the accident a secret. When the surgeon was stitching me together, the son of the house, a boy of twelve, came timidly to the door of my room. 'Tell Mr. Bret Harte it's all right,' he said, *he killed the hare.*'"

However, the reports made by the Consul to the State Department seem to indicate more attention to his duties than has commonly been credited to him. One of these communications, dated May 4, 1882, gives a detailed account of the peculiar Glasgow custom according to which the several flats or floors of tenement houses are owned by separate persons, usually the occupants, each owner of a floor being a joint proprietor, with the other floor-owners, of the land on which the building stands, of the roof, the staircase and the walls. Another letter states, in answer to a question by the Department, that there were at the time probably not more than six American citizens resident in Glasgow, and that only one such was known to the Consul or to his predecessor. This, in an English-speaking city of six hundred thousand people, seems extraordinary.

The most interesting of Bret Harte's communications to the State Department is perhaps the following:—

"On a recent visit to the Island of Iona, within this Consular District, I found in the consecrated ground of the ruined Cathedral the graves of nineteen American seamen who had perished in the wreck of the 'Guy Mannering' on the evening of the 31st of December, 1865, on the north coast of the island. The place where they are interred is marked by two rows of low granite pediments at the head and feet of the dead, supporting, and connected by, an iron chain which encloses the whole space. This was done by the order and at the expense of the Lord of the Manor, the present Duke of Argyle.

. . . .

"I venture to make these facts known to the Department, satisfied that such recognition of the thoughtful courtesy of the Duke of Argyle as would seem most fit and appropriate to the Department will be made, and that possibly a record of the names of the seamen will be placed upon some durable memorial erected upon the spot.

. . . .

"In conclusion I beg to state that should the Department deem any expenditure by the Government for this purpose inexpedient, I am willing, with the permission of the Department, to endeavor to procure by private subscription a sufficient fund for the outlay."

It is a pleasure to record that these suggestions were adopted by the State Department. A letter of acknowledgment and thanks was sent to the Duke of Argyle, and a shaft or obelisk with the names of the seamen inscribed thereon was erected by the United States Government in the latter part of the year 1882.

Bret Harte's Consular experiences with seamen recall those of Hawthorne at Liverpool, and he appears to have acted with an equal sense of humanity. In one case he insisted that two sailors who had been convicted of theft should nevertheless receive the three months' pay due them, without which they would have been penniless on their discharge from prison. He took the ground that conviction of this offence was not equivalent to desertion, and therefore that the wages were not forfeited. He adds: "The case did not appear to call for any leniency on the part of the Government toward the ship-owners. The record of the ship's voyage was one of unseaworthiness, brutality and inefficiency."

In another case, the Consul supplied from his own pocket the wants of a shipwrecked American sailor, and procured for him a passage home, there being no government fund available for the purpose.

A glimpse of his Consular functions is given in the opening paragraph of *Young Robin Gray:*—

"The good American bark Skyscraper was swinging at her moorings in the Clyde, off Bannock, ready for sea. But that good American bark—although owned in Baltimore—had not a plank of American timber in her hulk, nor a native American in her crew, and even her nautical 'goodness' had been called in serious question by divers of that crew during her voyage, and answered more or less inconclusively with belaying-pins, marlin-spikes, and ropes' ends at the hands of an Irish-American Captain and a Dutch and Danish Mate. So much so, that the mysterious powers of the American Consul at St. Kentigern had been evoked to punish mutiny on the one hand, and battery and starvation on the other; both equally attested by manifestly false witness and subornation on each side. In the exercise of his functions, the Consul had opened and shut some jail doors, and otherwise effected the usual sullen and deceitful compromise, and his flag was now flying, on a final visit, from the stern sheets of a smart boat alongside. It was with a feeling of relief at the end of the interview that he at last lifted his head above an atmosphere of perjury and bilge-water and came on deck."

When the Consul reached the deck he saw, for the first time, Ailsa Callender, one of the most charming of his heroines, and as characteristically Scotch as M'liss was characteristically Western. The Reader will not be sorry to recall the impression that Ailsa Callender subsequently made upon the young American, Robert Gray:—

"'She took me to task for not laying up the yacht on Sunday that the men could go to "Kirk," and for swearing at a bargeman who ran across our bows. It's their perfect simplicity and sincerity in all this that gets me! You'd have thought that the old man was my guardian, and the daughter my aunt.' After a pause he uttered a reminiscent laugh. 'She thought we ate and drank too much on the yacht, and wondered what we could find to do all day. All this, you know, in the gentlest, caressing sort of voice, as if she was really concerned, like one's own sister. Well, not exactly like mine,'—he interrupted himself grimly,—'but, hang it all, you know what I mean. You know that our girls over there haven't got *that* trick of voice. Too much self-assertion, I reckon; things made too easy for them by us men. Habit of race, I dare say.' He laughed a little. 'Why, I mislaid my glove when I was coming away, and it was as good as a play to hear her commiserating and sympathizing and hunting for it as if it were a lost baby.'

"'But you've seen Scotch girls before this,' said the Consul. 'There were Lady Glairn's daughters whom you took on a cruise.'

"'Yes, but the swell Scotch all imitate the English, as everybody else does, for the matter of that, our girls included; and they're all alike.'"

The shrewd, solid, genial, even religious Sir James MacFen, in *The Heir of the McHulishes*, and the porter in *A Rose of Glenbogie*, are native to the soil, and have no counterparts in America, east or west.

These three stories dealing with Scotch scenes and people prove the falsity of the assertion sometimes made that Bret Harte could write only about California:—he could have gone on writing about Scotland all his life, had he continued to live there, and the tales would have been as readable, if not so nearly unique, as those which deal with California. He liked the Scotch people, and was received by them with great kindness and hospitality. "On my birthday," he wrote, "which became quite accidentally known to a few friends in the hotel, my table was covered with bouquets of flowers and little remembrances from cigar-cases to lockets."

At this period Bret Harte made the acquaintance of William Black and Walter Besant, and with the former he became very intimate. In the life of William Black by his friend, Sir Wemyss Reid, there are many references to Bret Harte. The two story-writers first met as guests of Sir George Wombwell, who had invited them and a few others, including Mr. Shepard, the American vice-Consul at Bradford, to make a driving trip to the ruined abbeys of Eastern Yorkshire. The party dined together at the Yorkshire Club in York, which was the meeting point. "I remember few more lively evenings than that," writes Sir Wemyss Reid. "Black and Bret Harte, whose acquaintance he had just made, vied with each other in the good stories they told and the repartees they exchanged."

Shortly afterward Black wrote to Reid, "Bret Harte went down to us at Brighton, and if we didn't amuse him he certainly amused us. He is coming again next week."

Later he wrote again from the Reform Club in London, to Reid: "In a few weeks' time don't be surprised if Bret Harte and I come and look in upon you—that is, if he is not compelled for mere shame's sake to go to his Consular duties (! ! !) at once. He is the most extraordinary globule of mercury—comet—aerolite gone drunk—flash of lightning doing Catherine wheels—I ever had any experience of. Nobody knows where he is, and the day before yesterday I discovered here a pile of letters that had been slowly accumulating for him since February, 1879. It seems he never reported himself to the all-seeing Escott , and never asked for letters when he got his month's honorary membership last year. People are now sending letters to him from America addressed to me at Brighton! But he is a mystery and the cause of mystifications."

In the following July there is another mention of Bret Harte in one of Black's letters. "Bret Harte was to have been back from Paris last night, but he is a wandering comet. The only place he is sure not to be found in is the Glasgow Consulate."

But the Consul's wanderings were not so frequent as Mr. Black supposed. Bret Harte had almost a monomania for not answering letters; and his absence from Glasgow could not safely be inferred from his failure to acknowledge communications addressed to him there. A rumor as to the Consul's prolonged desertion of his post had reached the State Department at Washington, and in November, 1882, the Department wrote to him requesting a report on the subject. He replied that he had not been away from Glasgow beyond the usual limit of ten days, at any one time, except on holidays and Sundays. This report appears to have been accepted as satisfactory, and the incident was closed.

At one time Bret Harte was to have dined with Sir Wemyss Reid and William Black at the Reform Club; "but in his place," says the biographer, "came a telegram in which I was invited to ask Black and Lockyer, who had just spent a few days with him in Scotland, their opinion of the game of poker—evidence that they had not spent all their time in Scotland in viewing scenery."

The damp climate of Glasgow did not agree with Bret Harte, and so early in his residence there as July, 1881, he wrote to the State Department requesting leave of absence for three months, with permission to visit the United States, on the ground that the state of his health was such that he might require a complete change of scene and air. The request was granted, but the Consul did not return to his native country.

In March, 1885, Bret Harte wrote to Black as follows:—

"My dear Black,—I was in the far South, trying to get rid of an obstinate cold, when your note reached me, and haven't been in London for some time. I expected you to drop in here on your way up to 'Balnagownie's arms'—whoever she may be. I'm afraid I don't want any 'Ardgay' in mine, thank you. Why any man in this damp climate should want to make himself wetter by salmon-fishing passes my comprehension. Is there no drier sport to be had in all Great Britain? I shudder at the name of a river, and shiver at the sight of any fish that isn't dried. I hear, too, that you are in the habit of making poetry on these occasions, and that you are dropping lines all over the place. How far is that place—anyway? I shall be in Glasgow until the end of March, and if you'll dry yourself thoroughly and come in and dine with me at that time, I'll show you how 'the laboring poor' of Glasgow live. Yours always,

"Bret Harte."

But, alas for Bret Harte! when this letter was written, his labors at Glasgow were about to cease. In the year 1885 a new Administration entered upon its duties at Washington, and many Consuls were superseded, perhaps for good cause. Bret Harte was removed in July, and another man of letters, Mr. Frank Underwood of Boston, reigned in his stead.

CHAPTER XVII

BRET HARTE IN LONDON

In 1880, during one of his many visits to London, Bret Harte made the acquaintance of M. Arthur and Mme. Van de Velde, who were already enthusiastic readers of his works, and it was not long before they became his most intimate friends in England if not in the world. From 1885, when he went to London to live, until the death of M. Van de Velde in 1895, he was an inmate of their house for a great part of the time. Afterward, Bret Harte took rooms at number 74 Lancaster Gate, which remained his headquarters for the rest of his life; but he was often a guest at Mme. Van de Velde's town house, and at her country home, The Red House at Camberley in Sussex.

M. Van de Velde was a Belgian whose life had been spent in the diplomatic service of his country. For many years he was Councillor of Legation in London. Mme. Van de Velde, his second wife, is of Italian birth, an accomplished woman of the world, and a writer of reputation. She translated many of Bret Harte's stories into French, and is the author of "Random Recollections of Court and Society," "Cosmopolitan Recollections," and "French Fiction of To-day." A quotation has already been made from her discriminating essay on Bret Harte. Her influence upon him was an important factor in the last twenty years of his life. Mme. Van de Velde led him to take himself and his art more seriously than he had done since coming to England. He settled down to his work, put his shoulder to the wheel, and kept it there during the remainder of his life. For a man naturally indolent and inclined to underrate his own writings, this well-sustained industry was remarkable. Bret Harte was always more easily influenced by women than by men. He showed his best side to them, and they called out the gentleness and chivalry of his nature. No woman ever spoke ill of him, and among his most grateful admirers to-day are the California women who contributed to the "Overland Monthly," and who testify to the uniform kindness and consideration with which he treated them.

Bret Harte's habits were regular and simple. He smoked a good deal, drank very little, and took exercise every day. At one time he played golf, and at another he was somewhat interested in amateur photography. But his real recreation, as well as his labor, was found in that imaginary world which sprang to life under his pen. He was often a guest at English country houses, and was familiar with the history of English cathedrals, abbeys, churches, and historical ruins. He made a pilgrimage to Macbeth's country in Scotland and to Charlotte Brontë's home in Yorkshire. He loved Byron's poetry, and was once a guest at Newstead Abbey. He frequently visited Lord Compton, later Marquis of Northampton, at Compton Wyngates in Warwickshire near the battleground of Edgehill, and at Castle Ashby at Northampton. Reminiscences of these visits may be found in *The Desborough Connections* and *The Ghosts of Stukeley Castle*. He belonged to various clubs, such as The Beefsteak, The Rabelais, The Kinsmen; but during the last few years of his life he frequented only the Royal Thames Yacht Club.

"This selection seemed to me so odd," writes Mr. Pemberton, "for he had no love of yachting, that I questioned him concerning it. 'Why, my dear fellow,' he said, 'don't you see? I never use a club until I am tired of my work and want relief from it. If I go to a literary club I am asked all sorts of questions as to what I am doing, and my views on somebody's last book, and to these I am expected to reply at length. Now my good friends in Albemarle Street talk of their yachts, don't want my advice about them, are good enough to let me listen, and I come away refreshed by their conversation.'"

So Hawthorne, it will be remembered, cared little for the meetings of the Saturday Club in Boston, and was often an absentee, but he delighted in the company of the Yankee sea-captains at Mrs. Blodgett's boarding-house in Liverpool. "Captain Johnson," he wrote, "assigned as a reason for not boarding at this house that the conversation made him sea-sick; and indeed the smell of tar and bilge-water is somewhat strongly perceptible in it."

The truth is that an aversion to the society of purely literary men should naturally be looked for in writers of a profound or original stamp of mind. Something may be learned and some refreshment of spirit may be obtained from almost any man who knows almost anything at first hand,—even from a market-gardener or a machinist; and if his subject is what might be called a natural one, such as ships, horses or cows, it is bound to have a certain intellectual interest. But the ordinary, clever, sophisticated littérateur is mainly occupied neither with things nor with ideas, but with forms of expression, and consequently he is a long way removed from reality. It may be doubted if any society in the world is less profitable than his.

Mr. Moncure Conway, in his autobiography, gives an amusing reminiscence of Bret Harte's proneness to escape from what are known as "social duties." Mrs. Conway "received" on Monday afternoons, and Bret Harte had told her that he would be present on a particular Monday, but he failed to appear,—much to the regret of some persons who had been invited for the occasion. "When chancing to meet him," writes Mr. Conway, "I alluded to the disappointment; he asked forgiveness and said, 'I will come next Monday—*even though I promise.*'"

He had a constant dread that his friendship or acquaintance would be sought on account of his writings, rather than for himself. A lady who sat next to him at dinner without learning his name, afterward remarked, "I have always longed to meet him, and I would have been so different had I only known who my neighbor was." This, unfortunately, being repeated to Bret Harte, he exclaimed, "Now, why can't a woman realize that this sort of thing is insulting?... If Mrs. —— talked with me, and found me uninteresting as a man, how could she expect to find me interesting because I was an author?"

During the last ten or fifteen years of his life, Bret Harte seldom went far from home. He never visited Switzerland until September, 1895, and even then he carried his manuscript with him, and devoted to it part of each day. He took great delight in the Swiss mountains, often spoke of his vacation there, and was planning to go again during the summer of his death.

From Lucerne he wrote to a friend as follows: "Strangest of all, I find my heart going back to the old Sierras whenever I get over three thousand feet of Swiss altitude, and—dare I whisper it?—in spite of their pictorial composition, I wouldn't give a mile of the dear old Sierras, with their honesty, sincerity, and magnificent uncouthness, for one hundred thousand kilometres of the picturesque Vaud."

Of Geneva he wrote to the same correspondent: "I thought I should not like Geneva, fancying it a kind of continental Boston, and that the shadow of John Calvin and the old reformers, or still worse the sentimental idiocy of Rousseau, and the De Staëls and Mme. de Warens still lingered there."

But he did like Geneva; and of the lake, as he viewed it from his hotel window, he wrote, "Ask him if he ever saw an expanse of thirty miles of water exactly the color of the inner shell of a Mother-of-Pearl oyster."

Of Geneva itself he wrote again: "It is gay, brilliant, and even as *pictorial* as the end of Lake Leman; and as I sit by my hotel window on the border of the lake I can see Mont Blanc—thirty or forty miles away—framing itself a perfect vignette. Of course I know the whole thing was arranged by the Grand Hotel Company that run Switzerland. Last night as I stood on my balcony looking at the great semi-circle of lights framing the quay and harbor of the town, a great fountain sent up a spray from the lake three hundred feet high, illuminated by beautifully shaded 'lime lights,' exactly like a 'transformation scene.' Just then, the new moon—a pale green sickle—swung itself over the Alps! But it was absolutely too much! One felt that the Hotel Company were overdoing it! And I wanted to order up the hotel proprietor and ask him to take it down. At least I suggested it to the Colonel, but he thought it would do as well if we refused to pay for it in the bill."

The same correspondent, by the way, quotes an amusing letter from Bret Harte, written in 1888, from Stoke Pogis, near Windsor Castle: "I had the honor yesterday of speaking to a man who had been in personal attendance upon the Queen for fifty years. He was naturally very near the point of translation, and gave a vague impression that he did not require to be born again, but remained on earth for the benefit of American tourists."

Bret Harte's reasons for remaining so long in England have already been explained in part. The chief cause was probably the pecuniary one, for by living in England he was able to obtain more from his writings than he could have obtained as a resident of the United States. He continued to contribute to the support of his wife, although after his departure from this country Mrs. Harte and he did not live together. The cause of their separation was never made known. On this subject both Mr. Harte and his wife maintained an honorable silence, which, it is to be hoped, will always be respected.

A few years before her husband's death, Mrs. Harte came to England to live. The older son, Griswold Harte, died in the city of New York, in December, 1901, leaving a widow and one daughter. The second son, Francis King Harte, was married in England some years ago, and makes his home there. He has two children. Bret Harte was often a visitor at his son's house. The older daughter, Jessamy, married Henry Milford Steele, an American, and lives in the United States. The younger daughter, Ethel, is unmarried, and lives with her mother.

Beyond the pecuniary reason which impelled Bret Harte to live in England were other reasons which every American who has spent some time in that country will understand, and which are especially strong in respect to persons of nervous temperament. The climate is one reason; for the English climate is the natural antidote to the American; and perhaps the residents of each country would be better if they could exchange habitats every other generation.

England has a soothing effect upon the hustling American. He eats more, worries less, and becomes a happier and pleasanter animal. A similar change has been observed in high-strung horses taken from the United States to England. And so of athletes—the English athlete, transported to this country, gains in speed, but loses endurance; whereas our athletes on English soil gain endurance and lose speed. The temperament and manners of the English people have the same pleasant effect as the climate upon the American visitor. Why is John Bull always represented as an irascible animal? Perhaps he is such if his rights, real or assumed, are invaded, or if his will is thwarted; but as the stranger meets him, he is civil and good-natured. In fact, this is one of the chief surprises which an American experiences on his first visit to England.

More important still, perhaps, is the ease of living in a country which has a fixed social system. The plain line drawn in England between the gentleman and the non-gentleman class makes things very pleasant for those who belong to the favored division. It gives the gentleman a vantage ground in dealing with the non-gentleman which proves as convenient, as it is novel, to the American. The fact that it must be inconvenient for the non-gentleman class, which outnumbers the other some thousands to one, never seems to trouble the Englishman, although the American may have some qualms.

Furthermore, strange as it may seem, the position of an author, *per se* is, no doubt, higher in London (though perhaps not elsewhere in England) than it is in the United States. With us, the well-to-do publisher has a better standing in what is called "society" than the impecunious author. In London the reverse would be the case. New York and Boston looked askance upon Bret Harte, doubting if he were quite respectable; but London welcomed him. Bret Harte was often asked to lecture in England, and especially to speak or write upon English customs or English society; but he always refused, being unwilling, as Thackeray was in regard to the United States, either to censure a people from whom he had received great hospitality, or to praise them at the expense of truth.

Nor was his belief in America and the American social system weakened in the least by his long residence in England or by his enjoyment of the amenities of English life.

An English author wrote of him, while he was yet living: "Time has not dulled Bret Harte's instinctive affection for the land of his birth, for its institutions, its climate, its natural beauties, and, above all, the character and moral attributes of its inhabitants. Even his association with the most aristocratic representatives of London society has been impotent to modify his views or to win him over to less independent professions. He is as single-minded to-day as he was when he first landed on British soil. A general favorite in the most diverse circles, social, literary, scientific, artistic, or military, his strong primitive nature and his positive individuality have remained intact. Always polite and gentle, neither seeking nor evading controversy, he is steadfastly unchangeable in his political and patriotic beliefs."

Another English writer relates that "At the time when there was some talk of war between Britain and America, he, while deploring even the suggestion of such a catastrophe, earnestly avowed his intention of instantly returning to his own country, should hostilities break out."

No two men could be more opposed in many respects than Hawthorne and Bret Harte. Nevertheless they had some striking points of resemblance. Both were men who united primitive instincts with consummate refinement; and different as is the subject-matter of their stories, the style and attitude are not unlike. They had the same craving for beauty of form, the same self-repression, the same horror of what is prolix or tawdry, the same love of that simplicity which is the perfection of art.

Long residence in England seems to have had much the same effect upon both men. It heightened their feeling for their native country almost in proportion as it pleased their own susceptibilities. Hawthorne's fondness for England was an almost unconscious feeling. When he returned to America, there to live for the remainder of his days, he did not find himself at home in the manner or to the degree which he had expected. "At Rome," his son writes, "an unacknowledged homesickness affected him, an Old-Homesickness, rather than a yearning for America. He may have imagined that it was America that he wanted, but when at last we returned there, he still looked backward toward England."

That a man should find it more agreeable to live in one country, and yet be firmly convinced that the social system of another country was superior, is nothing remarkable. It is the presence of equality in the United States and its absence in England which make the chief difference between them. Even that imperfect equality to which we have attained has rendered the American people the happiest and the most moral in the world. To the superficial visitor, indeed, who has seen only a few great cities in the United States, it might seem that equality is not much more prevalent here than it is in England; but let him tarry a while in the smaller cities, in the towns and villages of the Union, from the Atlantic to the Pacific, and he will reach a different conclusion. An English writer of unusual discernment speaks of "that conscious independence, that indefinable assertion of manhood, which is the key to the American character."

One result of Bret Harte's long residence in England was the circulation in this country of many false reports and statements about him which galled his sensitive nature. He had many times declined to be "interviewed," and probably made enemies in that way. "But when," writes Mme. Van de Velde, "in a moment of good nature he yielded to pressing solicitations, and allowed himself to be questioned, the consequences were, on the whole, to his disadvantage. From that moment the door was opened to a flood of apocryphal statements of various length and importance; sometimes entirely false, sometimes tinged with a dangerous verisimilitude; often grotesque, occasionally malicious, but one and all purporting to be derived from unquestionable sources."

Mr. Pemberton hints at more serious troubles which afflicted Bret Harte's last years. "If he, in common with many of us, had his deep personal disappointments and sorrows, he bore them with the chivalry of a Bayard and a silence as dignified as it was pathetic. To a man of his sensitive nature, the barbed shafts of 'envy and calumny and hate and pain' lacerated with a cruelty that at times must have seemed unendurable. Under such torments he often writhed, but he suffered all things with a quiet patience that afforded a glorious example to those friends who, knowing of his wounds, had to be silent concerning them, and could offer him no balm."

During the year 1901 Bret Harte's health was failing, although he still kept at work. His disease was cancer of the throat. He hoped to go abroad the following summer, and he had written in a letter to a friend, "Alas! I have never been light-hearted since Switzerland." But early in 1902 his condition became serious, and he went to stay with Mme. Van de Velde at Camberley. The Spring was cold and sunless, and he grew worse as it advanced. Nevertheless he was engaged in writing a play with Mr. Pemberton, and was meditating a new story which should reintroduce that favorite of the public, Colonel Starbottle. In March a surgical operation was performed on his throat, but the relief was slight and temporary; and from that time forward Bret Harte must have known that his fate was sealed, although he said nothing to his friends and with them appeared to be in good, even high spirits.

April 17, feeling somewhat better, he sat down to begin his new tale. He headed it, "A Friend of Colonel Starbottle's," and wrote the opening sentence and part of another sentence. Dissatisfied with this beginning, he tried again, and taking a fresh sheet of paper, he wrote the title and one sentence. There the manuscript ends. He was unable to continue it, although after this date he wrote a few letters to friends. On May 5 he was sitting in the morning, at his desk, thus engaged, when a hemorrhage of the throat suddenly attacked him. He was put to bed, and doctors were sent for. He rallied from this attack, but a second hemorrhage, late in the afternoon, rendered him partly unconscious, and soon afterward he died peacefully in the presence of Mme. Van de Velde and her attendants.

There is something sad in the death of any man far from home and country, with no kith or kin about him, though ministered to by devoted friends. Even Bret Harte's tombstone bears the name of one who was a stranger to his blood and race. We cannot help recalling what Tennessee's Partner said. "When a man has been running free all day, what's the natural thing for him to do? Why, to come home." Alas! there was no home-coming for Bret Harte; and if, as may have been the case, he felt little or no regret at his situation, the sadness of it would only be intensified by that circumstance. Some deterioration is inevitable when a husband and father foregoes, even unwillingly, those feelings of responsibility and affection which centre in the family,—feelings so natural that to a considerable degree we share them even with the lower animals.

That Bret Harte's separation from his family was in part, at least, his own fault seems highly probable from his character and career. He abhorred sentimentality in literature, and the few examples of it in his writings may be ascribed to the influence of Dickens. Nevertheless, with all his virility, it must be admitted that his nature was that of a sentimentalist. A sentimentalist is one who obeys the natural good impulses of the human heart, but whose virtue does not go much beyond that. He has right feelings and acts upon them, but in cases where there is nothing to provoke the right feeling he falls short. He is strong in impulse, but weak in principle. When we see a fellow-being in danger or distress our instinct is to assist him. If we fail to do so, it is because we hearken to reason rather than to instinct; because we obey the selfish, second thought which reason suggests, instead of obeying the spontaneous impulse which nature puts into our hearts.

But suppose that the person to be succored makes no appeal to the heart: suppose that he is thousands of miles away: suppose that one dislikes or even hates him: suppose that it is a question not of bestowing alms, or of giving assistance or of feeling sympathy, but of rendering bare justice. In such cases the sentimentalist lacks a sufficient spur for action: he feels no impulse: his heart remains cold: he makes excuses to himself; and having no strong sense of duty or principle to carry him through the ordeal, he becomes guilty of an act (or, more often, of a failure to act) which in another person would excite his indignation. In this sense Bret Harte was a sentimentalist.

He would have risked his life for a present friend, but was capable of neglecting an absent one.

This contradiction, if it be such, affords a clue to his character. In spite of his amiability, kindness, generosity, there was in Bret Harte an element of cruelty. Even his natural improvidence in money matters can hardly excuse him for selling the copyright of all his stories as they came out, leaving no income to be derived from them after his death.

The sentimentalist, being a creature of impulse, gets in the habit of obeying his impulses, good or bad, and is apt to find some difficulty at last in distinguishing between them. He easily persuades himself that the thing which he wishes to do is the right thing for him to do. This was a trait of Bret Harte's character, and it naturally accompanies that lack of introspection which was so marked in him. There was a want of background, both intellectual and moral, in his nature. He was an observer, not a thinker, and his genius was shown only as he lived in the life of others. Even his poetry is dramatic, not lyric. It was very seldom that Bret Harte, in his tales or elsewhere, advanced any abstract sentiment or idea; he was concerned wholly with the concrete; and it is noticeable that when he does venture to lay down a general principle, it fails to bear the impress of real conviction. The note of sincerity is wanting. An instance will be found in the *General Introduction* which he wrote for the first volume of his collected stories, where he answers the charge that he had "confused recognized standards of morality by extenuating lives of recklessness and often criminality with a single, solitary virtue." After describing this as "the cant of too much mercy," he goes on to say:—

"Without claiming to be a religious man or a moralist, but simply as an artist, he shall reverently and humbly conform to the rules laid down by a Great Poet who created the parables of the Prodigal Son and the Good Samaritan, whose works have lasted eighteen hundred years, and will remain when the present writer and his generation are forgotten. And he is conscious of uttering no original doctrine in this, but of only voicing the beliefs of a few of his literary brethren happily living, and one gloriously dead, who never made proclamation of this from the housetops."

This is simply Dickens both in manner and substance, and the tone of the whole passage is insincere and exaggerated, almost maudlin. Lamentable, but perhaps not strange, that in the one place where Bret Harte explained and defended what might be called the prevailing moral of his stories, he should fall so far short of the reader's expectation!

The truth is that Bret Harte took nothing seriously except his art, and apparently went through life with as little concern about the origin, nature, and destiny of mankind as it would be possible for any member of that unfortunate species to feel.

And yet there was a noble side to his character. He possessed in an unusual degree what is, perhaps, the most rare of all good qualities, namely, magnanimity. No man was ever more free from envy and jealousy; no writer was ever more quick to perceive and to praise excellence in others, or more slow to disparage or condemn. He used to say, and really seemed to believe, that Mr. John Hay's imitations of his own dialect poems were better than the originals. All the misconstruction and unkind criticism of which he was the subject never drew from him a bitter remark. He had a tenderness for children and dumb animals, especially for dogs, and his sympathy with them gave him a wonderful insight into their natures. Who but Bret Harte could have penned this sentence which the Reader will recognize as occurring in *The Argonauts of North Liberty*: "He had that piteous wistfulness of eye seen in some dogs and the husbands of many charming women,—the affection that pardons beforehand the indifference which it has learned to expect."

In breadth and warmth of sympathy for his fellow-men Bret Harte had what almost might be described as a substitute for religion; what indeed has been described as religion itself. Long ago, an author who afterward became famous, touched with the fervor of youthful enthusiasm for his vocation, declared that "literature fosters in its adherents a sympathy with all that lives and breathes which is more binding than any form of religion." A more recent thinker, Mr. Henry W. Montague, has finely said that "The most important function of Christianity is not to keep man from sinning, but to widen the range and increase the depth of his sympathies."

Judged by these standards, Bret Harte could not be described as an irreligious writer. Who, more than he, has warmed the heart and suffused the eyes of his readers with pity for the unfortunate, with admiration for the heroic? "A kind thought is a good deed," remarked an oriental sage. The doctrine is a dangerous one; but if it is true of any man, it is true of an author. His kind thoughts live after him, and they have the force and effect of deeds. Bret Harte's stories are a legacy to the world, as full of inspiration as of entertainment.

It was not by accident or as the result of mere literary taste that he selected from the chaos of California life the heroic and the pathetic incidents. Those who know California only through his tales and poems naturally think that the aspect of it which Bret Harte presents was the only aspect; that the Pioneer life would have impressed any other observer just as it impressed him, the single difference being that Bret Harte had the ability to report what he saw and heard. But such is not the case. Bret Harte's representation of California is true; there is no exaggeration in it; but there were other aspects of life there which would have been equally true. If we were to call up in imagination the various story-writers of Bret Harte's day, it would be easy to guess what features of life on the Golden Slope would have attracted them, had they been there in the days of the Pioneers: how the social peculiarities of San Francisco, with its flamboyant *demi-monde* and its early appeal to the divorce court, would have interested one; how the adventures of outlaws and robbers would have filled the mind of another; and how a third would have been content to describe the picturesque traits of the Spanish inheritors of the soil.

Bret Harte does indeed touch upon all these points and upon many others,—not a phase of California life escaped him,—but he does not dwell upon them. His main theme is those heroic impulses of loyalty, of chivalry, of love, of pure friendship, which are strong enough to triumph over death and the fear of death, and which, nevertheless, are often found where, except to the discerning eye of sympathy, their existence would be wholly unsuspected.

For this selection the world owes Bret Harte a debt of gratitude; and none the less because it was made instinctively. The actions of a really perfect character would all be instinctive and spontaneous. In such a man conscience and inclination would coincide. His taste and his sense of duty would be one and the same thing. A mean, an unkind, an unjust act would be a solecism as impossible for him as it would be to eat with his knife. The struggle would have been over before he was born, and his ancestors would have bequeathed to him a nature in harmony with itself. The credit for his good deeds would belong, perhaps, rather to his ancestors than to himself, but we should see in him the perfection of human nature, the final product of a thousand imperfect natures.

Something of this spontaneousness and finality belonged to the character of Bret Harte. If he was weak in conviction and principle, he was strong in instinct. If he yielded easily to certain temptations, he was impregnable to others, because he was protected against them by the whole current of his nature. It would be as impossible to imagine Bret Harte taking sides against the oppressed, as it would be to imagine him performing his literary work in a slovenly manner. Both his good and bad traits were firmly rooted, and, it may be, inextricably mingled. Mr. Howells said of him that "If his temperament disabled him from certain experiences of life, it was the sure source of what was most delightful in his personality, and perhaps most beautiful in his talent." Bret Harte's stories are sufficient proof that he was at bottom a good man, although he had grave faults.

His faults, moreover, were those commonly found in men of genius, and for that reason they should be treated with some tenderness. When one considers that the whole progress of the human race, mental and spiritual, as well as mechanical, is due to the achievements of a few superior individuals, whom the world has agreed to designate as men of genius,—considering this, one should be slow to pronounce with anything like confidence or finality upon the character of one who belongs in that class. We know that such men are different from other men intellectually, and we might expect to find, and we do find that they are different from them emotionally, if not morally. A certain egotism, for example, is notoriously associated with men of genius; and a kind of egotistic or unconscious selfishness was Bret Harte's great defect.

Popular opinion, a safe guide in such matters, has always recognized the fact that the genius is a species by himself. It is only the clever men of talent who have discovered that there is no essential difference between men of genius and themselves. Writers of this description might be named who have summed up Bret Harte's life and character with amazing condescension and self-assurance. Meagre as are the known facts of his career, especially those relating to his private life, these critics have assigned his motives and judged his conduct with a freedom and a certainty which they would hardly feel in respect to their own intimates.

The very absence of information about Bret Harte makes misconstruction easy. Why he lived apart from his family, why he lived in England, why he continued to draw his subjects from California,—these are matters as to which the inquisitive world would have been glad to be informed, but as to which he thought it more fitting to keep silence; and from that silence no amount of misrepresentation could move him. Mr. Pemberton has recorded the congenial scorn with which Bret Harte used to repeat the motto upon the coat of arms of some Scottish earl. *They say! What say they? Let them say!*

And yet, if a writer has greatly moved or pleased us, we have a natural desire, especially after his death, to know what manner of man he was. Most of all, we long to ask that familiar question, the only question which, at the close of a career, seems to have any relevance or importance,—Was he a good man? In the present case, such answer as this book can give has already been made; and if any Reader should be inclined to a different conclusion, let him weigh well the peculiar circumstances of Bret Harte's life, and make due allowance for the obscurity in which his motives are veiled.

Upon one aspect of his career there can be no difference of opinion. His devotion to his art was unwavering and extreme. Pagan though he may have been in some respects, in this matter he was as conscientious a Puritan as Hawthorne himself. Every plot, every character, every sentence, one might almost say, every word in his books, was subjected to his own relentless criticism. The manuscript that Bret Harte consigned to the waste-basket would have made the reputation of another author. No "pot-boiler" ever came from his hand, and, whatever his pecuniary difficulties, he never dreamed of escaping from them by that dashing-off of salable stories which is a common practice among popular writers of fiction.

Such he was at the beginning, and such he continued to be until the end. Six months elapsed, after the publication of his first successful story, before Bret Harte made his second appearance in the "Overland Monthly." His friends in California have given us a picture of him, a youthful author in his narrow office at the Mint, slowly and painfully elaborating those masterpieces that made him famous. It was the same forty years afterward when the fatal illness overtook him at his desk in an English country-house. The pen that dropped from his reluctant fingers had been engaged in writing and re-writing the simple, opening sentences of a story that was never to be finished.

Bret Harte was one of that select band to whom the gods have vouchsafed a glimpse of perfection. All his life, from mere boyhood, he was inspired by a vision of that ideal beauty which is at once the joy and the despair of the true artist. Whoever realizes that vision, even though in an imperfect manner, has overcome the limitations of time and space, and has obtained a position among the immortals which may be denied to better and even greater men.

CHAPTER XVIII

BRET HARTE AS A WRITER OF FICTION

Bret Harte's faculty was not so much that of imagining as of apprehending human character. Some writers of fiction, those who have the highest form of creative imagination, are able from their own minds to spin the web and woof of the characters that they describe; and it makes small difference where they live or what literary material lies about them. Even these authors do not create their heroes and heroines quite out of whole cloth,—they have a shred or two to begin with; but their work is mainly the result of creation rather than perception.

The test of creative imagination is that the characters portrayed by it are subjected to various exigencies and influences: they grow, develop, yes, even change, and yet retain their consistency. There is a masterly example of this in Trollope's "Small House at Allington," where he depicts the slow, astounding, and yet perfectly natural disintegration of Crosby's moral character. The aftermath of love-making between Pendennis and Blanche Amory is another instance. This has been called by one critic the cleverest thing in all Thackeray; but still more clever, though clever is too base a word for an episode so beautifully conceived, is that dawning of passion, hopeless and quickly quenched, between Laura Pendennis and George Warrington, the two strongest characters in the book. Only the hand of creative genius can guide its characters safely through such labyrinths of feeling, such back-eddies of emotion.

A few great novels have indeed been written by authors who did not possess this faculty, especially by Dickens, in whom it was conspicuously lacking; but no long story was ever produced without betraying its author's deficiency in this respect if the deficiency existed. *Gabriel Conroy*, Bret Harte's only novel, is so bad as a whole, though abounding in gems, its characters are so inconsistent and confused, its ending so incomprehensible, that it produces upon the reader the effect of a nightmare.

In fact, the nearer Bret Harte's stories approach the character of an episode the better and more dramatic they are. Of the longer stories, the best, as everybody will admit, is *Cressy*, and that is little more than the expansion of a single incident. As a rule, in reading the longer tales, one remembers, as he progresses, that the situations and the events are fictitious; they have not the spontaneous, inevitable aspect which makes the shorter tales impressive. *Tennessee's Partner* is as historical as Robinson Crusoe. Bret Harte had something of a weakness for elaborate plots, but they were not in his line. Plots and situations can hardly be satisfactory or artistic unless they form the means whereby the characters of the persons in the tale are developed, or, if not developed, at least revealed to the reader. The development or the gradual revelation of character is the *raison d'être* for the long story or novel.

But this capacity our author seems to have lacked. It might be said that he did not require it, because his characters appear to us full-fledged from the start. He has, indeed, a wonderful power of setting them before the reader almost immediately, and by virtue of a few masterly strokes. After an incident or two, we know the character; there is nothing more to be revealed; and a prolongation of the story would be superfluous.

But here we touch upon Bret Harte's weakness as a portrayer of human nature. It surely indicates some deficiency in a writer of fiction if with the additional scope afforded by a long story he can tell us no more about his people than he is able to convey by a short story. The deficiency in Bret Harte was perhaps this, that he lacked a profound knowledge of human nature. A human being regarded as material for a writer of fiction may be divided into two parts. There is that part, the more elemental one, which he shares with other men, and there is, secondly, that part which differentiates him from other men. In other words, he is both a type of human nature, and a particular specimen with individual variations.

The ideal story-writer would be able to master his subject in each aspect, and in describing a single person to depict at once both the nature of all men and also the nature of that particular man. Shakspere, Sterne, Thackeray have this power. Other writers can do the one thing but not the other; and in this respect Hawthorne and Bret Harte stand at opposite extremes. Hawthorne had a profound knowledge of human nature; but he was lacking in the capacity to hit off individual characteristics. Arthur Dimmesdale and Hester, even Miriam and Hilda, are not real to us in the sense in which Colonel Newcome and Becky Sharp are real. Hawthorne's figures are somewhat spectral; they lack flesh and blood. His forte was not observation but reflection. He worked from the inside.

Bret Harte, on the other hand, worked from the outside. He had not that faculty, so strong in Hawthorne, of delving into his own nature by way of getting at the nature of other men; but he had the faculty of sympathetic observation which enabled him to perceive and understand the characteristic traits that distinguish one man from another.

Barker's Luck and *Three Partners*, taken together, illustrate Bret Harte's limitations in this respect. Each of these stories has Barker for its central theme, the other personages being little more than foils to him. In the first story, *Barker's Luck*, the plot is very simple, the incidents are few, and yet we have the character of the hero conveyed to us with exquisite effect. In *Three Partners* the theme is elaborated, a complicated plot is introduced, and Barker appears in new relations and situations. But we know him no better than we did before. *Barker's Luck* covered the ground; and *Three Partners*, a more ambitious story, is far below it in verisimilitude and in dramatic effect. In the same way, *M'liss*, in its original form, is much superior to the longer and more complex story which its author wrote some years afterward, and which is printed in the collected edition of his works, to the exclusion of the earlier tale.

In one case, however, Bret Harte did succeed in showing the growth and development of a character. The trilogy known as *A Waif of the Plains*, *Susy*, and *Clarence*, is almost the same as one long story; and in it the character of Clarence, from boyhood to maturity, is skilfully and consistently traced. Upon this character Bret Harte evidently bestowed great pains, and there are some notable passages in his delineation of it, especially the account of the duel between Clarence and Captain Pinckney. Not less surprising to Clarence himself than to the reader is the calm ferocity with which he kills his antagonist; and we share the thrill of horror which ran through the little group of spectators when it was whispered about that this gentlemanly young man, so far removed in appearance from a fire-eater, was the son of Hamilton Brant, the noted duellist. The situation had brought to the surface a deep-lying, inherited trait, of which even its possessor had been ignorant. In this character, certainly in this incident, Bret Harte goes somewhat deeper than his wont.

We have his own testimony to the fact that his genius was perceptive rather than creative. In those Scotch stories and sketches in which the Consul appears, very much in the capacity of a Greek chorus, the author lets fall now and then a remark plainly autobiographical in character. Thus, in *A Rose of Glenbogie*, speaking of Mrs. Deeside, he says, "The Consul, more *perceptive* than analytical, found her a puzzle."

This confirms Bret Harte's other statement, made elsewhere, that his characters, instead of being imagined, were copied from life. But they were copied with the insight and the emphasis of genius. The ability to read human nature is about the most rare of mental possessions. How little do we know even of those whom we see every day, and whom, perhaps, we have lived with all our lives! Let a man ask himself what his friend or his wife or his son would do in some supposable emergency; how they would take this or that injury or affront, good fortune or bad fortune, great sorrow or great happiness, the defection of a friend, a strong temptation. Let him ask himself any such question, and, in all probability, he will be forced to admit that he does not know what would be the result. Who, remembering his college or schoolboy days, will fail to recognize the truth of Thoreau's remark, "One may discover a new side to his most intimate friend when for the first time he hears him speak in public"!

These surprises occur not because human nature is inconsistent,—the law of character is as immutable as any other law;—it is because individual character eludes us. But it did not elude Bret Harte. He had a wonderful faculty both for understanding and remembering its outward manifestations. His genius was akin to that of the actor; and this explains, perhaps, his lifelong desire to write a successful play. Mr. Watts-Dunton has told us with astonishment how Bret Harte, years after a visit to one of the London Music Halls, minutely recounted all that he had heard and seen there, and imitated all the performers. That he would have made a great actor in the style of Joseph Jefferson is the opinion of that accomplished critic.

The surprising quickness with which he seized and assimilated any new form of dialect was a kind of dramatic capacity. The Spanish-English, mixed with California slang, which Enriquez Saltello spoke, is as good in its way as the immortal Costigan's Irish-English. "'To confer then as to thees horse, which is not—observe me—a Mexican plug. Ah, no! you can your boots bet on that. She is of Castilian stock—believe me and strike me dead! I will myself at different times overlook and affront her in the stable, examine her as to the assault, and why she should do thees thing. When she is of the exercise I will also accost and restrain her. Remain tranquil, my friend! When a few days shall pass much shall be changed, and she will be as another. Trust your oncle to do thees thing! Comprehend me? Everything shall be lovely, and the goose hang high.'"

Bret Harte's short stay in Prussia, and later in Scotland, enabled him to grasp the peculiarities of nature and speech belonging to the natives. Peter Schroeder, the idealist, could have sprung to life nowhere except upon German soil. "Peter pondered long and perplexedly. Gradually an explanation slowly evolved itself from his profundity. He placed his finger beside his nose, and a look of deep cunning shone in his eyes. 'Dot's it,' he said to himself triumphantly, 'dot's shoost it! Der Rebooplicans don't got no memories. Ve don't got nodings else.'"

What character could be more Scotch, and less anything else, than the porter at the railway station where the Consul alighted on his way to visit the MacSpaddens. "'Ye'll no be rememberin' me. I had a machine in St. Kentigern and drove ye to MacSpadden's ferry often. Far, far too often! She's a strange, flagrantitious creature; her husband's but a puir fule, I'm thinkin', and ye did yersel' nae guid gaunin' there.'"

Mr. Callender, again, Ailsa's father, in *Young Robin Gray*, breathes Scotch Calvinism and Scotch thrift and self-respect in every line.

"'Have you had a cruise in the yacht?' asked the Consul.

"'Ay,' said Mr. Callender, 'we have been up and down the loch, and around the far point, but not for boardin' or lodgin' the night, nor otherwise conteenuing or parteecipating.... Mr. Gray's a decent enough lad, and not above instruction, but extraordinar' extravagant.'"

Even the mysteries of Franco-English seem to have been fathomed by Bret Harte, possibly by his contact with French people in San Francisco. This is how the innkeeper explained to Alkali Dick some peculiarities of French custom: "'For you comprehend not the position of *la jeune fille* in all France! Ah! in America the young lady she go everywhere alone; I have seen her—pretty, charming, fascinating—alone with the young man. But here, no, never! Regard me, my friend. The French mother, she say to her daughter's fiancé, "Look! there is my daughter. She has never been alone with a young man for five minutes,—not even with you. Take her for your wife!" It is monstrous! It is impossible! It is so!'"

The moral complement of this rare capacity for reading human nature was the sympathy, the tenderness of feeling which Bret Harte possessed. Sympathy with human nature, with its weaknesses, with the tragedies which it is perpetually encountering, and above all, with its redeeming virtues,—this is the keynote of Bret Harte's works, the mainspring of his humor and pathos. He had the gift of satire as well, but, fortunately for the world, he made far less use of it. Satire is to humor as corporal punishment is to personal influence. A satire is a jest, but a cutting one,—a jest in which the victim is held up to scorn or contempt.

Humor is a much more subtle quality than satire. Like satire, it is the perception of an incongruity, but it must be a newly discovered or invented incongruity, for an essential element in humor is the pleasurable surprise, the gentle shock which it conveys. A New Jersey farmer was once describing in the presence of a very humane person, the great age and debility of a horse that he had formerly owned and used. "You ought to have killed him!" interrupted the humane person indignantly. "Well," drawled the farmer, "we did,—almost." Satire is merely destructive, whereas sentiment is constructive. The most that satire can do is to show how the thing ought *not* to be done. But sentiment goes much further, for it supplies the dynamic power of affection. Becky Sharp dazzles and amuses; but Colonel Newcome softens and inspires.

There is often in Bret Harte a subtle blending of satire and humor, notably in that masterpiece of satirical humor, the *Heathen Chinee*. The poet beautifully depicts the naïve indignation of the American gambler at the duplicity of the Mongolian,—a duplicity exceeding even his own. "'We are ruined by Chinese cheap labor!'"

Another instance is that passage in *The Rose of Tuolumne*, where the author, after relating how a stranger was shot and nearly killed in a mining town, records the prevailing impression in the neighborhood "that his misfortune was the result of the defective moral quality of his being a stranger." So, in *The Outcasts of Poker Flat*, when the punishment of Mr. Oakhurst was under consideration, "A few of the Committee had urged hanging him as a possible example and a sure method of reimbursing themselves from his pockets of the money he had won from them. 'It's agin justice,' said Jim Wheeler, 'to let this yer young man from Roaring Camp—an entire stranger—carry away our money.' But a crude sentiment of equity residing in the breasts of those who had been fortunate enough to win from Mr. Oakhurst overruled this narrower local prejudice."

Even in these passages humor predominates over satire. In fact,—and it is a fact characteristic of Bret Harte,—the only satire, pure and simple, in his works is that which he directs against hypocrisy. This was the one fault which he could not forgive; and he especially detested that peculiar form of cold and calculating hypocrisy which occasionally survives as the dregs of Puritanism. Bret Harte was keenly alive to this aspect of New England character; and he has depicted it with almost savage intensity in *The Argonauts of North Liberty*. Ezekiel Corwin, a shrewd, flinty, narrow Yankee, is not a new figure in literature, but an old figure in one or two new situations, notably in his appearance at the mining camps as a vender of patent medicines. "That remarkably unfair and unpleasant-spoken man had actually frozen Hanley's Ford into icy astonishment at his audacity, and he had sold them an invoice of the Panacea before they had recovered; he had insulted Chipitas into giving an extensive order in bitters; he had left Hayward's Creek pledged to Burne's pills—with drawn revolvers still in their hands."

Even here, however, the bitterness of the satire is tempered by the humor of the situation. But in Joan, the heroine of the story, we have a really new figure in literature, and it is drawn with an absence of sympathy, of humor and of mitigating circumstances which is very rare, if not unique, in Bret Harte.

One other example of pure satire may be found in his works, and that is Parson Wynn, the effusive, boisterous hypocrite who plays a subordinate part in *The Carquinez Woods*. With these few exceptions, however, Bret Harte was a writer of sentiment, and that is the secret of his power. Sentiment may take the form of humor or of pathos, and, as is often remarked, these two qualities shade off into each other by imperceptible degrees.

Some things are of that nature as to make
One's fancy chuckle, while his heart doth ache.

A consummate example of this blending of humor and pathos is found in the story *How Santa Claus Came to Simpson's Bar*. The boy Johnny, after greeting the Christmas guests in his "weak, treble voice, broken by that premature harshness which only vagabondage and the habit of premature self-assertion can give," and after hospitably setting out the whiskey bottle, with crackers and cheese, creeps back to bed, and is thus accosted by Dick Bullen, the hero of the story:—

"'Hello, Johnny! You ain't goin' to turn in agin, are ye?'

"'Yes, I are,' responded Johnny decidedly.

"'Why, wot's up, old fellow?'

"'I'm sick.'

"'How sick?'

"'I've got a fevier, and childblains, and roomatiz,' returned Johnny, and vanished within. After a moment's pause he added in the dark, apparently from under the bedclothes,—'And biles!'

"There was an embarrassing silence. The men looked at each other and at the fire."

How graphically in this story are the characters of the Old Man and his boy Johnny indicated by a few strokes of humor and pathos! Perhaps this is the greatest charm of humor in literature, namely, that it so easily becomes the vehicle of character. Sir Roger de Coverley and the Vicar of Wakefield are revealed to us mainly by those humorous touches which display the foibles, the eccentricities, and even the virtues of each. Wit, on the other hand, being a purely intellectual quality, is a comparatively uninteresting gift. How small is the part that wit plays in literature! Personality is the charm of literature, as it is of life, and humor is always a revelation of personality. The Essays of Lamb amount almost to an autobiography. Goldsmith had humor, Congreve wit; and probably that is the main reason why "She Stoops to Conquer" still holds the stage, whereas the plays of Congreve are known only to the scholar.

California was steeped in humor, and none but a humorist could have interpreted the lives of the Pioneers. They were, in the main, scions of a humorous race. Democracy is the mother of humor, and the ideal of both was found in New England and in the Western States, whence came the greater part of the California immigration. In passing from New England to the isolated farms of the Far West, American humor had undergone some change. The Pioneer, struggling with a new country, and often with chills and fever, religious in a gloomy, emotional, old-fashioned way, leading a lonely life, had developed a humor more saturnine than that of New England. Yuba Bill, in all probability, was an emigrant from what we now call the Middle West. Upon this New England and Western humor as a foundation, California engrafted its own peculiar type of humor, which was the product of youth, courage and energy wrestling with every kind of difficulty and danger. The Pioneers had something of the Mark Tapley spirit, and triumphed over fate by making a jest of the worst that fate could do to them.

Nothing short of great prosperity could awe the miner into taking a serious view of things. His solemnity after a "strike" was remarkable. In '52 and '53 a company of miners had toiled fruitlessly for fourteen months, digging into solid rock which, from its situation and from many other indications, had promised to be the hiding-place of gold. At last they abandoned the claim in despair, except that one of their number lingered to remove a big, loose block of porphyry upon which he had long been working. Behind that block he found sand and gravel containing gold in such abundance as, eventually, to enrich the whole company. The next day happened to be Sunday, and for the first time in those fourteen months they all went to church.

A "find" like this was a gift of the gods, something that could not be depended upon. It imposed responsibilities, and suggested thoughts of home. But hardship, adversity, danger and sudden death,—these were all in the day's work, and they could best be endured by making light of them.

California humor was, therefore, in one way, the reverse of ordinary American humor. In place of grotesque exaggeration, the California tendency was to minimize. The Pioneer was as euphemistic in speaking of death as was the Greek or Roman of classic times. "To pass in his checks," was the Pacific Slope equivalent for the more dignified *Actum est de me*. This was the phrase, as the Reader will remember, that Mr. Oakhurst immortalized by writing it on the playing card which, affixed to a bowie-knife, served that famous gambler for tombstone and epitaph. He used it in no flippant spirit, but in the sadly humorous spirit of the true Californian, as if he were loath to attribute undue importance to the mere fact that the unit of his own life had been forever withdrawn from the sum total of human existence.

Of this California minimizing humor, frequent also in the pages of Mark Twain and Ambrose Bierce, there is an example in Bret Harte's poem, *Cicely*:—

I've had some mighty mean moments afore I kem to this spot,—
Lost on the Plains in '50, drownded almost and shot;
But out on this alkali desert, a-hunting a crazy wife,
Was r'aly as on-satis-factory as anything in my life.

There is another familiar example in these well-known lines by Truthful James:—

Then Abner Dean of Angels raised a point of order, when
A chunk of old red sandstone took him in the abdomen,
And he smiled a kind of sickly smile, and curled up on the floor,
And the subsequent proceedings interested him no more.

This was typical California humor, and Bret Harte, in his stories and poems, more often perhaps in the latter, gave frequent expression to it; but it was not typical Bret Harte humor. The humor of the passage just quoted from *How Santa Claus Came to Simpson's Bar*, the humor that made Bret Harte famous, and still more the humor that made him beloved, was not saturnine or satirical, but sympathetic and tender. It was humor not from an external point of view, but from the victim's point of view. The Californians themselves saw persons and events in a different way; and how imperfect their vision was may be gathered from the fact that they stoutly denied the truth of Bret Harte's descriptions of Pioneer life. They were too close at hand, too much a part of the drama themselves, to perceive it correctly. Bret Harte had the faculty as to which it is hard to say how much is intellectual and how much is emotional, of getting behind the scenes, and beholding men and motives as they really are.

That brilliant critic, Mr. G. K. Chesterton, declares that Bret Harte was a genuine American, that he was also a genuine humorist, but that he was not an American humorist; and then he proceeds to support this very just antithesis as follows: "American humor is purely exaggerative; Bret Harte's humor was sympathetic and analytical. The wild, sky-breaking humor of America has its fine qualities, but it must in the nature of things be deficient in two qualities,—reverence and sympathy. And these two qualities were knit into the closest texture of Bret Harte's humor. Mark Twain's story ... about an organist who was asked to play appropriate music to an address upon the parable of the Prodigal Son, and who proceeded to play with great spirit, 'We'll all get blind drunk when Johnny comes marching home' is an instance.... If Bret Harte had described that scene it would in some subtle way have combined a sense of the absurdity of the incident with some sense of the sublimity and pathos of the scene. You would have felt that the organist's tune was funny, but not that the Prodigal Son was funny."

No excuse need be offered for quoting further what Mr. Chesterton has to say about the parodies of Bret Harte, for it covers the whole ground: "The supreme proof of the fact that Bret Harte had the instinct of reverence may be found in the fact that he was a really great parodist. Mere derision, mere contempt, never produced or could produce parody. A man who simply despises Paderewski for having long hair is not necessarily fitted to give an admirable imitation of his particular touch on the piano. If a man wishes to parody Paderewski's style of execution, he must emphatically go through one process first: he must admire it and even reverence it. Bret Harte had a real power of imitating great authors.... This means and can only mean that he had perceived the real beauty, the real ambition of Dumas and Victor Hugo and Charlotte Brontë. In his imitation of Hugo, Bret Harte has a passage like this: 'M. Madeline was, if possible, better than M. Myriel. M. Myriel was an angel. M. Madeline was a good man.' I do not know whether Victor Hugo ever used this antithesis; but I am certain that he would have used it and thanked his stars for it, if he had thought of it. This is real parody, inseparable from imitation."

The optimism for which Bret Harte was remarkable had its root in that same sympathy which formed the basis of his humor and pathos. The unsympathetic critic invariably despairs of mankind and the universe. This is apparent in social, moral, and even political matters. A typical reformer, such as the late Mr. Godkin, gazing horror-struck at Tammany and the Tammany politician, discerns no hope for the future. But the Tammany man himself, knowing the virtues as well as the vices of his people, is optimistic to the point of exuberance. After all, there is something in the human heart, amid all its vileness, which ranges mankind on the side of the angels, not of the devils. The sympathetic critic perceives this, and therefore he has confidence in the future of the race; and may even indulge the supreme hope that from this terrible world we shall pass into another and better state of existence.

CHAPTER XIX

BRET HARTE AS A POET

Whether Bret Harte will make his appeal to posterity mainly as a poet or as a prose writer is a difficult question, upon which, as upon all similar matters relating to him, the critics have expressed the most diverse opinions. There is perhaps more unevenness in his poetry than in his prose, and certainly more facility in imitating other writers. *Cadet Grey* is, in form, almost a parody of "Don Juan." *The Angelus* might be ascribed to Longfellow (though he never could have written that last stanza), *The Tale of a Pony* to Saxe or Barham, a few others to Praed, one to Campbell, and one to Calverley. Even that very beautiful poem, *Conception de Arguello*, a thing almost perfect in its way, strikes no new note. And yet who could forget the picture which it draws of the deserted maiden, grieving,—

Until hollows chased the dimples from her cheeks of olive brown,
And at times a swift, shy moisture dragged the long sweet lashes down.

Hardly less pathetic is the description of the grim Commander, her father, striving vainly to comfort the maid with "proverbs gathered from afar," until at last

... the voice sententious faltered, and the wisdom it would teach
Lost itself in fondest trifles of his soft Castilian speech;

And on "Concha," "Conchitita," and "Conchita," he would dwell
With the fond reiteration which the Spaniard knows so well.

So with proverbs and caresses, half in faith and half in doubt,
Every day some hope was kindled, flickered, faded, and went out.

Few, indeed, are the poets who have surpassed the tender simplicity and pathos of these lines; and yet there is nothing very original about them either in form or substance. But there are several poems by Bret Harte, perhaps half a dozen, which do bear the mark of original genius, and which, from the perfection of their form, seem destined to last forever.

The *Heathen Chinee*, little as Bret Harte himself thought of it, is certainly one of these. This poem, says Mr. James Douglas, "is merely an anecdote, an American anecdote, not more deeply humorous than a hundred other American anecdotes. But it is cast in an imperishable mould of style.... Mr. Swinburne's noble rhythm sang itself into his soul, and he gave it forth again in an incongruously comic theme. The rhythm of a melancholy dirge became the rhythm of duplicity in the garb of innocence. The sadness and the sighing of Meleagar became the bland iniquity of Ah Sin, and the indignantly injured depravity of Bill Nye. It was a miracle of humorous counterpoint, a marvel of incongruously associated ideas."

Too much, however, can easily be made of the part played by the metre of the *Heathen Chinee*. *Artemis in Sierra* is as good in its way as the *Heathen Chinee*, and the very different metre employed in that poem is made equally effective as the vehicle of irony and burlesque.

89

Mr. Douglas goes on to say that the Atalanta metre failed in the poem called *Dow's Flat*, "because there was no exquisite discord between the sound and the sense, between the rhyme and the reason."

But did it fail? Let these two specimen stanzas answer:—

For a blow of his pick
Sorter caved in the side,
And he looked and turned sick,
Then he trembled and cried.
For you see the dern cuss had struck—"Water?"—Beg your parding, young man,—there you lied!

It was *gold*,—in the quartz,
And it ran all alike;
And I reckon five oughts
Was the worth of that strike;
And that house with the coopilow's his'n,—which the same isn't bad for a Pike.

Almost all of Bret Harte's dialect poems have this same perfection of form, and in the whole range of literature it would be difficult to find any verses which tell so much in so small a compass. The poems are short, the lines are usually short, the words are short; but with the few strokes thus available, the poet paints a picture as complete as it is vivid. The thing is so simple that it seems easy, and yet where shall we find its counterpart?

These poems not only please for the moment, but they are read with pleasure over and over again, and year after year. Perhaps their most striking quality is their dramatic quality. They tell a story, and often depict a person. Truthful James, for example, is known to us only as the narrator of a few startling tales; and yet even by his manner of telling them he gives us a fair notion of his own character. The opening lines of *The Spelling Bee at Angels* are an example:—

Waltz in, waltz in, ye little kids, and gather round my knee,
And drop them books and first pot-hooks, and hear a yarn from me.
I kin not sling a fairy tale of Jinnys fierce and wild,
For I hold it is unchristian to deceive a simple child;
But as from school yer driftin' by, I thowt ye'd like to hear
Of a "Spelling Bee" at Angels that we organized last year.

As for Miss Edith, her character is shown in every line.

You think it ain't true about Ilsey? Well, I guess I know girls, and I say
There's nothing I see about Ilsey to show she likes you, anyway!
I know what it means when a girl who has called her cat after one boy
Goes and changes its name to another's. And she's done it—and I wish you joy!

THE HOME OF "TRUTHFUL JAMES," JACKASS FLAT, TUOLUMNE COUNTY, CALIFORNIA
Copyright, Century Co.

But these dramatic poems of Bret Harte are surpassed by his lyrical poems,—surpassed, at least, in respect to that moral elevation which lyrical poetry seems to have in comparison with dramatic poetry. Lyrical poetry strikes the higher note. It is the fusion in the poet's own experience of thought and feeling;—it is *his* experience; a first-hand report of one man's impression of the universe. Whereas dramatic poetry, with all the splendor of which it is capable, is, after all, only a second-hand report, a representation of what other men have thought or felt, or said or done. Not Shakspere himself has so elevated mankind, raised his moral standard, or enlarged his conceptions of the universe, as have the great lyrical poets.

Bret Harte cannot, of course, be ranked with these; nor, in saying that his lyrical poems are his best poems, do we necessarily assert for him any high degree of lyrical power. Perhaps, indeed, the chief defect in his poetry is an absence of the personal or lyrical element. He gives us exquisite impressions of human character and of nature, but there is little of that brooding, reflective quality, which affords the deepest and most lasting charm of poetry. His poetry lacks atmosphere; it lacks the pensive, religious note.

Bret Harte, one would think, must have been a romantic and imaginative lover, and yet in his poetry there is little, if anything, to indicate that he was ever deeply in love. Of romantic devotion to a woman, as to a superior being, we find no trace either in his stories or in his poetry. How far removed from Bret Harte is that mingled feeling of love and veneration which, originating in the Middle Ages, has lasted, in poetry at least, almost down to our own time, as in these lines from a writer who was contemporary with Bret Harte:—

When thy cheek is dewed with tears
On some dark day when friends depart,
When life before thee seems all fears
And all remembrance one long smart,

Then in the secret sacred cell
Thy soul keeps for her hour of prayer,
Breathe but my name, that I may dwell
Part of thy worship alway there.

Bret Harte was cast in a different mould. No doubts or fears distracted him. So far as we know, he asked no questions about the universe, and troubled himself very little about the destiny of mankind. He was essentially unreligious, unphilosophic, true to his own instincts, but indifferent to all matters that lay beyond them. And yet within that range he had a depth and sincerity of feeling which issued in real poetry. Bret Harte, with all the refinement, love of elegance, reserve and self-restraint which characterized him, was a very natural man. He possessed in full degree what one philosopher has called the primeval instincts of pity, of pride, of pugnacity. He loved his fellow-man, he loved his country, he loved nature, and these passions, curbed by that unerring sense of artistic form and clothed in that beauty of style which belonged to him, were expressed in a few poems that seem likely to last forever. It was not often that he felt the necessary stimulus, but when he did feel it, the response was sure. Of these immortal poems, if we may make bold to call them such, probably the best known is that on the death of Dickens. This is the last stanza:—

And on that grave where English oak and holly
And laurel wreaths entwine,
Deem it not all a too presumptuous folly,
This spray of Western pine!

Still better is the poem on the death of Starr King. It is very short; let us have it before us.

RELIEVING GUARD

Thomas Starr King. Obiit March 4, 1864.

Came the relief. "What, sentry, ho!
How passed the night through thy long waking?"
"Cold, cheerless, dark,—as may befit
The hour before the dawn is breaking."

"No sight? no sound?" "No; nothing save
The plover from the marshes calling,
And in yon western sky, about
An hour ago, a star was falling."

"A star? There's nothing strange in that."
"No, nothing; but above the thicket,
Somehow it seemed to me that God
Somewhere had just relieved a picket."

What impresses the reader most, or at least first, in this poem is its extreme conciseness and simplicity. The words are so few, and the weight of suggestion which they have to carry so heavy, that the misuse of a single word,—a single word not in perfect taste, would have spoiled the beauty of the whole. Long years ago the "Saturday Review"—the good old, ferocious Saturday—sagely remarked: "It is not given to every one to be simple"; and only genius could have achieved the simplicity of this short poem. "The relief came" would have been prose. "Came the relief" is poetry, not merely because the arrangement of the words is unusual, but because this short inverted sentence strikes a note of abruptness and intensity which prepares the reader for what is to come, and which is maintained throughout the poem;—had it not so been maintained, an anti-climax would have resulted.

Moreover, short and simple as this poem is, it seems to contain three distinct strands of feeling. There is, first, the personal feeling for Thomas Starr King; and although he was a minister and not a soldier, there is a suitability in connecting him with the picket, for, as we have seen, it was owing to him, more than to any other man, that California was saved to the Union in the Civil War. Secondly, there is the National patriotic feeling which forms the strong under-current of the poem, nowhere expressed, but unmistakably implied, and present in the minds of both poet and reader. Possibly, we may even find in "the hour before the dawn" an allusion to the period when Mr. King died and the poem was written; for that was the final desperate period of the war, darkened by a terrible expenditure of human life and suffering, and lightened only by a prospect of the end then slowly but surely coming into view. Thirdly, there is the feeling for nature which the poem exhibits in its firm though scanty etching of the sombre night, the lonely marshes, and the distant sky. The poem is a blending of these three feelings, each one enhancing the other;—and even this does not complete the tale, for there is the final suggestion that the death of a man may be of as much consequence in the mind of the Creator, and as nicely calculated, as the falling of a star.

91

The truth is that Bret Harte's national poems, with which this tribute to Starr King may properly be classed, have a depth of personal feeling not often found elsewhere in his poetry. In common with all men of primitive impulses, he was genuinely patriotic. "America was always 'my country' with him," writes one who knew him in England; "and I remember how he flushed with almost boyish pleasure when, in driving through some casual rural festivities, his quick eye noted a stray American flag among the display of bunting."

This patriotic feeling gave to his national poems the true lyrical note. Among the best of these is that stirring song of the drum, called *The Reveille*, which was read at a crowded meeting held in the San Francisco Opera House immediately after President Lincoln had called for one hundred thousand volunteers. In this poem the student of American history, and especially the foreign student, will find an expression of that National feeling which animated the Northern people, and which sanctified the horrors of the Civil War,—one of the few wars recorded in history that was waged for a pure ideal,—the ideal of the Union.

With these poems may be classed some stanzas from *Cadet Grey* describing the life of the West Point cadet, and this one in particular:—

Within the camp they lie, the young, the brave,
Half knight, half schoolboy, acolytes of fame,
Pledged to one altar, and perchance one grave;
Bred to fear nothing but reproach and blame,
Ascetic dandies o'er whom vestals rave,
Clean-limbed young Spartans, disciplined young elves,
Taught to destroy, that they may live to save,
Students embattled, soldiers at their shelves,
Heroes whose conquests are at first themselves.

It has been said that one function of literature, and especially of poetry, is to enable a nation to understand and appreciate, and thus more completely to realize, the ideals which it has instinctively formed; and in the lines just quoted Bret Harte has done this for West Point.

The poem on San Francisco glows with patriotic and civic feeling, and it expressed a sentiment which, at the time when it was written, hardly anybody in the city, except the poet himself, entertained. San Francisco in 1870 was dominated by that cold, hard, self-satisfied, commercial spirit which Bret Harte especially hated, and which furnished one reason, perhaps the main reason, for his departure from the State.

Drop down, O fleecy Fog, and hide
Her sceptic sneer and all her pride!

Wrap her, O Fog, in gown and hood
Of her Franciscan Brotherhood.

Hide me her faults, her sin and blame;
With thy gray mantle cloak her shame!

And yet it was impossible for Bret Harte, with his deep, abiding faith in the good instincts of mankind, not to look forward to a better day for San Francisco,

When Art shall raise and Culture lift
The sensual joys and meaner thrift,

And all fulfilled the vision we
Who watch and wait shall never see.

There is also a strong lyrical element in Bret Harte's treatment of nature in his poetry, as well as in his prose. What he always gives is his own impression of the scene, not a mere description of it, although this impression may be conveyed by a few slight touches, sometimes even by a single word. The opening stanza of the poem on the death of Dickens is an illustration:—

Above the pines the moon was slowly drifting,
The river sang below;
The dim Sierras, far beyond, uplifting
Their minarets of snow.

Ruskin somewhere analyzes the difference between real poetry and prose in a versified form, and quoting a few lines from Byron, he points out the single word in them which makes the passage poetic. In the lines just quoted from Bret Harte, the word "sang" has the same poetic quality; and no one who has ever heard the sound which the poet here describes can fail to recognize the truth of his metaphor.

This is always Bret Harte's method. He reproduces the emotional effect of the scene upon himself, and thus exhibits nature to the reader as she appeared to him. Emotion, it need not be said, is transmitted much more effectively than ideas or information. In fact, an objective, detailed description of a landscape, however accurate or exhaustive, will leave the reader almost as it found him; whereas a single word which enables him to share the emotion inspired by the scene in the breast of the writer will transport him at a bound to the spot itself.

The charm of life in California consisted largely in this, that it was lived in the open air. It was almost a perpetual camping out, made delightful by the mildness of the climate and the beauty of the surroundings. Even the cheerful fires of pine or of scrub oak which burn so frequently in the cabins of Bret Harte's miners, are kindled mainly to offset the dampness of the rainy season; and though the fire blazes merrily on the hearth the door of the hut is usually open. The Reader knows how "Union Mills" indolently left one leg exposed to the rain on the outside of the threshold, the rest of his body being under cover inside.

Bret Harte in his poems and stories availed himself of this out-door life to the fullest extent. When the Rose of Tuolumne was summoned from her bedroom, at two o'clock in the morning, to entertain her father's guest, the youthful poet, she met him, not in the stuffy sitting-room of the house, but in the moonlight outside, with the snow-crowned Sierras dimly visible in the distance, and "quaint odors from the woods near by perfuming the warm, still air."

The young Englishman, Mainwaring, and Louise Macy, the Phyllis of the Sierras, could not help being confidential sitting in the moonlight on that unique veranda which overhung the Great Cañon, two thousand feet deep, as many wide, and lined with tall trees, dark and motionless in the distance. If the Outcasts of Poker Flat had met their fate in ordinary surroundings, victims either of the machinery of the law or of man's violence, we should think of them only as criminals; but with nature herself as their executioner, and the scene of their death that remote, wooded amphitheatre in the mountains, they regain their lost dignity as human beings. How vast is the difference between John Oakhurst shooting himself in a bedroom at some second-class hotel, and performing the same act at the head of a snow-covered ravine and beneath the lofty pine tree to which he affixed the playing card that contained his epitaph!

In *Tennessee's Partner*, the whole tragedy is transacted in the open air, excepting the trial scene; and even the little upper room which serves as a court house for the lynching party is hardly a screen from the landscape. "Against the blackness of the pines the windows of the old loft above the express office stood out staringly bright; and through their curtainless panes the loungers below could see the forms of those who were even then deciding the fate of Tennessee. And above all this, etched on the dark firmament, rose the Sierra, remote and passionless, crowned with remoter passionless stars."

Nature, thank God, does not share our emotions, and, so far as we know, is swayed by no emotions of her own. But she inspires certain emotions in us, and is a visible, tangible representation of strength and serenity. Those who delight in nature are a long way from regarding her as they would a brick or a stone. A certain pantheism, such as Wordsworth was accused of, can be attributed to everybody who loves the landscape. There is a mystery in the beautiful inanimate world, as there is in every other phase of the universe. "A forest," said Thoreau, "is in all mythologies a sacred place"; and it must ever remain such. Let anybody wander alone upon some mountain-side or hilltop, and watch the wind blowing through the scanty, unmown grass, and it will be strange if the vague consciousness of some presence other than his own does not insinuate itself into his mind. He will begin to understand how it was that the Ancients peopled every bush and stream with nymphs or deities. Richard Jeffries went even further than Wordsworth. "Though I cannot name the ideal good," he wrote, "it seems to me that it will be in some way closely associated with the ideal beauty of nature."

Bret Harte did not trouble himself much about the ideal good; but he had in full degree the modern feeling for nature, and found in her a mysterious charm and solace,—"that profound peace," to use his own language, "which the mountains alone can give their lonely or perturbed children."

In one of the stories, *Uncle Jim and Uncle Billy*, he describes the unlucky and unhappy miner going to the door of his cabin at midnight.

"In the feverish state into which he had gradually worked himself it seemed to him impossible to await the coming of the dawn. But he was mistaken. For even as he stood there all nature seemed to invade his humble cabin with its free and fragrant breath, and invest him with its great companionship. He felt again, in that breath, that strange sense of freedom, that mystic touch of partnership with the birds and beasts, the shrubs and trees, in this greater home before him. It was this vague communion that had kept him there, that still held these world-sick, weary workers in their rude cabins on the slopes around him; and he felt upon his brow that balm that had nightly lulled him and them to sleep and forgetfulness. He closed the door, crept into his bunk, and presently fell into a profound slumber."

This kind of communion with nature depends upon a certain degree of solitude, and the mere suggestion of a crowd puts it to flight at once. Even the magnificence of the Swiss mountains is almost spoiled for the real lover of nature by those surroundings from which only the skilled mountain-climber is able to escape. Mere solitude, on the other hand, provided that it be out of doors, is almost always beautiful and certainly beneficent in itself.

He who lives in a desert or in a wood, on a mountain top, like the Twins of Table Mountain, or in an unpeopled prairie, may have many faults and vices, but there are some from which he will certainly be free. He will be serene and simple, if nothing more. "It is impossible," as Thomas Hardy remarks, "for any one living upon a heath to be vulgar"; and the reason is obvious. Vulgarity, as we all know, is merely a form of insincerity. To be vulgar is to say and do things not naturally and out of one's own head, but in the attempt to be or to appear something different from the reality. There can be no vulgarity on the heath, on the farm, or in the mining camp, for there everybody's character and circumstances are known; there is no opportunity for deceit, and there is no motive for pretence.

Moreover, the primitive simplicity of the mining and the logging camp, or even that of an isolated farming community, is not essentially different from the cultivated simplicity of the aristocrat. The laboring man and the aristocrat have very much the same sense of honor and the same ideals; and those writers who are at home with one are almost always at home with the other. Sir Walter Scott and Tolstoi are examples. But between these two extremes, which meet at many points, comes the citified, trading, clerking class, which has lost its primitive, manly instincts, and has not yet regained them in the chastened form of convictions.

It is no exaggeration to say that the society which Bret Harte enjoyed in London was more akin to that of the mining camp than to that of San Francisco. In both cases the charm which attracted him was the charm of simplicity; in the mining camp, the simplicity of nature, in London the simplicity of cultivation and finish.

CHAPTER XX

BRET HARTE'S PIONEER DIALECT

Occasionally Bret Harte uses an archaic word, not because it is archaic, but because it expresses his meaning better than any other, or gives the needed stimulus to the imagination of the reader. Thus, in *A First Family of Tasajara* we read that "the former daughters of Sion were there, *burgeoning* and expanding in the glare of their new prosperity with silver and gold."

Often, of course, the employment of an archaic expression confers upon the speaker that air of quaintness which the author wishes to convey. Johnson's Old Woman, for example, "'Lowed she'd use a doctor, ef I'd fetch him." The verb to *use*, in this sense, may still be heard in some parts of New England as well as in the West. "I never use sugar in my tea" is a familiar example.

Many other words which Bret Harte's Pioneer people employ are still in service among old-fashioned country folk, although they have long since passed out of literature, and are never heard in cities. Thus Salomy Jane was accused by her father of "honeyfoglin' with a hoss-thief"; and the blacksmith's small boy spoke of Louise Macy as "philanderin'" with Captain Greyson. These good old English words are still used in the West and South. In the same category is "'twixt" for between. Dick Spindler spoke of "this yer peace and good-will 'twixt man and man." "Far" in the sense of distant is another example: "The far barn near the boundary." "Mannerly" in the sense of well-mannered has the authority of Shakspere and of Abner Nott in *A Ship of '49*.

One of Bret Harte's Western girls speaks of hunting for the plant known as "Old Man" (southernwood), because she wanted it for "smellidge." "Smellidge" has the appearance of being a good word, and it was formerly used in New England and the West, but it is excluded from modern dictionaries.

Some expressions which might be regarded as original with Bret Harte were really Pioneer terms of Western or Southern use. "Johnson's Old Woman," for "Johnson's wife" was the ordinary phrase in Missouri, Indiana, Alabama, and doubtless all over the West and South. Thus a Missouri farmer is quoted as saying: "My old woman is nineteen years old to-day." "You know fust-rate she's dead" is another quaint expression used by Bret Harte, but not invented by him, for this use of "fust-rate" in the sense of very well was not uncommon in the West. In the poem called *Jim*, there are two or three words which the casual reader might suppose to be inventions of the poet.

What makes you star',
You over thar?
Can't a man drop
'S glass in yer shop
But you must r'ar?

This use of r'ar or rear, meaning to become angry, to rave, was frequent in Arkansas and Indiana, if not elsewhere.

The next stanza runs:—

Dead!
Poor—little—Jim!
Why, thar was me,
Jones, and Bob Lee,
Harry and Ben,—
No-account men:
Then to take *him*!

"No-account" in this sense was a common Western term; and so was "ornery," from ordinary, meaning inferior, which occurs in the next and final stanza.

When Richelieu Sharpe excused himself for wearing his best "pants" on the ground that his old ones had "fetched away in the laig," he was amply justified by the dialect of his place and time. So when little Johnny Medliker complained of the parson that "he hez been nigh onter pullin' off my arm," he used the current Illinois equivalent for "nearly." Mr. Hays' direction to his daughter, "Ye kin put some things in my carpet-bag agin the time when the sled comes round," was also strictly in the vernacular.

No verbal error is more common than that of using superfluous prepositions. "To feed up the horses," for instance, may still be heard almost anywhere in rural New England. On the same principle, Mr. Saunders, in *The Transformation of Buckeye Camp*, ruefully admits that he and his companion were thrown out of the saloon, "with two shots into us, like hounds ez we were." This substitution of into for in, though common in the West, is probably now extinct in the Eastern States; but a purist, writing in the year 1814, quoted the following use as current at that time in New York: "I have the rheumatism into my knees."

A few words were taken by the Pioneers from the Spanish. "Savey," a corruption of *sabe*, was one of these, and Bret Harte employed it. "Hedn't no savey, hed Briggs."

The wealth of dialect in Bret Harte's stories is not strange, considering that it was culled from Pioneers who represented every part of the country. But, it may be asked, how could there be such a thing as a California dialect:—all the Pioneers could not have learned to talk alike, coming as they did from every State in the Union! The answer is, first, that, in the main, the dialect of the different States was the same, being derived chiefly from the same source, that is, from England, directly or indirectly; and, secondly, the dialect of what we now call the Middle West—of Missouri, Indiana, Ohio, and Illinois—tended to predominate on the Pacific Slope, because the Pioneers from that part of the country were in the majority. It is almost impossible to find a dialect word used in one Western State, and not in another.

There are, however, some Western, and more especially some Southern words which never became domiciled in New England. The word allow or 'low, in the sense of declare or state, is one of these, and Bret Harte often used it. "Then she 'lowed I'd better git up and git, and shet the door to. Then I 'lowed she might tell me what was up—through the door."

And here is another example:—

"Rowley Meade—him ez hed his skelp pulled over his eyes at one stroke, foolin' with a she-bear over on Black Mountain—*allows* it would be rather monotonous in him attemptin' any familiarities with her."

("Rowley Meade," by the way, is an example of Bret Harte's felicity in the choice of names. No common fate could be reserved for one bearing a name like that.)

Lowell employs the word allow in its corrupted sense in the "Biglow Papers"; but he adds in a footnote that it was a use not of New England, but of the Southern and Middle States; and to prove the antiquity of the corruption he cites an instance of it in Hakluyt under the date of 1558.

"Cahoots" is another example. When the warlike Jim Hooker said to Clarence, "Young fel, you and me are cahoots in this thing," he was using a common Western expression derived remotely from the old English word cahoot, signifying a company or partnership, but not known, it is believed, in New England.

"When we rose the hill," "put to" (*i. e.* harness) the horse, "cavortin' round here in the dew," and "What yer yawpin' at ther'?" are found in almost every State, East or West. But "I ain't kicked a fut sens I left Mizzouri" is a Southern expression. "Blue mange" for *blanc mange* is probably original with Bret Harte.

One of Bret Harte's most effective dialect words is "gait" in the sense of habit, or manner. "He never sat down to a square meal but what he said, 'If old Uncle Quince was only here now, boys, I'd die happy.' I leave it to you, gentlemen, if that wasn't Jackson Wells's gait all the time." And Rupert Filgee, impatient at Uncle Ben Dabney's destructive use of pens, exclaimed, "Look here, what you want ain't a pen, but a clothes-pin and split nail! That'll about jibe with your dilikit gait."

"Gait" is a very old term in thieves' lingo, meaning occupation or calling, from which the transition to "habit" is easy; and it is interesting to observe that in one place Bret Harte uses the word in a sense which is about half-way between the two meanings. Thus, when Mr. McKinstry was severely wounded in the duel, he apologized for requesting the attendance of a physician by saying, "I don't gin'rally use a doctor, but this yer is suthin' outside the old woman's regular gait." Bret Harte's adoption of the word as a Pioneer expression is confirmed by Richard Malcolm Johnston, the recognized authority on Georgia dialect, for he makes one of his characters say:—

"After she got married, seem like he got more and more restless and fidgety in his mind, and in his gaits in general."

The ridiculous charge has been made that Bret Harte's dialect is not Californian or even American, but is simply cockney English. The only reason ever given for this statement is that Bret Harte uses the word "which" in its cockney sense, and that this use was never known in America.

Which I wish to remark,
And my language is plain,

is the most familiar instance, and others might be cited. Thus, in *Mr. Thompson's Prodigal* we have this dialogue between the father of the prodigal and a grave-digger:—

"'Did you ever in your profession come across Char-les Thompson?'

"'Thompson be damned,' said the grave-digger, with great directness.

"'Which, if he hadn't religion, I think he is,' responded the old man."

This use of "which" is indeed now identified with the London cockney, but it may still be heard in the eastern counties of England, whence, no doubt, it was imported to this country. Though far from common in the United States, it is used, according to the authorities cited below, in the mountainous parts of Virginia, in West Virginia, in the mountain regions of Kentucky, especially in Eastern Kentucky, and in the western part of Arkansas.

Professor Edward A. Allen of the University of Missouri says that this use of "which" is "not Southern, but Western."

Moreover, upon this point also we can cite the authority of Richard Malcolm Johnston, for the cockney use of "which" frequently occurs in his tales of Middle Georgia; as, for instance, in these sentences:—

"And which I wouldn't have done that nohow in the world ef it could be hendered."

"Which a man like you that's got no wife."

"Howbeever, as your wife is Nancy Lary, which that she's the own dear sister o' my wife."

"And which I haven't a single jubous doubt that, soon as the breath got out o' her body, she went to mansion *in* the sky same as a bow-'n'-arrer, or even a rifle-bullet."

Another authority on this point is the well-known writer of stories, Alfred Henry Lewis, a native of Arkansas. In his tales we find these expressions:—

"Which his baptismal name is Lafe."

"Which if these is your manners."

"Which, undoubted, the barkeeps is the hardest-worked folks in camp."

"Which it is some late for night before last, but it's jest the shank of the evening for to-night."

No writer ever knew Virginia better than did the late George W. Bagby, and he attributes the cockney "which" to a backwoodsman from Charlotte County in that State. "And what is this part of the country called? Has it any particular name?"

"To be sho. Right here is Brilses, *which* it is a presink; but this here ridge ar' called 'Verjunce Ridge.'"

Mark Twain's authority on a matter of Western dialect will hardly be questioned, and this same use of "which" is not infrequent in his stories. Here, for instance, is an example from "Tom Sawyer": "We said it was Parson Silas, and we judged he had found Sam Cooper drunk in the road, which he was always trying to reform him." Finally, that well-known Pioneer, Mr. Warren Cheney, an early contributor to the "Overland," testifies that "which" as thus used "is perfectly good Pike."

The rather astonishing fact is that Bret Harte uses dialect words and phrases to the number, roughly estimated, of three hundred, and a hasty investigation has served to identify all but a few of these as legitimate Pioneer expressions. A more thorough search would no doubt account satisfactorily for every one of them.

However, that dialect should be authentic is not so important as that it should be interesting. Many story-writers report dialect in a correct and conscientious form, but it wearies the reader. Dialect to be interesting must be the vehicle of humor, and the great masters of dialect, such as Thackeray and Sir Walter Scott, are also masters of humor. Bret Harte had the same gift, and he showed it, as we have seen, not only in Pioneer speech, but also in the Spanish-American dialect of Enriquez Saltello and his charming sister, in the Scotch dialect of Mr. Callender, in the French dialect of the innkeeper who entertained Alkali Dick, and in the German dialect of Peter Schroeder. For one thing, a too exact reproduction of dialect almost always has a misleading and awkward effect. The written word is not the same as the spoken word, and the constant repetition of a sound which would hardly be noticed in speech becomes unduly prominent and wearisome if put before our eyes in print. In the following passage it will be seen how Bret Harte avoids the too frequent occurrence of "ye" (which Tinka Gallinger probably used) by alternating it with "you":—

"'No! no! ye shan't go—ye mustn't go,' she said, with hysterical intensity. 'I want to tell ye something! Listen!—you—you—Mr. Fleming! I've been a wicked, wicked girl! I've told lies to dad—to mammy—to you! I've borne false witness—I'm worse than Sapphira— I've acted a big lie. Oh, Mr. Fleming, I've made you come back here for nothing! Ye didn't find no gold the other day. There wasn't any. It was all me! I—I—*salted that pan!*'"

Bret Harte's writings offer a wide field for the study of what might be called the psychological aspect of dialect, especially so far as it relates to pronunciation. What governs the dialect of any time and place? Is it purely accidental that the London cockney says "piper" instead of paper, and that the Western Pioneer says "b'ar" for bear,—or does some inner necessity determine, or partly determine, these departures from the standard pronunciation? This, however, is a subject which lies far beyond our present scope. Suffice it to say that it would be difficult to convince the reader of Bret Harte that there is not some inevitable harmony between his characters and the dialect or other language which they employ. Who, for example, would hesitate to assign to Yuba Bill, and to none other, this remark: "I knew the partikler style of damn fool that you was, and expected no better."

CHAPTER XXI

BRET HARTE'S STYLE

In discussing Bret Harte, it is almost impossible to separate substance from style. The style is so good, so exactly adapted to the ideas which he wishes to convey, that one can hardly imagine it as different. Some thousands of years ago an Eastern sage remarked that he would like to write a book such as everybody would conceive that he might have written himself, and yet so good that nobody else could have written the like. This is the ideal which Bret Harte fulfilled. Almost everything said by any one of his characters is so accurate an expression of that character as to seem inevitable. It is felt at once to be just what such a character must have said. Given the character, the words follow; and anybody could set them down! This is the fallacy underlying that strange feeling, which every reader must have experienced, of the apparent easiness of writing an especially good conversation or soliloquy.

The real difficulty of writing like Bret Harte is shown by the fact that as a story-teller he has no imitators. His style is so individual as to make imitation impossible. And yet occasionally the inspiration failed. It is a peculiarity of Bret Harte, shown especially in the longer stories, and most of all perhaps in *Gabriel Conroy*, that there are times when the reader almost believes that Bret Harte has dropped the pen, and some inferior person has taken it up. Author and reader come to the ground with a thud.

Mr. Warren Cheney has remarked upon this defect as follows:—

"With most authors there is a level of general excellence along which they can plod if the wings of genius chance to tire for a time; but with Mr. Harte the case is a different one. His powers are impulsive rather than enduring. Ideas strike him with extraordinary force, but the inspiration is of equally short duration. So long as the flush of excitement lasts, his work will be up to standard; but when the genius flags, he has no individual fund of dramatic or narrative properties to sustain him."

But of these lapses there are few in the short stories, and none at all in the best stories. In them the style is almost flawless. There are no mannerisms in it; no affectations; no egotism; no slang (except, of course, in the mouths of the various characters); nothing local or provincial, nothing which stamps it as of a particular age, country or school,—nothing, in short, which could operate as a barrier between author and reader.

But these are only negative virtues. What are the positive virtues of Bret Harte's style? Perhaps the most obvious quality is the deep feeling which pervades it. It is possible, indeed, to have good style without depth of feeling. John Stuart Mill is an example; Lord Chesterfield is another; Benjamin Franklin another. In general, however, want of feeling in the author produces a coldness in the style that chills the reader. Herbert Spencer's autobiography discloses an almost inhuman want of feeling, and the same effect is apparent in his dreary, frigid style.

On the other hand, it is a truism that the language of passion is invariably effective, and never vulgar. Grief and anger are always eloquent. There are men, even practised authors, who never write really well unless something has occurred to put them out of temper.

Good style may perhaps be said to result from the union of deep feeling with an artistic sense of form. This produces that conciseness for which Bret Harte's style is remarkable. What author has used shorter words, has expressed more with a few words, or has elaborated so little! His points are made with the precision of a bullet going straight to the mark, and nothing is added.

How effective, for example, is this dialogue between Helen Maynard, who has just met the one-armed painter for the first time, and the French girl who accompanies her: "'So you have made a conquest of the recently acquired but unknown Greek statue?' said Mademoiselle Renée lightly.

"'It is a countryman of mine,' said Helen simply.

"'He certainly does not speak French,' said Mademoiselle mischievously.

"'Nor think it,' responded Helen, with equal vivacity."

Possibly Bret Harte sometimes carries this dramatic conciseness a little too far,—so far that the reader's attention is drawn from the matter in hand to the manner in which it is expressed. To take an example, *Johnson's Old Woman* ends as follows:—

"'I want to talk to you about Miss Johnson,' I said eagerly.

"'I reckon so,' he said with an exasperating smile. 'Most fellers do. But she ain't *Miss* Johnson no more. She's married.'

"'Not to that big chap over from Ten Mile Mills?' I said breathlessly.

"'What's the matter with *him*,' said Johnson. 'Ye didn't expect her to marry a nobleman, did ye?'

"I said I didn't see why she shouldn't,—and believed that she *had*."

This is extremely clever, but perhaps its very cleverness, and its abruptness, divert the reader's interest for a moment from the story to the person who tells it.

One other characteristic of Bret Harte's style, and indeed of any style which ranks with the best, is obvious, and that is subtlety. It is the office of a good style to express in some indefinable manner those *nuances* which mere words, taken by themselves, are not fine enough to convey. Thoughts so subtle as to have almost the character of feelings; feelings so well defined as just to escape being thoughts; attractions and repulsions; those obscure movements of the intellect of which the ordinary man is only half conscious until they are revealed to him by the eye of genius;—all these things it is a part of style to express, or at least to imply. Subtlety of style presupposes, of course, subtlety of thought, and possibly also subtlety of perception. Certainly Bret Harte had both of these capacities; and many examples might be cited of his minute and sympathetic observation. For instance, although he had no knowledge of horses, and occasionally betrays his ignorance in this respect, yet he has described the peculiar gait of the American trotter with an accuracy which any technical person might envy. "The driver leaned forward and did something with the reins—Rose never could clearly understand what, though it seemed to her that he simply lifted them with ostentatious lightness; but the mare suddenly seemed to *lengthen herself* and lose her height, and the stalks of wheat on either side of the dusty track began to melt into each other, and then slipped like a flash into one long, continuous, shimmering green hedge. So perfect was the mare's action that the girl was scarcely conscious of any increased effort.... So superb was the reach of her long, easy stride that Rose could scarcely see any undulations in the brown, shining back on which she could have placed her foot, nor felt the soft beat of the delicate hoofs that took the dust so firmly and yet so lightly."

Equally correct is the description of the "great, yellow mare" Jovita, that carried Dick Bullen on his midnight ride: "From her Roman nose to her rising haunches, from her arched spine hidden by the stiff *manchillas* of a Mexican saddle, to her thick, straight bony legs, there was not a line of equine grace. In her half-blind but wholly vicious white eyes, in her protruding under lip, in her monstrous color, there was nothing but ugliness and vice."

Jovita, plainly, was drawn from life, and she must have been of thoroughbred blood on one side, for her extraordinary energy and temper could have been derived from no other source. Such a mare would naturally have an unusually straight hind leg; and Bret Harte noticed it.

As to his heroines, he had such a faculty of describing them that they stand before us almost as clearly as if we saw them in the flesh. He does not simply tell us that they are beautiful,—we see for ourselves that they are so; and one reason for this is the sympathetic keenness with which he observed all the details of the human face and figure. Thus Julia Porter's face "appeared whiter at the angles of the mouth and nose through the relief of tiny freckles like grains of pepper."

There are subtleties of coloring that have escaped almost everybody else. Who but Bret Harte has really described the light which love kindles upon the face of a woman? "Yerba Buena's strangely delicate complexion had taken on itself that faint Alpine glow that was more of an illumination than a color." And so of Cressy, as the Schoolmaster saw her at the dance. "She was pale, he had never seen her so beautiful.... The absence of color in her usually fresh face had been replaced by a faint magnetic aurora that seemed to him half spiritual. He could not take his eyes from her; he could not believe what he saw."

The forehead, the temples, and more especially the eyebrows of his heroines—these and the part which they play in the expression of emotion, are described by Bret Harte with a particularity which cannot be found elsewhere. Even the eyelashes of his heroines are often carefully painted in the picture. Flora Dimwood "cast a sidelong glance" at the hero, "under her widely-spaced, heavy lashes." Of Mrs. Brimmer, the fastidious Boston woman, it is said that "a certain nervous intensity occasionally lit up her weary eyes with a dangerous phosphorescence, under their brown fringes."

The eyes and eyelashes of that irrepressible child, Sarah Walker, are thus minutely and pathetically described: "Her eyes were of a dark shade of burnished copper,—the orbits appearing deeper and larger from the rubbing in of habitual tears from long wet lashes."

Bret Harte has the rare faculty of making even a tearful woman attractive. The Ward of the Golden Gate "drew back a step, lifted her head with a quick toss that seemed to condense the moisture in her shining eyes, and sent what might have been a glittering dewdrop flying into the loosened tendrils of her hair." The quick-tempered heroine is seen "hurriedly disentangling two stinging tears from her long lashes"; and even the mannish girl, Julia Porter, becomes femininely deliquescent as she leans back in the dark stage-coach, with the romantic Cass Beard gazing at her from his invisible corner. "How much softer her face looked in the moonlight!—How moist her eyes were—actually shining in the light! How that light seemed to concentrate in the corner of the lashes, and then slipped—flash—away! Was she? Yes, she was crying."

There is great subtlety not only of perception but of thought in the description of the Two Americans at the beginning of their intimacy:—

"Oddly enough, their mere presence and companionship seemed to excite in others that tenderness they had not yet felt themselves. Family groups watched the handsome pair in their innocent confidence and, with French exuberant recognition of sentiment, thought them the incarnation of Love. Something in their manifest equality of condition kept even the vainest and most susceptible of spectators from attempted rivalry or cynical interruption. And when at last they dropped side by side on a sun-warmed stone bench on the terrace, and Helen, inclining her brown head toward her companion, informed him of the difficulty she had experienced in getting gumbo soup, rice and chicken, corn cakes, or any of her favorite home dishes in Paris, an exhausted but gallant boulevardier rose from a contiguous bench, and, politely lifting his hat to the handsome couple, turned slowly away from what he believed were tender confidences he would not permit himself to hear."

Without this subtlety, a writer may have force, even eloquence, as Johnson and Macaulay had those qualities, but he is not likely to have an enduring charm. Subtlety seems to be the note of the best modern writers, of the Oxford school in particular, a subtlety of language which extracts from every word its utmost nicety of meaning, and a subtlety of thought in which every faculty is on the alert to seize any qualification or limitation, any hint or suggestion that might be hovering obscurely about the subject.

Yet subtlety, more perhaps than any other quality of a good style, easily becomes a defect. If it is the forte of some writers, it is the foible, not to say the vice, of others. The later works of Henry James, for instance, will at once occur to the Reader as an example. Bret Harte himself is sometimes, but rarely, over-subtle, representing his characters as going through processes of thought or speech much too elaborate for them, or for the occasion.

There is an example of this in *Susy*, where Clarence says: "'If I did not know you were prejudiced by a foolish and indiscreet woman, I should believe you were trying to insult me as you have your adopted mother, and would save you the pain of doing both in *her* house by leaving it now and forever.'"

And again, in *A Secret of Telegraph Hill*, where Herbert Bly says to the gambler whom he has surprised in his room, hiding from the Vigilance Committee: "'Whoever you may be, I am neither the police nor a spy. You have no right to insult me by supposing that I would profit by a mistake that made you my guest, and that I would refuse you the sanctuary of the roof that covers your insult as well as your blunder.'" And yet the speaker is not meant to be a prig.

There is another characteristic of Bret Harte's style which should perhaps be regarded as a form of subtlety, and that is the surprising resources of his vocabulary. He seems to have gathered all the words and idioms that might become of service to him, and to have stored them in his memory for future use. If a peculiar or technical expression was needed, he always had it at hand. Thus when the remorseful Joe Corbin told Colonel Starbottle about his sending money to the widow of the man whom he had killed in self-defence, the Colonel's apt comment was, "A kind of expiation or amercement of fine, known to the Mosaic, Roman and old English law." And yet his reading never took a wide range. His large vocabulary was due partly, no doubt, to an excellent memory, but still more to his keen appreciation of delicate shades in the meaning of words. He had a remarkable gift of choosing the right word. In the following lines, for example, the whole effect depends upon the discriminating selection of the verbs and adjectives:—

Bunny, thrilled by unknown fears,
Raised his soft and pointed ears,
Mumbled his prehensile lip,
Quivered his pulsating hip.

Depth of feeling, subtlety of perception and intellect,—these qualities, supplemented by the sense of form and beauty, go far to account for the charm of Bret Harte's style. He had an ear for style, just as some persons have an ear for music; and he could extract beauty from language just as the musician can extract it from the strings of a violin. This kind of beauty is, in one sense, a matter of mere sound; and yet it is really much more than that. "Words, even the most perfect, owe very much to the spiritual cadence with which they are imbued."

A musical sentence, made up of words harmoniously chosen, and of sub-sentences nicely balanced, must necessarily deepen, soften, heighten, or otherwise modify the bare meaning of the words. In fact, it clothes them with that kind and degree of feeling which, as the writer consciously or unconsciously perceives, will best further his intention. Style, in short, is a substitute for speech, the author giving through the medium of his style the same emotional and personal color to his thoughts which the orator conveys by the tone and inflections of his voice. Hence the saying that the style is the man.

If we were looking for an example of mere beauty in style, perhaps we could find nothing better than this description of Maruja, after parting from her lover: "Small wonder that, hidden and silent in her enwrappings, as she lay back in the carriage, with her pale face against the cold, starry sky, two other stars came out and glistened and trembled on her passion-fringed lashes."

No less beautiful in style are these lines:—

Above the tumult of the cañon lifted,
The gray hawk breathless hung,
Or on the hill a winged shadow drifted
Where furze and thorn-bush clung.

And yet, so exact is the correspondence between thought and word here, that we find ourselves doubting whether the charm of the passage lies in its form, or in the mere idea conveyed to the reader with the least possible interposition of language; and yet, again, to raise that very doubt may be the supreme effect of a consummate style.

Bret Harte was sometimes a little careless in his style, careless, that is, in the way of writing obscurely or ungrammatically, but very seldom so careless as to write in a dull or unmusical fashion. To find a harsh sentence anywhere in his works would be almost, if not quite, impossible. A leading English Review once remarked, "It was never among Mr. Bret Harte's accomplishments to labor cheerfully with the file"; and again, a few years later, "Mr. Harte can never be accused of carelessness." Neither statement was quite correct, but the second one comes very much nearer the truth than the first.

Beside these occasional lapses in the construction of his sentences, Bret Harte had some peculiarities in the use of English to which he clung, either out of loyalty to Dickens, from whom he seems to have derived them, or from a certain amiable perversity which was part of his character. He was a strong partisan of the "split infinitive." A Chinaman "caused the gold piece and the letter to instantly vanish up his sleeve." "To coldly interest Price"; "to unpleasantly discord with the general social harmony"; "to quietly reappear," are other examples.

The wrong use of "gratuitous" is a thoroughly Dickens error, and it almost seems as if Bret Harte went out of his way to copy it. In the story of *Miggles*, for example, it is only a few paragraphs after Yuba Bill has observed the paralytic Jim's "expression of perfectly gratuitous solemnity," that his own features "relax into an expression of gratuitous and imbecile cheerfulness."

"Aggravation" in the sense of irritation is another Dickens solecism which also appears several times in Bret Harte.

Beside these, Bret Harte had a few errors all his own. In *The Story of a Mine*, there is a strangely repeated use of the awkward expression "near facts," followed by a statement that the new private secretary was a little dashed as to his "near hopes." Diligent search reveals also "continued on" in one story, "different to" in another, "plead" for "pleaded," "who would likely spy upon you" in an unfortunate place, and "too occupied with his subject" somewhere else.

This short list will very nearly exhaust Bret Harte's errors in the use of English; but it must be admitted, also, that he occasionally lapses into a Dickens-like grandiloquence and cant of superior virtue. There are several examples of this in *The Story of a Mine*, especially in that part which relates to the City of Washington. The following paragraph is almost a burlesque of Dickens: "The actors, the legislators themselves, knew it and laughed at it; the commentators, the Press, knew it and laughed at it; the audience, the great American people, knew it and laughed at it. And nobody for an instant conceived that it ever, under any circumstances, might be different."

Still worse is this description of the Supreme Court, which might serve as a model of confused ideas and crude reasoning, only half believed in by the writer himself: "A body of learned, cultivated men, representing the highest legal tribunal in the land, still lingered in a vague idea of earning the scant salary bestowed upon them by the economical founders of the government, and listened patiently to the arguments of counsel, whose fees for advocacy of the claims before them would have paid the life income of half the bench."

That exquisite sketch, *Wan Lee, the Pagan*, is marred by this Dickens-like apostrophe to the clergy: "Dead, my reverend friends, dead! Stoned to death in the streets of San Francisco, in the year of grace, eighteen hundred and sixty-nine, by a mob of half-grown boys and Christian school-children!"

In the description of an English country church, which occurs in *A Phyllis of the Sierras*, we find another passage almost worthy of a "condensed novel" in which some innocent crusaders, lying cross-legged in marble, are rebuked for tripping up the unwary "until in death, as in life, they got between the congregation and the Truth that was taught there."

Bret Harte has been accused also of "admiring his characters in the wrong place," as Dickens certainly did; but this charge seems to be an injustice. A scene in *Gabriel Conroy* represents Arthur Poinsett as calmly explaining to Doña Dolores that he is the person who seduced and abandoned Grace Conroy; and he makes this statement without a sign of shame or regret. "If he had been uttering a moral sentiment, he could not have been externally more calm, or inwardly less agitated. More than that, there was a certain injured dignity in his manner," and so forth.

This is the passage cited by that very acute critic, Mr. E. S. Nadal. But there is nothing in it or in the context which indicates that Bret Harte admired the conduct of Poinsett. He was simply describing a type which everybody will recognize; but not describing it as admirable. Bret Harte depicted his characters with so much *gusto*, and at the same time was so absolutely impartial and non-committal toward them, that it is easy to misconceive his own opinion of them or of their conduct. From another fault, perhaps the worst fault of Dickens, namely, his propensity for the sudden conversion of a character to something the reverse of what it always has been, Bret Harte—with the single exception of Mrs. Tretherick, in *An Episode of Fiddletown*—is absolutely free.

It should be remembered, moreover, that Bret Harte's imitations of Dickens occur only in a few passages of a few stories. When Bret Harte nodded, he wrote like Dickens. But the better stories, and the great majority of the stories, show no trace of this blemish. Bret Harte at his best was perhaps as nearly original as any author in the world.

On the whole, it seems highly probable—though the critics have mostly decided otherwise—that Bret Harte derived more good than bad from his admiration for Dickens. The reading of Dickens stimulated his boyish imagination and quickened that sympathy with the weak and suffering, with the downtrodden, with the waifs and strays, with the outcasts of society, which is remarkable in both writers. The spirit of Dickens breathes through the poems and stories of Bret Harte, just as the spirit of Bret Harte breathes through the poems and stories of Kipling. Bret Harte had a very pretty satirical vein, which might easily, if developed, have made him an author of satire rather than of sentiment. Who can say that the influence of Dickens, coming at the early, plastic period of his life, may not have turned the scale?

That Dickens surpassed him in breadth and scope, Bret Harte himself would have been the first to acknowledge. The mere fact that one wrote novels and the other short stories almost implies as much. If we consider the works of an author like Hawthorne, who did both kinds equally well, it is easy to see how much more effective is the long story. Powerful as Hawthorne's short stories are—the "Minister's Black Veil," for example—they cannot rival the longer-drawn, more elaborately developed tragedy of "The Scarlet Letter."

The characters created by Dickens have taken hold of the popular imagination, and have influenced public sentiment in a degree which cannot be attributed to the characters of Bret Harte. Dickens, moreover, despite his vulgarisms, despite even the cant into which he occasionally falls, had a depth of sincerity and conviction that can hardly be asserted for Bret Harte. Dickens' errors in taste were superficial; upon any important matter he always had a genuine opinion to express. With respect to Bret Harte, on the other hand, we cannot help feeling that his errors in taste, though infrequent, are due to a want of sincerity, to a want of conviction upon deep things.

And yet, despite the fact that Dickens excelled Bret Harte in depth and scope, there is reason to think that the American author of short stories will outlast the English novelist. The one is, and the other is not, a classic writer. It was said of Dickens that he had no "citadel of the mind,"—no mental retiring-place, no inward poise or composure; and this defect is shown by a certain feverish quality in his style, as well as by those well-known exaggerations and mannerisms which disfigure it.

Bret Harte, on the other hand, in his best poems and stories, exhibits all that restraint, all that absence of idiosyncrasy as distinguished from personality, which marks the true artist. What the world demands is the peculiar flavor of the artist's mind; but this must be conveyed in a pure and unadulterated form, free from any ingredient of eccentricity or self-will. In Bret Harte there is a wonderful economy both of thought and language. Everything said or done in the course of a story contributes to the climax or end which the author has in view. There are no digressions or superfluities; the words are commonly plain words of Anglo-Saxon descent; and it would be hard to find one that could be dispensed with. The language is as concise as if the story were a message, to be delivered to the reader in the shortest possible time.

One other point of much importance remains to be spoken of, although it might be difficult to say whether it is really a matter of style or of substance. Nothing counts for more in the telling of a story, especially a story of adventure, than the author's attitude toward his characters; not simply the fact that he blames or praises them, or abstains from doing so, but his unspoken attitude, his real feeling, disclosed between the lines. Too much admiration on the part of the author is fatal to a classic effect, even though the admiration be implied rather than expressed. This is perhaps the greatest weakness of Mr. Kipling. That a man should be a gentleman is always, strangely enough, a matter of some surprise to that conscientious author, and that he should be not only a gentleman, but actually brave in addition, is almost too much for Mr. Kipling's equanimity. His heroes, those gallant young officers whom he describes so well, are exhibited to the reader with something of that pride which a showman or a fond mother might pardonably display. Mr. Kipling knows them thoroughly, but he is not of them. He is their humble servant. They are, he seems to feel, members of a species to which he, the author, and probably the reader also, are not akin. Now, almost everybody who writes about fighting or heroic men in these days,—about highwaymen, cow-boys, river-drivers, woodsmen, or other primitive characters,—imitates Mr. Kipling, very seldom Bret Harte. Partly, no doubt, this is because Mr. Kipling's mannerisms are attractive, and easily copied. That little trick, for example, of beginning sentences with the word "also," is a familiar earmark of the Kipling school.

But a stronger reason for imitating Mr. Kipling is that the attitude of frank admiration which he assumes is the natural attitude for the ordinary writer. Such a writer falls into it unconsciously, and does not easily rise above it. The author is a "tenderfoot," discoursing to another tenderfoot, the reader, about the brave and wonderful men whom he has met in the course of his travels; and the reader's astonishment and admiration are looked for with confidence.

Vastly different from all this is the attitude of Bret Harte. He takes it for granted that the Pioneers in general had the instincts of gentlemen and the courage of heroes. His characters are represented not as exceptional California men, but as ordinary California men placed in rather exceptional circumstances. Brave as they are, they are never brave enough to surprise him. He is their equal. He never boasts of them nor about them. On the contrary, he gives the impression that the whole California Pioneer Society was constructed upon the same lofty plane,—as indeed it was, barring a few renegades.

When Edward Brice, the young expressman, "set his white lips together, and with a determined face, and unfaltering step," walked straight toward the rifle held in Snapshot Harry's unerring hands, the incident astonishes nobody,—except perhaps the reader. Certainly it does not astonish the persons who witness or the author who records it. It evokes a little good-humored banter from Snapshot Harry himself, and a laughing compliment from his beautiful niece, Flora Dimwood, but nothing more. We have been told that Shakspere cut no great figure in his own time because his contemporaries were cast in much the same heroic mould,—greatness of soul being a rather common thing in Elizabethan days. For a similar reason, the heroes of Bret Harte are accepted by one another, by the minor characters, and, finally, by the author himself, with perfect composure and without visible surprise.

Bret Harte makes the reader feel that he is describing not simply a few men and women of nobility, but a whole society, an epoch, of which he was himself a part; and this gives an element of distinction, even of immortality, to his stories. Had only one man died at Thermopylæ, the fact would have been remembered by the world, but it would have lost its chief significance. The death of three hundred made it a typical act of the Spartan people. The time will come when California, now strangely unappreciative of its own past, and of the writer who preserved it, will look back upon the Pioneers as the modern Greek looks back upon Sparta and Athens.

THE END

Made in the USA
Las Vegas, NV
05 January 2023

65030365R00057